THE YOUNG MONTROSE

James Graham, the great Marquis of Montrose, is one of the noblest figures of history, a brilliant leader of men, a world-acclaimed strategist, a talented moderate in a bigoted age, a man of as great probity as of charm and the loyalist of the loyal – yet, a strangely modest man at heart. And by no means a plaster saint, by any count. If Charles the First had had even one other servant of the stature of Montrose, probably British history would have been very different. But one man alone could not alter all, when intolerance, despotism, folly and weakness held the stage – even though James Graham tried hard, and almost succeeded.

In this two-part novel Nigel Tranter takes the fascinating, gallant, yet desperate story of this man from the initial snub he received from the monarch he was to devote his life to serve, to the detriment of his own marriage, wellbeing and peace of mind, through all the reluctant involvement in national affairs, through intrigue, violence, treachery, to battle, more battle, and eventual near-triumph. But expensive triumph, for James Graham and those he loved, with all Scotland almost in his grasp and his hated enemy, Archibald Campbell, Marquis of Argyll, defeated and discredited, and England and Oliver Cromwell next on the list. But that was to reckon without Fate . . .

The Young Montrose

Nigel Tranter

CORONET BOOKS
Hodder and Stoughton

Copyright © 1972 by Nigel Tranter

First published 1972 by
Hodder and Stoughton Ltd.

Coronet edition 1974
Third impression 1980

Printed and bound in Great Britain for
Hodder and Stoughton Paperbacks, a
division of Hodder and Stoughton Ltd.,
Mill Road, Dunton Green, Sevenoaks, Kent
(Editorial Office: 47 Bedford Square,
London, WC1 3DP) by
Hunt Barnard Printing, Ltd.,
Aylesbury, Bucks.

ISBN 0 340 16213 9

PRINCIPAL CHARACTERS
In Order of Appearance

JAMES GRAHAM, FIFTH EARL OF MONTROSE: twenty-third chief of the Grahams, aged twenty-four. *An Greumach Mor*.

JOHN GRAHAM, LORD KILPONT: son of the first Earl of Airth (or eighteenth Earl of Menteith).

KING CHARLES THE FIRST

JAMES, THIRD MARQUIS OF HAMILTON: chief of the Hamiltons, later first Duke.

WILLIAM HAMILTON, EARL OF LANARK: brother to above.

WILLIAM LAUD: Archbishop of Canterbury.

ARCHIBALD NAPIER, FIRST LORD NAPIER OF MERCHISTON: Scots statesman, brother-in-law of Montrose.

JOHN, LORD GRAHAM: eldest son of Montrose.

JAMES, LORD CARNEGIE: son of the Earl of Southesk, brother-in-law of Montrose.

DAVID CARNEGIE, FIRST EARL OF SOUTHESK: father-in-law of Montrose.

LADY MAGDALEN CARNEGIE, COUNTESS OF MONTROSE

JAMES GRAHAM: second son of Montrose.

PATRICK GRAHAM, YOUNGER OF INCHBRAKIE: known as Black Pate, friend and kinsman of Montrose.

JOHN LESLIE, SIXTH EARL OF ROTHES: Scots statesman and Covenant leader.

REV. ALEXANDER HENDERSON: Minister of Leuchars and Covenant leader.

SIR THOMAS HOPE OF CRAIGHALL: Lord Advocate.

ARCHIBALD JOHNSTON OF WARRISTON: advocate and Covenant leader, later Lord Warriston.

JOHN CAMPBELL, FIRST EARL OF LOUDOUN: Covenant leader, later Chancellor of Scotland.

REV. ANDREW CANT: Minister of Pitsligo, leading Scots divine.

REV. DAVID DICKSON: Minister of Irvine, leading Scots divine.

GEORGE GORDON, SECOND MARQUIS OF HUNTLY: chief of Clan Gordon.

JAMES GORDON, VISCOUNT ABOYNE: second son of above.

LORD LEWIS GORDON: third son of Huntly.

GEORGE, LORD GORDON: eldest son of Huntly.

ARCHIBALD CAMPBELL, EIGHTH EARL OF ARGYLL: *MacCailean Mor*, chief of Clan Campbell, later first Marquis,

ALEXANDER LESLIE: Field-Marshal, later first Earl of Leven.

ROBERT ARNOT, or BALFOUR, SECOND LORD BALFOUR OF BURLEIGH: Scots statesman and general.

QUEEN HENRIETTA MARIA: wife of King Charles.

PRINCE RUPERT OF THE RHINE: nephew of King Charles, Royalist commander.

PRINCE MAURICE OF BOHEMIA: brother of above, Royalist general.

SIR WILLIAM ROLLO: son of Laird of Duncrub, lieutenant of Montrose.

ALASTAIR MACDONALD, YOUNGER OF COLONSAY: nicknamed Colkitto, commander of Irish gallowglasses.

DAVID DRUMMOND, MASTER OF MADDERTY: heir of Lord Madderty, brother-in-law of Montrose.

JAMES OGILVY, FIRST EARL OF AIRIE: chief of Ogilvys and staunch kingsman.

SIR DAVID OGILVY: son of Airlie.

SIR THOMAS OGILVY: son of Airlie.

COLONEL NATHANIEL GORDON: soldier of fortune.

COLONEL MAGNUS O'CAHAN: Irish lieutenant of Colkitto.

WILLIAM KEITH, SEVENTH EARL MARISCHAL: chief of Keiths and Covenant commander.

JOHN MACDONALD OF MOIDART, CAPTAIN OF CLANRANALD: great Highland chief.

ALAN CAMERON OF LOCHEIL, CAPTAIN OF CLAN CAMERON: great Highland chief.

IAN LOM MACDONALD: the Bard of Keppoch.

PART ONE

I

JAMES GRAHAM STOOD, TAPPING THE TOE OF HIS HIGH-HEELED silken shoe on the waxed floor, and eyed his fellow men and women with scant approval. He was not aware that this showed rather plainly – or indeed, at all – on his handsome features; nor even that impatience was evident in his toe-tapping. For he was a young man of principle as well as of determined courtesy, and desired to offend none, except perhaps in chivalrous fashion and in a suitable cause. But these people were, in the main, deplorable to a man of any sensibility, women as well as men, unfortunately. James Graham approved of women, normally.

That there were not a few Scots amongst the posturing, painted, scented, chattering crew, was probably half the trouble. James Graham was philosophically and broad-mindedly prepared to find the English courtier more or less like this – just as he had made thoughtful allowances for the inanities and perversions of Paris, Seville, Venice, Padua, Florence, and even the Papal Court at Rome, from which he had just come; but to see Scots like John Maitland, Master of Lauderdale, with rouged cheeks and painted lips; Patrick Leslie, Lord Lindores, simpering and ogling behind upraised scented gloves; and the handsome Elizabeth Murray, though she could be no more than sixteen, not only with her gown cut so low that her breasts escaped whenever she stooped or bowed – which she did with marked regularity – but chose to find her garters in constant need of adjustment, with consequent extra stooping and disarray; all this was unedifying. The last might be all very well, indeed perhaps commendable, in private. But not in public, not in the Palace of White-hall, surely. Here it seemed not only a betrayal of sound Presbyterian Scotland, but in the worst of taste. Not that the thronging, overdressed crowd found it so, most evidently, since all were of a similar pattern. As though determined to demonstrate that the wretched Puritans had no place here. Yet the King was a sober and religious man, much more godly than was James Graham – and Scots-born at that. That he should tolerate this sort of behaviour at his Court was scarcely believable. His flighty little French wife, of course, was otherwise, they said – and the doting Charles denied her nothing. No doubt this was Henrietta Maria's doing.

The Graham had had half an hour of this already, and wondered how much more he could, or should, stand. He was a young man not used to being kept waiting. Hamilton had said to be here at six prompt. In that half-hour he had barely spoken to a soul; just stood, apart a little, feeling out-of-place and somehow conspicuous – which last at least was no illusion, for James Graham in any company was conspicuous, of a sheer beauty of countenance which, though wholly masculine and virile, was allied to a proud grace of bearing that never failed to draw all eyes – even though fullest appreciation thereof was not necessarily the reaction of every one of his own sex.

Though he recognised many, he did not really know anyone here – nor indeed greatly desired to. Perhaps something of this attitude escaped him, despite his carefully courteous intentions. Three years on the Continent had made a stranger of him, even to the Scots present – and he had been only just of age, after all, when he left on his rather unusual Grand Tour. Nor had he ever previously visited the Court at London. It seemed that he had missed little thereby.

His foot was tap-tapping again, when a voice at his elbow turned him.

'Egad, James – it's yourself! On my soul, I scarce knew you! I heard you were home. But . . .'

'Home, Johnnie . . .?' the other repeated, high brows higher. But he quickly relented, and smiled, warmly – and thereby transformed the proudly beautiful face into one of quite extraordinary attraction and charm. 'It is good to see a kent face – and an honest one! They seem scarce here! What brings you to Whitehall, Johnnie? A long way from the Carse of Forth.'

'What brings anyone to Court, James? The hope of betterment. Of justice, if you like.' The Lord Kilpont grimaced plain, boyish features. 'Not that I look like to win either, 'fore God! And yourself? What brings you, of all men?'

'Not betterment. Nor yet justice, I think,' the other returned – and his slightly scornful enunciation of the word betterment was eloquent. Then, as so often, he shook his head briefly, as though to throw off an involuntary reaction in favour of an amended and kinder one. 'I am sorry that you are not finding success, Johnnie. Or justice. For, i' faith, if all I hear is true, that you much deserve. Your father's ill-treatment was a crying scandal. Are you hoping for a reversal of the forfeiture?'

'Nothing so great. Only some small office of profit, some help with our creditors. The Customs of Airth and Alloa, perhaps. We are near penniless, James. Things have gone from bad to worse, while you have been gone. My father is a done and broken man. He will not last long, I fear. He is dunned, day in, day out. But he is too proud to ask the King's mercy, or aid. So I come. But to little benefit . . .'

'Poor Menteith! I did not know that it was so bad. I heard only snatches of it all, garbled. In Padua, I was then. This of Menteith is sore tidings . . .'

'Hush, man! Do not mention that name. Even to breathe the word Menteith today is next to high treason! My lord of *Airth* only, if you please!'

James Graham eyed his far-out kinsman with a perplexed frown. 'You mean this, Johnnie? Surely not! Surely Charles is not thus. A godly man, all say, and honest. Noble, indeed . . .'

'Perhaps. But weak, James – or, if not weak, with great weaknesses. Stupidities, 'fore God! The worst, that he relies on favourites who are fools or knaves. More of the first than the other, I do believe – but the end is the same! Aye, Charles Stewart looks noble enough, sounds noble – but how noble are his acts? Ask William Graham, my father!'

Lord Kilpont, a year younger than his chief, was son and heir to William, who until two years before had been eighteenth Earl of Menteith, one of the greatest nobles and proudest names in Scotland; and who, because in a rash moment, flushed with wine, had been heard to boast that his own blood was more truly royal than the King's, had been summarily forfeited, deprived of his ancient earldom with all its great revenues, and allowed to retain only his small

13

barony of Airth, in the Carse of Stirling, with the scornfully new-minted title of Earl of Airth – this by King Charles's personal command, who, on the advice of sundry ill-wishers of Menteith's, was pleased to sense a threat to his throne and dignity in the Graham's bibulous boast, true as it was. For the Grahams were of royal descent, and closer to the main stem of the ancient Scots ruling line than was Charles Stewart himself. The new Earl of Airth, who should also have been Earl of Strathearn, a semi-royal and illustrious earldom, was a ruined man.

The imputation that the dignified and stately monarch was weak – and worse, stupid – disturbed James Graham. 'I think you mistake, my friend,' he said. 'His Grace was ill-advised in this, to be sure. I have not all the truth of it – I was a year gone when it was done, was I not? All that I may do, to put it right, I will do. But – you go too far, naming the King weak and stupid. Charles Stewart is no weakling, no fool, I swear. God forbid!'

'You have not spoken with him, I think? Even seen him?'

'No. But all declare him worshipful, wise, good.'

'I could name you some who do not!' Kilpont said grimly. But at the other's expression he wisely changed the subject. 'And you, James – what do *you* seek from His Grace?'

'Seek? I seek nothing. Only to offer him my services. As is my simple duty.'

'Your services . . . ?'

'To be sure. What else? I am Montrose.'

'Mm. *An Greumach Mor!* In Scotland that means much,' the Viscount acceded. 'But here . . . ?'

'It is in Scotland, naturally, that I would serve him. Not here.' The other's glance around him was sufficiently eloquent. 'Are you of Hamilton's mind, then, about the King?'

'Hamilton? Does that one *have* a mind? Pray, James – of a mercy, do not speak my name in the same breath with that . . . lickspittle! That empty-headed, ill-disposed, vapouring toady!'

'Save us, Johnnie – what's come to you, man? You were not always so sour! Myself, I do not greatly love Hamilton – but he is great with the King. Has his ear. And is the foremost man in Scotland today, they say.'

'In Scotland! That mincing popinjay would no more set

14

his dainty foot in Scotland today than in Muscovy! He is the worst of all the crew of fawning, lying, sycophants who surround the King. All you may say is that Scotland is well quit of James Hamilton and his like!' Clearly, boyish as he still looked, Kilpont was a very different man from the laughing, heedless twenty-year-old James Graham had left behind him. Then he paused in his vituperation to ask, 'What was it you meant about my lord Marquis? His mind, anent the King?'

'Merely that he warned me that the King was much offended with Scotland, these days. That I should take care how I mention his ancient kingdom to His Grace – lest it serve me but ill. Myself, I cannot believe this. Scotland, after all, is his true realm. Where he was born, where his line belongs. It is but thirty years since the Stewarts have sat on this English throne. That he should hate Scotland is unthinkable . . .'

'So Hamilton said that?' Kilpont fingered the wispy hair on his chin which he was trying to grow – with an envious glance at the neatly luxuriant moustache and trim under-lip beard of his friend and chief. 'I wonder why, egad? He has his reasons, that one, no doubt.'

'You believe it to be untrue, then? Yet you hinted, did you not, that here my name may mean but little . . .'

Montrose paused, as another man came sauntering up to them, an exquisite this, in sky-blue satin and brocade, lace, jewelled buckles, earrings and ivory-handled, shoulder-high, ribboned walking-staff.

'Save us, Basil – you too!' he exclaimed. 'Got up like a mummer at a fair, as bad as the rest! I vow, all you require now is a dancing-bear!'

'At Court, one must be a courtier, my dear James – or nothing! And I would be *something,* as you know,' the newcomer declared, laughing, and flourishing a lace-edged, scented handkerchief. A plump-featured, silky-haired, genial young man, he pointed, with the head of that ridiculous staff. 'You, now – you serve yourself but ill, dressed so. I swear it! Even the beauteous and poetic Earl of Montrose! You will but seem to rebuke others – and so smell curst Calvinist to His Majesty. See if you do not.'

James Graham looked down at his own attire, and shrugged. 'I think I am very well,' he said. 'It served well enough for half the Courts of Europe. Why not here?'

'Why not indeed?' Kilpont agreed. 'You are the most distinguished-seeming man in this Audience Chamber, for a wager!'

And that, in fact, was true. Distinguished was the apt word for this man. Without seeking to do so, he ever bore himself with a distinction, a separateness, and assurance of carriage which was something different again from the lithe natural grace and the fine features. That he should be dressed all in black, slashed with silver – even though of satin and velvet – apart from the deep white lace collar and ruffles at wrists, did further set him apart, and dramatically so, in the kaleidoscopic riot of colours in that great hall, although this was in fact his normal style for high occasions.

'Truly said,' the Englishman acceded. 'But distinction can be costly – against the undistinguished! I have said so before, James – being not troubled that way myself! But ... I have not the privilege of this gentleman's name ...?'

'Ha – of course. A kinsman, John Graham, Lord Kilpont, heir to the Earl of Menteith ...'

'A mercy, James – I told you! Not that. Never that. The name is as forbidden as that of MacGregor! Airth, if you please – to my sorrow!'

'Very well. Heir to the first Earl of Airth, though eighteenth otherwise! A sorry story. And this, Johnnie, is my good friend Basil, Viscount Fielding, who was my companion through most of the lands and cities of Europe. Heir to my lord Earl of Denbigh.'

Kilpont nodded, and Fielding made an elaborate leg, with which was associated a twirling of his staff and a flourish of the handkerchief.

'Honoured,' the latter commented. 'You Scots are so deucedly good at figures! I fear that I could never count. Eighteenth, you said? And that from the fifth Earl of Montrose ...!'

'But eighth Lord Graham, and twenty-third chief of the name, *An Greumach Mor*,' Kilpont interpolated carefully.

'Quite – oh quite! As I say – I never could add. As well, since my father is one of the new men. The first Earl! Makes it easy for me, you see ...'

'Enough of such nonsense,' Montrose said. 'The English can count, I think, as well as we, when it comes to most matters. Gold pieces, for instance. Acres. Houses. Servants.

Pay no heed to Basil's mockery, Johnnie – his tongue is the worst of him. For myself, it is the *King's* counting that concerns me. Of time! Hamilton said to be here by six o'clock. Now it is nearer seven.'

'His Majesty never appears before seven, I am told,' Fielding mentioned. 'He is a staid man, of set custom and habit. Not like his appalling and unpredictable sire. Ah – forgive me! He was a Scot also, of course! My tongue, again . . .'

'Is that truth? That the King never comes before seven o'clock? Then why did Hamilton have me here at six?' James Graham's pleasantly modulated, almost musical, voice, with the slight Highland intonation, went level, thin.

'I told you. The man's a fool,' Kilpont insisted. 'Hamilton. Or . . . perhaps he designed to keep you waiting!'

'Hamilton? The Marquis? Is he your sponsor, James?' Fielding asked. 'A strange man as I should know! My brother-in-law, no less! Married Margaret my sister – at the age of seven!'

'Sponsor, no.' That was short. 'Montrose needs no sponsor with his liege lord. I but sought his guidance, as how conveniently to approach His Grace. We are related at a distance. And his brother, Lanark, was with me at college . . .'

A sudden fanfare of trumpets from without interrupted him. The chatter in the huge gilded apartment stilled, and all eyes turned towards the top end, where great doors were flung open. Two files of Yeoman of the Guard, in scarlet and black, marched in, pikes on shoulders, to pace onward down the chamber. Right and left before them the company fell back, leaving a clear and red-lined central avenue. Behind, a gorgeously apparelled usher in heraldic tabard stalked in, and as the fanfare died away, thumped his rod on the floor.

'Silence for His most excellent Majesty Charles, by the Grace of God, King!' he cried. And everywhere men bowed low and women sank in deepest curtsy.

It was all highly impressive, dignified, suitable. Unfortunately, what followed was less so. A crowd of men came surging into the hall, some backing, sidling, even skipping, as they eddied round a small central group of three, bowing, flourishing, gesticulating, in a fatuous display of adulation. And within this capering perimeter the trio sauntered, one tall, in a peach-yellow satin, one short and tubby in rich, vaguely clerical habit, and one slender and slight in purple

2   17

velvet, wearing a wide-brimmed black hat with a large curling golden ostrich-feather. Because of the hat, and the fact that its wearer was not very tall, Montrose, like most others, could not see the man's features behind his escort.

If this entrance lacked something in dignity, no less so did the waiting company's reception. Straight from their bowing and curtsying, there was a jostling rush forward, men and women pushing and elbowing each other to be foremost on either side of the lines of inward-facing Yeomen of the Guard. James Graham, astonished, found himself shouldered aside in the scramble, and although he had been waiting in a good position all this while, now was quickly edged into the background.

'Come – or we will not win near the King,' Kilpont exclaimed, starting to push, in turn.

'Never!' the other jerked. 'Think you Montrose should act so? In such rabble!'

'You heard Fielding. At Court, do as the courtiers do! See – *he* does.'

'Let him. I bide here.'

'Then the King will not see you. What you came here for.'

'So be it, then. But . . . Hamilton knows that I am here.'

The Marquis of Hamilton was the tall man in yellow at the King's right; and because of his height, he could see over the heads of most of the crowd. Already, almost as soon as he entered the room, his glance had caught that of his fellow Scot – and though he looked away at once, without any sign, Montrose knew that he had recognised him. He was a fine figure of a man, though ridiculously overdressed and prinked up with a plethora of ribbons, bows, rosettes, costume-jewellery and the like on top of his peach satin slashed with scarlet. The royal right hand rested on his puffed and pearl-seeded sleeve.

It was some little while before James Graham could catch a glimpse of the King's face, when he momentarily took off his hat to greet a genuflecting lady presented to him by one of his troupe. But at the sight, the younger man's offence and ill-humour left him, melted promptly like snow in the sun. For Charles Stewart was all and more than he had hoped to see, his features noble, splendid, stately, kingly indeed, but never proudly arrogant or distant. Sensitive, compassionate, almost sad, his great lustrous Stewart eyes looked beneath his lofty forehead and delicately arching brows. The face was long and narrow, an impression accentuated by the pointed beard, longer than was usual for the period, and the shoulder-length curling auburn hair; and the general expression was grave. But the smile, when vouchsafed, was warm and kindly. Every inch and line and movement of the man was implicit with dignity.

''Fore God, man – you said he was stupid! Weak and stupid! I think your troubles must have cost you your wits, Johnnie!'

'Perhaps.' The other shrugged. 'He looks a king, yes. But he acts . . . otherwise. You will learn!'

The King passed slowly up the avenue formed by the Guard, pausing here and there to speak to some low-bowing man or dipping woman either singled out by himself or presented by one of his posturing minions – and always, when it was a woman, he briefly removed his great feathered hat with a gesture of the most gracious courtesy. Quite soon he was past a point level with Montrose, and no sign or glance given.

'You see,' Kilpont said. 'You are not noticed. Here it is deil tak the hindmost!'

'Wait, you,' the other answered.

They had a lengthy wait, for Majesty was in no hurry, and many people were spoken to and presented. Before long, James Graham's toe began to tap-tap the floor again.

When Charles at length turned, at the far end of the room, to move slowly back, the tubby man with the slightly clerical look about his plum-coloured velvet and lace, seemed to take over from Hamilton in making the majority of presentations. And he found more to catch his eye than had the Marquis – especially amongst the women – to the Graham's ill-concealed impatience.

'That man – who is he? A churchman – but with a good conceit of himself!'

'That is William Laud, the Archbishop. The King's close confessor! An Armenian – and the most unpopular man in England! Yet Charles loves him well – even better than Hamilton, they say. He has turned the Church here upside-down. And is seeking to do the same in Scotland . . .'

'Scotland? The Archbishop of Canterbury? What has such to do with Scotland?'

'Well may you ask! But King Charles heeds him in all things. And Charles is still King of Scots.'

Slowly the courteous monarch worked his way down the long room again. And despite himself, James Graham edged a little forward. When he saw Basil Fielding briefly enjoying the royal attention, he subconsciously smoothed the lace at his throat and the ruffles at his wrists, waiting to catch Hamilton's signal the while. But the Marquis looked anywhere but at Montrose; and the King gradually passed by.

'God's curse!' the Graham swore, beneath his breath. 'This is too much!'

Kilpont eyed his chief sidelong, and decided to hold his tongue.

Biting his lip, Montrose watched his sovereign's gracious retreating back.

Fielding came pushing his way to his friend's side again. 'James! Sink me – what's this? he exclaimed. 'You are ignored. This is beyond all belief. The Earl of Montrose – spurned. On your first visit to Court. You should have pushed forward, man. As I did. As all do . . .'

'I should not,' the other snapped. 'Besides, they know that I am here. Hamilton does. He looked at me. And his brother, Lanark, mincing there. I saw him peering – and pretending not to. Yet he has brought half a dozen to the King . . .'

'It is damnable. See – people are looking. Staring. I heard many whispering your name . . .'

'Let them . . .'

'James – if you slipped round there, to near the door, behind these, you would win close enough. As they go out. There is still time . . .'

'I will do no such thing. Think you I must dodge and jouk and crawl for any man? Even Charles Stewart?'

'But . . . if he does not know that you are here?'

'Then it is Hamilton's doing. And, 'fore God, I will not crawl for Hamilton!'

In silence the trio waited. And now there was no question but that many eyes were turned in their direction. Close by, a woman tittered.

Then, as the King was about to leave the room, and trumpeters were raising their instruments for the valedictory fanfare, Hamilton stooped, and spoke in the royal ear, turning to glance back directly at Montrose.

Charles Stewart paused, turned also, grave-faced, and waited.

Everywhere a sudden hush fell on the great company. Fielding grabbed his friend's arm.

James Graham stood where he was, head high, motionless, as grave-faced as his monarch.

Moments passed thus, sudden tension in the air. Hamilton was an abruptly changed man, prominent eyes darting, nibbling at his silky moustache. Then, frowning, he flicked a gloved hand at his younger brother, the Earl of Lanark, a flick that ended in a finger pointing at Montrose. William Hamilton came hurrying, pushing his way through the throng, to where the Graham stood.

'My lord . . .' he gasped, all but panted. 'James – His Grace . . . His Majesty will see you now. Come. Come quickly – in God's name !'

The other waited a second or two longer, then bowed formally. He moved forward unhurriedly.

'Haste ye, man.' Lanark, already well ahead, turned anxiously, to mutter, 'You'll not keep the King waiting !'

The Graham said nothing to that, and increased his pace no whit.

The dandified Lanark reached the royal presence a deal before his charge. His brother looking angry, flushed, began to speak, then changed his mind. The King's expression, like his bearing, had not changed.

'Your Majesty, have I leave to present my lord Earl of Montrose?' Hamilton jerked, at last.

'Ah, yes. I know of my lord,' Charles said mildly, inclining his head. He neither smiled nor frowned. But he extended his hand.

James Graham bowed low, and reached out to take the royal hand. But he did not take it in the usual way, to raise to his lips; instead he placed the long slender fingers between his own two palms, and bowed over it, in the traditional gesture of fealty.

'Your Grace's true and devoted servant to command,' he said, low-voiced.

The King, regaining his hand, considered the younger man from those lustrous sad eyes, but without his famed warmth. 'I did not see you come to honour my Coronation at Edinburgh, near three years ago, along with my other Scots lords,' he observed, his voice even.

'To my sorrow. I was then in Padua, Your Grace.'

'Indeed. Then I trust that Padua served you will. I bid you a good day, my lord of Montrose.' Charles inclined his head again, and turned away.

'Sire . . . !' Montrose exclaimed, and then bit back the flood of words which surged to his lips, as the King strolled off through the wide doorway, and the ring of his entourage closed round him.

The clamour of talk and exclamation rose again in the Audience Chamber behind, as the trumpets rang out.

Biting his lips, James Graham stared after the sovereign lord he had come to offer service and loyalty to, the service of a great and powerful house, great wealth, great man-power, and blood as proud as the Stewarts'. Then he flung himself round, and went stalking long-strided down the huge apartment, past the re-forming Yeomen, looking neither right nor left, caring nothing for the stares, the smirks or the tinkling laughter, making for the entrance at the far end.

He was down crossing the open palace courtyard before Kilpont caught up with him.

'Save us, James – here's your bonnet!' the other panted, clapping on his own wide hat. 'A plague on them – that was ill done! A studied insult! But, why? Why? To *you?*'

Montrose vouchsafed no answer.

'A mercy – no need for such haste, surely!' Kilpont was almost having to run to keep up with his companion's great striding. 'It was Hamilton's doing – that I swear. He has put the King against you. I was watching him. Charles is a fool, yes – but he does not lack civility. Even to me he was more civil than that – although he has not heeded my pleas. It was Hamilton . . .'

'The King it was who spurned me – not Hamilton!' the other got out, from behind clenched teeth. 'Whatever Hamilton may have said or done, it was Charles Stewart who decided. Decided to reject Montrose. Before all. I did not proffer my hand and fealty and name, to *Hamilton!*'

At the bitterness in his friend's voice, so unusual, so out-of-character, Kilpont shook his head.

'I am sorry, James – sorry. But . . . what next? Will you try again? Discover what Hamilton is at – and face him with it? Challenge the arrogant lickspittle! Approach Charles again . . .'

'I will not. I ride for Scotland tomorrow, as fast as horse-flesh will carry me. Shake the dust of this place off my feet. And wish that I had sailed home direct from France! That I had never thought to visit this London, to pay my duty. It is Scotland again, for me – tomorrow.'

'Damn it, if I will not ride with you, James! On my oath, I will! I've had enough of this city of fawning spaniels and toad-eaters! And I gain no advantage for my father, here. A breath or two of our snell Scots air – that is what we both need. And leave London to its stews, its stinks and its jackals and trucklers. Especially its Scots ones!'

The other nodded. 'Aye – I long to feel the wind off the heather again, the scents of bracken and pine, hear the crackle of whins in the sun. I have been away too long, Johnnie. It is time I was home. Time . . .'

2

JAMES GRAHAM HAD NEVER HAD ANY PRONOUNCED AFFECTION for Edinburgh, a city he had little known or had occasion to know. In friendly small Glasgow he had lived as a child, in the house of Lord Justice Clerk Elphinstone, with his own Mugdock Castle near by to the north. Of Perth he was fond, near his favourite home of Kincardine Castle, on the southern verge of Strathearn; and Stirling, to the south of this, was almost a Graham town. Montrose itself, where he had been born, though a smaller place, always pleased him. And St Andrews, where he had studied and spent his high youth gloriously, he loved as the finest little city, not only in Scotland but in all Christendom – better than Paris, Rome, Venice or Padua. But in Edinburgh, on its hills above the silver Forth, he somehow felt alien, chilled – not so much by its everlasting winds which, after all, were no colder than those of St Andrews – but by some quality in the folk, the temper of its people. He ever felt small, under the soaring tenements, the dizzy grey stone 'lands' which huddled so close on the climbing ridge between Holyroodhouse and the frowning Castle, projecting inwards over the narrow streets and wynds, so as almost to cut out the very sky – but never those winds. Yet this early May day of brittle sunlight, sting-ing showers and rain-washed colour, as he rode in beneath Arthur's Seat, past the Abbey and Palace, and up the Canon-gate and under the Netherbow Port, he almost embraced the place to him, acknowledging its magnificent setting, cherish-ing even its smells – and the blustering winds which made them more bearable than those of London and Paris – look-ing kindly on its craggy-jawed, bonneted men and shawled women, however little his benevolent glances were returned, and shook the glistening raindrops from his travelling-cloak with more cheer than he had shown for days. It was Scot-land, stern and stark and authentic, but vivid, challenging and self-sufficient as was nowhere else that he had come across in all his three years of travels – his own place, the land his love for which he had only truly discovered when far away.

He and Kilpont parted company in the Grassmarket, the latter to ride on westwards, out again by the West Port and so by Corstorphine and Linlithgow to Airth, short of Stirling, in whose small castle his sick and broken father roosted in-consolate; while Montrose, with young Graham of Morphie his esquire, Master John Lambie his secretary, his body-servant Dod Graham, and the six armed troopers who had ridden as his guard the length and breadth of Europe, turned southwards up the Candlemaker Row, climbing steeply, to issue from the city at the Bristo Port, and jingle at a trot across the Meadows, swinging westwards around the emi-nence where workmen were still busily erecting the great Geordie Heriot's Hospital, begun eight whole years ago and not finished yet. And now they were climbing on to the Burgh Muir, all whins and broom and rocky outcrops, where the burghers' thin cattle grazed, and the insolent herd-boys threw stones and lewd pleasantries at the horsemen, ready to dodge for safety amongst their shaggy charges at first sign of retaliation. Even this, today, commended itself to James Graham. Surely only in Scotland, where the independent

24

spirit ruled all, would herd-laddies throw stones at a belted earl and his party of armed cavaliers.

Across the Burgh Muir, the ground ever rising, with the Braid and Pentland Hills soaring behind and further gladdening the travellers' hearts after too long in at countries, they passed near the turrets and steep roofs of Wrightshouse, the Napier house of a kinsman. But they did not halt, pressing on to a long ridge of yellow-blazing whins, crackling in the sun as Montrose had ached to hear so many a time. And here they saw, on the slightly downward slope beyond, a tall stone tower rising sheerly out of the orchards and formal pleasance-gardens, a strong, stout battlemented keep of five storeys and garret within the parapet, complete with wall-walk, curtain-walled courtyard and gatehouse, trim, self-contained, indomitable – and not a little arrogant – typical of the land and the people.

At sight of it Montrose reined in a little, and his fine eyes clouded. 'Merchiston,' he murmured, to himself. 'Och, Margaret!' Then he shook his head under the splendid wide-brimmed and feathered hat, and kneed his mount on.

Under the gatehouse arch of Merchiston Castle they rode clattering into the cobbled courtyard, a stout porter in leather doublet and the inevitable blue bonnet coming bustling out to take the head of Montrose's magnificent stallion.

'Hech, my lord, my lord – it's yoursel'!' he cried. 'Man, Lord James, you're back! Guidsakes – here's a blessed day!'

'Aye, Wattie – I'm back. At last. To find you fatter than ever. Fat as an in-pig gilt, I vow!'

'Och, comfortable just,' the other averred complacently, handing the Earl down, 'Nae mair'n that. Yoursel', you look braw, my lord – braw. Aye, you've changed. The right cavalier now, beardie and all! She . . . she wouldn'a . . . och, man – my leddy . . . !' He shook his greying head, and turned ruddy face away.

'Aye, Watty – as you say.' That came thinly, stiffly. Then he touched the porter's shoulder, lightly. 'Is your master at home?'

'Ooh, aye. He's up in his ain bit chamber, at the top o' the house. He's aye there, writing, writing. He has little heart for aught else, the man, these days. Awa' up wi' you.'

Leaving the others to their own devices, Montrose climbed the detached forestair, crossed the little removable timber gangway, and so entered the keep at first-floor level – a device which ensured a second line of defence should the outer curtain-wall be breached. Then on up the narrow, winding turnpike in the thickness of the walling – eight-foot thickness – lit only by arrowslits, the steps hollowed by mailed feet. At the top, the little garret watch-chamber within the dizzy parapet wall-walk, was the room with the splendid views which his brother-in-law had made his study. He knocked and entered.

The greying, lean, grave-faced man in the shabby clothing turned at his deck by one of the dormer windows, to look, peer, and then jump up, rather sombre features lit up.

'Jamie! Jamie!' he cried. 'God is good – Jamie Graham! It's yourself.' His voice little different from that of his gate-porter below, Archibald first Lord Napier of Merchiston, Privy Councillor, Treasurer Deputy of Scotland for life, former Lord Justice Clerk and still extraordinary Lord of Sessions, came forward to greet the younger man in warmest welcome.

They embraced each other with undisguised affection, for they were the greatest of friends, these two, despite the discrepancy in age. Napier, when a man of forty, had married Montrose's second sister Margaret when she was eighteen, making her an excellent husband. More than that, he had made a second father for the boy who had lost his own sire at fourteen, and had to take on the formidable business of being *An Greumach Mor,* chief of all the Grahams, and fifth Earl of Montrose while still with five years of his teens to run. Lord Napier was long past the fathering stage, as that of legal guardian – but he remained the wise and trusted friend.

'Archie! Here's joy.' James Graham held the other back, to look at him – and only just stopped himself from blurting out how he had aged in three years. He recognised, too, that he perhaps should not have used that word joy. 'It has been a long time,' he said. 'Too long, Archie.'

'Aye, too long, lad.'

The other looked away, moistening his lips. 'Margaret,' he said. 'I am sorry. Dear God – I am sorry!'

Napier nodded. 'We are the poorer, Jamie. Perhaps, somewhere, some are the richer? Who knows? Your father. Mother. But . . . it is scant comfort.'

Margaret Graham had died less than a year after her

brother's departure for the Continent, after a dozen years of marriage, leaving three children and the still-born infant whose birth killed her. Like any husband in the circumstances, Archibald Napier could not absolve himself altogether from blame.

'She was the best of us,' Montrose said. 'The kindest, truest, most excellent. I grieve for us all – but for you above all.'

'God's will be done,' the other answered quietly.

'Was it God's will, then? You, a judge. Great in the Kirk. Tell me.' And then, at sight of the older man's perplexed and sorrowful face, he reached out impulsively to grasp his arm. 'I am sorry, Archie Forgive my ill tongue. I have learned to question much that before I accepted, these last years – perhaps too much. I did not mean to hurt you further.'

'Do not blame yourself, Jamie. But . . . questioning fate, destiny, what is ordained by the Lord God Omnipotent, serves nothing, brings no comfort but only more sorrow. This I have learned the sore way, God knows. A man must learn to accept.'

'But you yourself taught me to be a seeker. Ever a seeker, not an acceptor. Did you not?'

The other inclined his head. 'Aye. But now I seek God's *purpose* with men. And to accept His will – if I may. But – enough of this, lad. What of your other seeking? Your other sister? What of Katherine, Jamie? You still have not found her?'

Montrose shook his head. 'Not a trace. No word – nothing. As I wrote to you, I found John Colquhoun, at last. In Venice. But alone. Katherine was not there. She had gone. He said, he said that she had run off with another man! He knew not where.'

'God have mercy on her!' Napier whispered.

Montrose's prolonged Grand Tour had been rather more than just that. It had been a quest, a search, and a terrible one. Undertaken under the guise of finishing his education in the accepted fashion, to lessen the scandal of it all. And undertaken hurriedly, and against much good advice – including the Lord Napier's, which was why he had not been in his earl's place at King Charles's coronation at Edinburgh only a month or so after his hasty departure. For another brother-in-law, Sir John Colquhoun of Luss, chief of that

27

name and husband of the Lady Lilias, eldest of the five Graham sisters, had suddenly elected to desert his wife and family, abandon his estates, sheriffdom and responsibilities, and abscond to the Continent – and, what was worse, had taken with him the Lady Katherine Graham, the unwed younger sister of twenty. To the scandal of all Scotland. Outlawed by the shocked Privy Council, excommunicated by the outraged Kirk, Colquhoun and his sister-in-law disappeared beyond the seas. And nothing would serve young James Graham but that he there and then must advance the date of his projected educational tour of the capitals of Christendom, and go in search of his erring sister.

'I did not fight John Colquhoun,' he said, slowly. 'I had promised myself that I would have his life. But, seeing and hearing him, I perceived that would profit nothing. Nor help Katherine, nor yet Lilias. The man was broken, distraught, pitiful. I scarce knew him. He was a man deserted.'

'Deserted! Colquhoun? What are you saying, Jamie? Do you know what you are saying?'

'All too well, I know. *He* had been deserted – both by my sister, and by his creature Carlippis, who had been his evil genius throughout. The poor besotted fool!'

Appalled, Napier stared at the younger man. 'You . . . you are making your sister a wanton, then? A heartless wanton . . . !'

'I know not what my sister is. I *thought* that I knew her. We were close – but a year between us. She was ever my companion, as children. And ever she was spirited. Strange, in some fashion. But, this . . . ! God's mercy – what is she?'

'You are not saying that she went off with the Italian? Or German – whatever he was. That necromancer of Colquhoun's. A mere servant! With that wretched charlatan?'

'I do not know. Except that they left John Colquhoun secretly. And at the same time. And both went none know where.'

'If it had not been yourself telling me, I'd not have believed it! Katherine! Little Katherine. But nineteen years. And you learned no more of her?'

'I sent out messengers, enquirers, from Venice, Florence, Rome. All the time I was studying at Padua, I was seeking word of her. False scents I followed, in plenty. Nothing came of any. I was told of a young Scotswoman who had appeared at the Court of King Louis, calling herself the Comtesse de Medoc. Medoc might, at a stretch, be for Mugdock, where Katherine was born. I threw up my studies at Padua, and went to Paris with Basil Fielding, Denbigh's son. But the woman was Irish, not Scots. A young widow of a true Medoc. I remained at the French Court. Still seeking. Then your letter came, telling me that it was time that I returned to Scotland. That matters were not well here, and that I should be home.'

'Aye.' Heavily Napier said it. 'And that is the truth. I am sorry, lad. Grieved that all this sore trouble should have struck you – struck us all. Grieved to have fetched you home to more trouble. Grieved for this realm of Scotland . . .'

'You said in your letter that matters were going but ill. In kirk and state.'

'Ill, yes. But – see you, here is no way to welcome you home, Jamie. You will be weary, needing refreshment. How long do you bide with me?'

'A night, two. No more, Archie. Then I must ride north to Kinnaird. I sent word to Magdalen that I was coming.'

'To be sure. I must not keep you from her – blithe as I would be to have you bide.'

'Magdalen – all is well at Kinnaird?'

'Aye. No trouble there, at least, the good Lord be praised. She will rejoice to see you. She has missed you sorely, Jamie.' The older man shot a keen, searching glance at the younger. 'It has been a long time, lad. For a woman.'

'For us all, Archie – for us all. But I do blame myself – even though I esteemed them to have little need of me, up there.'

'More than you think, James. But – come you down. You must eat and drink. You will have your folk with you. My house is yours . . .'

It was evening before, fed and rested, Montrose could again be alone with his brother-in-law. They walked together in the mellow walled garden to the south of the castle, amongst clipped box and apple-trees, with the first swallows darting about them in the clear northern light – all of which affected the homecomer not a little.

'I urged you, in my letter, to make shift to see King Charles,' Napier said. 'Did you so, Jamie?'

'I saw King Charles,' the other answered.

At the tone of voice, the older man looked sidelong at his companion.

'You scarce sound enchanted? Did something go amiss?'

'Amiss, yes. Whether my face, my name, or the style of me, I know not. But His Grace would have none of me. Scarce threw me a word. Rejected me out-of-hand, before all his Court.'

Napier had stopped. 'You . . . you cannot mean this, in truth? That the King rejected you? *You*, Montrose! One of the greatest lords in Scotland. I cannot believe it, Jamie . . .'

'It is the truth. More than rejected – spurned. Deliberately. I was there to offer him my leal support and duty, my whole strength, my all. For the word is that he may need it! But, it seems that he wants none of it. Even though my family has borne up the Scots throne for centuries. Johnnie Kilpont says that it was Hamilton's doing. That Hamilton had poisoned the King's mind against me – I know not why. I have never given offence to Hamilton, that I know of .But . . . even so, Charles could have heard me, made his own judgment. My liege lord . . .'

'This is beyond all.' Shaking his head, Napier moved on slowly along the garden path. 'His Grace needs every true man he may find, indeed. Though most of all, honest advice – dear God, how he needs that! And he will not get it from Hamilton, and his like. But – how was it? What did he say . . . ?'

Clipped of voice, stiffly – for it went sorely against a young man's pride, especially one reared as Montrose had been, to power and authority almost from infancy – he told all, as they paced beneath the trees on the drifts of fallen apple-blossom.

Napier heard him out, frowning, sighing. 'Save us – I fear, Jamie. Fear for Scotland. Fear for the King's Grace – for us all. When a man can make so many mistakes, can scarce do anything aright – how shall the realm survive? And yet, he is honest, I am convinced. Means well. And is not a fool. Indeed, I conceive him honourable, truly princely in most matters. A man apart . . .'

'As did I. And so he appears, looks, sounds. But behaves, it seems, differently!'

'He is badly advised – we all know that. He has no judg-

30

ment as to whom to trust, to take into his confidence. He surrounds himself with time-servers, place-seekers, windbags. This I know only too well. He lacks his father's shrewdness. King James was as graceless a king as ever sat upon a throne – but he was shrewd. He would never have done what Charles is doing. Splitting his ancient realm in twain for the sake of a clerk's rigmarole, a prayer-book!'

'Kilpont said something of this. But he had not the rights of it, I am sure.'

'Aye – that is why I wanted you home, Jamie. I daresay young Kilpont was none so far out. This is the trouble that threatens Scotland. Dire trouble, and all for a few printed words on paper. The King, egged on by this wretched prelate Laud, this Archbishop he has made, is insisting that the Kirk changes its form of worship to the same as the Church of England! Indeed, he would have no Kirk of Scotland, but have us all worshipping God the same way, he says – his way, Laud's way. We must accept his bishops – these we have already, this while, but we scarcely bow down to them. But now he has seven of them on his Privy Council. And we are to use a new prayer-book of Laud's in our kirks, and give up the Presbyterian form of worship and church government. This, by royal command. On pain of treason!'

'But . . . but it is not possible! None can do such a thing. Not the King. Not any archbishop. Not any man on God's earth! Scotland's faith, her worship, is her own.'

'Charles says otherwise. He claims that he is head of the Church, as of the realm . . .'

'The Church of England, maybe – but not of Scotland! None but Christ Himself is head of Scotland's Kirk!'

'Aye – so we, the Kirk, have told him. But he will have none of it. He has appointed a Court of High Commission, to rule for him in matters ecclesiastical. He has appointed Archbishop Spottiswoode of St Andrews as Chancellor of Scotland, instead of the Earl of Kinnoull – the first churchman to hold the office since the Reformation of blessed memory. He has made a new diocese of Edinburgh, and declared the High Kirk of St Giles to be its Cathedral, and ordered cast down the partition-wall between the chancel and the nave. He will have none of the presbyters – we are all to be Episcopalians, bowing to his bishops whether we will or no.'

'But . . . he cannot make us, 'fore God! He cannot change a nation's religion – one man!'

'He can try. And lacks not the means, or the will to enforce it. John Livingstone, Lord Balmerino, you know. He protested, sought to rally others to protest. The King called it high treason. Had him warded and tried – aye, and condemned. To death, no less! For gainsaying the royal right to say how we should worship. But, man – there was siclike an uproar over it, that even Charles Stewart took second thoughts and issued a royal pardon. But, see you – it *was* only a pardon, not a reversal of his edicts. And, it seems, he has learned nothing by it. A new ordinance to regulate the worship of the Kirk was signed, in London, earlier this year. And this very month a Book of Canons was sent up to us, for obedience. These Canons to have the force of law. Moreover, there is this Liturgy to follow. That is Charles Stewart, by the Grace of God, King! And, stirring up this bees' bike, he yet spurns Montrose's hand and help!'

'Is he run mad, the man?'

'Well may you ask! But I think not. It is that he has a set and unyielding mind. And believes that he is right – always he is right. And has none, that he will listen to, who will tell him to his face that he is wrong! Letters we have written – but they achieve nothing. Save to put our necks at risk! I fear that we have that most dangerous of rulers, Jamie – a righteous, unbending autocrat, who believes that he, and he only, knows the mind of our God! His father before him, James the Sixth, called himself Christ's Vice-regent. The son, I swear, *believes* it!'

'And yet, he appeared a gentle man, noble. He served me less than kindly – but in himself appeared to be kindly, no autocrat, no tyrant.'

'As you say. Here in Scotland, when he came to his coronation near three years past, all men conceived him as worthy, upright. Noble, as you say. Indeed, I believe that in most things he is so – save this of religion. And here, the sorrow of it, his uprightness becomes menace, no less. In his inmost heart, Charles is brittle, unbending. It grieves me to say it, for I have served him and his father all my days. But now, it seems, none may serve him save sycophants and toadies. That, James, I will never be.'

At the heavy solemnity of his friend's voice, Montrose

shook his head. 'This all makes of my small trouble a mere nothing, Archie,' he said. 'The vexations of a halfling! I see well how the greater trouble will grow, if it is not checked. Myself, I care not greatly whether a man approaches his God through a bishop or a presbyter. Indeed, it may be that neither need come between any true worshipper and his creator, any more than need a Romish saint – only the Lord Christ's intercession being necessary. But . . . I would give my blood to defend the right of every man to choose for himself. This of the King could split the realm.'

'Well and truly said. But, indeed, what Charles is doing is not so much splitting his realm now as uniting it. Uniting it against himself. You mind how he forced through the Act of Revocation, in 1625 – to compel the lords and lairds, who had won the Old Church's lands at the Reformation, to yield them up again. For the support of his new bishops. That drove a sore wedge between King and nobles. We both lost no little by it, Jamie. Not a lord but is in fury against having to pay tithes to the Kirk and rent to the Crown. But this concerned the churchmen and ministers no whit. Nor the common folk. Indeed, they chuckled, as we know well. But now, the King is forcing his bishops and prayer-book down the throats of Kirk and people. He will have all Scotland against him, lords, Kirk and folk. Save only, it may be, the Catholics – ominous allies, on my soul! Our good and upright liege lord is sowing the seeds of hatred, Jamie. And heeds no good counsel.'

'You have told him, besought him?'

'When he was here, for his coronation, I spoke – and received but small thanks, as you may guess. Since, I have written letters. As is no more than my duty, as one of the King's ministers of state. And as result am losing the King's regard, certain offices. I have had to give up my Orkney estates, which I had of the Crown. Intriguers at Court have them now. I am no longer Deputy Treasurer . . .'

'But that was yours for life, was it not?'

'Aye, for life. But King Charles is displeased with me, and I was forced to resign the office. I was compensated with monies – but what is that, when I no longer have my master's trust? Not that I care greatly for office, or aught else, since Margaret died – but I have much experience, and ought to be able to advise the King. I am still of the Privy

Council – but no longer is the Scots Council's word
heeded . . .'

'Dear God – the folly of it ! The waste.'

'It is more than folly, waste, lad. It could spell disaster.
Scotland will never thole this burden. The freedom for which
our fathers fought, from Bruce's, Wallace's days, till this –
it is not to be lost at the scrape of a royal pen. More especially
with an English cleric's hand behind it ! It must not be, *will*
not be ! I am the King's most leal subject, but if he insists on
this, by force – which God forbid ! – I, and many another
like me, on whom he could have relied, will not stand idly
by and see it done.' The older man's voice shook a little. 'To
this end, James, to this evil end, I have brought you home.'

For long moments they looked at each other, there in the
shadowy garden, sombre-eyed, silent; until, in unspoken
agreement they turned and went indoors, the glowing May
night gone sour on them.

3

IT WAS NOT AT MUGDOCK IN THE CAMPSIE FOOTHILLS NORTH
of Glasgow, nor yet at Kincardine in the southern skirts of
Strathearn, nor even at Old Montrose on the Mearns sea-
board, that James Graham ended his three years' journeying; but at another's house, not his own, in the wide valley of
the South Esk in Angus between the Grampians and the sea,
admittedly not far from Montrose but unconnected there-
with – Kinnaird Castle, seat of the Carnegies, whose lord had
recently been raised to the status and dignity of first Earl of
Southesk. To this great house in its spreading parkland,
where the Esk coiled to join that strange landlocked tidal
basin of Montrose Bay, the Graham and his little entourage
rode down over the braes of Rossie Muir three evenings later
– and again with very mixed feelings. It was a fair place, rich,
settled, secure, and though it was not his home, he knew it

34

as well as any house of his, and loved it well. His mind had dwelt on it long and often, and on what it contained, these past many months, even ached to see its warm brown-stone towers, cattle-dotted parks and spreading orchards, and to hear the voices that would assuredly welcome him there. But now that he in fact approached it, he knew strange doubts, qualms, almost reluctance. It had been so long. So much had changed. He was indeed a different man from the youngster who had ridden away, a man travelled, experienced, tried, mature, where he had been little more than an enthusiastic but callow stripling. All must inevitably be much altered – and not only in himself.

They had been seeing for some time the two columns of blue smoke ascending high in the early evening air, before it dawned on him that these were not woodsmen's fires but, sited on an eminence just to the west of the castle, must be twin beacons, bonfires. He had sent word of his coming, from Edinburgh; and these must have been blazing all day to welcome him back. The recognition brought something of a lump into Montrose's throat.

While still almost a mile from the great house, they saw the file of horsemen come spurring out from under the gate-house arch, to drum over the drawbridge timbers and come southwards at a canter, obviously to meet him. Keen eyes had been watching. When a banner unfolded itself, to stream in the breeze and flutter bravely at the head of the oncoming party, James Graham's own eyes misted a little. Even at that range he could see that it was of black and gold – and the only black-and-gold heraldic banner of earl's size in all broad Scotland bore the undifferenced arms of the chief of the Grahams, *An Greumach Mor*. Besides himself, only one other could, or would, ride under that ensign.

As they drew near it could be seen that of the five who rode to meet them one was no more than a child, a small figure though mounted on no pony; one was a richly dressed youngish man slightly older than Montrose himself; one was a burly man of early middle-age, who bore the banner; and the other two were grooms. Much moved, James Graham slowed his horse to a walk.

A few yards off, the man with the banner signed to the boy, who promptly pulled off his mount with some style, at the same time managing to doff his plumed hat with a

35

flourish – even though it knocked against his horse's head and ears in the process and almost fell from a small hand. Undeterred, flushing a little, the large eyes bright, the lad jerked a bow from the saddle.

'Greetings, my lord,' he said. 'I hope that I see your lordship well. And not wearied. My lady-mother sends her dev . . . devotion.' That was of a gabble, but he got it out.

'Johnnie!' Montrose said. It was not often that this adequate man made so inadequate response.

The twenty-four-year-old father and the six-year-old son sat their sidling horses and stared at each other. Inevitably they were almost strangers. The toddler of three whom the man had left behind him bore little resemblance to this fine-featured, rather delicate-looking lad with the big eyes and serious expression. Foolishly Montrose had continued to think of him as he had last seen him. And the young Lord Graham had scarcely been able to remember his sire at all – save by the portrait by Master Jamesone, which hung in his mother's chamber; and this fine gentleman hardly resembled that eager youth.

With an effort the man restrained himself from spurring forward to clasp that small, proud yet anxious figure to himself. That would never do – not when the boy had come thus formally to meet him, under that banner, playing the man, beside the Chamberlain, bringing his mother's greeting.

'I rejoice to see you, son,' he said, controlling his voice, like the rest of him. 'So tall. So well grown. And well favoured. I thank you for coming to meet me. You sit your horse fairly.'

The lad flushed with pleasure. 'He has been saddled all day awaiting you,' he said, in a rush. 'My Uncle James – my Lord Carnegie, I mean – taught me to ride. He says that I am better than you were, at six years . . .' That tailed off in something of a gasp, as realisation dawned that perhaps this might be thought scarcely tactful in the circumstances.

'Ha! That could well be,' Montrose acceded gravely. 'It is good to hear.' He turned to the other, younger, man. 'So you are Lord Carnegie now, Jamie. Of course. So much has happened. Davie's sad death. I am sorry – a tragedy. And your father's elevation. I still think of *him* as Lord Carnegie. Accept my congratulations. And my thanks for making a horseman out of my son.' That last was said courteously, but just slightly formally, considering that they were brothers-in-law. These two, although brought up as near neighbours and close family friends, had never greatly loved each other. Carnegie's extra three years had made for a certain superiority and condescension, which had tended to be frustrated by the fact that he was only a second son – and of a first lord, at that – while, from the age of fourteen, the other was fifth Earl of Montrose, chief of all the Grahams, and moreover insufficiently humble for his years. The raising of his father, the Lord Carnegie, to be first Earl of Southesk, at the King's Scottish coronation in 1633, only a few months after Montrose's departure, and the death of the elder brother, David, less than six months later, had only partially evened the score.

Carnegie had been eyeing the other closely, and not failing to note all the splendid good looks, the poise, authority and maturity of the man. He recognised all too clearly, but without elation, that some further adjustment of attitudes would be necessary. His voice was curter than probably he intended.

'No thanks required. And I have taught him more than that, I hope. Lacking his father, someone must needs do so ! Hm . . . welcome back to Kinnaird. It has seemed a long time.'

'Long, yes.' Eyes grey and considering locked for a moment or two with eyes brown and smouldering. Then Montrose turned to the somewhat older man with the flag, thick-set, ruddy-complexioned and plainly dressed. 'It is good to see you, Sir Robert. Kind in you to come. You at least have not changed, I swear !' That was said with a smile. 'See – I have brought back your heir to you, as you have brought me mine !'

Graham of Morphie bowed, scarcely glancing at his own son, Montrose's esquire. 'I could do no less than come, my lord James. I have looked to this day for long. You are well returned. Greatly needed. I rejoice to see you home.'

Morphie was the nearest of the Graham lairds to Kinnaird and Montrose, his property lying only some six miles to the north, at Marykirk of the Mearns. Sir Robert had been left in charge of the great Montrose estate as Chamberlain, during his chief's absence. A solid, able man, he had been one of the curators, with Archie Napier and David Carnegie, appointed by the old Earl of Montrose to look after the boy he left as heir. And he was married to the Earl of Southesk's sister.

'All tell me it is time that I returned,' Montrose said, a little grimly. 'You also, Robert. You will have your reasons?'

'Aye, my lord.' That was heavy. 'I shall not be sorry to shift a wheen burdens from my shoulders to yours! Praise to God, they look now sufficiently broad to bear them!'

'Mm.' Brows raised, the Earl shrugged. 'So be it, then. I have now to look to my own interests – thanking you who have looked to them for me.' He nodded to both men. 'Come, Johnnie – take me to your mother.'

Urging his mount forward, he was able to close with the boy, at last, and slip an arm around the slight shoulders momentarily, without any suggestion of unmanliness. Then, side by side they rode down the long slope to the marshland, to splash across the Pow Burn, and on, over the wide parklands to Kinnaird Castle on its terrace.

A great company waited to receive them, assembled within the inner bailey, beyond the drawbridge and gatehouse, of all ranks and standing, men, women and children too. The return of the Graham was an occasion indeed.

In the centre stood a big bulky man in his sixties, florid, choleric, with white hair and a bushy beard – David, new Earl of Southesk, eighth Laird of Kinnaird, first Lord Carnegie, Privy Councillor, High Sheriff of Forfar, Extraordinary Lord of Session and father-in-law of James Graham. He stood with arms akimbo, and looked threatening; but then David Carnegie usually looked threatening. He was flanked by two young women, one bold-eyed and handsome, the other modest and plumply comely – his Countess and third wife, and his daughter Magdalen. Each held a two-year-old toddler by the hand, girl and boy.

'Greeting, my lord Earl!' Montrose called dismounting, and doffing his hat with a flourish. 'I need not ask if I see *you* well. Growing younger year by year, I swear!' He bowed to the Countess of Southesk. 'My lady – you bloom! My lord looks to suit you as well as you him! Your servant.' And to the other, still younger woman, a year younger than himself, in fact, he raised an open hand. 'Magdalen, my dear.'

One countess, his own, dipped deeply, and murmured, 'My lord,' low-voiced. The other stared openly, assessingly, and whistled, barely beneath her breath, in scarcely ladylike fashion, saying nothing.

'So you are back, boy! You have taken your time, have you no'?' Southesk cried. None other than he would have thought to call Montrose boy – and even he looked just a little bit askance as he said it, perceiving that there were changes here which could not be entirely ignored. 'We looked to see you near a year back. What held you?'

'I am flattered that you so greatly missed my poor presence, my lord,' the other answered easily. 'But matters of sufficient import delayed me, I assure you.'

'Aye. Well, there's matters o' sufficient import amiss for you, here in this Scotland, man. For any man! You've come home to trouble, see you.'

'So I have heard. On all hands.' He shrugged, ruefully. 'And, I vow, you might think it all *my* doing, from the way it is laid on me! But . . . of that later.' Montrose looked round at all the assembled company, and made a comprehensive bow, flourish of his plumed hat, and friendly smile. 'My salutations to you all,' he called. 'It is good to see you again. I am glad to be back. My thanks for your reception of me. Hereafter I shall speak with you all. But meanwhile, my lady-wife demands her errant lord's attention – and merits it, you will concede! You will bear with us?'

It was superbly done, with assurance, simplicity, courtesy yet authority, such as the James Graham who had departed three years before could never have achieved. It took charge of the situation for them all, even for old Southesk, his Countess and his son. *An Greumach Mor,* Earl of Montrose, was now to be permitted to greet his wife with some measure of privacy. None found cause for complaint or discomfort.

None, that is, save perhaps for the Lady Magdalen Carnegie herself. Always a shy and retiring creature, she was apparently quite overwhelmed by this handsome, self-possessed, almost commanding presence that had come back to her after so long. Almost in a panic she bit her lip, clutching the toddler to her knees, all but shrinking back as Montrose came forward to her, eyes darting towards her father, her brother, even her small son, to anyone, for aid.

Her husband saw it, and understood, at least partially. He turned to young Johnnie, hand out, and together they moved up to the woman.

'My dear,' he said gently, 'this young man has already conveyed to me your greetings and welcome. Most worthily. How fine a son you have bred for me. I am grateful – from my heart I am. And here – here is another, on my soul! Another good Graham for Scotland!'

That saved her. 'Yes. Yes, this is Jamie, my lord.' She was constrained to stoop, and make a great fuss of picking up the little one in her arms, and so could face her husband with the child as a sort of buffer. 'Is . . . is he not a fine lad? And like you, a little. Like you . . . you were.' She gulped. 'Not now – but were. Your nose. I am sure that he has your nose. So, so long. No, no – not too long. But . . . your nose. And mouth. Yes, your mouth also. Jamie – he is strong. Stronger than Johnnie. Oh, Johnnie is stronger now. But as a bairn. When you left, Johnnie was not strong. You remember that. I . . . I . . .' She was gabbling. And realising it only too clearly, abruptly stopped and became unutterably silent.

He nodded gravely. 'Yes, indeed. That I remember well. Which makes it all the better that you have made of Johnnie so much the man.' He patted his heir on the head, and reached out to take the younger child from her. 'So this is the second James Graham! We will have to learn to know each other, he and I. But you will teach us.' He felt down with his other hand, and raised hers to his lips. 'You have much to teach me, my dear.'

She did not answer, but something of the panic had left her. She was able to slip that kissed hand under his arm, to take her elder son by the elbow, and so face all the chattering throng, after a fashion, Magdalen, Countess of Montrose with her man and bairns. They bowed, left and right, moving towards the keep doorway.

It was long, however, before they could be alone together – nor, indeed, were either of them over-eager for that moment. It was Southesk's house, and as well as much eating and drinking to see to, he had bones to pick with young Montrose, with his son, with his brother Sir John Carnegie, who presently arrived from Ethie Castle to the south. David Carnegie was a great picker of bones – which perhaps partly accounted for his youngest daughter's chronic distrust of herself. At any rate, he kept his male company at table well into the night, long after the ladies had retired – even after his young wife, new married just before Montrose had left

40

on his travels, reappeared on the minstrels' gallery above the
Great Hall for a few moments, sought to attract her lord's
attention, failed, and raising eloquent eyebrows implying
complicity with the watching James Graham, departed.

When at last he managed to escape, and made his way
across the courtyard, in the wan northern half-light, to the
flanking-tower which his wife and children occupied, he went
quietly. But light still gleamed from the window of the
first-floor bed-chamber. And when he entered, seeking to
keep the door from creaking, it was to find Magdalen lying
awake on the great four-poster bed, staring up at the dusty
canopy. She did not look at him, after the first quick glance.

'I believed that you would be asleep,' he said. 'I have been
long. Your father had much to talk over. I am sorry. I have
come home, it seems to a realm seething with unrest like a
porridge-pot on a hob!'

'Yes,' she said.

'If you are wearied, Magdalen, would be alone, I will
sleep tonight in the boys' chamber?'

'No,' she said.

'Very well.' He sat on the edge of the bed, looking down
at her. It has been a long time, my dear,' he said slowly.

'Yes.'

'Your letters – I thank you for them. You are good with
letters.'

'Better, better than with . . . other things.'

'Do not say it. You never thought sufficiently highly of
yourself. *I* think more kindly.'

'Yet . . . you stayed away. For long.'

'Yes. There was so much to be done. To be seen. To be
learned. And I am scarce likely ever to go back. A different
world, Magdalen. A wider, richer world. Of great experien-
ces, of treasures, of thought and learning. Of a quality of
living far beyond anything we know here in Scotland. It
behoves any who will have rule in this realm to learn of it
all they may.'

She did not answer.

'This custom, to make the Grand Tour, is wise, lass. It
broadens a man. Those who are born to lead require such
broadening. Without it, those they lead can only suffer . . .'

'My brother Jamie. He went likewise. On his Tour. And
came home in but one year. From Padua.'

41

'Did he not come home when Davie died? As new heir. But – what of it? I am not Jamie Carnegie. Moreover, I had a task, a quest, which he had not.'

'You never found her? Katherine? No trace?'

'No trace,' he agreed, sombrely.

'I am sorry for that.' For the first time, she turned her eyes on him. 'You were close, I know. Closer to her than to any. It must hurt you sorely.'

'Yes. I did all that a man could. Searched the length and breadth of Europe. Had enquirers in every land. I wonder if, indeed, she still lives.'

'Poor Kate . . .'

'No – not poor Kate! Whatever else she is, or was, not poor! She lived ever richly, rashly, but to the full. Expended herself, never counting the cost. Foolish, often. Headstrong, yes. Unkind at times. But in herself, her life, rich. Not poor Kate.'

The woman turned her head away. 'Perhaps. And you – you are of the same stamp. As . . . as sure of yourself. And I am . . . otherwise. It is poor Magdalen, I think!' Her voice choked a little. 'You would not . . . have spent three years searching for me!'

Shaking his head unhappily, he eyed her. '*You* would never have required such search. Run away with your own sister's husband. And then abandoned him, likewise. Gone off, heedless of all, God knows where! You would not, could not. But, had Magdalen Carnegie indeed done that, I would have gone seeking for her, likewise.'

'Would you? I wonder! No – Magdalen Carnegie stays at home. A good wife. Dutiful. Waiting. Always waiting. Her husband's pleasure. A dutiful wife, mother of his bairns. Dutiful mother. Waiting – since the day we were wed. Bairns ourselves!'

'Waiting, lass? Waiting – for what? Not, I think, just for this return of mine?'

'Dear God – I do not know!' She twisted round to face him again, and a hand came out from beneath the bedclothes to grasp his lace-edged wrist, the nails digging into his flesh. 'Oh, James, James – I do not know! Sweet Christ have mercy upon me – I do not know!' she sobbed.

Frowning, the man bent to kiss that flushed brow, to stroke that thick, lustrous hair soothingly. He was not the only one whom the years had changed, it seemed. It was all true. They had been wed as little more than children. At seventeen, with his Mastership of Arts from St Andrews secured, his curators, Archie Napier, Graham of Morphie and David Carnegie, had decided that the Earl of Montrose ought to be married. What better choice than the sixteen-year-old youngest daughter of Carnegie, childhood play-mate, neighbour, family friend – a sound match for both. Neither were really consulted – but, at that age, neither would have dreamed of objecting. Next to their sisters and brothers, they knew each other better than they knew anyone else, and had always been good enough friends. So all had been suitably arranged, the marriage settlement drawn up and signed, lands and dowry apportioned. Graham of Morphie had commissioned the famous George Jamesone to paint a portrait of the bridegroom. Exactly a year later, an heir was born, Johnnie – the object of the exercise. It had all been quite notably suitable, satisfactory, successful.

Magdalen, and therefore her young husband, had con-tinued to live at Kinnaird – although he often had to be away visiting his other great estates in the south. The house of Old Montrose, three miles to the east, was old indeed – though that was not what the name meant. It should have been Ald Montrose, from the Gaelic *alt moine ross,* the burn of the mossy point. But, more than old, it was large, rambling and neglected, indeed part derelict, for the Grahams had other and more favoured castles in south and west, and the town-house in the burgh of Montrose itself, where James Graham had been born, served them adequately as occa-sional base in these parts. Old Lord Carnegie would not hear of his young daughter departing for far parts, moving into the decayed barracks down the road, or setting up house amongst the burghers of Montrose town. There was plenty of room at Kinnaird where the young couple could live con-veniently under the authoritative eye of father and curator. And it was so. Possibly that was a large part of the trouble.

Montrose did not withdraw his arm. With the other hand he continued to stroke her hair. 'You are overwrought, my dear,' he said. 'Tired. Upset. It has been too long a day. But you will feel better. Tomorrow. You will see. We shall talk then. I have much to tell you. Today has been too much for you.'

Her smothered sobs were all his answer.

'Sleep now, Magdalen lass. That is your need. I will go bed down in the boys' chamber above. I shall do very well there . . .'

'No! No – you will not!' Fiercely she cried it.

'It would serve best, I think. For tonight . . .'

'I say no.' Suddenly she threw back the bedclothes strongly, and revealed herself as lying naked, a well-made young woman, heavy-breasted but fair, her abundant white flesh warm in the mellow lamp-light. 'See – I am a dutiful wife. I told you so. Told you that I waited for you!' Her voice broke again.

He moistened his lips, and took some time to reply. 'Is this . . . what you waited for, then?' he got out. 'I think not, my dear.'

'Yes. Yes, I say.' She spread herself on the bed, in a sort of defiant invitation, but with her flushed face and tear-dewed eyes turned away from him. She spread her body in deliberate invitation – yet her abhorrence was in every inch of her flaunting yet shrinking person.

The man, who was no monk, was deeply moved. And as deeply perplexed, his body at odds with his mind and heart.

But whatever of repugnance he sensed in her, he could by no means reject that offer and demand. To do so was unthinkable. He rose, and commenced to remove his clothing. She had covered herself again by the time that he was naked and had extinguished the lamp and turned back to her.

As he moved in beside her on the warm bed, she remained still, almost breathless, but with her head turned away from him. He sought gently to caress her, to soothe the tension from her. But before long he desisted, achieving nothing and but taxing himself. He took her then, but even so seeking to waken her passion, to rouse response, until his own need overwhelmed him. She did not answer a word, a whisper, or murmur of his, throughout.

Afterwards, for long, they both lay gazing up at the shadowy canopy, wordless, listening while the curlews called wearily, endlessly, from the Montrose marshes to the east. More than once the man almost spoke, and then drew back from fruitless words.

It was she who at length broke the silence. 'You must bear with me, James,' she said slowly, carefully. 'I am no wife for

44

such as you, I know well. But I try – God knows how I try! You are right, no doubt. Tomorrow will be better, I promise you.'

'Aye – all the tomorrows, lassie. They will be better. Now that I am home again, we shall start afresh, you and I. Who knows, the years may prove well spent, for us. Who knows, in them I may have learned more than just statecraft, the arts of rule and war, and the ways of a wider world. Give me a chance to prove it, my dear.'

'But what have *I* learned? Only that you have grown the further from me, James.'

'Then – help me to grow back, Magdalen,' he urged. 'Your help I need. Need, girl.'

He felt her shake her head on the pillow. But also, presently, he felt her relaxing a little, then more noticeably. In time, he slept, with an arm around her soft, still body.

It was hours later before Magdalen Carnegie closed her eyes.

4

THINGS WERE INDEED BETTER IN THE MORNING, AND ALL THE mornings – since these two were determined that they should be. They learned to live with each other again, to accept, to compromise, to withhold judgment, to help, strengthen, even comfort. The two boys were their greatest aid in this, as well as their prime inducement. With them as link they drew almost close. Marriage, even successful marriage, has been built on less than this.

That neither aimed quite so high as that was at once their safeguard and their tragedy.

The fact that Magdalen was largely free, at last, of Kinnaird and her family, undoubtedly greatly helped. Montrose had castles and estates over the length and breadth of the land; more than that, branches of his house and clan still more widely dispersed. After so long an absence, it was necessary to visit all, make innumerable decisions on the spot, put much to rights, show himself to his people. Almost everywhere he went he took his Countess and his sons, to introduce and display them, as was expected of him. Consequently they were not much at Kinnaird, or at the town-house in Montrose either, during that summer and autumn of 1636 – to the marked advantage of their union.

But if matters personal and private were thus lightened somewhat in these months, matters national and public were not. Everywhere James Graham went the talk was the same, resentment, murmurings, the stirrings of revolt. By and large, the people of Scotland, of all ranks and degrees, were angry. They were loyal enough. Indeed, it was remarkable how loyal they remained, considering that their king, James the Sixth and his son Charles, had deserted them for London, so clearly preferring everything English, and considering their old realm scarcely worth even visiting. But to the Scot, religion was highly personal and precious, not any mere formality, or separate compartment of life which could be accepted or more or less shrugged off for the sake of peace. The metaphysical implications of his faith were part and parcel of his being. New forms of worship or theology were not to be imposed on him from without, by king, parliament or hierarchy – more especially from England. For that very reason the Reformation had come later to Scotland than to almost any other nation in Christendom; but when it did come it had been more basic, comprehensive, drastic. Now their religion was not only being interfered with, but actually changed, by dictate from London, made to conform with that of England. It was not to be borne.

All this was bad enough. But there was another aspect of the situation which was worrying – especially for one placed in Montrose's position, straddling as it were the Highland Line, both in the location of his estates and the background of his blood and race. The Reformation had never really penetrated to the true Highlands effectively, certainly not to the remoter areas – except for the Campbells' Argyll. Therefore, these London edicts were of little or no interest in the Highlands. But, unfortunately, the Gordon chief, the Marquis of Huntly, not actually a Highlander himself but a strong Catholic and having great influence in all the North, was declaring himself wholly and vigorously in favour of the King in all this – and seeing that others did likewise. So that there was a serious division forming in Scotland, to the country's hurt, Highland versus Lowland, North versus the rest, Catholic versus Protestant. It was ominous and dangerous as it was grievously disappointing for all who had the unity of the realm at heart.

With the days shortening, Montrose took his little family and entourage to settle down at Kincardine Castle, on the southern verges of Strathearn. Magdalen was uneasy about this, still under her father's spell and afraid that it would cause offence. Moreover, all her life she had never lived anywhere else but at Kinnaird. But James Graham was determined on it, that they were not going back to Kinnaird, declaring that it was not suitable that the Earl of Montrose should roost always in another's house as though he had no place of his own. Kincardine was his favourite property, as it had been his father's before him.

So the old grey castle, on the rocky bluff above the wooded ravine of the Ruthven Water, was opened up and refurbished, and again young voices rang within its ancient walls, to challenge the singing of tree-top birds and the rush of falling water. The headlong Ruthven came boiling out of Glen Eagles, in the Ochils foothills of south Perthshire, to swing eastwards in its deep sylvan hanging glen above the Strathearn head-town of Auchterarder, before falling into the Earn at Aberuthven. In this winding sheltered valley, with the magnificent prospects of the Highland mountains across the wide strath, the Graham castle soared high on a rocky promontory, an eagle's nest of a hold, of lofty, mellow stone walls, crowstepped gables, steep roofs and pepper-pot turrets. Small compared with Kinnaird, or even Montrose's own Mugdock, Dundaff or Fintry, towering upwards instead of sideways, within its cramped and oddly shaped courtyard, it was a modest seat for so great a lord; but it was strong enough, and most pleasing in character as in surroundings. And it was central, not only for the various Graham lands, but for Stirling, Edinburgh, Glasgow, Perth and St Andrews, places where things were apt to happen in Scotland.

It was one golden day of belated autumn, in mid-November, with all Strathearn aglow with colour, that Montrose, returning to Kincardine with the sinking sun from

47

hunting hinds in the Ochils, found company awaiting him. He rode over the drawbridge into the little courtyard above the dizzy drop, with Kilpont, whose home at Airth was only a score of miles to the south, and Black Pate Graham, Younger of Inchbrakie near by, who had taken over from Young Morphie as personal esquire, to find the place crowded with a dozen and more horses, their grooms and armed attendants hanging around them, indicating that it was no unimportant company.

In his hall, James Graham found Magdalen entertaining, in some evident embarrassment, two very oddly paired visitors, who in their different ways seemed to discompose her almost equally. One was burly, almost gross, of late middle years, untidy, dressed in shabby finery, a coarse-featured, red-faced, noisy man with little pig-like eyes that were very shrewd – John Leslie, sixth Earl of Rothes, and strangely enough, the most popular man in Scotland. The other was tall, thin, dark and soberly dignified, with sternly ascetic features, fine eyes and an expression of harshly restrained intensity, clad all in black.

Montrose had met Rothes only once before, when he was still a student at St Andrews; but the older man greeted him like a friend, a crony, of long standing, punching his shoulder, belabouring his back, and spluttering couthy assertions of admiration, esteem, affection. James Graham, a fastidious man, sought not to allow his distaste to show.

'Laddie, laddie – you're braw, right braw! Fair magnificent, indeed! Guidsakes – you've come on! Here's John Leslie's hand. A right swack man's come back to your bed, lassie! You'll ken the differ, I'll be bound? Hey?' Rothes almost always affected the broadest Doric.

Montrose extricated himself with difficulty from the other's salutations, at the same time seeking to come to the rescue of his flushing wife. '*I* am the more fortunate, my lord,' he said. 'The better for being home. I hope I see your lordship well?'

'You see an auld done runt, by God!' the burly man roared. 'Ask *my* wife! But, och – no' so done yet that the sight o' this weel-favoured quean doesna raise the man in me, by the powers! I was just by way o' telling hersel' the same . . .'

'Hm. No doubt, my lord. And this . . . ?' Montrose turned to the other man.

'Ooh, aye – this is nane other than the Reverend Henderson. Maister Alexander Henderson himsel'. Minister o' Leuchars, in my county o' Fife. A scholar, see you – and a tower o' strength in the Kirk today. He's desirous o' a bit word in your lug, James. As am I.'

'I have heard of Master Henderson – and only heard good,' Montrose said, holding out his hand. 'You honour my house, sir.'

The minister bowed stiffly, his eyes searching, but said nothing. The younger man felt that he was being weighed and assessed.

'You will not have eaten? Your horses were still steaming in my yard. No doubt my wife has bidden you bide the night with us?'

'Hech, eye. Mind you, I'd have accepted her bonnie hospitality even sharper had I heard frae her that you werena coming hame this night! But a man must sup his gruel as it's ladled out. Aye, we'll bide.'

'My lady Montrose has been entirely kind. And very patient. I am grateful,' Henderson said, and his voice was unexpectedly rich and vibrant.

Magdalen hurried from the hall.

Later, the three men sat before a log fire in the small upper chamber which Montrose had set aside as a study and lined with books, parchments and documents which he had collected and sent home during his years on the Continent – a collection which obviously much interested Alexander Henderson at least. A large flagon of wine occupied a small table beside them, and Rothes was working his way steadily through it, though the other two only sipped their liquor. The older earl's bawdy stories and outrageous and scurrilous anecdotes had been non-stop throughout the preceding meal, and still went on – his host and fellow guest bearing with them as best they might, the former with a civility in which patience was evident, the latter with a sort of steely impassivity.

Then, quite abruptly, Rothes changed his tune, and the little darting eyes he turned on Montrose were gimlet-sharp and in no way clouded with wine.

'How stand you with the man Charles Stewart?' he demanded starkly.

The younger man stroked long fingers over mouth and tiny

49

pointed beard, taking his time to answer that barked question. 'I am a loyal subject of His Grace,' he said, at length.

'Aye – nae doubt!' That was a snort. 'So are we all – while we value our heads! Balmerino proved the wisdom o' that! I'm no' speaking of your loyalty, James. It's your wits I'm concerned with. Archie Napier tells me that this Montrose has a head on him. And, forbye, notions beyond the ordinar'. Are you for the Kirk, man – or the bishops?'

'Must I be for one and against the other, my lord? I was never greatly concerned with forms of worship, before I left on my travels. And in the different lands of Christendom, I saw nothing which made me to believe that a man's salvation depended on the form of words he used to speak with his Maker, nor yet on the colour of a priest's clothing. Is it so different in Scotland?'

'Och, lad, dinna fence with words...'

'My lord Montrose,' Henderson intervened, quietly stern. 'You require freedom to worship Almighty God in your own way? Is that what you say?'

'It is, sir.'

'And are you prepared to uphold such right, for others as well as yourself?'

Carefully Montrose scrutinised the lean, strangely sensitive face leaning forwards towards his own. 'I have not, I confess, deeply considered whether I am, or not, sir,' he said. 'But I concede that, probably, I ought to be.'

'Ha – there speaks a canny chiel!' Rothes cried. 'No' that I'm blaming you, lad. The man I respect uses his head. Scotland needs men with cool heads more than men with hot tongues, in this pass.'

'Scotland needs *every* man, in this pass,' the minister amended evenly.

The Graham looked from one to the other. 'This pass...?' he repeated. 'Is there a pass? Which demands our defence? Yet?'

'There is.' Rothes banged down a thick fist on the table, to make the flagon jump. 'By God, there is! I am new back frae London, man. Charles Stewart is riding for a fall. He will heed none but the man Laud and his lackey Juxon – he that's new Bishop of London in Laud's stead. These two English jumped-up clerks have our liege lord licking their prelatical feet! It makes me spew – spew, I say!'

'It is unedifying, yes. But – this pass, you speak of . . . ?'

'It is this thrice-damned prayer-book! You must have heard of it? Laud has had two Scots lickspittles, Wedderburn, Bishop o' Dunblane and Maxwell, Bishop o' Ross, to concoct the rat-rhymes and paternosters. They have finished their presumptuous blasphemies, and now Laud and Juxon have had their fell turn at it. And presented it to Charles. And he, our sovereign lord, has swallowed it all, with its mummery and its incantations and its rituals. It is being printed, and is to be imposed on Scotland forthwith. By the royal edict. On pain o' excommunication. Before Easter next.'

'Excommunication? Surely not? How can this be? Who is to be excommunicated?'

'Every parish minister, in the first place. The prayer-book itsel' isna yet printed. But the Book of Canons is, that is to go with it and enforce it. I've seen this, man – had in it my two hands. It's wicked.' All trace of the coarse, loud-mouthed buffoon had for the moment disappeared, and with it most of the broad Doric, as Rothes leant over, pointing a stubby finger at Montrose. 'These Canons are signed and sealed by the King, as head o' Christ's Church – by his way o' it. They declare that every parish minister in Scotland will have provided himsel' with at least two copies o' the prayer-book before Easter – on pain o' excommunictaion and banishment. Banishment, mind. To be used thereafter, in every kirk – on pain o' the same penalties. And any who may raise their voice against it, or fail to adhere to it, to be banished likewise.'

Montrose shook his head, wordless.

'Nor is that all, my lord,' Henderson put in. 'All presbyteries are to be put down – the courts and government of the Kirk. Even though the Scots bishops themselves accept them. Bishops alone are to govern the Kirk of Scotland.'

'It is scarcely to be believed,' the younger man said slowly.

'But it is the truth, for a' that. I tell you, Montrose, I've seen the printed and signed Canons.'

'Scotland – the realm will not accept it! Nobles and Kirk alike. The whole people . . .'

'You think not, lad? Pray God that you are right. Pray God! But, I say, it is up to us, man, who have the leadership in this land, to *see* that the realm does not! Charles will have

51

done what the Edwards and the Henrys never could do — wiped out this ancient realm and put us under the English heel. That is the size o' it. That it should be under the heels o' damnable English prelates is the measure o' our abasement, by God!'

James Graham looked from one to the other. 'What do you wish for me?' he asked, quietly.

'Just that the Graham does not fail his ancestors, lad. At Dunbar, at Stirling Brig, at Bannockburn, at Flodden-field, at Pinkie Brae, Graham has stood — aye, and fallen if need be — for the freedom o' this sair-harried realm. Do *you* stand aside, man?'

Levelly, Alexander Henderson spoke. 'All we ask, my lord, is that you lend your name and support, when the time comes. For a stand for our liberty, our right to worship God in our own way, our determination that none shall take from us our birthright as free men.'

Montrose inclined his handsome head. 'I could do no less,' he said.

'Praise be! Aye, lad — so I believed. And so said Archie Napier. Here is right excellent augury. We came to you amongst the first, James — for where the Graham leads, lesser men will follow. And it is the lesser men, the common folk, the townsmen, that we must rally, see you. Charles himsel' has rallied the nobles against him, by his Act o' Revocation, his taking o' the tithes and teinds o' our lands to pay for his bishops. He will unite the Kirk against him by this Liturgy and doing awa' with the presbyteries. But, the common folk . . .'

'Fear not for the common folk, my good lords,' Henderson interrupted. 'King Charles has assured of them rising also, I think!'

'You say so?'

'Yes. Or the man Laud has done it for him! This of the surplices. In his Canons, you tell me, it is ordained that every minister of the Gospel discards his black Geneva gown and dons a white linen surplice. Likewise on pain of excommunication. I tell you, he could scarce have served us better! Here is something which the ordinary man and woman can see and understand. Compared with the rest, it is little or nothing I agree. But they, the common folk, will see it as popery, the trappings of idolatry. That, and these pictures which your lordship tells me are to be painted in the prayer-book, on the initial letters of each page and prayer – cherubs, angels and the like. Imagery, devices of the Devil. Aye, smile my lords – but, I tell you, who am of the people myself, that this will serve better than all your doctrine and pronouncements. Aye, or *my* sermons! This they will see as bowing down to idols! The folk will rise in their wrath.'

Rothes shrugged. 'So be they rise,' he said. 'But they must learn o' them, first.'

'They will learn, never doubt it. We – the ministers of God's Kirk – will not fail to equip ourselves with the King's white surplices, I promise you! Though we will never wear them. They will hang from every pulpit in the land, as text for our discourses. The prayer-books too, when they come. We will not use them – but every kirk will show them to the people, with their pictures and popery...'

'Ha – and there is more for you to display, Henderson man. Now I mind o' it. A Kalendar o' Scots saints. *Saints,* mark you. Such Kalendar to be printed with each book, by the King's personal command! Saints, and their days, for observation, veneration, worship! Show that!'

Obviously this was news to Alexander Henderson. He looked shocked, no less. 'Saints ... !' he gasped. 'Is ... is the man clean out of his wits?'

'You may ask! That is Charles, by the Grace o' God, King! Aye.' John Leslie reached for the flagon. 'So there you have it, James. We can rely on you? When the time comes?'

'You can rely on me not to stand dumb, my lord. Not to withhold my protest. Beyond that, I do not commit myself. I am the King's man, in all else. A loyal subject. Protest, I will support. Insurrection and revolt are another matter. I bid you both remember it.'

There was a long moment's silence.

'Pray God it comes not to that,' Henderson said, at length. 'But a man must be prepared to more than speak for his beliefs.'

'Aye, man – to be sure,' Rothes put in, rather hurriedly. 'But time enough to think o' that, when the talking fails.'

'Talking reason, must *not* fail,' Montrose declared strongly. 'The King must be shown the folly of his policy. Shown that he will rouse the whole Scottish realm against him...'

'Think you he hasna been told so, time and again? Balmerino told him – and near lost his head! *I* have told him – to my cost! Your good-brother Napier has told him, written letters aplenty – to no result but his own loss o' power and position. Charles ignores all – but has around him a pack o' toadies and lackeys who shout Amen to his every word. Aye, and keep the truth frae him.'

'Then he must be shown that these are false advisers. His true enemies, not his friends – Hamilton, Lanark, Traquair and their like. Time-servers. We must send the King not one letter, or two. But the voice of the whole realm must speak. Honestly, loyally, respectfullly – but firmly. A declaration. Scotland has done it before. The community of the realm of Scotland. From Arbroath. In good King Robert's time – a Declaration of Independence.' Montrose sat forward, his fine eyes alight now. 'That letter was to the Pope of Rome. Now we must needs send one to King Robert's own descendant ten generations removed. Signed by all true men whose names mean anything in Scotland. Such, the King could not ignore or dismiss. This, I say, should be done. And quickly. Before more evil befalls.'

'Mm.' Rothes rubbed his multiple chins. 'We'll hae to think on this. It might be worth the trying.'

'More than a letter or a declaration,' Henderson said. 'A covenant. A declaration is only that. Binds its signatories only to a belief, an assertion. But a covenant, binding men to action, should their demands be refused – that is something different.'

'Demands?' Montrose repeated. 'I said nothing of demands. Loyal subjects cannot *demand* from the Lord's Anointed.'

'Requests, then. A word, my lord.'

'An important word, sir. Significant. Let us be clear in our minds what we are about – that there be no misunderstanding. I will have nothing to do with demands upon the King's Grace. I will declare that I believe the King's policies are wrong – and rejoice if many others so declare with me. But I will not set myself up against my liege lord, to his hurt or constraint. Let that be understood, now and hereafter.'

'To be sure, James – to be sure,' Rothes nodded, after a barely perceptible pause. 'It shall be as you say . . .'

5

NEITHER KING CHARLES NOR THE LEADERS OF HIS OUTRAGED
Scots people were, in fact, so efficient and effective as they
intended. The book of the Canons was duly distributed –
printed in the end at Aberdeen – with all its dire commands
and intimations of punishments, ecclesiastical and civil,
should they be disobeyed; but the winter passed, Easter itself,
April, May, June, and still the reason and object of it all,
the prayer-book and Liturgy, did not appear. Delays in the
printing and binding were blamed; possibly the inclusion of
those ominous coloured pictures and cherubs was largely
responsible. And there were rumours of Scots sabotage, certain Privy Councillors' names being linked with the delays,
Rothes and Napier amongst them. Even sundry English
Puritans were said to have a hand in the business. The thing
became something of a joke, as time went on, hardly to be
taken seriously – despite all the dreadful warnings that re-
sounded from practically every pulpit in Scotland. Only the
surplices appeared, shaped and sewn, it is to be feared,
mainly by busy Presbyterian fingers, to hang as dire and
inflammatory symbols in front of the said pulpits. Alexander
Henderson and his colleagues at least played their part.

And yet, even so, the forces of righteous defence were little
more competent and efficacious, or up-to-time, than was the
assault from London. Although Rothes, Loudoun, Lindsay
and others had mobilised major support throughout the
Lowlands for massive protest, and the theory of a great
declaration or petition to the King was accepted, nothing was
actually done to implement it; as the threat hung fire, so not
unnaturally did the counterblast. Many wordy forms of
protest and declamation were composed, as a sort of exercise
– Montrose and his secretary John Lambie penned two or
three themselves; but none grew into the organised and

widespread national testimony which was required – almost to the relief of the authors, those at Kincardine included.

So summer came again, and men found many things to do more immediately preoccupying than either religious or political disputation. Amongst other distractions, James Graham learned that he was to become a father once again – and rejoiced that Magdalen was greatly uplifted at the prospect.

Then, in mid-July, a letter arrived from the Earl of Rothes, to declare that the waiting and inaction was over. The prayer-book had arrived in quantity, the Scots bishops were commanded, and determined, to bring them into use forthwith, and had selected Sunday the 23rd of July for, as it were, vesting day. All the books could not be distributed round the country by then; but their spiritual lordships had decided that there would be a great service of dedication and celebration in the Cathedral of Edinburgh – in other words, the High Kirk of St Giles – before the Privy Council, the judges of Session, the Lord Provost and magistrates, and as many of the congregation as there remained room for. All persons of note in the kingdom were urged to be present – and Rothes suggested that Montrose and others like-minded could do much worse than attend. He had a town-house in Edinburgh and would be glad there to return the hospitality received at Kincardine.

So, with mixed feelings, James Graham presented himself at the lofty greystone 'land' in the Horse Wynd, off the Cowgate of Edinburgh, at Leslie's Ludging, on the Saturday evening – and was surprised to find it full to bursting. Half of the nobility of Scotland appeared to be crammed into its tiered rooms, even lining its twisting turnpike stair. Amidst much noise, argument, declamation and laughter, Montrose distinguished the Earls of Dunfermline, Home, Eglinton, Lindsay, Loudoun, Lothian, Sutherland and Wigtown; the Lords Balmerino, Stormont, Boyd, Yester and Elcho; and great lairds like Sir George Stirling of Keir, Douglas of Cavers, Fraser of Philorth, Mure of Rowallan and Home of Wedderburn. Sober-garbed and markedly out-of-place amongst this dazzling throng of cavaliers, were one or two of the Edinburgh ministers.

Many of the company were known to him, of course; some of them indeed friends from college days at St Andrews –

such as Wigtown, Lindsay, Sutherland and the former Glamis, now Earl of Kinghorne. Amongst the older men there were not a few members of His Grace's Scots Privy Council, although it was significant that none of its Lords Spiritual were present.

The talk was all about the morrow's confrontation. The Chancellor was evidently expecting trouble. He had sent orders to the Lord Provost and magistrates of Edinburgh to have the Town Guard out in force 'to ensure the peace of the King's lieges'. The Chancellor, chief minister of the Crown in Scotland, and convener of its parliament, was the Primate, Archbishop Spottiswoode of St Andrews who, three years before the old Earl of Kinnoul died, had been appointed to this key position, to the great offence of the nobility, the first cleric to be Chancellor since the Reformation. Spottiswoode himself would not be present – he would be introducing the prayer-book in his own cathedral of St Andrews; Bishop Lindsay of Edinburgh would preside – and his chief, the young Earl of Lindsay, was coming under not a little raillery for nurturing such a snake in the bosom of his clan.

Montrose was unable to get a word alone with Rothes, but could gain no impression of anything constructive being done, especially any idea of drawing up a declaration or covenant to send to the King. He put the matter to practically all he spoke with, and found no real opposition to the notion – although most seemed to feel that it would be useless, doomed to rejection by the obdurate Charles. When the Earl of Loudoun likened it to a Band, he got immediate favourable reaction. Bands, or bonds, meant something positive to these men. But Montrose demurred. A Band implied action against something. And the only target for that action, here, could be the King. That was not to be contemplated.

Montrose was glad to discover Archie Napier amongst the aristocratic throng, and in a corner confided to him that he feared that matters looked like getting out-of-hand. He was not going to be a party to civil war – and that is the way that matters were trending. There were too many hot-heads here, however gilded. Wiser councils must be brought forward, and made to prevail.

His brother-in-law shook his grey head. 'I know it, James. I pray that we can in the end win the day and see moderation prevail. Wine is talking loud here. At a council-table, could we but get to one, heads and voices would be cooler.' He frowned. 'And the King – he serves the cause of moderation nothing! He is deaf to all our pleas, and blind to his own good. He will resile not one inch from his folly.'

'But he *is* the King, still. The Lord's Anointed.'

'Aye – there's the grip of it.' Napier turned, as an imposing figure approached them. 'Ha! And here's the King's Advocate, no less! Sir Thomas – I think you will not know my good-brother, Montrose. James – the Lord Advocate, Sir Thomas Hope of Craighall.'

James Graham eyed the newcomer with interest, a big, portly, dark-visaged man, with a fleshy face and narrow-set, dark, keen eyes, scarcely prepossessing of appearance but clearly a man to be reckoned with, quite apart from being principal law officer of the Crown in Scotland. The fact that the Lord Advocate was coarse-looking, and sounded it, had thick lips, a wide mouth and a wild black and bushy beard, would only deceive the ignorant or the very unwary. Montrose knew that this was one of the most potent characters in two kingdoms – if scarcely the best-loved. Potent in more ways than one, for he had fourteen children – and what was more, two of them were already Lords of Session, to sit upon the High Court bench before which their father came to plead as King's Advocate; a fact which allowed him to plead with his head covered, an unprecedented privilege, since it would be considered derogatory for a man to take his hat off to his sons.

The younger man bowed, wordless.

'I know *of* his lordship,' Hope greeted 'Who does not? You are well returned to Scotland, I think, young man.' The Advocate splattered a little from those thick red lips as he spoke.

'You say so, sir? I appear to have returned to a seething pot of troubles, indeed.' Montrose drew back almost involuntarily, not liking what he saw – and surprised indeed to see the King's Advocate in this company, though he could hardly say so.

'Trouble, yes. But trouble is the forcing ground of change, of progress, of greatness, my lord.' Hope had a strangely light voice for a man of his appearance and reputation – and somehow managed not to sound sententious. 'Trouble is to be

grasped in strong hands, not jinked and jouked. Is it no',
Archie?'

'Presupposing the strong hands are available. And allied
to cool wits.'

'Spoke like an Extraordinary Lord o' Session, my old
friend! So we must needs seek strong hands, in this stir, must
we not? Aye, and cool heads. But they're scarce, Archie,
scarce.'

'You are right, Tom. That is just what we were saying,
James and I. Cool heads, a conference table. Not a stramash
of high words and flourishes.' Napier waved a hand round at
the crowded room. 'Such as we have here.'

'Cha – there may be cool heads, aye, and strong hands too,
in the land. But they maun be allied to a voice which men
will *heed*, Archie. We may conceive our ain voices clear
enough, and our heads likewise! We may even think ourselves wise, on occasion. But will Scotland heed us? Follow
us? I think not. Even you, Archie, born second Lord Napier,
these will never follow!' The Lord Advocate waved a scornful hand at the aristocratic throng. 'As for me, I am a low-
born base fellow, son of an Edinburgh burgher. What belted
earl will follow Tom Hope? Even though sometimes they'll
admit themselves fear't of me! No – the voice of Scotland
needs must be a voice high-born, younger too, of the blood
of the old leadership. Only such will our stubborn fellow
countrymen follow – and not only the nobility. The com-
monality are just as bad. I have been looking for such these
long months.'

'The Earl of Rothes has taken an active role . . .' Montrose
began.

'John Leslie!' Hope cut him short with a snort. 'Leslie –
he isna such a fool as he sounds, I grant you. But nor is he
of the stuff of leadership. Young men would never follow
the like – nor would he try to make them. And it is young
men, not old, who will decide this present matter.'

'What do you mean, sir? Saying that *young* men will
decide it? You do not mean resort to arms, surely? You, the
King's Advocate, do not advocate revolt? Rebellion? Against
the King?'

'Young man – I am the King's servant. I will do nothing,
nothing mark you, to injure His Grace. But like my lord
Napier here, I conceive him to be so ill-advised as to be in

59

danger of losing his Scottish kingdom. In such pass, it is my duty, as I see it, the duty of all true lieges, to save him from those who so advise him and poison his mind. From his own misguided notions forbye. And this will not be done without stark deeds. Not rebellion, pray God. But resolute, right positive action. And for that, the voices of old men will not suffice.'

Neither of his hearers spoke for a few moments. Montrose was more struck by the man's sombre words and grave tones, however light the voice, than by anything that he had yet heard since his return to Scotland. When the principal law officer of the realm, the man, next to the Chancellor, representing the King's authority, spoke so, admitted that he had been looking for strong leadership for months, to counter the royal edicts, matters had indeed come to crisis-point.

Montrose and Napier were back near-by next morning, well before the set hour of ten, to take their places in St Giles High Kirk. Nine a.m. was the usual hour, but there had been an earlier service, at eight, that Sunday the 23rd of July, in order that the common folk of the parish might have their ordinary worship and be got safely out of the way, so that there might be ample accommodation for the important people before whom the new prayer-book was to be used for the first time. Also that there might be no risk of unseemly disturbance. Normally there were no seats for the congregation – although elderly ladies and sick folk often brought their own stools with them – but there were stalls set aside for especial worshippers; and since it was inconceivable that earls and great lords should have to stand like other folk, these had today been suitably reinforced. Montrose and his brother-in-law, therefore, sat comfortably at the front of the north transept, right at the great central crossing where the massive fluted pillars supported the church's mighty lantern-tower, the south transept directly in front of them, the huge nave on their left, but the choir on their right screened off with tapestries and hangings – this because it was at present undergoing reconstruction and restoration to its former state. St Giles, before the Reformation, had been one great church, though with many side-chapels and chantries; but the Reformers had changed all that, dividing it up into three separate places of Presbyterian worship for city parishes. Now, under the new episcopal regime, it was one church again; but the choir area was not yet fully restored, in keeping with cathedral status. In front of the tapestry barrier was placed today a large Communion-table, with crucifix, candles, cloth and frontal, looking suspiciously like an altar, rows of throne-like chairs flanking it on either side. And a little farther forward, under the crossing's groined vault itself, rose a carved wooden pulpit, with below it an ornate lectern or reading-desk.

The great cruciform church, undoubtedly large enough to be any bishop's cathedral, was already all but full. Half the aristocracy of Scotland, with all the notabilities of Edinburgh and Lothian, stood around. There was a mighty chatter of tongues, calling out, exchange of greetings and pleasantries, laughter, more suitable for a fairground than a church. Montrose said as much to Rothes, whom he found installed as his neighbour.

'And whose blame might that be? It's no' godly, I'll grant you. But if the bishops will make o' the kirk a place as full o' mummery and show as a playhouse, then theirs the consequence, say I. Eh, Archie?'

Napier looked around him distastefully, at all the colour, style and fashion. 'I'd say there's more come here today to see and be seen, than to worship God, John.'

'Aye, so. But we're no' here to worship, are we? We're here, on the King's royal command, transmitted by His Beneficence the Archbishop o' St Andrews, Chancellor o' this realm. To witness the institution o' a royal edict. Nothing more. No' to worship our Maker.'

Montrose cleared his throat. 'It may be so. But I hope nevertheless, my lord, that we get through this in decency. If we take it upon ourselves to question, and seek change, the King's commands, it must be on a plane of highest principle. And it must be seen of all to be so. If we give a lead in this, it must be with dignity. I mislike the bearing, the attitudes, I see here this morning. In a house of prayer.'

'Uh-huh. Nae doubt you're right, James. But all men – aye, and all women, for that matter – maybe havena just your fine sentiments and lofty ideals! We're no' all Jamie Graham o' Montrose!'

Directly, then, the other put it to him. 'You have not arranged any disturbance, my lord? Any demonstration, within this church, against these ordinances? I hope not. For it is no place for such. It could do our cause much harm. Set moderate men against us. You must see it?'

'Och, man – I've no' arranged anything !' Rothes declared. But there was a slight emphasis on the personal in that. 'We're here, as commanded, to hear this new prayer-book read. If folk dinna like it, and choose to make that plain, am I to blame . . . ?'

'My lord,' Montrose said urgently, 'you have taken the lead in this matter. You are one of the foremost nobles in the land. And one of the best liked, the most respected. Many will trim their sails to yours. You cannot say that what happens here is no concern of yours, no blame of yours. If folly prevails here, you must bear part of the responsibility. As indeed must I. And Archie. If you know of aught which might serve our cause ill, cause offence to moderate men – then I say it is your duty to seek halt it, before it is too late.'

'Duty, a' God's name ! *You* see fit to tell me my duty?'

'I do, my lord. Since you saw fit to come to tell me mine, at Kincardine, last November. And hence I am here.'

'And I? Suppose I conceive my duty otherwise, sir?'

'Then I suggest that you have not considered it sufficiently. Your duty cannot be to allow happen anything which might force men to abandon our cause. Men . . . such as myself !'

Rothes swallowed, his double chins quivering. Then, without another word, he rose abruptly from his pew and stalked off.

'You did that featly, stoutly, Jamie,' Napier said. 'I know no other who could, or would, have forced Rothes so. You are heeding Tom Hope's words, I think?'

'I am but looking to my own name and reputation. And yours, Archie. If Leslie wants Graham to dance, he must pipe a tune that Graham will heed ! *You* sent him to me, my friend – you should have told him so.'

His brother-in-law nodded mildly, a faint smile about his lips. 'I am glad that I sent him,' he said.

The great church was nearly full, all the stone-flagged nave being tightly packed with people. Montrose, presently, gestured towards the front of these serried ranks. 'Is that not strange?' he said. 'All this notable crowd of the quality. Yet there, in the forefront, in the best places of all, these wifies sitting there on their stools. Common folk of the town, are they not? Yet you said that such were being kept from this service? That they had their service earlier? Of set purpose.'

It was true. Whatever the official fiat about the ordinary congregation being given their normal and non-prayer-book service early this momentous day, the fact was that the first three or four rows of the close-packed ranks of the standing quality was composed of most evidently common folk, women all, sitting on little folding stools and looking entirely assured and pleased with themselves.

'You mistake, Jamie,' Napier explained. 'These are not Edinburgh wifies – not of the general run. Common folk they may be. They are maids – ladies' maids and tiring-women. It is a custom here. They come early to the kirk, with their mistresses' stools, to win a good place for their betters. Then, just before the service starts, their ladyships can come in at their ease and take over the stools – and the maids go home and make the beds or prepare the dinner! All most suitably devised, in Edinburgh fashion!' He looked beyond. 'Only today, I fear, the good ladies will be highly outraged, and denied their divine worship! For, as you see, the place has become so tight jammed that there will be no room for even the most formidable dame to win through. I think the abigails must needs serve as deputies throughout! Bishop Lindsay will be as distressed as the mistresses – what ever the Lord God thinks!'

'Save us – that is Edinburgh for you! Small wonder it gets the name it has. I . . .'

Montrose's voice was drowned by a hullabaloo from without, shouts and catcalls growing ever louder, and through it the tuck of drum. The former much prevailed over the latter – and it did not sound like cheers and applause.

'A mob,' James Graham said, frowning. 'Trouble in the streets.'

'It is the Town Guard, marching to their drums. But I fear it is not the Guard that is being shouted at!'

Inside the church the noise abated notably as attention was concentrated on what went on outside. It seemed as though the good folk of Edinburgh, even though denied their normal forenoon service, were not going to be left out entirely from the day's proceedings.

The door of the north transept was thrown open and, preceded by the city macebearer, the Provost in scarlet and ermine and the magistrates in their robes, came in, pacing rather faster than their usual procession and looking distinctly ill-at-ease, not to say out-of-breath. Two files of the Town Guard marched inside with them, and the doors were closed, shutting out the noise somewhat. As the magistrates moved to their allotted places, Rothes returned to his seat.

'Folk out there who think differently frae James Graham!' he said grimly. 'Henderson had the rights of it.'

'What do you mean?'

'I mean that these outside, the common folk, are shouting against Popery and idolatry, man. They're no' caring about the prayer-book. It's the surplices and the pictures they're crying at. Half the town's there, yelling abominations and damnation to the Papes!'

'The more fools them, then!'

'It may be. But ignore them at your peril, my lord! Yon yowling's no' *your* voice. But it's the *other* voice o' Scotland, for a' that!'

A fanfare of trumpets, from outside the south transept, stilled all conversation. The doors at that side were thrown open, while all who had seats in the church got to their feet. The noise of the crowd was much less noticeable than when the north porch door had been open, for this south entrance gave on to the enclosure of Parliament Square, a narrow area which could be barred off from the High Street. Out from Parliament Close across the way, the Lord Advocate, with Sir George Elphinstone of Blythswood, the Lord Justice Clerk, pacing slowly and with great dignity, led the procession of the King's judges, the Lords of Session.

'All this to hear a prayer-book read!' Montrose said.

'Wait you,' Rothes advised. 'There's word that Spottiswoode's here himsel', after all.'

'The Archbishop? From St Andrews? Then – he must see this as of vital importance,' Napier said. 'A trial of strength, perhaps?'

'They would bind us. Seek to commit us to acceptance of this thing, by sheer weight o' consequence.' Rothes snorted. 'They tell me that Spottiswoode came, meaning to lead in the whole Privy Council. But most o' it has chosen to sit in the body o' the kirk, like you and me, Archie – so he'll hae to make do wi' a wheen bishops!'

64

The judiciary seated, there was another fanfare, and again the south doors were opened. First came in a delicate-looking young man, seeming almost to wilt under the brilliant splendour of a Lion Rampant tabard, carrying a baton of office.

'Save us – Balfour! Sir James Balfour of Denmiln, the Lyon!' Montrose exclaimed. 'The very trappings of royalty. Can they do this?'

'Aye, they can – it means that Spottiswoode is here as Chancellor o' Scotland, and King's representative, no' just as Archbishop and Primate,' Rothes said. 'So what is done here today has all the authority of the state behind it.'

'Scarcely that – since it lacks that of parliament,' the Graham amended. 'Here is the royal authority, yes. The great officers of state. The judiciary. The Church. But not parliament. Let us not forget it.'

A galaxy of magnificently robed prelates paced in stately fashion behind the Lord Lyon King of Arms and his heralds, vivid in rich colours, jewel-encrusted, golden croziers and crosses winking in the July morning sun. The first pair, one heavy and white-haired, the other tall, dark and stooping, wore taller, more elaborate mitres than the pairs behind, their trains borne by handsomely attired pages. To the singing of a great choir of men and boys in white surplices, who came on after, this gorgeous company entered.

'Both archbishops! Glasgow too!' Napier exclaimed. 'And four other bishops – Galloway, Dunblane, Dunkeld and Brechin. So they are not introducing the prayer-book in their own dioceses. All concentrated on Edinburgh today. Even Tom Hope did not know of this.'

'As well that parade o' play-actors came straight ower frae Parliament Close, and no' by the High Street door!' Rothes commented grimly. 'Or they'd have lost some o' their gewgaws by this! Look at them!'

Because these, like the judiciary before them, came in from the end of the south transept, the people crowded in the nave did not see them for a few moments. When they did come into sight, making for the row of chairs set on the north of the Communion-table, a great corporate sigh arose from the congregation. There was exclamation amongst it, condemnation, even a sort of unwilling admiration, but no real uproar. Clearly many were not unimpressed by the sheer magnificence of the spectacle, especially the women on the stools in front. Nothing like this had been seen in St Giles for eighty years, since the Reformation of blessed memory.

Montrose's parallel sigh of relief was premature. The choir had now come into view. And where the gorgeous copes, chasubles, stoles and mitres of the prelates had got by without clamour, through their unaccustomed splendour, the simple white surplices which clothed the humble singers were as red rags to bulls. Not to the mass of this congregation, but to those representatives of the common people at the front. To a woman they rose from their stools, and cried out, pointing, hooting, skirling at the hated symbols which their ministers had been denouncing as Popery for months. Pandemonium ensued.

But the authorities were not unprepared for trouble, whatever touched it off. The choristers, after wavering momentarily, paced on, singing the louder. At a sign from the Lord Lyon King of Arms, the Town Guard present, who had been lining the walling around the crossing, stepped forward, halberds at the ready, threateningly. And from the south porch another blast of trumpets, louder than before, shook the great building.

Between them, these moves served their turn. The abigails and serving-women quietened, perceived that authority frowned on them and them alone, and that the quality behind them were looking and sounding indignant, not at the choristers but at themselves for usurping their right of protest. One or two continued to glare, one shaking a bony fist; but most resumed their seats, and none continued with the shouting.

While still the singing continued, in at the same south door came the cathedral clergy and celebrant's procession, crossbearer, acolytes, servers and priests with the holy vessels and elements, followed by the canons, the Dean, and, bringing up the rear, the plump, rosy person of Bishop Lindsay of Edinburgh, in purple cope and mitre. He paced forward, wielding his crozier with great assurance and authority but with very wary eyes. The doors shut finally behind him.

All in turn bowing before the Communion-table and the crucifix behind to the faint murmuring of the congregation, the priests and canons took their places on the chairs facing the senior prelates. The Bishop climbed into the pulpit, and Dean Hannah moved into the reading-desk immediately below. He was a little man, with a fiery red complexion and a long nose – and could be seen to be wearing a white linen surplice under the short dalmatic and stole. He held a book in his hands gingerly, as though it might well burn his fingers.

As the singing died away, there was to be heard a steady undertone of muttering from the assembled worshippers.

The Bishop raised a beringed hand. 'By command of the King's most excellent Grace, and in the name of the Father, the Son and the Holy Ghost. Amen,' he intoned in a rich, sonorous voice.

Nobody contested that.

'The service will be that contained in the Book of Common Prayer ordained to be read in this and every other church of His Grace's realm of Scotland, by the King's command, that of His Grace's Privy Council, and of the College of Bishops.'

The company stirred restively.

The Bishop looked down on the Dean, coughed, and gestured.

Dean Hannah made some play of opening the book, finding the place with the blue satin and gold-frilled marker, and cleared his throat. 'Let us pray,' he said.

All around the Communion-table, the clerics and choristers and acolytes sank to their knees, the prelates and canons on specially provided kneelers, the rest on the floor.

The congregation thus early were faced with decision. Standing tight packed as they were it would have been difficult to kneel anyway, with more space taken up by legs than by feet. One or two may have sought to do so, at the back, for there was some slight commotion. Only those at the very front were in any position for ready kneeling – the maids, the Provost and magistrates, the judges and the great lords. Cautiously Edinburgh's civic fathers watched to see what their betters would do. One or two of the judges began to bend their knees, and then perceived that neither the Lord Advocate nor the Lord Justice Clerk were doing so, and almost imperceptibly straightened up again. All eyed the stalls of the earls, questioningly.

This problem of kneeling had not occurred to Montrose, any more than to most of his companions. He realised that innumerable eyes were on him. He bowed his head, and remained standing. Something like a moan rose from the great gathering.

'Let us *pray!*' the Dean repeated, his voice considerably higher-pitched.

From above him, the Bishop's deeper voice snapped, 'Proceed!'

'Ah. Hm. Aye. Almighty God, unto whom all hearts be open, all desires known, and from whom no secrets are hid: Cleanse the thoughts of our hearts by the inspiration of Thy Holy Spirit, that we may perfectly love Thee and worthily magnify Thy Holy Name: Through Christ our Lord,' he said hurriedly.

The assembly, standing, listened. It was a prayer that they all knew, with nothing new about it. After all, most of them had been using a liturgical service for years, John Knox's Liturgy.

Then followed the Summary of the Law. 'Our Lord Jesus Christ said: Hear O Israel, the Lord our God is one Lord ...'

Only the clergy and choristers made response: 'Lord have mercy upon us, and write these Thy laws in our hearts, we beseech Thee.' But they intoned it strongly, hearteningly, and the Dean stood up a little more straight, his voice recovering.

'Lord have mercy upon us!'

'Well might ye say it!' one of the women made response, before the formal 'Christ have mercy upon us!' drowned the rest.

The congregation stirred, like a restive goaded beast.

Shocked, the Dean's voice went squeaky again. 'Lord ... Lord ... have mercy ...'

A woman's excited laughter, from the back, set off a surge of exclamation and comment.

The Dean tried to continue, raising his voice higher and higher – but with it all the noise increased. Presently Hannah gave up the attempt, and gazed about him anxiously, wringing his hands.

In the pulpit, Bishop Lindsay was speaking – but could not make himself heard. Then one of the stools was knocked over, as a woman rose to shout something – and the clatter of it produced one of those abrupt moments of silence which can follow a new and violent sound. And into it the Bishop could be heard clearly commanding, 'The collect, man! Get on with the collect for the day.'

The word 'collect' from the pulpit did indeed seem to collect and distil all the pent-up animosity and tension in the place. There was a rumbling growl from many throats, and above it all a penetrating woman's screech.

'Colic, ye say! Deil colic the wame o' ye, *I* say! Out on ye – Anti-christ!'

A great shout of laughter rose from the company, wholly and finally dissipating any residual atmosphere of worship from the assembly. But the laughter came from the assembled quality, not at all from the common folk with the stools in front. They were roused to rage, rather than amused – partly, possibly, by that very laughter behind them, which might seem to mock them. The maids were all on their feet now.

'Idolatry! Idolatry!' one screamed. 'It's Baal entered upon us!'

'Aye – Rome! Rome's come to Emburgh!'

'Papes! Papes! Fause-tongued thieves! Out on ye . . . !'

The Bishop rose in the pulpit, waving the golden crozier indignantly. 'Silence! Silence, in God's holy house. How dare you!' he cried. 'In the Name of God – peace!'

'I'll peace you, you crafty auld fox! You fat belly-god! Beast o' Rome!'

Stricken by such impious insults bawled in his cathedral, Bishop Lindsay gasped helplessly, at a loss for words or deeds. He turned, to gaze at the archbishops, for help, guidance. But the switching of the attack to his superior seemed to have aroused Dean Hannah to anger, where that on himself had produced only fear.

'Be quiet! Be quiet, I say!' he shouted. 'Shameless women! Daughters of Jezebel! Dare you interrupt God's servants? Defile Christ's Holy Eucharist . . . ?'

'Dare *you* read the Mass in my lug!' a short, dumpy, apple-cheeked woman yelled back. And on an impulse, she stooped, picked up the overturned stool at her feet, and hurled it with all her strength at the Dean.

It was not a particularly good throw, for she hung on to the stool an instant too long, as female throwers are apt to do. So that it flew low, struck the lectern a glancing blow, and finished up clattering against the pulpit base. But it made a lot of noise, and had as much impact on the proceedings as though indeed it had scored a direct hit on its target.

There were a few moments of utter and appalled silence. Then tumultuous uproar broke out in the High Kirk of St Giles.

Suddenly everybody was shouting at once – and a large proportion seemed to be on the move also. The Provost bellowed for the Town Guard to clear the church. Most of the congregation surged forward – since it could not surge backwards or sideways, and motion was abruptly imperative. Prelates, judges and magistrates saw their escape route to the south porch likely to be blocked, as a result, and in their turn surged thitherwards, stumbling over kneelers, desks and church-furniture in an undignified scurry, long robes kilted high. The little Dean, who seemed to be the prime object of fury, found himself attacked by a horde of viragoes and, retiring in the face of it, defended himself as best he might, wielding the prayer-book.

Above him, islanded in his pulpit amid this turbulent sea of wrath and panic, Bishop Lindsay, hand to mouth, appealed through convulsive fingers, for aid, to the Most High, the Provost, magistrates and Town Council, the Lord Lyon King of Arms, and any and all right-thinking persons.

Montrose, shocked and dumbfounded, nevertheless recovered his wits quickly – but decided that the Dean was in greater need than his superior. He pushed his way through the milling throng to the aid of the little man, commanding order and cessation of folly forthwith, with all his notable and inborn authority. It was less effective than usual, admittedly, but he did make some impression, especially when Sir Thomas Hope and Napier materialised at his side. They got the Dean extricated, between them, and Hope led him away.

Rothes edged his way to Montrose's side. 'So much for dignity and seemliness, James!' he said. 'Have you ever seen the like?'

'I have not. Nor wish to see it again!' the younger man returned. 'It is a stain on the name of this kingdom . . .'

'Och, it's no' so bad as that, lad. If it's a stain, it will wash off! But – it changes matters. By God, it does! There will be no going back, now. No time for dainty half-measures. Mark my words – all Scotland will hear of this by the morn's morn. Of bishops and archbishops running for their smooth skins before the godly Mistress Geddes! Popery fleeing before

70

the forces o' righteousness. And, mark you, the common
folk's righteousness, no' ours! This will ring round the land
– that it was the Edinburgh wifies who did it, no' John Leslie
and James Graham!'

'For that I will thank God, at least!'

'You say so? I wonder.' He had to shout above the uproar.
'I say, I wonder. Think you it best that the folk should lead
in Scotland? No' the nobles? Will you win your moderation
that gait? Use your wits, man.'

'Mm.'

Archie Napier had come up. 'John's right,' he said,
urgently. 'I have just had a word with Tom Hope. He is
saying the same. That we will have to act quickly now – or
the whole cause could get out-of-hand. As this morning has
done. This could be like a heather-fire, burning all, bad and
good alike. We must control it – if we can ...'

6

THERE WAS INDEED MUCH TALKING, AND SOME ACTION IN
Scotland thereafter. The country rang with that Sunday's
doings in Edinburgh – and with the name of Jenny Geddes,
stool-thrower and bishop-feller, who suddenly became something of a national heroine. Not with the gentry, of course,
who could by no means countenance such abandoned behaviour. But amongst the ordinary people the die was now
cast, the issue clear-cut, the anti-episcopal cause their very
own.

That it must not remain so was the concern of thinking
folk who sought the realm's weal. Leadership there had to be,
demonstration that mob-rule would not serve. Which
demonstration was not easy – for in fact this display of mob-
rule *had* served, most effectively, at least for limited objectives. For after that Sunday no attempts were made to read
the new prayer-book from any pulpit in Scotland, the

bishops lay very low, and Archbishop Spottiswoode repaired in haste to London for fresh instructions.

So there was much debate, argument and suggestion, in castle and manor, town-house and manse; also much recrimination and dissension. Montrose's scheme for a petition of rights at last saw fulfilment – although it was not until the 18th of October that it was finally signed, sealed and sent off to the King. It was wordy, and rather uninspiredly styled *Scotland's Supplication and Complaint Against the Book of Common Prayer, the Book of Canons, and the Prelates;* not at all what James Graham had visualised. He signed it, nevertheless. None really believed that it would convince King Charles of the error of his ways.

It was not until almost a month later, when not so much as an acknowledgment had been received, that positive and effective action was taken by the born leadership of the country, after so much feeble bickering and delay. For almost every day there were scenes, crowds rioting, magistrates shut up in the Tolbooth of Edinburgh, prayer-books burned, the Lord Treasurer, the Earl of Traquair mobbed and his staff of office broken, old Bishop Sydserf almost killed. Great crowds flocked on Edinburgh from far and near, agitating against the cleric-dominated Privy Council. Sir Thomas Hope, putting at risk all his career, declared that Scotland was not so much misgoverned as not being governed at all. He suggested that the Privy Council's request for a committee of complainers was apt, permitting the calling of a Convention. He suggested that it be done forthwith, as pursuant of the Privy Council order, his own name and style being sufficient authority.

And so, on the 18th of November, 1637, a great Convention of all those entitled to attend a parliament was called in the Parliament Hall of Edinburgh. By no means all who were invited attended, many holding that to do so would brand them as having taken sides against the monarch. But sufficient did so to produce a large and representative assembly – larger than many a true parliament. Out of it all came the decision, not unanimous but carried by a large majority, that a standing commission of the Convention be set up, not just as a committee to speak before the Privy Council, but as a much more meaningful, permanent and effectve body. It would consist of representatives of the four constituent sections of the Convention, the nobles, the lairds, the Kirk and the burghs, these all to meet together, but each at a separate table for their order, thereat to take council for and action towards the proper regulation of the realm's affairs until parliament itself appointed otherwise. It was, in effect, a provisional government.

Montrose found himself appointed to the Table of the Nobles, but declined the convenership, when it was proposed by Rothes, who himself refused the position. It was then filled by John Campbell, Earl of Loudoun.

So, at last, the rudderless ship of state began to sail on a recognisable course, however unacceptable to some. Montrose himself by no means approved of all that was decided upon : but having spoken out against courses he objected to, he could do no less than go along with the majority decisions thereafter. It was the voice of Scotland, spoken in more democratic fashion than any there had known previously; and while he would not fail to seek to influence it, he would not controvert it.

Quickly the results were seen. Mob violence diminished, the people quietened, the Privy Council was left in no doubt as to strength of opinion throughout the country against the royal ordinances, and the ministers of the Kirk sobered somewhat in their pulpit agitation. The Lord Treasurer Traquair, a stupid man, departed for London, if not wiser, at least better informed.

Strangely, where King Charles had shown little concern over riot and fury in his nothern kingdom, he reacted sharply to these latest developments. Royal commands and edicts came flooding north. All petitioners and objectors soever were commanded to disperse on pain of treason; and not to reassemble without the Privy Council's consent. To amplify this, the Council itself was ordered to remove itself from Edinburgh and meet in Linlithgow. And as further intimation that the King meant business, the law courts were also commanded to leave Edinburgh. The capital was to be isolated as a plague-spot – and warning was served on the Lord Advocate and judges. Finally, Charles, with firm courage if nothing else, announced that he took complete and personal responsibility for the new prayer-book, insisted upon its immediate introduction, and gave the sternest orders to all ministers to impose it at all costs. It was to be war, at least to the paper-knife.

The Tables, meeting under the threat of treason, decided at last to take up seriously the idea of a great national covenant, no mere supplication or petition this time, but a manifesto of the people's rights, a clarion call to action, and a bond of engagement. Montrose, torn by doubts, assented.

Even such wordy warfare exacts its price on the individual – and James Graham learned something of the cost, other than to his peace of mind, when he returned home to Kincardine after that third major sitting of the Tables, at the beginning of December. He was surprised to find Magdalen, with the boys, all packed and ready to leave – despite the fact that she was nearly eight months pregnant.

'My dear,' he exclaimed, 'where are you bound?'

'Home,' she told him briefly.

'But – this is your home.'

'Is it? I think not.'

At her tone, he eyed her thoughtfully. 'Magdalen – what is to do?'

'My father is come. He will take us back to Kinnaird. For Yuletide.'

'Southesk here?'

'He is gone today to Inchaffray. To speak with the Lord Madderty. Awaiting your return. He will be back anon. We ride tomorrow.'

'But . . . I had no thought to go to Kinnaird. For Yule. Nothing has been said of this, nothing discussed.'

'You have been little here, to discuss anything.'

'I have been much thronged with work.'

'You are ever much thronged with work, James.'

'These are fateful, anxious days . . .'

'They have been long, weary days. For me.'

'I am sorry. You are drawing near your time. It must be grievous for you. But that will soon be by with. And then . . .'

'And then – what betterment? Waiting for the next!'

'My dear, you are distraught.'

'Distraught, yes. Distraught with waiting. For you! I waited all the years you were gone beyond the seas. And still I wait, idling my life away. So – I go to Kinnaird.'

'Idling, girl? With our two sons to rear? And this my house

to keep? Not so large as Kinnaird – but not small. Sakes – you will have less to do at Kinnaird! In another's house.'

'It is at least my home. As this crow's-nest can never be!'

'I did not know that you so misliked it here. It seems to me a bonnie house enough . . .'

'Then why not bide in it?' she flashed. 'If you like it so well. You are scarce ever here. *I* might esteem it better if I shared it with my husband!'

He bit back the hot words that sprang to his lips. 'Magdalen,' he said slowly, carefully, 'the kingdom is in grievous state. It demands the service of all its true sons. I am an earl of Scotland. One of those on whom rest the greater responsibility. Chief of a great clan. I have set my hand to the task of seeking to right some of the realm's wrongs. With others. I could do no less. Would you have me, the Graham, fail in my simple duty?'

'Have you not simple duty to more than the realm?'

'I have, yes. More than duty – love and affection, and my own concerns. But, meantime, I have no choice but to do what I was born to do.'

'Were you, the Graham, born to rebel against your king? You, one of his earls, who should be his main support?' That came out in a rush. 'My father is another of the earls of Scotland. Though a new one! He sees not his duty so!'

Montrose took a deep breath. 'Do I hear your father's voice speaking there?' he asked, at length.

'My father can say as he will. He never lacks for words! But even a woman, even Magdalen Carnegie, can think her own thoughts. I . . . oh, James, I believe you do wrongly! You are another man, since you returned from foreign lands. I feel . . . I feel that I do not know you, any more.'

At her abrupt alteration of tone and manner, the cracking of her hard-maintained front, the man reached out to grasp her arm.

'Magdalen – do not say it. I am still James Graham, your husband, father of your bairns, sharer of your bed, of *our* life. If I have changed, it is only that I have grown older, changed from a youth to a man. But – it is a man you would wish as husband, is it not? No callow youth. A man, who knows his own mind – or seeks to do so. Is that so ill?'

'If it means that you grow away from me – yes.'

'I cannot remain the bairn I was when I left you, girl.

75

But, then – nor are you the same. You are changed, like-wise . . .'

'And whose fault is that? *I* have stayed where I was, where I belonged. I have not become a renegade!'

'Renegade!' Almost he laughed. 'Dear God – James Graham renegade!' Then he frowned. 'That word, at least, is not your own. That I swear! So, my lord of Southesk names me renegade? He, who ever makes his own laws and rules!'

'You have turned against the King.'

'I have told you, Magdalen – it is not true. I am the King's loyal subject – and will ever be so. But when the King does ill, grievously ill, to the hurt of his people and of his own name and rule, is it not my duty to seek change his course?'

'Who are you to judge the King?'

'You cannot have it this way and that. If I, as an earl of Scotland, one of the *Righ,* the princes, the lesser kings, of which Charles is the *Ard Righ,* the High King – if I must be foremost in the King's support – then I also must be one who advises the King as to right and wrong, in his rule in this land. Else I am a mere vassal; worse, a paid servant to carry out his will, right or wrong. Which, pray God, I will never be!'

'Oh, words – great, swelling words!' she cried. 'I cannot trade such words with you, James. You are ever too clever for me. But, this I say. That I believe you do ill. And . . .' she set her less than prominent jaw obstinately, 'and tomorrow we go to Kinnaird.'

'Even though I say otherwise?' he asked. 'It is not con-venient for me to go farther from Edinburgh, at this pass. I must return there for another meeting, in ten days' time.'

'The more reason that I am at Kinnaird, then. Since I am to be left alone again. As always!'

'Magdalen – I do not think that Kinnaird is the place for you. Under your father's eye and tongue. You know it – we have spoken of it, often. If you will not stay here at Kin-cardine, come to Edinburgh with me, meantime. We can take a lodging in the city. For this winter, which must be of great import . . .'

'No! What would I do in Edinburgh? Amongst all your clever plotters and intriguers? I want no part in your plot-ting. Any more than in your rabbles and riots! I am going home – at least for a time.' Chokingly but finally, she said it, and turning, ran from him, actually ran.

He began to hurry after her, but then thought better of it. Shaking his head, he went heavy-footed in search of his sons.

Nevertheless, after an unsatisfactory night in his wife's bed, James Graham rode north for the Mearns, with his Countess, his sons and his father-in-law, having thought on it until his head spun. He was not a man to shirk the price that had to be paid – any price.

7

EDINBURGH MIGHT BE DEMOTED, IN NAME, FROM BEING capital, by the King's command; but seldom before had the old grey city above the Forth been so much the centre and heart of the country. The Privy Council – or the Lords Spiritual part of it – might meet occasionally and fearfully in Linlithgow or Stirling; but the meetings which mattered to Scotland were taking place all the time in Edinburgh; not only those of the Tables themselves, but public and private assemblies, conclaves and groups of the nobility, clergy, burgesses and ordinary folk, conferring, protesting, demonstrating. People streamed to the city from all parts – or not quite all parts, for the Highlands in the main remained disinterested, and Aberdeenshire and the North-East hostile. This latter attitude was accounted for partly by the fact that St Andrews, the former ecclesiastical metropolis and most ancient university, was the main centre of Presbyterianism – and therefore its rival, Aberdeen University, must needs support Episcopacy, to be different; and partly owing to the great influence thereabouts of the mighty Catholic house of Gordon, whose chief, the Marquis of Huntly, inevitably chose to link the Crown with the Papacy.

That winter of 1637/38, Montrose saw more of Edinburgh than he had ever done. After the birth of another son, whom they named David, in early January, he was more frequently in the city than at Kinnaird – where he found the atmosphere a little trying. The great National Covenant was in process of being drawn up; and since its sentiments and provisions were all-important, James Graham was concerned that his hand should not be absent from the wording. Also, he was beginning to regret that he had allowed the Earl of Loudoun to be appointed the convener of the Nobles' Table, with the influence this position was assuming. Loudoun, the first earl, had been Sir John Campbell of Lawers, a harsh and overbearing man, and notably anti-King. Montrose was seeking, at this stage, and on the urgings of Napier, Rothes and even Sir Thomas Hope, to restrain him from too intemperate an attitude. If the Campbell had had his way – like some of the more extreme ministers – it would have been outright armed rebellion, and the royal authority denied and dismissed.

Such was the situation when, on the 19th of February, John Stewart, Earl of Traquair, Treasurer of Scotland, arrived back in Scotland from London – but not at Edinburgh. He went to Stirling, and in the presence of the truncated Privy Council, had the Lord Lyon King of Arms read a new proclamation from the King, at the Mercat Cross, giving force of law to various aspects of Charles's policy. However, the Lyon and his heralds were ordered to come to Edinburgh and read the proclamation there on the 22nd – although discreetly.

Since one of the clauses was that all petitioners and protestors against the King's ecclesiastical policy were to be banished the city and forbidden to meet together on pain of treason, it was high time for swift decisions.

Edinburgh buzzed like a bee's-bike disturbed; but though there was strong pressure for drastic, indeed violent action, Montrose, Rothes, Napier and Henderson – guided in the background by the Lord Advocate – managed to have moderation to prevail. Meantime. The royal proclamation would be heard and its proclaimers not subjected to riot or contempt. But the Tables' own proclamation would be read thereafter, and the new National Covenant brought forward for signature in turn.

So, on Thursday the 22nd, Edinburgh was packed to bursting point, to witness this first direct confrontation, the first formal exchange of salvoes in the war of words between Monarch and people. At an hour before noon, as the bells still jangled the hour, the steady tuck of drum heralded the Town Guard, specially reinforced for the occasion, marching up the crowded High Street to the Mercat Cross outside St Giles. They had to force their way less than gently, with halberds and pikes and flat of swords, so dense was the throng; but everywhere the ministers were mixing with the people, urging restraint, a quiet reception, and the upholding of the dignity and authority of their Tables. In the main they were successful, extraordinarily so considering the intensity of the emotion aroused. There were a few scuffles, some shouts and catcalls, one or two stones thrown; but the Guard and its charges got through without major upset – these charges including the unhappy Provost and magistrates of Edinburgh, some of whom were themselves members of the Burghs' Table, Lord Lyon Balfour and his brilliantly tabarded heralds, and, impassive-featured, pacing majestically, Sir Thomas Hope of Craighall, His Grace's Advocate.

Around the platformed Mercat Cross, of course, the crowd was most dense and most illustrious. Here, standing tight-packed as herrings in a barrel, was a large part of the country's aristocracy, gentry, clergy, guildry, merchantry – and, of course, innumerable of the citizenry and country folk in for the proclamations, with screeching children, barking dogs, pedlars, hucksters, pickpockets, cutpurses, indeed all the community of the realm. It was a cold grey day, with an east wind off the sea and an occasional smirr of rain – Edinburgh in February. Every window of the tall flanking tenements and lands held its quota of womenfolk.

Through all, the Town Guard pushed. Leaving the magistrates and the Advocate at the foot of the octagonal, arched and parapeted base of the Cross, the Provost and Lord Lyon, with four heralds and two trumpeters, climbed the little winding stair to the platform, above the heads of the crowd. And there, as uncomfortably cramped as were their hearers below, the trumpeters took over from the drummers who had rat-a-tatted continuously hitherto, and blew a long and blaring fanfare.

Provost William Dick, one of the wealthiest merchants in the land, raised his hand. 'My lords, masters, citizens and burghers,' he shouted, 'as chief magistrate of this city, I

79

require that you give ear and respectful hearing to the most honoured Lord Lyon King of Arms, who speaks by order of the King's Grace.'

One or two witticisms greeted this, for the Provost had a slight impediment in his speech which turned his Rs into Ws. But the trumpets soon cut that short.

Sir James Balfour of Denmiln and Kinnaird unrolled his parchments, and in a high clear voice, began :

'In the name of Charles, by the grace of God, King – hear me. It is hereby declared, ordained and decreed, that . . .'

He got no further. A great sigh rose from the assembled multitude, grew into a murmur, a groan that increased and began to change into an ominous growling. Shouts began to punctuate this heavy, angry sound – but they were in the main the shouts of the ministers calling for quiet, for attention, a decent respect, some of the nobility joining in. Gradually they were heeded, and an uneasy hush prevailed again.

Sir James Balfour, with an anxious frown, tried again. He got a little further, this time, managing to read the royal preamble. But when he proclaimed that the King took fullest and personal responsibility for the introduction of the new Liturgy, the murmuring began once more. Raising his voice, the Lord Lyon announced that King Charles could not possibly discuss or debate such matters within his own divine right and prerogative. Desperately, as the noise swelled, Balfour shouted the provisions that all petitioners and indeed all strangers, must disperse and leave Edinburgh forthwith, under pain not only of his royal displeasure but under all the penalties of treason. Loud, deep and steady was now the outcry from thousands of throats. Clearly no efforts of the ministers were going to have any effect now.

Montrose, whose handsome features had been growing more and more set, turned to Napier. 'They will never hear him now,' he jerked. 'We must get Balfour away. We cannot have the Lyon rabbled – the King's spokesman. Henderson, and the other ministers, swore that they could control the crowd. This is damnable . . . !'

'What did you expect?' That was Rothes, at his other side. 'The temper o' this realm will not suffer talk the likes o' that, now. Not this day.'

'We must demonstrate the authority, the moderation, of

the Tables,' the younger man insisted. 'If I could get up there . . .' He gestured towards the Cross platform. But it was closely surrounded by the thick cordon of the Town Guard, who were most obviously under orders to let no one through.

'Thank God – Balfour is getting out !' Napier exclaimed. 'See, he is folding up his papers.'

Clearly, the Lord Lyon saw the uselessness of continuing – and he was not the man to provoke any more trouble than he must. He signed to his trumpeters, and they blew a final and somewhat ragged flourish. He turned and pushed his way down the stairway.

The triumphant cheers of the crowd swelled and maintained. So soon as the trumpets sounded for the last time, there was a stir fairly close to the Cross, upstreet – nearer to Montrose's own stance, indeed. Here there was another sort of platform, semi-permanent, of timber, on which the scaffold was erected for executions. It had been brought out today, but its top kept clear. Up on to this now clambered four men, the Earl of Loudoun, Sir George Stirling of Keir, Master Alexander Henderson and Archibald Johnston of Warriston, lawyer – the conveners of the Tables. The latter was waving a large paper.

Gradually the noise subsided.

'Thank God !' James Graham murmured. 'Now – let us hope Warriston keeps his head. And tongue ! He is scarce the wisest choice . . . !'

Archibald Johnston, laird of the small property of Warriston, north of Edinburgh, looked indeed an unlikely choice to be spokesman of the combined Tables of Scotland's Convention. Young – exactly Montrose's own age of 25 – he was slight, painfully thin, stooping, pale, with long, lank black hair and burning eyes, a born fanatic if ever there was one. His was a strange character, nervously intense, utterly unconcerned with time – he was said to remain on his knees in prayer all many a night, for as long as fourteen hours at a stretch – immoderate, uncaring of the opinions of others. Yet he had a brilliant mind, a great legal knowledge, and a phenomenal grasp of detail, together with a fiery eloquence which tended to spare others no more than himself. An advocate, already he was renowned at the bar – though little liked. He had been chosen spokesman today as representing the city of Edinburgh on the Table of the Burghs, and as one of the actual compilers of the wording of the new Covenant – which Covenant indeed he was here to declare. Montrose had been almost the least certain as to the wisdom of his appointment.

Warriston raised his hand for silence – and strangely enough got it quite quickly. Despite his meagre frame he had a commanding presence of a sort, and a deep, resonant voice which carried infinitely better than either the Lyon's or the Provost's.

'My friends,' he cried, 'good folk – you have heard the voice of power and majesty. Aye, and the voice of error and shame, likewise! Even though it be in the King's name. I say to you, that yon was not in truth the voice of Charles Stewart, the King's Grace, that you heard. But the voice of the man Laud, and his minion Juxon, English apostate clerks, knaves, reprobates who . . .'

A great roar of approval drowned his words.

When he could, he went on, drawn features working. 'Not only Laud and his English jackals mislead the King. For their own shameless ends, Scots prelatical dogs do likewise. Spottiswoode, Wedderburn, Maxwell, Sydserf! Renegade Papists, idolators, chamberlains of Satan, the worse in that they are of our own nation, betraying their fellows and the blessed reformed faith, worshippers of Baal . . .'

'I feared it!' Montrose groaned. 'The man cannot contain himself. He is drunken on his own words! I told them. I told *him* . . . !' He raised his arm high. 'If I could but catch his eye. Calm him . . .'

But in the press no man's hand was going to be seen by any other. Montrose started to push his way nearer to the scaffold-platform.

'You'll no' get near him,' Rothes declared.

He was right. The younger man made but little headway. But, of all things to be there in the middle of the High Street, was an upended barrel. How and why it came to be there was a mystery. But, stumbling over it, and cursing it as so many another had done, Montrose perceived that it might serve his turn. He climbed up on to its less than stable top – while Rothes, at his back, held it, and him, steady.

'Man, James,' he chuckled, 'who'd ha' thought to see *Greumach Mor* hoisted on a barrel! Watch you – or you'll no' be at rest till you are lifted up above the rest o' us on three fathoms o' a rope!'

James Graham did not heed that sally. He was only about twenty yards from Warriston now; and, raised above his fellows thus, the other could not fail to see him – or the warning, minatory finger. The orator faltered just a little in his diatribe.

Warriston's hesitation and glance drew the attention of others to Montrose, of course. But, strangely enough, the crowd misconstrued, assuming that the great Earl of Montrose was so carried away with enthusiasm for all this eloquence that he must needs show it thus. He earned a cheer for himself, in consequence, and popular approval as the first of the high nobility to make plain his position.

His gesture, however, was not ineffectual. Warriston recollected, and thereafter applied himself to his brief. This was to summarise in digestible form the contents of the National Covenant which they had prepared, to use it as a counterblast to the royal proclamation, and to intimate that it would be set out on parchments and ready for comprehensive signature in a day or two's time.

In great, ringing tones he proclaimed the kernel of the Negative Confession against Popery, of 1581, heady, denunciatory stuff which, since it had been signed by Charles's own father, James the Sixth, made it a safe basis for this new manifesto, declaring that, as a confession of faith, they and all true Christian men did condemn the monuments of bygone idolatry.

That went down well.

The second part of the Covenant listed all the Acts of the Scots Parliament passed since the Reformation to protect and support the true faith and Presbyterian form of worship – all again signed by King James and even one or two, reluctantly, by Charles himself in his first years on the throne. These would have made but dull reciting to a crowd; but Warriston managed to summarise some of them effectively, and to emphasise that these, and only these, were in fact the law of the land, and as such must be upheld by all loyal and law-abiding subjects.

It was skilfully done, and had the effect of leaving the hearers in no doubt, not only that their course was right and lawful, but that by setting at naught and controverting the expressed provisions of parliament, the King was in fact breaking the law as well as his own coronation oaths, and betraying his father's memory equally with his realm's integrity. Even Montrose was moved to applaud.

The third and final section of the Covenant was an affirmation of loyalty.

'We, noblemen, barons, gentlemen, burgesses, ministers and commons,' he intoned slowly, distinctly, 'considering the dangers to the true religion, to the King's honour, and to the public peace, by the manifold innovations and evils contained in our late supplications, complaints and protestations, do hereby profess before God, His holy angels and the whole world, that we shall constantly adhere to and defend the aforesaid true religion, and forebear from the practice of all innovations introduced into the worship of the Lord God. Aye, and to labour by all means in our power lawfully to recover the purity and liberty of the Gospel as it was established. Also, to stand to the defence of our dread sovereign, the King's Majesty, his person and authority, as we do the laws of his kingdom. This we, the undersubscribing, promise and swear by the great name of the Lord God, that religion and righteousness may flourish in the land, to the glory of God, the honour of the King, and the peace and comfort of us all.'

Warriston paused, looked over at Montrose, and in a different and much less dramatic voice added, almost expressionlessly, 'God save the King's Grace.'

Considering the turgid nature of his material, and the fact that it was written to be read, not spoken, even the speaker must have been surprised by the enthusiasm of its reception. Men cheered, waved and capered, women skirled and clasped each other, bonnets were thrown into the air. Perhaps only the Scots, with their love of metaphysics, rhetoric and wordy debate, could have worked themselves up to such pitch over the like. With even Montrose cheering, Warriston stood back, trembling.

The Earl of Loudoun took his place, briefly, to announce that the said National Covenant would be transcribed on parchment and brought for signature to the kirkyard of the Greyfriars, here in Edinburgh, in four days' time, when this great step forward would be taken in the work of God and of the King's realm of Scotland.

So, the following Wednesday, the 28th, since no hall or building was large enough to contain all the people who must
assemble for the occasion, the National Covenant of 1638
was subscribed and signed in the extensive graveyard of
Greyfriars Church, which crowned the hill above the valley
of the Cowgate to the south. The crowd was not quite so
dense as that at the Cross, for guards at the gate could here
keep out the mere spectators and gapers, indeed the ordinary
citizens who could contribute nothing to *this* day's work,
being in the main unable anyway to read or write. For all
that, there were fully a thousand present, come to subscribe
this dread bond and affirmation, signature of which might
indeed place a noose around their necks – for none could fail
to recognise that this document and declaration ran directly
counter to the recent royal proclamation, with its explicit
threats of treason. Whoever signed this Covenant, at least
would not do so lightly. Nevertheless, not a few children had
been brought to Greyfriars that day, to see the making of
what could not fail to be history.

Henderson set the tone and tenor of the proceedings by
mounting one of the many flat table-stones of the graveyard
and calling the great company to prayer in loud and ringing
voice. Head thrown back, fine eyes alight, fists clenched and
often upraised to heaven, he not so much entreated and
besought his Maker as assailed Him in the name of their
mutual and sacred cause and duty. Harshly powerful, his
words direct, unfaltering, his sincerity undeniable, he committed the Lord God to the side of liberty, justice and Presbyterianism, at length and in detail. After this, the very angels
of light might not mistake.

Then John Campbell, Earl of Loudoun, mounted the
gravestone, even as the Amens rang out vehemently, seeking
to cut them short. He was, however, no orator, and before
he was finished folk were chatting amongst themselves and
tending to move around to keep warm. Frowning, the earl
wound up prematurely by calling upon all present to append
their names to the document – and then, at a tug from
Warriston, recollected, and added that before they could
honestly do so, of course, they must hear its terms, all its
terms. At a slight groan from those who could hear, he com-

manded Archibald Johnston of Warriston to read the Covenant through.

The young advocate put things to right, despite the bad start, the chill draughts of the place, and the tendency of his hearers to stamp on the grass, rub and even blow on their hands. Once again his histrionic abilities were brought dramatically into play, and what could have been a rather dull, wordy and repetitious disquisition, despite its un-doubted noble sentiments and sincerity, became a clarion call, a resounding testimony of a nation's love of freedom, a cause to die for it need be. So carried away by emotion became this strange orator, as he went on, that sometimes tears coursed unheeded down his sallow cheeks, his voice choked, and there were agonising pauses when it seemed that he could not go on. Montrose, to whom this sort of thing was totally alien and embarrassing, was astonished to perceive that, instead of putting people off, and making the occasion something of a charade, this treatment was in fact arousing the company to a high pitch of almost febrile enthusiasm. The pauses and gulping silences seemed only to enhance the tension. And cold was forgotten.

A voice murmured in the Graham's ear. 'Now you will perceive what we, in the courts, must needs contend with! There is a chiel who will have my office, if he can!'

It was Sir Thomas Hope, at Montrose's back, wrapped in a fur robe and sober black.

'How honest is he, think you? Is this play-acting? Or sincerity?'

'Oh, he is sincere enough, I think. Though, i' faith, I believe that I would prefer that he was not! A man so moved to hot feeling, as this, could endanger any cause. If allowed high place. And Warriston will not be content with lowly. But . . . he will get your Covenant signed for you, this day. Mark my words!'

Yet, despite his words, and despite the ringing, almost hysterical acclaim which greeted the end of the reading, when Loudoun, like a douche of cold water, curtly demanded signatures, the great crowded kirkyard was abruptly stricken with immobility. A silence descended. No single man stepped forward to be the first to sign this noble and applauded document. It was as though sudden realisation had dawned that this, however splendid, would most certainly be branded by the King and the Privy Council as a highly treasonable statement, and expressly contrary to the royal command.

'Does the Graham not lead in this?' came quietly at Montrose's shoulder, as none volunteered.

'Gladly,' the younger man said. 'But surely it is for Rothes to be first? Or yourself, sir? On whose advice this was drawn up.'

'Na, na – Tom Hope signing that paper could no longer remain King's Advocate, man. I will serve your cause better in that office than by writing my name yonder.'

'Perhaps. But Rothes . . . ?' Montrose looked over at that man enquiringly.

Rothes smiled, almost mockingly, but shook his head. 'After you, James,' he chuckled. 'If needs I must!'

'Very well.' Raising his voice, James Graham called strongly, 'Give me the pen, my lord.'

A great sigh arose from the company.

Taken from Warriston the large parchment was spread out flat on top of another table-stone by Archibald Henderson and Andrew Cant. Taking the quill from Loudoun, dipping it in the portable ink-horn, James Graham strode forward and, bending low, wrote the word Montrose bold and clear, just below the end of the statement, at the left-hand side.

'Praise God! And bless you, my lord,' gravely good-looking Andrew Cant said quietly, at his side. 'Scotland could ever rely on the Graham! Where you lead, a whole realm will follow.'

Doubtfully the younger man shook his head, straightening up. 'I fear, sir, that you expect too much of me.' But there was no doubt about him when Loudoun made to take the quill from his fingers. 'Wait you, my lord,' he said. He turned, and held the pen out to Rothes.

That squat man wagged his head ruefully. 'You are a hard man, James,' he complained. 'The Graham's head Charles Stewart might think twice to chop. But Johnnie Leslie's he'd have off like a thrissle's! His Grace has never loved me.' Nevertheless, he took the quill and signed, a notably crabbed, small signature for so extrovert a man, squeezed in to the left of the other, where there was scarcely room anyway – an odd choice when there was a whole sheet to choose from. Montrose looked at the older man thoughtfully.

After these two, there was no longer any holding back – save in the matter of due precedence. Since two earls had signed first, it was accepted that the other earls should come next. Cassillis, Home, Lothian, Wemyss and Loudoun set down their names in quick succession. The lords followed, Yester, Boyd, Elcho – Wemyss's son – Lindsay, Melville and Balmerino. Archie Napier did not sign, pointing out like Hope, that if he did so, he could scarcely remain a member of the Privy Council; and his membership there might yet be of more value to the cause than his signature on a paper. The long queue of the lesser barons and lairds was now forming up, in turn. This business obviously was going to take a long time.

'There is one face missing here, today, that I'd looked to see,' Sir Thomas Hope said, as they stood watching the long line of signatories. 'Where is Archibald Campbell?'

'Why should he be here? He has shown no least interest, attended no meetings.'

'There are more ways of showing interest than by attending meetings, my lord. My information is that my lord of Lorne is exceeding interested. Word of everything that is said and done is carried to him forthwith. Hot-foot, indeed. I vow that he will know by the morn's morn who first put pen to that paper.'

'Not in far-away Argyll, surely . . . ?'

'He is not in Argyll. These last weeks he has been at Castle Campbell, near Dollar. Not ten miles across the Ochils from your own house of Kincardine. Do not say that you did not know it! *MacCailean Mor* and *An Greumach Mor* sitting cheek by jowl in the Ochils. Do not tell me this is news to you, my lord!'

Montrose frowned. 'I have not been staying at Kincardine. My wife is at her father's house of Kinnaird I . . .' He paused. 'Archibald Campbell is not yet *MacCailean Mor*,' he said, in a different voice.

'To all intents he is. His feckless father disgraced, turned rabid Catholic in his dotage, indulging in foolish plots and banished Scotland. By decree the Lord Lorne has been given – or has acquired – all his father's powers, the management of the largest lands in this realm and complete control of

88

Clan Campbell. He is *MacCailean Mor* in everything but name. He is only a step from being the powerfullest man in Scotland.'

'Mm.'

'Did you expect him here today, Tom?' Napier asked.

'I conceived that he could not afford to stay away! I was wrong, it appears.'

'I do not take you, sir,' Montrose said. 'What has the Campbell to gain here? All here put their necks at risk, but stand to gain nothing. Save perhaps some peace in their souls! What is here for the Campbell?'

'What but the leadership and power in this land?' the Lord Advocate replied. 'Since it lost its kings to London, Scotland has lacked its leadership. The Campbell will lead in Scotland, if he may. And this cause and bond, this Covenant, could give him – or another – that leadership. If played aright.' And he looked directly at the younger man.

'I have said, and still I say, that *I* do not seek such position,' Montrose declared flatly, almost doggedly.

'You cannot deny your birthright, my lord. Any more than can Archibald Campbell. I think that you would not wish to see *him* ruling in Scotland?'

The other was silent.

'It is my belief that Lorne but waits his chance. To take this cause into his own two hands. Then use it to rule Scotland.' Hope paused. 'And, who knows, Scotland might do worse! For a strong hand, any strong hand, could be better than no hand at all. Or a thousand weak ones!'

James Graham chewed on that for a while, as he was meant to do. 'I do not say that I accept that,' he observed, at length, watching Douglas of Cavers, Sheriff of Teviotdale, append his signature. 'But . . . Campbell has done nothing. For this Covenant. Even though, as you say, he may be interested, watchful, he has done nothing, taken no part. Not even come to sign it. How can you think that he intends to use it?'

'He would not sign it for the same reason that I do not,' Napier said. 'He is a member of the Privy Council, likewise. Made so, though young, while you were abroad, James. He would cling to that position, meantime, I have no doubt.'

'Exactly,' Hope agreed. 'Archie Campbell is exceeding godly, for a man of his years – the more so since his father married again and turned Papist. I know no sterner Presbyterian in the land! He will, *must* approve this cause. But he is a clever man, something of a fox. And will prefer, if fingers are to be burned while lighting this fire, that it should be other fingers than his own. When he is assured of your success – then he will step in. And as Privy Councillor, Justiciar of Argyll and Chief of Clan Campbell, his step will be no light one !'

'And if we are less than successful?'

'Then he will prove to be the King's man, after all, his name unsoiled. He will have sought to save Scotland for Charles. And so gain the rule over it from a grateful monarch. So – he bides his time.'

'I think, sir, that you do not like Archibald Campbell any more than do I !' Montrose said slowly.

'Like? Liking, my lord, who or what, is nothing to the case. I am not concerned with likes and dislikes, but with facts. I conceive that it is my duty to contrive that the rule of law prevails in this realm, in the best measure possible. For that I need a strong hand at the helm – else there is chaos, as now. That I should like that hand is not necessary.'

'And you have chosen to push me towards that leadership? However lacking in strength *my* hand !'

Thinly, Hope smiled. 'The choice, my lord, is . . . limited,' he said, and turned away.

They were still signing that parchment, by the light of torches, at eight o'clock that February night.

8

THE JUNE MORNING WAS LOUD WITH THE TRILLING OF LARKS in the blue, the humming of bees in the gorse and broom, the calling of cuckoos from the thorn scrub – and the singing of James Graham, Earl of Montrose. For this man, in the right company, with stirring works to do – especially in the saddle and not cooped up indoors in long-winded talk – was a totally different character, blithe, genial, frank and relaxed, a most excellent companion. And today, the 7th of June, riding south-westwards from Edinburgh's Burgh Muir, on the Pentlands road that led eventually to Lanark, he had all these conditions in his favour. It was action of a sort, at least, after all the talking, wherein he was his own man, and in his own kind of good company – very much his own. In fact 120 mounted and armed Stirlingshire and Strathearn Grahams, under Black Pate Graham of Inchbrakie. So, broad-brimmed, plumed cavalier hat hanging at his saddle-bow, long curling chestnut hair blowing in the breeze, he sang in a rich and tuneful tenor; and Inchbrakie at his side, a swarthy, ruggedly good-looking man a year older than himself, and probably his closest friend, chimed in with a deep husky bass, here and there, when he could catch the lilts of the strange foreign airs his chief had brought home from his travels. A little way behind, in fairly tight formation, the Graham troopers laughed and chattered as they trotted, a cheerful, gallant company. Nevertheless, all except the two leaders wore jacks, or breastplates of steel, and morion-type helmets, their lance-tips glittering in the sunshine.

'The banner, James?' Black Pate mentioned, at an interval between songs. He used the Christian name when they were alone together, but was meticulous with his honorific and lordings when others could hear. 'Having brought it, should you not have it flying?'

'Time enough, Pate, when we see them, for the play-acting. That banner has been hanging in my father's hall too long, unused. Scotland has been no place for banners this century of our Lord! I fear that it will split from its staff at a blow of wind! And how would Graham look then? We must needs have a new one, if there is to be much of this.'

'I will set my wife to work on it,' the other said, tactfully not suggesting that the Lady Magdalen should have the task. 'It comes to me that we may need it.' Inchbrakie sounded as though he hoped, rather than feared it.

Consciously repressing the spirit that hoped likewise, Montrose shrugged. 'Let us pray otherwise.' He deceived nobody.

'It is barely an hour to noon,' his friend said. 'Where do you look to meet Hamilton?'

'Who knows, with that man? He passed the night at Carnwath. Hamilton is of a sluggish temper, I think. Myself, I'd have been in Edinburgh by this. But the Marquis may like his bed of a morning. We may look for him anywhere between here and Cairns Castle. Unless we meet a messenger from the minister of Carnwath first!'

The Covenanters, as they were beginning to call themselves, were in the happy position of finding themselves exceedingly well-informed as to what went on, at least in the Lowlands of Scotland. This because the country was divided up into innumerable parishes, and in each there was a parish church whose incumbent was, in nine cases out of ten, a whole-hearted supporter of their cause. So that nothing of importance could happen in any corner of the land without some keen-eyed divine sending the Tables in Edinburgh word hot-foot – a great convenience. It had certainly proved so in this instance. The Marquis of Hamilton's doings had been followed and chronicled, step by step, since he crossed the Border in late May. And with particular interest.

For this was King Charles's answer. He had sent up a royal commissioner to Scotland, ostensibly to enquire on the spot into complaints and problems; but in fact, as was sufficiently well known, to gain time. When the Covenant, signed eventually all over Scotland, had been sent to him, the King's first reaction had been righteous and sorrowful wrath. Then he had sent to Scotland for certain advisers to come and inform him as to what was wrong with his Scots people. Charles was never good at choosing men, clearly no judge of character; and on this occasion, allegedly on Hamilton's advice, he had sent for those who would give him the kind of advice he desired – Traquair, Roxburgh, Spottiswoode and a parcel of bishops. But one summons surprised Scotland – Archibald Campbell, Lord Lorne. What made Charles so choose, and what Lorne told the King, were equally uncertain; but the Campbell came back from London, his thin lips shut like a clam. And presently a temporising missive followed, from the King, making certain minor concessions about the prayer-book and the law courts, but demanding the immediate withdrawal and denunciation of the Covenant itself. Also the announcement that a royal commissioner would be sent up in due course, to hear all views and deliver a proclamation to the King's local Scots subjects. It was all a much more reasonable and hopeful reaction than had been feared – were it not for the warnings of spies at Court, who declared unanimously that Charles was only playing for time, while he settled his differences with his English parliament with whom he was at logger-heads over the Ship Money issue and other questions; and a later warning that it was the Marquis of Hamilton who was on his way north, as Commissioner and that he was in fact bearing two proclamations, one of a very different tone from the other, these to be read as the circumstances indica-ted. Clearly Charles Stewart was still a force to be reckoned with.

His Commissioner had certainly borne out the spies' warn-ings, as to devious behaviour. Instead of making directly for Edinburgh, to see the people with whom he was to treat, he had swung off westwards at the Border and headed for Lanarkshire and his own territory of Hamilton. And there he had lingered for a week. But not altogether idly. The word was that he was gathering men, armed men, from his great estates. Presumably he wished to argue from strength, while in Edinburgh, in the time-honoured Scots fashion, with a fighting tail behind him.

But at Hamilton the Marquis discovered what is apt to happen to even great lords when they desert their lands and show no interest in their estates save as a source of rents. All accounts agreed that he had had the utmost difficulty in raising any sort of force. And the most reliable estimates had it that all he had managed to collect was less than a hundred exceedingly reluctant warriors. With these he apparently intended to descend upon the capital. No doubt there were plans for reinforcements to come in from elsewhere, for there were reports of musterings in other parts of the country.

It was a difficult situation for the Tables. Save for its hot-heads, the last thing that the Covenanters wanted was to be the first to resort to armed force. And any attack on the King's Commissioner would be most patent treason and revolt. On the other hand, to allow an armed company of any size into the capital, especially one which could, in the King's name, demand the allegiance of the Town Guard, was a grave danger. Arrest and imprisonment for most of the principal signatories of the Covenant would be only the first almost certain result.

So Montrose, who could most swiftly whistle up a sizeable force of men, had been asked to handle the matter. Nothing could have pleased him better, in the circumstances. He sent for Black Pate.

They rode, then, jingling over the long, green Pentland hillfoots, as though with not a care in the world, scattering sheep and stirks, laughing, waving to the country folk, Montrose himself setting the tone and tenor. He had accounts to settle with James Hamilton.

They were near Malleny, and threading open thorn-scrub woodland, when keen eyes spotted, far ahead, the glint of sunlight on steel. This quickly developed into a long, strung-out file of horsemen, crossing the moorland beyond, not in any tight formation like the Grahams but straggling, scattered.

'So-o-o!' Inchbrakie commented, eyes narrowed. 'Would we could make an ambush of it! We could roll them up like babes in a plaid!'

'Would you, a leal subject, ambush His Grace's High Commissioner? Shame on you, Pate!'

Nevertheless, quarter of a mile on, where the woodland grew thicker with ash and birch mixed, Montrose reined up. 'We will wait here a-while,' he declared. 'Why ride on when we must then come back?'

'Aye.' The other grinned. 'You'll no' want the men dismounted though, I take it?'

'It is scarce worth it,' his chief agreed, glancing assessingly about him. 'See – a score of men down each side of this track. Each one length apart. Facing inwards. And lances couched. The rest drawn up in close ranks, ten abreast. Still facing west. That should serve.' Although his tone was entirely conversational and unhurried, there was somewhere at the back of it the ring of sure, almost joyous command.

With a short bark of a laugh, Inchbrakie began to marshal his men into the required hollow-square formation, closing and flanking the track, which here bent away through the woodland beyond, out of sight. The word was passed for complete quiet.

So when, after a longer wait than most anticipated, the Marquis of Hamilton and the first of his company came trotting round the corner, it was to find themselves abruptly confronted, and their way barred, by a solid phalanx of

94

disciplined, armed and silent men, in such a position that there was no turning sideways either. There was a great pulling up and reining in of horses, with outcry and alarm – and consequent confusion behind, round the bend where the on-comers could see nothing of what went on. Chaos reigned on one side, utter and steely calm on the other.

Montrose, however, was anything but steely. He rode forward from the open front of his square, sweeping off the hat he had re-donned in a complicated flourish, his bow from the saddle profound, his smile all-embracing. A half-length behind Black Pate followed, the now unfurled Graham standard fluttering above him.

'Welcome, my lord Marquis! Welcome, in the name of the Convention of the Estates of Scotland! I am desolated that we could not express our welcome earlier. But we looked for the King's Commissioner at the Border – not coming from Lanarkshire!'

'What . . . what a God's name is this!' Hamilton exclaimed, dividing his alarmed glance equally between front and rear, and obtaining reassurance in neither direction. He was no coward – indeed he had been decorated for leading cavalry charges in the Swedish wars of Gustavus – but this sort of situation was enough to upset the most phlegmatic. 'Montrose – I say what is this?'

'What but a greeting, my lord? As *I* say. A respectful greeting for the King's Royal Commissioner – if belated. I have the honour to be sent by the Joint Tables of the Convention, to bid you welcome to Scotland, and to escort you to Edinburgh in fitting style. Er . . . God save the King.'

Like a sudden clap of thunder the 120 voices behind him rapped out a staccato 'God save the King,' and as abruptly resumed silent immobility. Hamilton jumped, rather prominent blue eyes popping.

'I . . . ah . . . devil take me! I need no escort of yours, Montrose!' The Marquis, though less exquisite than on the last occasion Montrose had seen him, was still overdressed for the road, in velvet, lace, ribbons and jewellery.

'Look on this not as mine, my lord, but as the Convention's. And now yours. At your service.'

Hamilton's own people were now crowding round the bend behind him. There was, of course, insufficient room for them, what with the trees and the stern ranks of flanking

95

troopers. The confusion grew worse every moment. In the face of the solid, motionless, lance-couched ranks in front, the newcomers made a sorry sight.

'I require no such service,' the Marquis, recovering himself somewhat now, declared. 'And certainly not from the King's enemies.'

'The King has scarce an enemy in all Scotland,' the younger man assured him. 'I hope that it was the King's *friends* that you came to speak with, my lord?'

The other coughed.

'See, sir – here is my kinsman Inchbrakie, as loyal a subject as His Grace possesses in all his realm.'

Black Pate genuflected elaborately. 'Your servant, my lord Marquis. We have been much concerned for you.'

'I know not why, sir.'

'We heard, with joy, that your lordship was approaching the Border, eight days past,' he said, grave-faced. 'Bringing His Grace's royal proclamation to Edinburgh. Then, neither hint nor hair of you, all these days! Can you wonder at our fears for you? All Edinburgh, all Scotland, in a stir? The King's Commissioner amissing. And the King's proclamation likewise. They feared that the wild English had got you. Their Border thieves are notable rascals.' Black Pate Graham was one of the toughest characters in Perthshire. His heartfelt anxiety, mixed with reproach, for the Marquis, had to be heard to be believed.

Hamilton heard but scarcely believed. He cleared his throat. 'Not so,' he said. 'I regret any concern. But ... private matters demanded my attention. At Hamilton. My estates. It was necessary.' Realising, perhaps, that this might sound rather like an apology – and to a mere Graham laird – he turned again on Montrose. 'You might have spared yourself your trouble, my lord. In coming to meet me,' he added thinly.

'Trouble nothing. It is all satisfaction, I assure you,' the other declared handsomely. 'After all, it is long since I had the pleasure of sight of you. It was at the Palace of Whitehall, was it not? One night two years back? When you made my poor presence known to the King's Grace!'

The Marquis looked away, frowning. 'It was unfortunate,' he said. 'The King was ... was less than himself, that night. Of a dark humour.'

'To be sure. Distressing. I saw your lordship doing all in your power to guide him in the matter. Your great influence with His Grace is known to all. I do not forget your efforts that night!'

Hamilton, it was clear, had had enough of the subject. And of the entire encounter. 'No doubt,' he said shortly. 'And now, Montrose, if you will move your men aside, I will continue on my way to Edinburgh.'

'As you wish.' Montrose nodded to Black Pate, who raised a hand to the square of watching Graham troopers. Obedient to the signal, they moved.

It was not really a complicated manoeuvre. The two flanking lines merely turned to face forwards instead of inwards, on their previous courses, westwards; while the solid phalanx at the end of the box opened into two sections in their turn, but reined round to face the other way, eastwards. As Montrose urged Hamilton on, the former flanking files swung in quickly, determinedly, at his back – so that, save for two gentlemen attendants and one groom, the Marquis was cut off from his long and confused tail of supporters.

'Forward!' James Graham called. And, pleasantly, to Hamilton. 'On to Edinburgh, my lord.'

The tight-knit company of 120, closely surrounding the two noblemen, set off at a swift jingling trot, eastwards.

'But – s'wounds, man – how dare you! Stop! Halt, I say!' Pressed on from behind by forty horsemen, the Commissioner – or, at least, his horse – had no option but to move forward with the rest. 'What is this? Stop! I command it.'

'We must escort you to Edinburgh. As we were commanded. And as your lordship just declared. That is why we came. A guard of honour.'

'I have my own escort.'

'Our sorrow that you were forced to the trouble of providing it, sir. Now all is well. Send them home, my lord Marquis.'

'No! This is outrage! Would . . . would you lay hands on the King's Commissioner?'

'Lay hands . . . ? Save us – outrage? You jest, my lord – that is it, you jest! We provide most sure and heedful escort, never fear. An hour, little more, and you will be in Holyroodhouse. All is prepared for your comfort.'

In some agitation, Hamilton looked behind. He could not

see very well, for the forty Grahams; but it was clear enough that no attempt was being made, or likely to be made, by his leaderless and bewildered company, to rescue him. In no particular formation, they were beginning to trot along behind, uncertainly, no trouble to anyone.

'This is beyond all!' the Marquis complained. But obviously there was nothing that he could usefully do about it.

'How does His Grace?' Montrose enquired conversationally. 'We hear much of his policies but little of his royal self. He is well?'

The other, staring about him, did not vouchsafe an answer.

'It is this realm's sorrow that we do not see more of him. Much would be gained in understanding and affection, were he to visit Scotland more frequently. Tell His Grace so, my lord, when you return. This is his own true realm, as England never can be. As it is yours! It will repay closer attention, I swear.'

The Marquis's grunt was eloquent.

Montrose did not permit himself to be silenced. In the best of good-humour he chatted as they trotted on, asking questions, making points, offering advice, a man totally at ease and in control. His victim, although he did not co-operate, could not but listen and seem to consider, however stiff his back, hemmed in closely as he was.

Pate Graham presently rode up. 'Your men are straggling badly, my lord,' he reported. 'Some are a mile behind. Their part is done. Have I your authority to order that they return to Lanark? To Hamilton?'

'No!'

'There is no accommodation for them at Holyroodhouse,' Inchbrakie went on imperturbably. 'Fodder and stabling will be hard to come by, in a city already full to overflowing for your lordship's visit. And these will serve no useful purpose there.'

'My lord Marquis knows best what to do with his people, Pate,' Montrose observed judicially. 'Perhaps he will quarter them at Colinton. Or at Dalkeith. Or at Salt Preston. Since Edinburgh is so full. Costly – but his lordship is a man of great means, we know. Care no more for it.'

'As you will, my lord. Although – these towns you name

are already crowded also. Haddington, perhaps – but it is half a day's ride from Edinburgh . . .'

Hamilton, who was notoriously unwilling to spend money, save on his personal adornment, was looking ever more unhappy. He kept glancing behind him, but gaining no comfort.

'Do not concern yourself,' Montrose told him. 'A deep purse covers much. They will do very well at Haddington. Or Linlithgow, perhaps. And you could dismount them. Quarter the men in one place and the horses another. Inconvenient, but . . .'

'I am on the King's business, sir. My men will be quartered at the King's expense. Or the realm's,' the Marquis interrupted.

'Ah. How fortunate. Does the Privy Council know it? My lord of Traquair, the Treasurer, is in London, as you know. And my good-brother, Napier, of that Council, still acts Deputy Treasurer when need be. Any payment would have to be passed by him. But . . . I will have a word with him, my lord. Be assured.'

After a few silent moments the Marquis turned in his saddle and called to one of his gentlemen behind. 'Craignethan – send the men back to Hamilton,' he snapped.

'As to your own quarters in Holyroodhouse, my lord, you should be entirely comfortable,' James Graham went on pleasantly. 'My lord Rothes has seen to that. You know Rothes, of course . . . ?'

Since Rothes and Hamilton had been deadly enemies for many years, that was another conversational gambit which fell flat instead of lightening the road to Edinburgh.

In James the Fourth's grey old palace of Holyroodhouse at the foot of Edinburgh's Canongate, James Hamilton sought to play the king, in a tentative, exploratory fashion. There were some who held that his haughty and unbending manner was not just a natural arrogance but was rehearsal for the future : that in the event of Charles Stewart losing his life, or his throne, he, Hamilton, would claim it. For he was, indeed, of royal descent, being great-grandson of that Regent Arran and Duke of Chastelherault who had long been heir to the throne during the minority of Charles's father, remotely descended from James the Second. Some even went so far as to suggest that his misleading of the King in the matter of advice, was calculated, so as to cost Charles the throne of Scotland which he himself would better fill. While this last was probably nonsense, Hamilton was clearly inordinately proud of his royal blood, and found regal posturings much to his taste.

When he was ready, the King's Commissioner commanded that representatives of the Tables appear before him, to answer questions. He would have no crowd descend upon him, however, and ordered that three nobles and three ministers come as deputation. Loudoun, Rothes and Montrose were chosen, with the Reverends Henderson, Dickson and Cant. Johnston of Warriston accompanied them, but only as clerk and legal adviser.

They were received with stiff condescension and formality – reciprocated by the ministers and Loudoun, although Rothes was all mocking whimsy and Montrose imperturbably genial. They were conducted to the throne-room on the first floor, where they were kept waiting for the best part of half an hour, until Hamilton, extravagantly magnificent in the cloak and ribbon of the Garter, over pale blue satin, despite the summer warmth, stalked in, accompanied by Archbishop Spottiswoode, Bishop Lindsay, the Marquis of Douglas – married to a Hamilton – the Earl of Abercorn, another Hamilton, the Earl of Roxburgh, and the Lord Ruthven. There were no greetings. Hamilton paced to the throne, scarcely glancing at the waiting group, waved his supporters to stand on either side of him – but slightly behind – and sat down, carefully arranging his splendid starred cloak to drape around him. No word was spoken.

Loudoun cleared his throat. As Convener of the Joint Tables, he ostensibly led the delegation. 'My lord Marquis,' he jerked, 'on behalf of the Convention of the Estates of Scotland, I offer you greeting and salutation.'

'I thank you,' the other replied shortly. 'It is customary for the King's representative and Commissioner, acting in the King's place, to be addressed as Your Grace.'

'Hm.' Loudoun glanced at his colleagues doubtfully, put right off his not very certain stride.

That was how Hamilton wanted it. This was *his* audience. 'His Majesty has sent me to investigate the state of disaffection and insurrection in this his realm, and the causes of it,' he declared flatly. 'And to recommend what action is required.' He repeated the word action, a shade ominously. 'His Majesty is much distressed by all the ill conduct which prevails today in Scotland, and especially by the contumely of those who signed the treasonable and threatening Band called the Covenant. I am required to make full investigation into this matter. It is my hope that I may inform His Majesty that it is not in fact a conspiracy, but the foolish mistakes of misguided men!' The prominent pale blue Hamilton eyes surveyed them significantly. His statement had been made in an even monotone, as of a man memorising a lesson – for in fact Hamilton was little more of an orator than was Loudoun. Almost relievedly raising his voice, he added, 'You will now answer my questions.'

Loudoun grunted, but said nothing.

'My lord,' Rothes put in, 'we came to parley, to discuss, not to be inquisitioned. Did *you* came as the King's Commissioner? Or as the King's *Inquisitioner?'*

There were gasps from the throne-dais at that. Hamilton, moistening his lips, took his time to answer. 'Earl of Rothes,' he said thickly, 'if you expect response from me, address me as Grace!'

'Damned if I will!' Rothes muttered, but below his breath.

Alexander Henderson cleared his throat. 'My lords – this will serve us nothing,' he said.

Montrose took a hand. 'Marquis of Hamilton, His Grace's Commissioner,' he said cordially, 'we all rejoice to see you here as King's representative. And to congratulate you upon your appointment as Keeper of this palace of Holyroodhouse. And as such, as *both,* would pay you fullest respects. As to this matter of style and address – as you know, here in Scotland, it has always been our wont to address only the monarch in person as Grace. We seek that you will bear with us in this. In England, however, we believe that they use the term Majesty. Indeed you have used it here, yourself. Majesty presents no difficulty to our thrawn Scots tongues, as does Grace. And you, sir, in your style and magnificence, look truly majestic. I therefore, for one, have no objection to name you Majesty. If it please Your Majesty!'

If Rothes's curt intervention had aroused gasps, this amiable and mannerly contribution produced much louder ones – and not only from the dais. Everywhere men gulped, and stared. Hands rose, lace handkerchiefs fluttered. Only

Rothes looked less than shocked – indeed chuckled coarsely.

Oddly enough, most alarmed of all appeared to be the Lord High Commissioner. 'No! No!' he cried. 'Not that! A God's name, man – have a care! That is the King's alone.'

'But, Majesty – so is Grace. More so, here in Scotland . . .'

'No, sir – I will not have it. Do not say it. I command that you do not style me so. You hear?'

'As you will. You conceive Grace to be a lesser style than Majesty, then, my lord Marquis? Here, in Scotland? Would you have our kings less high, less important, than those of England?'

The other blinked. 'Not so. I said nothing such. You put words into my mouth, Montrose – ill words. I will not have it. I am the King's loyalest and humble subject.'

'As you will, my lord Marquis. As are we! So we need have no more confusion over titles and styles. And proceed amicably to our business.'

'Yes. Very well. So be it. Ah . . . hrrm . . .' It was Hamilton's turn to be put off his stride.

'We understand, my lord Commissioner,' Montrose went on quickly, smoothly, 'that His Grace intends to make certain concessions to our requests. As set forth in the petitions and the Covenant. For which we are most loyally grateful. In the matter of the prayer-book. And of the Canons. Likewise the return of the law courts to Edinburgh. Is this so? We await your lordship's announcement with interest.'

At the stir behind him, Hamilton banged on the arm of the throne, frowning. 'Not so fast! Not so fast!' he complained. 'I am here to question you – not you me! These concessions – I have said nothing of concessions. You go too fast. They are only possible. Not sure. Certain. To be granted only if I am satisfied.'

'Quite so, my lord. The concessions are conditional. But they are clear, are they not? We have heard, from sound sources, that the reading of the Liturgy in churches is to be no longer compulsory. That the Canons anent surplices, saints days and the like are relaxed. That the law courts may return from Linlithgow. These are the King's concessions?'

'Mm. They *may* be. It is possible. But only on conditions. On condition that your Covenant is given up. Abandoned. Disavowed. Only so.'

There was what amounted to a growl from the three

ministers. 'That, sir, we will in no wise do! For any concessions soever!' Alexander Henderson cried strongly.

'Never!' David Dickson agreed. 'The Covenant stands!'

'It is a treasonable document,' Hamilton asserted. 'You have risked your necks in putting your names to it. Of His Majesty's clemency he permits that you may withdraw from it. Retract. And be forgiven. It is more than you deserve, I say. But the Covenant must be withdrawn.'

'Is that your last word, my lord?' Andrew Cant asked quietly.

'It is.'

'Then we but waste our time here,' Dickson declared. 'The Lord has hardened the King's heart. This is a stiff-necked servant of a stiff-necked master! There is nothing for us here. Let us be gone, in the name of God!'

Loudoun nodded. 'On these terms it is profitless to talk. We shall bid our Commissionership a good day.'

'Wait, my friends,' Montrose intervened. 'It were as well, I think, to ascertain whose is the hard heart and the stiff neck. The master's, or the servant's? Since the master is not here.' He had not forgotten something that Hamilton had let slip, on their ride to Edinburgh – that, as a 'kindly Scotsman' himself, if they were both reasonable and firm in their attitude, they might win something of what they fought for. Hamilton had been a rather frightened man when he said that, and possibly only seeking to buy time. But it could have been a revealing remark. 'It comes to me that the King would not have authorised concessions such as these had he been so stiff-necked as now seems. A man who will make one concession will make another, be it reasonable. And to demand that a national covenant, signed by all but a whole realm, be abandoned out-of-hand, is not reasonable. We have heard that my lord Hamilton brought *two* proclamations in his pouch. Both signed by the King. His the choice which to read. Perhaps my lord has forgotten the second proclamation?'

There was a tense silence in the throne-room.

Then the Archbishop of St Andrews leant and spoke in the frowning Commissioner's ear. He spoke at some length. When he drew back, the Marquis of Douglas, at the other side, whispered likewise. Both looked anxious, urgent.

The Covenanters stood, waiting.

At length, Hamilton spoke stiffly. 'Very well. This once I will be merciful. Will exercise the clemency His Majesty entrusted to me. To my discretion. The Covenant is not, cannot be, acceptable to the King. But I will allow the concessions to stand, meantime. Allow that they be made known and permitted. For the present, I can do no more. I shall return to London. With this of the Covenant. To lay before His Majesty. He may command otherwise thereafter. It is probable. He may countermand the concessions. You understand? More I cannot do.'

'More we cannot ask, meantime,' Montrose acceded. 'We thank you. But knowing your lordship's great influence with the King, we will hope, with some confidence, that His Grace will be at least as careful for the feelings of his kindly Scots subjects.' Deliberately he used Hamilton's own former phrase.

To that there was no response.

Alexander Henderson spoke. 'We have brought sundry matters, propositions, outstanding questions, for consideration. To put before your lordship. The Laird of Warriston, here, has them all wrote down. Would you wish us to expand upon them now? Or to leave them with you to read and think upon?' In the circumstances he forbore from calling them 'articles of peace', as they had been referred to in committee.

'God's wounds – no! Leave them, man.' The Commissioner half-rose from his seat, in alarm at the notion of further wordy debate. 'Let them lie. We shall look at them. My lord Archbishop. And others. Leave it. Er . . . this audience is now closed. You have my permission to retire.'

If Hamilton would have preferred the deputation to move out backwards, he was disappointed, and had to be content with a selection of bows, some perfunctory.

They were hardly outside the great double doors when Rothes was slapping Montrose on the back. 'Man, James!' he hooted. 'Yon was magnificent! Threatening to call the man Majesty! You had that bladder of lard fair dumbfoonert! Fear't for his neck. We must see that Charles Stewart gets to hear o' this. That his beloved Hamilton was like to be styled His Majesty, in Holyroodhouse! It may not greatly advance *our* cause – but I swear it will no' advance James Hamilton's!'

'It served its turn,' the younger man agreed, unsmiling. 'But it was unimportant, quite. What matters is that these concessions be promulgated and made effective. They will never dare withdraw them afterwards.'

'Think you them so important?' Loudoun growled. 'When we know that Hamilton and the King but play for time? Time to muster and arm! All else is but play-acting.'

'I cannot think that you are right in this,' the Graham said. 'Even King Charles would not make war on his own people and realm.' But his voice lacked its accustomed calm assurance.

9

FOUR WEEKS LATER, WITH THE KING'S COMMISSIONER returned to London, Montrose was in the saddle again, riding north this time – to play something of the commissioner himself. Once more he had Black Pate and a force of Grahams to escort him; but this time there were many more of them, and he had the Lord Kilpont as another lieutenant. As well as these, however, he had a different kind of companion on this occasion – the triumvirate of ministers who were now the acknowledged spokesmen of Scotland's Kirk, the Reverends Henderson, Dickson and Cant. They were on their way to Aberdeen.

The Tables, and the Covenant leadership, were concerned about that grey northern city. Led by the University doctors of divinity, the ministers, and almost all Aberdeen in their wake, had taken up an anti-Covenant attitude. They were not so much for Episcopacy as against Presbyterianism, and the theories propounded by the Universities of St Andrews, Glasgow and Edinburgh. And the former Catholic Gordon influence was strong, with Hamilton known to have been in contact with the Marquis of Huntly, their chief, as to armed aid. Montrose had been made a freeman of the city at the early age of seventeen, and was fairly well known there, his Old Montrose estates being only some forty miles to the south. So now, the Graham, with copies of the Covenant in his baggage, was to convince the hard-headed townspeople, and if possible Huntly, to sign; and his clerical colleagues to show the professors the errors of their ways.

He had spent the night at Kinnaird, and now rode northwards past the fine new castle Sir Thomes Burnet of Leys had built out of an old ruin at Muchalls, along a rocky coastline. He had not imposed his following, even the three ministers, on Southesk and Magdalen, but installed them all in the town of Montrose, at his own charges, riding back alone to Kinnaird. Magdalen had reverted very much to being daughter rather than wife, and there was no doubt as to whom she accepted as prime authority; but she was obviously glad to see her husband, and their lovemaking that night had been more successful than for long. There had even been tears at parting. The children were all growing apace, and most evidently delighted with their handsome father, young John, eight years old, pleading to be taken with the cavalcade to Aberdeen. Their grandfather, Southesk, was less appreciative, declaring bluntly that his son-in-law was meddling in matters too great for him, and that he would be lucky if it was only his fingers that got burned. That his daughter should be wed to a man who set himself up against his king was beyond Southesk's understanding – and no declarations to the contrary affected him in the slightest. Nevertheless James, Lord Carnegie, came spurring after Montrose as he left in the morning, declaring that he wished to accompany him. His brother-in-law found this an odd request. They had never been friends; and though Carnegie's attitude towards his overbearing father was normally a sulky suspicion, the fear was that here he might have been sent to spy upon Montrose. His wife, after all, was a daughter of the Earl of Roxburgh, one of Hamilton's associates and very anti-Covenant. The Graham's refusal of his company, though couched in friendly terms, was obviously not well received.

So now Montrose rode towards the crossing of Dee in much less assured and single-minded state than when he had ridden south to meet Hamilton. He rather wished that he had never called in at Kinnaird. Family relationships and public duty did not seem to harmonise.

He was far from comforted by the conversation which developed between the three ministers riding behind him, and to which Kilpont was obviously listening interestedly. It concerned King Charles, how much responsible he was personally for his policies, and what would happen if he sent an army over the Border against his Scots subjects. It was the sort of talk which greatly grieved the Graham, but of which he was hearing more and more. When David Dickson declared that, in the event of war, the King should be deposed, declared abdicate as far as his Scottish realm was concerned, and the young Prince Charles elevated in his stead, Montrose could stand it no more.

'Sir,' he exclaimed, turning in his saddle, 'in my presence such words will not be spoken! The King is the King. To whom I – and you – have vowed fealty and allegiance. Whether we agree with his policies or no. The King's person is sacred. He is the Lord's Anointed.'

'A Popish doctrine, my lord,' Dickson snapped.

'Not only Popish, sir. Christian. The Kirk assents. Agrees that the monarch is divinely appointed and sustained . . .'

'Only on condition that he maintains the true and reformed religion.'

'On condition? *My* oath of fealty was certainly not so conditioned! If you, sir, and those who think like you, would ride the same road as Montrose, you will respect His Grace's royal position, and utter no talk of deposition and forced abdication. Understand it, if you please.'

'My lord – we were only speaking of what might happen in the unhappy event of war,' Henderson put in placatingly. 'I believe that it will not come to that. We are loyal subjects. The King will respect the feelings of his people, in the end.'

'But if he does not?' Dickson insisted. 'If he sends armies against us? Shall we not fight back? Shall we let them lay us low? And if we do fight, we are in arms against the King. What then, my lord?'

'We will not be in arms against the King. *I* will not – that I promise. We may resist religious practices imposed upon us against our consciences. But not rise in arms against the monarch.'

'It is a fine distinction, Earl of Montrose!'

'Not in *my* mind. I ask you all to remember it.'

In that spirit they came to the Dee.

Warned of their impending arrival, a great company awaited them at Bridge of Dee, the Provost and magistrates of the city and some hundreds of the townsfolk. But it was noticeable that none wore clerical black.

Provost Patrick Leslie greeted Montrose respectfully, almost effusively, declaring that the city was his, as its honoured freeman. He was affable to Kilpont and Inchbrakie also – but it was noticeable that he had little more than a glance to spare for the three ministers. He was handed a letter from his kinsman and chief, the Earl of Rothes, urging him to do all in his power, both in the city and in the country round about, to aid that noble and true-hearted cavalier the Earl of Montrose – and this he protested vehemently that he would do, in the name of God and of the Saints Nicholas, Mary and Machar, the patrons of New and Old Aberdeen respectively – a reference which drew frowns from the clerics.

On this somewhat equivocal note they crossed Bishop Elphinstone's great seven-arched bridge and into the purlieus of the granite city.

Before they reached the Town House and Tolbooth in Golden Square, where apparently a banquet awaited the visitors, Montrose was already going warily. Provost Leslie was skilfully avoiding all references to religion and politics, and behaving as though their freeman had come on a private visit.

To put matters to a test, Montrose interrupted the determined adulatory flow. 'I have a copy of the National Covenant with me, Mr Provost,' he said. 'It is my hope that you will sign it, before all. As lead to others. And urge that your magistrates do likewise. Aberdeen has been backward in this matter.'

Leslie drew a deep breath. 'My lord,' he all but croaked. 'No! Your pardon – but no. I . . . I pray to be excused. Not to sign.'

'Why, man? What ails you at it? Is it a matter of conscience?'

'Ah . . . umm . . . conscience?' The Provost bit his lip perceiving a pitfall. 'No,' he decided, after an agitated moment. 'Not conscience. But . . .'

'You are not a Catholic?'

'No, no. I am of the Kirk. All know it, well. It is not that, my lord. It is, ah, difficult.'

'Most of this realm has found it right and proper. None so difficult. Why you?'

'We, we are King's men, here.'

'And do you say that I am not, sir?'

'Sakes – no! Never that, my lord Earl – never that! But some are not. Some would have the King down. Some see this Covenant as a condemnation of King Charles. I cannot sign such a thing.'

'I tell you it is not so. Do you know better than do I, sir? Would Montrose pull down his King? If your chief, my lord Rothes, can sign, why not you?'

'My lord Rothes is . . . is far away. Others are not!'

'Ah! Do not tell me that you, a Leslie, kin to Rothes, fear a pack of college professors?'

'Hech – not them! There are others, my lord. More . . . more potent!'

'So! You mean, the Gordons?'

'Aye – the Gordons. My lord Huntly is near, where my lord Rothes is far! And can field a hundred men for every one of Leslie.'

'Mm. I will be seeing the Marquis of Huntly. But, Mr Provost, do not tell me that the great city of Aberdeen must do as the Gordon says, if it would do otherwise? You have trained bands, have you not? A Town Guard? A walled and strong city.'

Leslie said nothing. They were halted now, before the tall Tolbooth, the narrow streets crowded with watching – but not cheering – townsfolk, through which the cavalcade had had to force its way. The Provost dismounted, to aid his visitor down.

Montrose shook his head. He had been reared near enough to the Highland Line to be careful about eating the salt of any man with whom he might be at odds, and so having hands tied by the claims of hospitality.

'No, sir,' he announced. 'I regret any discourtesy. But I am here of a set purpose, my friend. At the command of the Tables of the Convention. To gain Aberdeen for the Covenant. Does the Provost of Aberdeen sign? Or does he not?'

'I cannot, my lord. Bear with me.' The other wrung his

hands. 'Perhaps hereafter. When you have spoken with my lord Marquis. Meantime – come. A banquet is prepared for you and yours. All is ready. Come, enter my lord . . .'

'My sorrow – but no. I will not sit down with those who conceive me a traitor to my King! Nor those who betray their own realm and religion, through fear.'

'But . . . but . . .' The Provost turned unhappily to stare at his fellow magistrates, all lined up to conduct their guests within.

'But nothing, sir,' Montrose said, making his voice stern. 'Here is a matter of principle. When you tell me that you will lead your citizenry in signing this paper, then I will rejoice to eat your meat. Till then, sir, I bid you a good day.'

'But your men, my lord? All your great company . . . ?'

'We shall find quarters for them in the town, never fear. At my own charges.' He turned. 'Pate – see to it. Quarters. And not only for the men. Who is for the Covenant in Aberdeen? With a large house? Your kinsman, the Earl Marischal? The Lord Forbes?'

'The Marischal is from home, I understand.' Inchbrakie's mother was grand-daughter of the fourth Earl Marischal. 'And Forbes is old, ailing, and bides at Forbes Castle. But Pitsligo is sound, and his wife my cousin, sister to the Marischal.'

'Then let us seek Pitsligo's town-house. The Provost will inform us where it lies . . .'

In the end they found admirable quarters in the great mansion of William Keith, seventh Earl Marischal, which was indeed the prior's palatial suite of the former Greyfriars Monastery which the Marischal had gained at the Reformation, the present yong earl's sister, Lady Pitsligo, gladly throwing it open for the visitors. Settled therein, the ministers set out for the University in Old Aberdeen, seeking interview with the professors and divines.

They came back later, much later, and in no joyful mood, able to boast no more success than had Montrose with the magistracy. The doctors would have nothing to do with the Covenant, although many of the students appeared to be in favour. What was worse, a meeting of the city ministers had decided against allowing the visitors the use of any of their pulpits for the next day, Sunday – one of the main objectives of the expedition, whereby they could reach the ears of the people. Whether it was love for King Charles, belief in episcopacy, or fear of the Gordon, Aberdeen was solid against the Covenant.

But the apostles thereof were by no means beaten. They hired town-criers and sent out messengers all through the city to announce a great service next day, or series of services, which would continue non-stop throughout the day from morning till night, each of the three Covenanting divines taking it in turn to preach and lead the prayers. This to be held in the large central courtyard of the Earl Marischal's lodging, wet or fine. All who professed the Reformed faith of Christ Crucified were urged at least to come and listen and pray for God's guidance.

Fortunately that Sunday dawned dry, even though a chill haar blanketed all from the North Sea. From an early hour crowds thronged the Greyfriars vicinity, and there was considerable uproar when large numbers could not gain admittance to the courtyard. Montrose's Graham troopers had to be employed in crowd-control duties. Not all, it is to be feared, were there in search of God's guidance or in Covenanting zeal; but at least the common folk of Aberdeen turned out in force; and as the day wore on, thousands heard an increasingly hoarse triumvirate of divines expound the Creator's purpose with them, men in general, and the erring city of Aberdeen in particular. There were some unmannerly interruptions; but the Grahams soon coped with these. And available Covenants soon were satisfactorily filled with signatures – even though some scoffers declared that they would be getting Hielant tinks to set their sooty marks on it next! Certainly it was not the leadership or intelligentsia of the city that were signing.

Montrose quite quickly had enough of this marathon of joint worship and persuasion, and set off on a round of visits, with his pleasantly uninhibited and hearty hostess, Lady Pitsligo, to bring a little pressure on neighbouring lairds.

By evening he was fully convinced – as the lady had told him from the beginning – that the Covenant would get nowhere in the North-East until the Cock o' the North himself, George Gordon, second Marquis of Huntly, was persuaded, if not to sign it, at least to withdraw his strong and declared opposition to it. The Gordon power was all-important. With 200 Gordon lairds within a thirty-mile radius of Huntly, their chief could count on over a thousand men rallying to his call in a couple of days, five thousand in a week. And not just bareshanked Highland caterans, but jacked and armed horsemen. Here was the shield and buckler behind which Aberdeen University defied St Andrews, Glasgow and Edinburgh.

On the Monday morning, then, Montrose rode the forty miles to Huntly, by Don, Ury and the Braes of Foudland, rounding the dominant peak of Benachie under the great skies of that rolling far-flung land. He rode practically un-escorted. It would have been pointless, indeed foolish, to take any large armed party on this errand, since the Gordon could so readily outmatch it. Anyway, the ministers were probably in greater need of the protection. He took Kilpont with him, however, and half a dozen troopers.

The town of Huntly and its great castle – more properly the Castle of Strathbogie – lies secluded in the folds of the green foothills of the great mountains that form the roof of Scotland, a world unto itself. Here the Gordon chiefs main-tained a strange, out-dated, semi-barbarous but princely state, undisputed lords of life and death over a vast area. Highland and Lowland.

Long before they reached Strathbogie, Montrose's little party found themselves being escorted by a large and ever-growing company of heavily armed and fierce-looking clans-men, who seemed to be concerned, not with greeting the newcomers but with demonstrating who was master here-abouts. These were dismounted Highlanders, and trotted along beside the horsemen untiring as they were speechless, a somewhat off-putting convoy. Presently they were joined by a mounted squadron of about two hundred, under a cavalier-like personage of great magnificence, who intro-duced himself courteously enough as Gordon of Straloch, Chamberlain to the Gordon, High and Mighty Marquis of Huntly and Lord of Strathbogie; and as politely asked the visitors' business on Gordon territory. He did not show the least surprise, however, when he was told that this was *An Greumach Mor,* Earl of Montrose, seeking word with the said Gordon.

In this fashion, then, they dipped down into the green valley of the Deveron, in now fertile and populous country beneath the high hills, and entered the narrow streets of Huntly, a place of peat-reek, smells, flies, yelling children and barking dogs. The enormous castle, with its widespread outworks, flanking-towers and soaring keep, loomed above all at the junction of Bogie and Deveron, ancient although all the upper storeys had been rebuilt in the latest architectural vogue from France not long before – elaborate stone-work, mullions, string-courses, oriels, dormers and so on. Like its lord, Huntly Castle was an odd mixture.

Obviously the Gordon had known all about his visitors coming, for he was waiting at the end of his drawbridge to meet them, in full and extraordinary fig. Probably no one else in Scotland dressed quite like George Gordon, second Marquis of Huntly. A tall, finely built and handsome man of middle years, with features a shade too fine and narrow to be strong, and eyes just a little foxlike in their slant, he had a pointed beard rather longer than usual, like the King's. He was inclining somewhat to stoutness but was still a splendid figure of a man. He wore tartan trews, cut on the cross and tight-fitting, to show off long, good legs; and with them a large, jewelled, wild-cat skin sporran. Above was a tartan waistcoat of a different hue, worn under a deep-skirted, military-style riding-coat with heavy turned-back cuffs and gold buttons. If this was not enough, on a warm summer's day, a great tartan plaid of still another variety was slung and pinned down, over one shoulder, by a large sparkling brooch of Celtic design, with the ribbon of the Garter crossing it diagonally and untidily. To crown all, he wore on his curling, shoulder-length, fox-red hair an enormous beaver hat with two curling ostrich feathers in the colours of his house, blue and gold.

'Greetings to the Graham!' this dramatic personage declared, in ringing tones. 'Welcome to my poor house. Here's Gordon's hand. I knew your father, poor man. And your witch of a mother. Man, who would have thought that they would have produced the like of yourself!'

A little bemused by both his host's appearance and reception, Montrose dismounted and shook the proffered hand. He expressed his satisfaction and honour in being received in person by the great Marquis of Huntly, Cock o' the North, and introduced Kilpont, whose father would be well known to the Gordon. Apparently the former Earl of Menteith was indeed, for Huntly promptly held forth on the follies of that unfortunate, and hoped that his son had more sense – all in the best of humours however. Then, more or less as an after-thought, he selected two of the no fewer than eleven youths and children who were milling around amongst as many deer- and wolf-hounds and smaller dogs, casually identifying them as Aboyne and Lewis – the Viscount Aboyne, second son, and the Lord Lewis – though which was which was not clear.

Montrose was paying his respects to these two, and also to a somewhat slatternly but sharp-eyed dark girl who seemed to be the eldest of the brood, but Huntly's booming voice interrupted. He had turned to his hounds, and it rapidly became apparent that these were his favourite subject and study. One by one he named them, carefully, describing in detail their pedigrees, prowess and particular points, occasionally referring back for comparison and amplifica-tion – all under the admiring regard of a whole court of Gordon lairds and cadets, of varying types and degrees, and some hundreds of assorted supporters. As the recital went on and on, the visitors stirred a little. Montrose was uncertain whether this was normal procedure or a subtle form of side-tracking.

It was another of the youths, a boy smaller than either of the two who had been introduced, with a preternaturally grave expression but a bright eye, who came to the rescue. 'Father,' he said calmly, 'these lords are weary with long riding. On a hot day. Should they not receive refreshment?'

'Eh? What do you say? Dammit, boy – hold your tongue! What's the hurry? Quiet! Would you have the Graham deem you lacking in manners? See, my lords – this Luath is one of the finest bitches in all the North. She has bred some of my best hounds – but still can out-run and pull down a tall stag. Seumas is of her breeding . . .'

The brave Gordon son tugged at his impressive sire's plaid. 'My lord of Montrose has a parchment, sir,' he announced. 'I see it peeping from his saddle-roll. I swear it is the Covenant itself! Brought for you to sign. Is is not, my lord?'

'Since you ask, young man – it is! Many have signed it in Aberdeen. My lord your father's name would much grace it.'

'No doubt, Montrose – no doubt!' Huntly said testily. 'But

I mislike it, see you. I told your Colonel Munro as much, when he came here with the paper. It is not for me, all this talk of religion and faith and covenants. I prefer my hounds! A man knows where he is with them. Now – see this tall fellow, sired by younder Keiran. There is breeding for you! Look at the length of leg, the depth of chest . . .'

'Excellent, I am sure, my lord Marquis. But the Gordon has more to offer this realm than fine hounds, I swear! In Scotland many look to you for lead. Will you not give it to them, sir?'

'Not against the King's Grace.'

'Think you *I* would bring this Covenant to you if it was aimed against the King's Grace? The Graham is as loyal as the Gordon!'

'Others do not say so, my lord.'

'Then others lie, sir. Have you *read* the Covenant?'

'All those words! Why no, sir.'

'If you will do so, you will discover no single word against His Grace. That I assure you. More than that. See – here is a statement, an endorsement, on this copy, signed by myself and my colleagues of the Ministers' Table – Henderson, Dickson, Cant. I will read it to you.' Montrose picked up the parchment. 'We declare before all, that we neither had nor have any intention but of loyalty to His Majesty, as this Covenant bears.' He held it out to Huntly. 'This we wrote for some in Aberdeen who also had not read the wording. Will it not serve to content you, my lord?'

It was Huntly who suddenly thought of refreshment now. 'We must think on this. But – shame on me to have kept you thus, lacking meats, wine, sustenance. Come, my lords – my house is yours. Come.'

The young Gordon who had first suggested it, gravely led the way. The Great Hall of the castle was even more chaotic than the forecourt. All the children, ranging from perhaps eighteen down to five years, came in, the supporting lairds too, and all the hounds, to add to the house- and lap-dogs, cats, two monkeys and, of all things, a tame heron which stalked about looking disgusted, with its own tub of live frogs for provender. Housegillies and varied servants were everywhere, all on entirely familiar terms with their lord and his family – although one of the smallest girls took pleasure in pointing out to the visitors, through a cobwebbed window, to where three naked men dangled from a dule-tree on the moot-hill beside the Deveron – they had been insolent, she explained. Huntly, of course, as well as having the usual baronial powers of pit and gallows, was hereditary Justiciar of the North, and could more or less hang whom he pleased. In all this teeming and vigorous scene three more daughters of the house came to blows and hair-pulling over which should serve what to the great Montrose. Needless to say, there was no Marchioness of Huntly; the poor lady had died, probably thankfully, in giving birth to the youngest of the brood nearly five years before. She had been a Campbell.

In the perpetual confusion and noise, it took some time for Montrose to realise that the dark youth in the stained and almost ragged clothing, who had dared to interrupt his father, was in fact, despite his size, the eldest son of the house, the heir, the Lord Gordon. It was typical of this odd establishment that it was the seventeen-year-old *second* son who was Viscount Aboyne, his year-older brother bearing the lesser title. This was because Huntly himself had been created viscount before he succeeded his father as marquis, and had passed this title on to his favourite, leaving his heir the traditional Lord Gordon. It was this young man's close study of the Covenant parchment – something nobody else seemed in the least interested in – which drew the Graham to him.

'Do you find aught against the King in that, my friend?' he asked quietly, amidst all the hubbub.

'No, my lord,' this other George Gordon answered seriously. 'To me it seems sufficient loyal. And to make good sense.'

'Ha! Then tell your father so.'

'That would serve nothing,' the youth observed simply. 'Better that you tell him, I think, that this paper seeks religious freedom for all. Liberty to worship according to a man's conscience. Even for Catholics. If so it does?' Montrose found two very level dark eyes fixed on his own. 'Can you so tell him, my lord?'

His guest fingered an arrowhead of beard. 'It is a statement of the reformed faith,' he said slowly. 'But I acknowledge that a Catholic's conscience can be as true and honest as a Protestant's. Therefore what is fair for the one should be fair for the other.'

'Aye. But that is not what I asked! Can you tell my father

116

that if this paper is accepted by the King, and what it says becomes the law in Scotland, then those who would follow the old faith may do so, as their conscience guides them, without hurt or harassment? Episcopalians likewise?'

Montrose drew a deep breath, eyeing this most unlikely son of his father. 'That I cannot swear to, friend, since it has not been debated. So far, none have spoken so honestly, so bold to the point, as have you. It would require to be considered and passed by the Tables. But this I can say – that such it should be. To my mind it is no less than due. How a man worships his God is his own affair. None should constrain other, be it the King, the Kirk, or the Pope of Rome. To this I would set my hand. To this I will testify.'

'My father may require more, my lord. But *I* would trust Montrose,' the Lord Gordon said quietly. 'I am not of age to sign this. But would if I might.' He handed back the parchment.

James Graham gripped the slender shoulder for a moment, before turning back to the others.

When he could gain Huntly's more or less undivided attention, he put the matter to him. Would he accept the Covenant if it was declared to include religious freedom for all? Catholics, Presbyterians and Episcopalians alike? Would he sign it with a rider to that effect?

The Cock o' the North burst into a spate of indeterminate noise, a flood of words signifying nothing in particular – though eloquent enough to Montrose. This man was not going to be pinned down. Whether feckless or crafty, the Gordon would not commit himself.

One last effort Montrose made. 'My lord Marquis,' he said, 'in this matter Scotland speaks with an all but united voice. The Covenant will win. For the King will not use armed force against the majority of his Scots people. In that day, you would not wish it to be said, I think, that the Gordon, almost alone, was against it? And prevented the North-East from signing it!'

'Me? I prevent none from signing, man! That I do not do so my own self need hinder none.'

'You say so? I rejoice to hear it. Others may sign it, if they will? And you are not concerned?'

'If they will . . .'

'The word of a noble lord,' the other interjected quickly.

He raised his voice for all to hear. 'My lord Marquis declares that he cares not who signs the Covenant!' he cried. 'That his abstention need hinder none. The word of a generous man! For this many will thank the Gordon.'

Blinking in some surprise at his sudden popularity, Huntly shook his head vigorously, and made more of his indeterminate noises.

Now Montrose was anxious only to disengage and be off. He had as much as he was likely to get, at Strathbogie – and could lose it again all to easily. But getting away from that strange establishment was not easy, and Huntly's hospitality, once broached, was comprehensive, even embarrassing. It looked as though they were automatically expected to stay for days. It was only by insisting that it was vital for him to be back in Aberdeen by noon next day that the Graham managed to detach himself – and even so they were provided with a large Gordon escort all the way back to the very city gates.

This time it was the young Lord Gordon who led. And all the way he asked questions, sought information, views, discussed points, a young man of intelligence with a mind of his own, despite his unimpressive appearance. Montrose took to him. He would make a very different chief for Clan Gordon from his father.

10

THE COVENANTERS PRESENTLY FOUND COMPENSATION FOR their non-success in the North-East, in word from London that the King was prepared to accede to their demand for the calling of a much-overdue General Assembly of the Church of Scotland – a summons which required the royal authority. This was splendid news, for whatever reason Charles was granting it. But the satisfaction in Scotland was somewhat allayed by the subsequent announcement that the

King would not attend in person but was sending the deplorable Hamilton again, as Lord High Commissioner. Nothing was said about the Covenant itself.

While there were the usual warnings that Charles was only playing for time in granting this procedural concession – although constitutionally he had no reason to withhold it – and that he was in fact preparing to outwit the Scots, Montrose at least preferred to believe that the King could be responding to reason, and behaving in honest and kingly fashion.

The great gathering was set for Glasgow, at the end of November. There had been no such General Assembly since 1619, although this was the constitutional and democratic court and ruling body of the Kirk of Scotland. Indeed, there had been only six in all, since King James removed south to London in 1603. All had been unsatisfactory, improperly constituted and conducted, each more dominated than the last by royal-appointed bishops. This one was going to be different. Much would hinge on it.

Montrose himself was duly elected as lay commissioner for Auchterarder, in which Strathearn parish stood Kincardine Castle. But when he set out for Glasgow, he rode again with Graham troopers at his back – at the Tables' request; for there were rumours that their enemies would overturn the entire proceedings by main force if no other means was open to them; and Glasgow was likely to resemble an armed camp. That 20th day of November, 1638, all Scotland seemed to be on the road to the little town between the Molendinar and the Clyde, that huddled beneath its great High Kirk, formerly St Mungo's Cathedral, wherein decision was to be taken.

In the narrow streets and lanes of Glasgow, packed as never before in its history, drama was foreshadowed. Black-clad ministers were everywhere; but that was to be expected – although the number who actually bore sword or dirk at their girdles came as a surprise to Montrose at least. It was the enormous numbers of men-at-arms and mail-clad supporters that most vehemently dominated the scene, however. They swarmed like locusts, wearing every sort of livery and colours. Every lord and laird in the land seemed to have descended upon this town of 12,000 inhabitants, each with his 'tail' of armed men. Or not quite every lord, perhaps –

for Huntly and the Gordons, for instance, was not represented; nor the Earl of Erroll's Hays, the Maxwells and Herries or other near-Catholic clans. But there were Hamiltons by the hundred, Border Kerrs of the Earl of Roxburgh, Traquair's Stewarts, Douglases of Clydesdale and Ogilvys of Airlie. It looked as though all the Glasgow decisions would not be taken inside St Mungo's Kirk.

Nevertheless, it was not so much all these that made the greatest impact on Montrose; his tight-disciplined Graham troopers under Black Pate of Inchbrakie would be a match for any of them. It was the sight of such large numbers of kilted, plaided and bare-kneed Highlanders in the streets that struck him most forcibly, and the answer to his enquiries as to their identity, the information that they were Campbells from Argyll. It was with a thoughtful mien that the commissioner from Auchterarder, after settling in at the lodging he was sharing with Archie Napier in the Drygate, went in search of fuller details.

Rothes, commissioner for Kirkcaldy in Fife, told him. 'Our cause must be prospering,' he declared, with his usual cynicism. 'The Campbell elects to bestow his support upon it! At last, openly, and for all to see. Man, is it no' great? Lorne, newly become *MacCailean Mor* and Earl o' Argyll by his fool father's death, celebrates the occasion! He discovers the Covenant is like to win in Scotland, and honours its Assembly with his presence. So now Charles Stewart can read the writing on the wall!'

'You are sure that it is *our* side that he joins? Not the government's? Hamilton's? Why bring so many men to Glasgow to join our cause?'

'With the Campbell you can never be certain-sure, I grant you. But – would yon one choose to join the King's party at this stage? Hey? Wi' the tide flowing our way? No' Archibald Campbell, I say! He wants a hand in what is decided here.'

'That could still be on the other side...'

Next morning, Wednesday the 21st of November, when the General Assembly, the first for nineteen years, was ceremonially opened in the nave of the vast church above the Molendinar Burn – which the Archbishop of Glasgow called his Cathedral of St Mungo and Master William

Annan its own minister called the High Kirk of Glasgow – the Earl of Argyll still provided no clear indication as to his intentions. When Montrose and Napier, having had to battle their way through unruly crowds to get in, took their seats in the body of the church as ordinary commissioners, beside Rothes and Eglinton, there was no sign of the Campbell.

There was a blare of trumpets, as the vestry door was flung open, to herald the entry of the Lord High Commissioner and his suite. All rose to their feet for the King's representative. Argyll was still not to be distinguished in the great throng. It was many years since James Graham had seen him, but he did not think that he would fail to recognise the man.

Once again Lord Lyon Balfour and his heralds led in the procession. Sundry officials came first. Then the Lords of the Privy Council – who by decision of the previous packed and unrepresentative Assemblies had been given leave to attend and vote. This, however, proved to be a very reduced attendance for many members of that august body had elected to either stay away or to sit elsewhere – as had the Lord Napier; and, more significant, not one of the thirteen Lords Spiritual, the bishops, all now members thereof, came in.

'Ha! See that!' Rothes cried out – for the din was already loud as a cattle-market. 'They too have seen the writing on the wall! No' a bishop to show his episcopal nose! Canny chiels – they ken what's good for them.'

'Thank God for that, at least,' Napier said. 'That gives us thirteen more votes. They knew they would be out-voted, and made to look small. Aye, out-talked and out-reasoned likewise. So they have chosen the better part, for once . . .'

But Montrose was not joining in the surge of exclamation which rose from all the vast company at this first hint of success for the Covenant – for the mighty church was packed, its two hundred and fifty or so commissioners only a very small proportion of the assemblage, and every aisle, side-chapel, and gallery, even the clerestory walks, crowded with far from silent spectators. He had drawn quick breath at quite another aspect of the Privy Council entrance – for second to come pacing in was the burly, bushy-bearded figure of David, Earl of Southesk.

'Look there,' he interrupted his other brother-in-law. 'Southesk has come. Come out of his retirement. When did you last see him at a Council meeting? That means he is here to take a strong line. And it will not be for us. He conceives us enemies of the King. And his son, Carnegie, will vote as his father wills, under his father's eye. The old man dominates all his family.'

Glancing sidelong at his friend, Napier nodded. 'Southesk could influence many,' he agreed. 'Especially from Angus and the Mearns. I had not thought to see him here . . .'

But Rothes was tugging at Montrose's arm on the other side, and pointing. Modestly, last of the Privy Councillors to pace in, was a slight stooping figure, limping a little, a soberly dressed, unassuming-seeming man, with a pale long face, long narrow nose and high brow beneath foxy-red, straight, thin hair. He might have been a clerk to the Council, an unfrocked minister perhaps. He kept his head lowered diffidently, the picture of a retiring nobody – but Montrose at least did not require to see the pronounced squint in the left eye, or the tight sour mouth beneath that drooping nose, to know differently.

'Archibald Campbell!' he breathed. 'By all the Powers – Argyll! Save us – it is himself! He is . . . worse! Six, seven years it is, since I saw him. And he is . . . worse!'

'Aye – *MacCailean Mor* himsel'!' Rothes said. 'The tod emerges frae his earth! How's yon to be the greatest man in Scotland?'

'Poor Scotland, then! But he is not that – yet! Praise God!'

It was strange, James Graham's ingrained loathing of this man. He was not one to hate readily; and the fact that the Campbells and Grahams were hereditary foes did not weigh heavily with him. They had only met once or twice, in their younger days, and even then they had not actually come to verbal blows, whatever their eyes said. The Campbell was only six years the elder – although he looked much more – and because of his physical defects might have been expected to be an object of sympathy and commiseration to the other's essentially considerate and kindly temperament. But the antipathy seemed to be born in him. From first sight he had abhorred and shrunk from this man. And there had been little doubt that the feeling was mutual.

'You will note,' Montrose said from between stiff lips, 'that my lord of Argyll chooses to sit, not as a commissioner for

Inveraray, but as one of the King's Privy Council, at this Assembly! Are you so sure now how he will vote?'

Even Rothes looked thoughtful.

There were ten members of the Privy Council taking their seats in a row on the dais at the chancel steps, where once the rood-screens had been, below the High Commissioner's throne but above the Moderator's chair and the Clerk's table. But at the last moment a fantastically curled, beribboned and painted exquisite came hurrying in alone, with tap-tapping, shoulder-high, streamered staff and lace handkerchief – no doubt scented – which he waved before his nose to counter the smell of less rarefied humanity. A howl of mirth went up, at the sight.

But Montrose and those beside him did not laugh as this apparition minced up, to take another of the Privy Council seats. It was the Earl of Lanark, Hamilton's brother, whose appearances in Scotland nowadays were a rarity indeed. That such as he should have come north to attend a General Assembly of the Kirk was so unlikely as to be scarcely credible; and could only mean that the opposition was in fact scraping up votes wherever it could. Presumably the King had made him a Privy Councillor specially for the occasion. If that was so, then they must have at least a hope of out-voting the Covenanters, or there was no point in the business. This had not been seriously considered as a possibility, up till now, in the Kirk's own Assembly. But the other side were experts in subversion. The very fact that Carnegie and his father were also here, and both with votes, struck a like note. Lanark, in the circumstances, was no laughing matter.

Another blast of trumpets, and Hamilton himself came stalking in, as king-like as ever, resplendent in a long velvet royal-blue cloak trimmed with ermine and held up by two pages, with a huge gemmed star of the Garter on its shoulder, and below it a riot of cloth-of-gold, satin, jewellery, bows, rosettes and contrasting slashings. Even his curled, ringleted, long hair was tied with coloured bows. He carried it off rather better than his brother, because he was taller, and well-built; but even so the absurdity shouted aloud – as did not a few of the Glasgow citizens in the spectators' galleries, church or none.

Pacing to his throne above the Privy Councillors, the

123

Marquis, after gazing at the scene with unease and distaste in almost equal proportions, proceeded to read his commission from the King, in a flat monotone. It proved to be in unexpectedly conciliatory terms, referring to Charles's well-beloved Scots lieges, his delight in his ancient kingdom, his support for the true Reformed religion, the concessions he had already made in that respect, and his deep interest and concern in the debates and decisions of the good fathers and brethren of his Church in Scotland, at which his trusted and entirely loved cousin, the most noble James, Marquis of Hamilton, Knight of the Garter, Lord of the Bedchamber, Master of the Horse, Chief Steward of Hampton Court, and Privy Councillor of both kingdoms, would most faithfully and ably convey his royal views and guidance. He blessed them all, and commended their deliberations to God.

Seldom was blessing pronounced in a less beatific tone of voice.

The procedure for General Assemblies was fixed and unalterable. It was deemed suitable that a proper and pious attitude should be engendered throughout, first of all, by an initial sermon. This also had the advantage of allowing all concerned time to survey the scene, size up the possibilities, and plan their campaigns – discreetly, of course, and paying at least some small attention to the preacher meantime.

The preacher, with surprising energy for one of his years, thundered and gesticulated on. Montrose got the notion that Argyll, not thirty feet away, kept staring at him personally – although with his squint, one could never tell. He stirred uncomfortably. Most of the other Privy Councillors were now asleep.

At length even the Reverend Mr John Bell ran out of strength and breath, though never of material; and thankfully Hamilton announced that the next business was the appointment of a Moderator to chair the proceedings.

Promptly David Dickson proposed their most revered and admired guide-in-God, Alexander Henderson, Minister of the Parish of Leuchars in Fife, than whom none could be more worthy and able.

Amidst ringing applause Andrew Cant seconded. Since one or the other of these two would have been the only obvious alternative nomination, there was no other name put forward. Rather reluctantly the High Commissioner declared Henderson to be the Moderator, the first for nine-teen years, and asked him to come forward and take the chair. A great sigh of relief arose from the body of the church. From now on the conduct of the Assembly at least was in sure hands.

Henderson, after making a brief speech of thanks, ex-pressing the gratitude of all for the King's gracious message, and his concessions intimated, and declaring that the Lord High Commissioner's appointment was such as to ornament the proceedings – a shaft which drew no lack of grinning appreciation – went on in changed, assured and businesslike fashion. He proposed that Archibald Johnston of Warrison, advocate, should act as Principal Clerk to the Assembly.

It was unthinkable that the Moderator's first move should be countered, and Warriston, tense in scowling embarrass-ment, stumbled forward to take his place at the table below the Moderator's chair. A number of lesser clerks and assessors followed him, with papers.

Henderson then welcomed all duly appointed com-missioners to this great, belated and historic Assembly, em-phasising that 'duly appointed' slightly. As was customary he went on, all commissions must be scrutinised, that God's work be surely and honestly done, by the due and proper representatives of Christ's Church and people. This would take some considerable time, possibly the rest of the day; and he proposed that the Assembly should adjourn until the Scrutinising Committee's work was done. Did any say otherwise?

After that sermon, none said otherwise, especially the Privy Councillors.

Since the Scrutinising Committee must be wise, experien-ced and impartial, the Moderator then suggested that its convener should be the Reverend David Dickson, of Irvine, whose knowledge of procedure was unrivalled. Half a dozen delegates rose to second, but Henderson pointed out mildly that this was not a proposal to vote upon, but the Moderator's procedural appointment for the better forwarding of the Assembly's business. Mr Dickson should select an impartial team of assessors, and proceed with their task during the adjournment. It might well take such time as to forbid reassembly until the morrow.

There was a murmur at that, variously compounded.

Behind Henderson the Lord High Commissioner cleared his throat ominously.

Unperturbed, the Moderator went on. 'Before we adjourn, some may wish to guide the scrutineers in their task, having perhaps special knowledge of misappointments and wrongous attendances. It is suitable that His Grace's High Commissioner should so intimate first, if he is a mind to.'

Hamilton was very much of a mind to. Spluttering a little he rose to his feet, then recollecting his royal state, quickly sat down again. 'I make objection,' he said thickly. 'Many are here who should not be. Any fool can see it! This Assembly has been packed. And sounds that it may be *more* packed!'

'I regret to hear it, my lord Marquis. This must be rectified. Perhaps your lordship will be more explicit?'

'Explicit? Man – look around you! This is an Assembly of the Church. Yet many here, I swear, represent only themselves! Or seditious parties that would endanger both the Church and the King's realm.'

'Then they must be rooted out. If you will name me names . . . ?'

'Names? What need for names, man? Look! There are more laymen here than ministers, I do believe. And many carry arms, despite my express proclamation forbidding it.'

'Arms are unsuitable in the house of the Lord,' Henderson agreed. 'But I would remind your lordship that this is a Presbyterian church, and laymen, elders, have a full say in its rule and direction. I respectfully suggest, however, that your High Commissionership is mistaken. We have the numbers of all commissioners attending. There are 142 ministers and 98 elders. The commissions of all shall be scrutinised.'

Hamilton huffed and puffed. 'I misdoubt the appointment of many here, sir. How it has been contrived.'

'Then, my lord, appoint your observers to the Scrutinising Committee, that you may be satisfied. But, I pray, give me instances, names . . . ?'

Hamilton muttered, but otherwise remained silent.

Henderson turned to look out over the company. 'If His Grace's Commissioner has no names to put before the committee, I believe that others have. As indication how there have been wrongous appointments. I call upon my lord of Montrose.'

Amidst sudden tension, Montrose rose. 'Mr Moderator,' he said slowly, 'it has been brought to my attention that there has been a mischance in the election of one of the commissioners for Brechin, in which Presbytery I am a heritor. I understand that John Erskine, Laird of Dun, was duly elected. But the Lord Carnegie now sits in his place.' He sat down.

There was a gasp and a thrill of excitement went through the gathering. Few were unaware that Carnegie was the speaker's brother-in-law.

Southesk half-rose from his seat, glaring at his son-in-law – but subsided as the Moderator's calm voice resumed.

'Is this confirmed by the Clerk?'

Warriston rose, fumbling with his papers. 'Yes, sir. I . . . I have it here. Appointment by Brechin Presbytery. John Erskine of Dun. Duly passed by the Tables, with the following note . . .'

'Tables! Passed by the Tables, 'fore God!' Hamilton roared, banging the arm of his throne. 'Hear that! Passed by the Tables. What need for further debate? Unless passed by these damned, unlawful and treasonable Tables, no man is acceptable here! A packed Assembly! Can you deny it?' He pointed directly at Montrose, not at Henderson. 'Deny it, I say!'

In the throbbing silence, Montrose perceived that Henderson was leaving it to him. He rose again. 'Is there fault in this?' he asked quietly. 'Since the King's Grace has refused to call a parliament these many years, the realm has had to be governed by some. This Privy Council, with half its members bishops, rejected by Church and people, has not done it. The Convention of Estates appointed these Tables, therefore, lacking other means. On the best legal advice! To call them unlawful and treasonable, my lord Marquis, is to betray lack of understanding. And it is right and proper that the Tables should consider who was appointed to this Assembly. No felon, malefactor, Armenian, unbeliever or Catholic may attend, by law. If the Tables did not exercise watch, who would? You, sir? Or my lords of the Privy Council?'

It is safe to say that no Lord High Commissioner had been spoken to so since the Kings of Scots had ceased to attend the Assemblies in person. Hamilton gulped and swallowed, prominent eyes popping.

'This . . . this is beyond all !' he got out.

'You asked for a denial, my lord. You have it.' Montrose sat down.

'All comments and remarks will be permitted only by and through the Chair,' Henderson rebuked them both, mildly. 'Mr Clerk, you will note this matter of the Lord Carnegie for the Scrutiny Committee.'

'I protest, sir !' That was the Earl of Southesk hotly. 'At this disgraceful attack upon my son. He is here of right. Erskine's was a rigged election. I myself had it amended.'

'The matter will be closely considered by the Scrutiny Committee, my good lord, never fear . . .'

'Fear, man? Fear ! Think you Carnegie fears what any pack of clerks and preachers may decide !'

'My lord, this, I would remind you, is an Assembly of the Church, where the decisions of clerks and preachers, as you name them, has some small relevance. I urge you, and all, to remember it. Now . . .'

'And *you* remember this. Any attempt to unseat my son will cost you dear. None yet meddled with Carnegie and did not live to regret it !' It was at Montrose that the old earl glared, however.

Rothes rose. 'I move the adjournment, Mr Moderator,' he said.

There was a score of seconders.

'It seems a fitting moment,' Henderson acceded, calmly grave. 'But, perhaps, before we leave, I should wish especially to welcome to our deliberations my lord Earl of Argyll, whose renown is known to all. His presence here, and his adherence to God's cause of freedom, true religion and justice, is of the utmost value. All honest men will rejoice, I am sure.'

The applause was less vociferous than might have been. As an attempt to edge the Campbell – who had sat silent, head bent, preoccupied, throughout – into declaring himself, indeed to commit him to the Covenant cause, it was laudable but less than successful. *MacCailean Mor* raised his reddish head for a moment, in briefest acknowledgment, and then looked down again. That was as far as his commitment went, meantime.

Henderson bowed towards the High Commissioner. 'With your agreement, sir, this Assembly stands adjourned.'

asked – if a court, could they, *must* they not, try? Try not only causes, policies, matters of belief and doctrine, but men? Men who introduced error and stumbling into the Kirk?

This set the gathering by the ears – especially when all over the great church there were shouts of 'The bishops! The bishops!' The Moderator sternly called all to order – but said nothing to indicate that it might not come to a trial of the King's bishops. Montrose stirred uncomfortably, and presently rose to declare that a witch-hunt was unsuitable, and the last thing that was required in this delicate situation. For once, he gathered no applause. Henderson skilfully channelled the discussion into series of procedural issues – and gained consistent majorities for each step in a progress towards complete Assembly power, prerogative and jurisdiction. The Lord High Commissioner and the Privy Councillors remaining glared, protested, condemned, threatened – but were consistently voted down. Hamilton even had a private battle with the Moderator, claiming that he had the votes of six assessors as well as his own – which Henderson ruled against, declaring that in God's kingdom, King Charles was one man, not seven!

The day was well advanced before Montrose noticed, inconspicuous in one of the public galleries, the reddish hair and sallow features of the chief of all the Campbells, listening attentively.

'So – Argyll removes himself from the Privy Council seats, and the voting!' he murmured, to Napier. 'But stays to watch and listen. See him yonder?'

'A strange man. Henderson will rejoice. A victory for him, I think. Argyll must conceive the issue to be going our way.'

'But still does not commit himself! That such a man, so timorous, should cut so wide a swathe in Scotland! It is scarce believable.'

'Do not deceive yourself, Jamie. Argyll is not timorous. Cautious, yes, but not timorous. I know him better than do you. Trust Tom Hope's judgment of him – he is a notable judge of character. He said that he would lead in Scotland – remember it! There is a man all must watch. He is strong, despite his manner, in more than men and lands. Henderson knows it. He must have him on the Covenant side.'

At the next day's session the Earl of Argyll came down

On the way out, Montrose found himself treated as something of a hero – to his distaste and curt rejection. He knew well that his heroics in the cause that day would cost him dear.

Next forenoon, when the full gathering reassembled, after a long wait for the High Commissioner, it was evident that Alexander Henderson's tactics were proving only partially successful. Admittedly, there were notable gaps amongst the commissioners, indications that the Scrutiny Committee had not been slothful. But the Lord Carnegie was still in his place as commissioner for Brechin, and Erskine of Dun still in the spectators' gallery; Brechin Presbytery's changed decision seemed to have been confirmed as genuine, and Montrose's reluctant gesture gone for nothing. Moreover, sitting beside Carnegie was now his uncle Sir John Carnegie of Ethie, newly arrived in Glasgow but apparently authentic commissioner for Arbroath. He was not known as having strong views – but it was unlikely that he would vote against his brother's line.

However, when the Privy Councillors trooped in, there were seen to be significant gaps in that august body. The Earl of Southesk himself was missing; it seemed that his anger at the previous day's proceedings had necessitated bleeding by a chirurgeon, and he was confined to his bed. More actually significant perhaps, the Earls of Wigtown, Morton and Argyll were also missing. When Hamilton took his seat, his features were dark with ill-suppressed rage. Not a few hoped that he also might require the services of a chirurgeon.

Proof of a change of balance in the proceedings was fairly quickly forthcoming. The Covenant leadership put matters to the test by moving the acceptance of the Scrutiny Committee's decisions. After some undignified wrangling, in which the High Commissioner himself took large part, the motion was passed by a fairly large majority. It was notable that the two Carnegies voted against.

Encouraged, Henderson moved on to establish the constitution and power of the Assembly, a vital matter when there had been no proper precedent since 1603. This was the supreme court of the Church of Scotland, and its members had to know their authority and limitations. It was quickly

9   129

from his discreetly modest perch, and took a seat, not with the Privy Council again but prominent amongst the nobles who were not actual commissioners – beside Morton his uncle, and Wigtown, indeed. It turned out that he was not a representative of Inveraray Presbytery, after all – although he easily could have been, since his word was law in that area. He was remaining at the Assembly as a private individual and forgoing his Privy Council vote. It was a strange decision, typical perhaps of the man – but at least it was clear indication of his disassociation with Hamilton and the King's policy. Apart from Montrose, the Covenanters were elated.

These two had to come face to face some time. It happened that evening when the Covenant leaders were invited to attend a gathering at the Earl of Loudoun's house in the Gallowgate, one of the few nobles who maintained a large town mansion in Glasgow, to discuss alarming information that the King, even while his representative was presiding over this Assembly, was making preliminary moves for the mustering of a great army; and since its assembly-place was set for Newcastle, within a short distance of the Scottish border, concern was not irrational. Argyll was one of the first persons Montrose saw, on entry to the house – he was Loudoun's kinsman and chief, of course. The Campbell saw him, likewise – but neither moved forward in greeting.

It was Henderson who presently brought them together. 'My lords,' he said, catching Montrose's arm, 'to have *MacCailen Mor* and *An Greumach Mor* in the same room, is something of an occasion, I think! You are well acquaint, I have no doubt?'

'We have met,' James Graham bowed, stiffly formal for him.

'My lord of Montrose's reputation is better known to me than his person,' the other observed. 'I am a man of retiring habit, of course.' Argyll's voice was as unexpected as the rest of him, a soft lilting Highland sibilance superimposed upon a naturally nasal rasp, allied to a slight hesitation.

'The more we value your lordship's presence with us, here,' the minister announced. 'Is it not so, my lord of Montrose?'

'Indeed, yes. It is a time for all men to declare themselves.'

'It is a time for all men to consider their position,' the Campbell amended thinly.

'There has been long for considering positions, my lord. Years. It is now time for action, I think.'

'Action against the King, sir?'

'Not against the King. Never that. Against the rule of bishops, and the suppression of parliament.'

'Will His Grace perceive the difference?'

'If he does not, his Scots Privy Councillors should inform him.'

'His Scots Privy Councillors must first assure themselves that it is so.'

'If any are still in doubt, it is because they choose to be.'

'His Grace himself has said, "No bishops, no king"!'

'Then His Grace is mistaken. So far as Scotland is concerned. For fifty years there were no bishops. Yet King James sat his throne safe enough.'

'So you are set to pull down the bishops, my lord?'

'Pull down? For myself, I care not whether there be bishops or not, in Scotland. So long as they do not attempt to rule the Kirk, change our worship, sway the King and dominate the Privy Council.'

'You would permit them to remain, lacking these powers?'

'I would, yes. If it would please the King. And those who think like him. Shorn of these powers they could do little harm.'

'There I think you err, my lord,' Henderson, who had been listening to this exchange carefully, interpolated. 'They should be rooted out quite. The Kirk has no place for them. They are a relic of Popery, and must go.'

'Which of you speaks with the voice of this Covenant?' Argyll asked. 'The Moderator? Or my lord of Montrose? When you have decided it, you may inform me.' And bowing, the Campbell limped away to alternative company.

They looked at each other. 'We are not clever enough for that one,' Henderson commented, frowning.

But next day, nevertheless, Argyll had his answer. Whether Henderson was determined to have it so, or whether this would have been the programme anyway, almost from the start of the proceedings the pressure was on the bishops, the office thereof and individual holders of it. Deliverance after deliverance was pronounced on the subject – and they were charges rather than questions for debate. In vain did the Lord High Commissioner object; the Moderator ruled his submissions as out of order. Then Hamilton revealed that the bishops had anticipated this attack, by subscribing a declinature to it beforehand, which he now insisted should be read. As no bishops had risked putting in an appearance, he called upon one of his own clan, the Reverend Dr Robert Hamilton, of Glassford parish, Lanarkshire, to read it. Again the Moderator ruled otherwise. This was not the time. Let the case against the office of bishop be heard first; then there would be opportunity for answer, defence, and this declinature.

Angrily the High Commissioner declared that he would not sit there and preside over a trial of the King's bishops. They were the highest officers of the Church, and the Church's Assembly had no right or authority to assail them.

Politely Henderson grieved to say that he believed His Grace's Commissioner was mistaken. The Assembly *had* powers to question and try bishops, if necessary to depose them. Bishops, or any other minister of the Church.

In the uproar at this statement, Hamilton could not make himself heard. When the Moderator at length gained him quiet, he shouted that it was all wind, vain mouthings, empty threats. It was disgraceful that the Moderator should make baseless statements, impossible of proof.

'Proof, my lord? If you wish proof, you shall have it.' Henderson signed to Warriston.

Then, to the wonder of all, the Clerk tapped a stack of yellowing papers on his table, to announce that these were the records of the General Assemblies of 1560 to 1590, thought to have been destroyed. It was known that the bishops and Crown authorities had indeed destroyed as much of the Presbyterian regime's records as they could. These vital Assembly proceedings had been assumed to have been amongst the first casualties. Their production, like this, was a great triumph for the Covenanters. On Henderson's promptings, Warriston read out the Act of the Dundee Assembly of 1580, duly signed by the King, abolishing the office of bishop, in the Kirk; and thereafter act after act of various others, all with the royal subscription, confirming this and wiping out all traces of the status and privileges of such prelates; likewise all subsidiary offices and titles such as deans, archdeacons, chanters and the like, all apt to be lumped under the heading of 'popish trash'. Shaken, Hamilton and the Privy Councillors sat silenced.

'This is a properly-called and lawful General Assembly of the Kirk,' the Moderator went on thereafter. 'So far as authority goes, we have absolute right to deal with bishops as we think fit. By these previous acts of Assembly the office had been shown to have had no warrant or authority in Holy Scripture, but brought in by the folly and corruption of men's inventions. Does this Assembly wish to proceed with the matter? Or to let it lie?'

The great and continuing shout left no doubt as to the wishes of the Assembly as a whole. So far as Scotland was concerned, the office of bishop was as good as abolished.

That night, Glasgow seethed like an ant-hill disturbed. The armed supporters of the various factions were involved in many clashes, and men everywhere were in a fever. The gauntlet was being thrown down, with a vengeance.

That vital decisions had crystallised overnight was immediately apparent next forenoon. So soon as the High Commissioner came in and was seated, he spoke.

'Mr Moderator – I have announcement to make. As the King's representative. The discussion of yesterday was, I rule, treasonable and not to be tolerated. If, today, there is any move towards the abolition of the office of bishop, or attempt to attack absent prelates, I shall, in the King's name, dissolve and close this Assembly as illegal.'

This bombshell shook even Alexander Henderson. When he could make himself heard, he protested. 'You cannot do this! None can dissolve an Assembly of Christ's Kirk save its own members. You have not the power.'

Hamilton banged his chair. 'I need not you, sirrah, to teach me my powers! Or my duty. I have the King's royal authority, which none can contest. This Assembly will end, if any further attack on the bishops is mounted. And meantime, I insist that the declinature of the bishops be read forthwith.'

To gain time for thought and consultation, Henderson acceded to that.

The unhappy Dr Hamilton, from Clydesdale, rose to announce that the following was signed by their lordships the Archbishops of St Andrews and Glasgow, and the Bishops of Edinburgh, Galloway, Ross and Brechin. Then, in something of a gabble, he launched into a lengthy written disquisition on the sanctity and scriptural authority of the order of bishops, with readings from the Epistles. It was clear, he said, that the King, as head of Christ's Church in these realms, alone had power over bishops, and that no Assembly, court or tribunal whatsoever, might question the royal appointments or the acts of the said bishops. The great gathering sat restive, hostile, but giving the very self-conscious reader a hearing.

All the while a succession of individuals came up to the Moderator's chair, for whispered consultation, Rothes amongst them. When he came back to his seat, he shrugged.

'Aye, then – the die is cast!' he informed. 'For better or for worse.'

'There is only one decision Henderson can make,' Montrose agreed gravely. 'I take it that he has made it?'

'God grant that it is the right one,' Napier murmured. 'Since it is like to cost us all dear!'

On the Moderator's formal enquiry, the deafening rejection of the declinature by the Assembly made counting votes superfluous.

Henderson turned to the High Commissioner. 'Sir, this court of the Church is of a sure mind. It rejects the bishops' statement, and I believe must go on to reject the bishops themselves. Furthermore, as Moderator, I declare that you have no power to keep this Assembly from discussing what it has the right to discuss and vote upon, by ample and due precedent, as quoted. You cannot lawfully dissolve it, on such grounds.'

'I can. And will. If it seeks to try the King's bishops. Does it?'

'I cannot advise that it may not. If so it desires.'

'So be it, then. You have brought it on your own rebellious heads.' Hamilton rose to his feet. 'In the name of His Majesty the King, I declare this Assembly finally and entirely dissolved. You will all disperse forthwith. The royal authority is withdrawn.' He bowed stiffly to the Privy Councillors, and turning, in deadly silence stalked to the vestry door, and out.

Glancing at each other in considerable dismay and confusion, the remaining Privy Councillors and great officers of state rose and went streaming after the Marquis.

'All will stand, while His Grace's Privy Councillors retire,' Henderson said, sternly.

Tha firm voice, measured, authoritative, pulled the shocked gathering together. Men drew deep breaths, and obeyed.

With the Lord Lyon King of Arms last to leave, this time minus any trumpet fanfares, Henderson spoke again. 'Be seated. Mr Clerk – to the next business, if you please.'

The general gasp of sheer excitement and admiration was tribute to this calm assumption that all was in order, and the situation unchanged. But not all was admiration. Dr Hamilton rose.

'Sir – Mr Moderator! This is impossible!' he cried. 'This Assembly has been dissolved. It cannot go on.'

'I rule that it can, sir. It is a duly authorised Assembly. Because His Grace's Commissioner has seen fit to withdraw, it by no means invalidates our authority. There are some hundreds of the *Kirk's* commissioners still present. You may put it to the vote, if you will.'

And so the Church of Scotland took the law into its own hands, abolished the office of bishop, and deposed collectively and individually, all who held such office. It was done formally and methodically. The holders of all bishoprics were named, declared to have accepted and exercised an office which the Kirk had officially condemned, and were therefore expelled and banned from in future holding any other ministerial office. Moreover, the present bishops' moral lapses were notorious, and were listed. Archbishop Spottiswoode, for instance, was accused of carding and dicing on the Sabbath, and tippling in taverns; the Bishop of Aberdeen of simony, the selling of benefices; the Bishop of Brechin of drunkenness, and offences against a woman and child; the Bishop of Moray of having people dancing naked in his house, and himself 'dancing prettily in his shirt'. Others variously stood accused of flagrant offences such as adultery and incest. All were deposed – and not only deposed, but excommunicated, save for the Bishop of Dunkeld who had given his Presbytery signs of repentance. Finally it was decreed that no minister of the Kirk could in future act on the Privy Council, attend parliament, or serve as judge or justice, the Church being a society independent of the State. This, of course, meant the abolition of the Church's

Estate of Parliament, a constitutional change of enormous significance.

So it was done. Never had there been such an Assembly. It was to go on for many days yet, passing numerous acts for the better government of the Kirk, the rectification of wrong, and the spiritual welfare of the people. But its main work was done. It would go down as the Assembly that defied the King and abolished his bishops.

It ended on its twenty-seventh session, no less, and on an unexpected note. At the very last, after the Moderator's valedictory and inspiring sermon, with only the formal prayer and parting benediction to come, who should rise from his spectator's seat, where he had sat attentively and silent throughout, but Archibald, Earl of Argyll. He spoke, at last, modestly, almost humbly, declaring that some might criticise him for his long delay in openly joining the supporters of the Covenant; which, however, was not for want of affection for so good and noble a cause, but perchance he was able to serve it better outside of it, and in the Privy Council. But when all efforts had failed with the King, his Commissioner and the said Council, he could stay no longer on the outside, but must now join with them all in the true cause of Kirk and freedom, or risk indeed being called a false knave. He therefore now assured the Assembly of his sympathy, his approval of its actions, and his convictions of its success. He exhorted all there to go back to their presbyteries and parishes and therein to do their duty and speak out valiantly for what had been decided. And to be ready to take more active steps if called upon. He urged that meantime they respect all due and lawful authority, however, lest they put themselves in the wrong. And that they pursued, in especial, peace and unity amongst themselves; for the enemy would undoubtedly seek to sow dissension and discord. With all his heart, he sought God's blessing upon them and what they had taken in hand.

It was a quite extraordinary speech, declared in the soft yet rasping voice, varying from almost servility to paternalism. And almost as extraordinary was the applause it produced – for none had failed to watch the silent, preoccupied, almost shrinking presence throughout, wondering, remembering that this was by any standards one of the most powerful figures in the land. This last-moment statement of adherence to their cause, and homologation of what at such great risk they had done, undoubtedly came as an enormous relief and encouragement to many. By those few strange words, Archibald Campbell suddenly turned himself into a hero of the Assembly, almost on a par with Alexander Henderson himself.

'And there you have it!' Rothes commented grimly. 'Hear how they cheer the man! The reward for biding his time. There's a chiel who kens when to jump, and how!'

'Tom Hope was right,' Napier agreed. 'That man will lead Scotland yet, if he may.'

'Lead? I think you misuse the word, Archie,' Montrose said levelly, his fine features strangely drawn. '*Use*, perhaps. Exploit. Manipulate. But to lead, it is necessary that a man be in the forefront, is it not? Here is no leader.'

'Perhaps I should have said master . . .'

Henderson was speaking. 'We rejoice that the Earl of Argyll thus joins, heartens and advises us,' he said. 'It is fitting climax to a great work. We have, in this Assembly, set God's house in order in this land. We have done our simple duty, spared none, nor ourselves. We have cast down the walls of Jericho; let him that rebuildeth them beware of the curse of Hiel the Bethelite. Now, my brethren and friends – go in peace. And may the blessing of God Almighty, the Father, the Son and the Holy Ghost, go with you all. Amen.'

II

IT ALL ADDED UP TO A DECLARATION OF WAR, OF COURSE – however many in Scotland, including James Graham, refused to see it that way. Hamilton went back to his master in a fury, declaring that of the Covenant leadership none was more vainly foolish than Montrose, but that Argyll would likely prove the most dangerous man in the state, and advising the strongest measures against rebels and traitors. The assembling of forces at Newcastle, which had been rather hanging fire and more of a token threat than a reality, began to take on serious proportions when the Catholic Earl of Arundel, son of Norfolk, was appointed commanding general, the Earl of Essex lieutenant-general, and the Earl of Holland, general-of-horse, the main muster being transferred to York.

In the circumstances, while protesting their loyalty to the Crown, the Tables had either to make military preparations of their own, or to knuckle under. This last was inconceivable, even to Montrose. They asked the King for a parliament, but this was curtly refused – Charles adding that no further General Assemblies would be permitted either until the bishops were reinstated and present. So the Tables, and Scotland, set about preparing to defend themselves.

Oddly enough, the Scots, Church-dominated as they were, proved to be better at the business than was the King – who, of course, was at odds with much of his English realm, his parliament and the Puritans. At least they went about it in prompt and businesslike fashion. And they had one great advantage, apart from enthusiasm for freedom and burning convictions that they were right – they could call upon a great pool of experienced professional soldiers. For generations it had been the custom for Scots younger sons to sell their itching swords abroad as mercenaries, for they were a warlike as well as a religious people – the two seem often to go together – and found internal feuding insufficiently rewarding as a steady profesison. The Continental wars had long been a source of employment for the Scots, and many of the European monarchs would have been hard put to it to officer their armies without them. The campaigns of the great Gustavus Adolphus of Sweden, in especial, had been a notable forcing-ground for military talent. So now the Scots mercenaries were called home from all over Christendom – and not asked to come for nothing either. The Covenanters had been amassing funds for months, with a voluntary levy on all land-holders and a nation-wide appeal at parish level. Money flooded in, and the militarists flooded home.

The greatest catch in this respect was, of course, Sandy Leslie, a clansman of Rothes and younger son of Leslie of Balgonie, acknowledged to be one of the greatest soldiers of the age, outmatching Wallenstein himself, and now field-marshal of the forces of Gustavus. He was tempted to come home as commander-in-chief of the armies of the Covenant.

Meanwhile Scotland was divided up into areas of recruitment, and Montrose given the most vital and dangerous sector, as far as internal security went – Angus and the Mearns, flanking the disaffected Aberdeenshire on the south. So at last he opened up his neglected and semi-decayed house of Old Montrose as headquarters, and at least temporarily gathered his little family around him again.

It would be pleasant to recount that this was a joyful domestic interlude; but perhaps that was more than could be hoped for. Magdalen and the children came, dutifully enough at his request, the few miles from Kinnaird – even she admitting that her husband could scarcely use her father's house as base for his treasonable activities. But her disapproval of his involvement was even more pronounced than before – and after the business at Glasgow, her father and brother were scarcely on speaking terms with her husband, a distressing situation for a young woman torn by a sense of neglect, by self-doubts and divided loyalties. She would do her duty as a wife – but obviously not much more meantime. And her very evident belief that she was married to a renegade and sedition-monger was no help to strained marital relations. They both tried, and tried hard, to make their union meaningful, in more than the mere necessary production of children to heir the Graham name and tradition; but such strivings are not always a true basis for marital bliss.

Not that James Graham was able to devote a large proportion of his time to improving domestic harmony. He was, in fact, exceedingly busy whipping up and training armed men from his Angus area. In this he had the useful aid of the young Earl Marischal, at Dunnottar Castle, farther north – indeed dangerously near Aberdeen – and of the Earl of Kinghorne, head of the ancient Lyon family of Glamis. Also, of course, many of his own Graham lairds, including Black Pate and Sir Robert of Morphie. But he also had the opposition of the Ogilvys, powerful indeed in the Angus glens, whose chief, the Earl of Airlie, was a king-at-any-price man. And, of course, the Carnegies. Matters did not come to actual blows; but it was a tug-of-war business, and men recruited one day might be discovered to have changed their minds the next. And, in the absence of any obvious immediate military threat, enthusiasm was apt to be confined to the ministers, rather than the would-be warriors.

This was the situation at the beginning of March when a courier reached Old Montrose from Edinburgh and the Tables – which meant in effect the ruling triumvirate, Loudoun, Rothes and Henderson. The news was serious and circumstantial. An armed clash looked to be unavoidable and imminent. King Charles himself had come up to Newcastle, and the army now there was reliably put at 21,000-14,000 infantry under the Catholic Earl of Arundel, Norfolk's son; 2000 cavalry under the Earl of Holland; and a special sea-borne force of 5000 under Hamilton himself, for which ships were assembling. This last was to sail up to link with Huntly, who was appointed Lieutenant of all the North-East, from the Esk to the Pentland Firth, and was to raise it for the King so as to take the Covenanters in the rear while the main army invaded over the Border. Moreover the Marquis of Strafford was to descend on the Clyde area, by sea from Cumberland, with an unspecified force; and the Earl of Antrim to invade Argyll and the North-West from Ireland. All assaults to be synchronised. The Scots intelligence services, at least, were proving their worth. The Earl of Montrose was herewith appointed General Officer in command of the North-East, with full powers, and the duty of dealing with Huntly – and Hamilton when he should arrive.

Somewhat shattered by this commitment, in his present circumstances, James Graham found occasion furiously to think.

Out of his cogitations, his first action was to call meetings of the known supporting lords, lairds and burgh representatives, one for the Angus area, one for the Mearns, and one for the anti-Gordon and pro-Covenant people immediately to the north of Huntly's domains, Forbeses, Frasers and Keiths, as a threat in Huntly's own rear. He chose Forfar, Stonehaven and Turriff as the meeting-places – the latter at the very north of Aberdeenshire, near the Banff border, as a secret venue – and appointed the 14th of February for the meetings. He would attend both of the southern ones personally; but for that a Turriff he sent Johnnie Kilpont and the young Earl of Kinghorne as lieutenants, to convene it and convey his views and commands. Meantime he greatly accelerated his recruiting, now with promise of actually fighting, and with the definite appointment of officers and responsibilities. Grahams were sent for from other areas, far and near.

On the 13th, in the late afternoon of the very day before the meetings a messenger arrived from Keith, the Earl Marischal at Dunnottar, to say that the word had leaked out somehow, and all Aberdeen knew that the northern Covenant leadership would be assembling in Turriff the next day; not only that, but that Huntly himself, with 2000 hastily assembled Gordons, was going to descend upon the said meeting, show who was master in the North-East, and strike the first blow for King Charles against his upstart rebels.

Appalled, Montrose cursed the folly of loud-mouthed irresponsibles. But he wasted no time in recriminations. Almost before the courier was finished, he was shouting for Black Pate and his 200 Graham horse. Somebody else could attend the other meetings.

Turriff was sixty-odd miles north of Montrose, as the crow flies, almost double that by road. Moreover, Aberdeen city and all the Gordon country lay between. No level-headed man would suggest that a troop of horse could go from one to the other in less than two days' very hard riding, and without having to fight their way into the bargain. But James Graham roused, was less than level-headed. Without so much as waiting for his evening meal, he kissed his wife and baby son an abrupt farewell, saluted his older two sons, and ran out into the stableyard buckling on steel breastplate as he ran. Vaulting into the saddle, with only young Morphie there ready, he did not wait for his troop either, but yelled instructions to Pate to follow on, and clattered off straight into a canter.

Montrose rode north by west, up out of the wide vale of the South Esk, making straight for the mighty barrier of mountains that formed the fifty-mile-long north wall of Strathmore, the Grampian Line which enclosed the Highland heart of Scotland. Crossing the South Esk by Bridge of Dun, he began the long, long climb that was to take him from sea-level to over 2500 feet. By Stracathro, where Edward of England had humiliated King John Baliol, he rode, to the bridge over the North Esk at Inchbare, and so on to Edzell, the red-stone village and castle of the Lindsays within the jaws of Glen Esk. It was important for his hastily made plans that he should ascertain who was in residence and command here this night; for old Lord Edzell, of Session, was a strong King's man; whereas his son, the head-strong David Lindsay, was as keen for the Covenant, more to spite his father than anything else, perhaps. And not only did Edzell Castle command the entrance to long Glen Esk, but Lindsay towers and little strongholds were dotted all the way up, barring it and the high pass beyond, to those the Lindsays did not love. Hence this dash here unattended. Fortunately, the old judge, who spent most of the winter at Edinburgh and the law courts, was not present; and his son was not only sympathetic but bored and looking for diversion. He insisted on joining Montrose in this venture, with a small, scratch contribution of tough Lindsay horsemen. When Black Pate and the Graham troopers came beating up, there was no further delay. The combined party faced one of the most taxing equestrian assignments that the East of Scotland could produce, the Mounth passes.

Lonely Glen Esk led them north-west for some seventeen miles, through the high mountains, by a passable track, an old drove road indeed. Its strategically sited towers, however, would have sealed off access to a still stronger company than this – hence the need for Lindsay co-operation. Had the old lord been in charge at Edzell, a less dramatic and easier route, by the Cairn o' Mounth, to the east, would have been necessary – but with much more risk of trouble with the Gordons.

By nightfall they were climbing out of Glen Esk's nor-therly fork, Glen Mark, well above the solitary Loch Lee, and out on to the great bare hillsides. Old snow was still lying at this level, over 1500 feet, but the track was marked at quarter-mile intervals by posts – although some were down, and in the dusk, confusing as to direction. But the Lindsays, on their own ground, were little at a loss – and at least the snow gave off an eerie white glimmer which served in lieu of light.

For a full hour they climbed, slowly now, by a route few would have deemed possible for horseflesh and in winter dark – though the Graham mounts were, of course, garrons or half-garrons, the short-legged, surefooted sturdy Scots mountain-horses, of which there were none tougher. High up on the windy, bitter-cold shoulder of Mount Keen, at nearly 2600 feet, in a spectral wilderness of snow peaks sensed rather than seen, they paused to regroup. So far there were no casualties, though some were tending to lag. Montrose spoke, cheerfully, encouragingly, the biting wind catching at his breath. Ahead of them, by a long, broken and slow descent of seven miles, lay the deep valley of the Dee, at Ballater – Gordon territory.

Avoiding the Pass of Ballater, and the small Gordon castles of Knock and Abergairn, they forded the Dee at Polhillock shallows, the valley-foot seeming to be deeply dark in contrast to the open heights. Unchallenged, an hour short of midnight, they began to climb again almost at once, up Glen Gairn. Up and up, round the vast flanks of the Morven hills they struggled now, back into the snows, again almost to the 2000 feet line, their route now less known to any. Many times they lost the track, and wasted precious time beating about in that hellish, frozen desert of ice and granite outcrops. As well, of course, that the underlying peat-hags were indeed frozen, or they could not have made any progress in the darkness. It took them over two hours more to cover the ten miles from the Dee to the Don valley, near Cock Bridge, where Corgarff Castle guarded this strategic crossing. It was a hold of the Earl of Mar, not the Gordons; but the travellers gave it a wide berth nevertheless, and forded the river discreetly half a mile downstream – a dangerous preference. More mountains lay ahead of them.

Dawn found them weary, going but slowly now, straggling out, but getting into lower ground again, in the foothills of the Cabrach, with the stripling Deveron winding in the misty valleys, and the border of Banffshire near. From here Turriff was only some twenty-five miles away – but with Strathbogie and the Huntly area directly in the way. A roundabout route through the low Foudland Hills was necessary, and then a dash across the still lower and populous lands of the Ythan valley and Auchterless, going heedfully indeed, with Gordon properties and castles thick around them. They could no doubt deal with the forces which any Gordon laird could throw against them at short notice – but not without delay, and word being carried to Huntly. Many folk did see them, in their progress thereafter, of course, and stared, wondering – but the travellers interfered with none. And who would have been foolish enough to challenge such armed and determined company, however travel-worn, lacking at least like numbers?

An hour before the Covenanters' meeting was arranged to start, at noon, Montrose's scouts reporting the approach to be clear still, they rode down the green haughs of the Idoch Water and up the brae into Turriff, men all but asleep in their saddles, horses stumbling, pecking, foundered. But they had achieved what it is safe to say had never been visualised as possible, much less attempted by a horsed squadron – an eighty-mile mountain circuit of Aberdeenshire in eighteen hours non-stop.

The Covenanting lairds of the North, quite unsuspecting of any danger, were as surprised as they were delighted to see the visitor. But Montrose quickly disillusioned them, more critical and less gracious than his usual. He did not blame them for leaking the news – although somebody had done so – but he pointed out that, had proper watch been kept here, with scouts out, his own party's arrival would not have surprised them as it had done. Kilpont and Kinghorne he especially blamed, for having failed to take any steps for the defence of the gathering, however secret they believed it to be. They were not wholly defenceless, of course, for the Lord Pitsligo, Viscount Frendraught, the Master of Forbes and others had brought their usual 'tails' with them; and with lesser lairds, grooms and servants, they totalled not far off 800 men.

None having considered defensive positions, Montrose decided that the ancient parish church of St Congans, with its kirkyard, crowning a green rise to the south-east of the village, was the only place. The minister would approve. Everyone to move in there, with the horses in the manse walled-garden adjoining. Meanwhile, local Forbes scouts out, in pairs, to give warning of any enemy approach.

The newcomers thereafter lay down amongst the tomb-stones, and slept the sleep of the exhausted.

Montrose was awakened a couple of hours later, with the word that scouts reported the approach of a great host from the south-west, hidden in the deep valley of the Deveron – thousands, it was declared, mostly foot. Only Huntly could produce that sort of host in this country.

Grimly the Graham shook the sleep from heavy eyes. Even allowing for exaggeration by the scouts, it looked as though his military career was likely to be a short one; yet he was not going to start it by any ignominious flight, without striking a blow. That was not for *An Greumach Mor*. It seemed improbable that they could repel any major attack, for long – yet what other honourable course was open to them?

He placed his people to man the kirkyard walls to best advantage, using the little belfry-tower of the church for his command-post. But he did not waste his Graham troopers thus, sending them over to the manse garden, under Pate, from which they might make a suitable cavalry diversion if the occasion offered. Then they could only wait.

And so, with bagpipes playing and horns ululating, a vast and straggling host presently began to come flooding out of the dip of the Deveron valley. It gave no least impression of being an army, being more like a huge fair on the move, carefree, undisciplined, in holiday spirit. Admittedly there were groups of mounted men amongst it all, and innumerable banners, with the glint of arms everywhere; but there was no sort of military formation, nothing of wariness or tension, no hint of any unified control – or indeed *any* control. As more and more came into sight, there seemed to be many in excess of the originally estimated 2000; but somehow there was little impression of menace in the multitude. Whether or not Huntly was with it, in person, was not apparent.

As some of his colleagues exclaimed at it all, Montrose, pointing out that the Gordon presumably had expected to disrupt a meeting and arrest its members rather than fight a battle, nevertheless could not explain why such numbers should be mobilised for this; unless Huntly merely desired to make a demonstration of strength in the area.

Presently at least some sort of elementary planning was evinced, as the host began to spread itself out in a great semi-circle to south and east of the village, presumably to prevent any dash for freedom in that direction: the River Deveron would effectively cut off flight at the other side, with its only bridge almost certainly held.

At what stage the Gordons realised that their approach was to be opposed by armed and alerted force was hard to

146

say. It was not even clear just where the leadership was, for banners were wide-scattered.

A part of the great throng had come very close, almost to the foot of the kirk-brae, before seeming to realise that the frieze of figures lining the kirkyard wall above had, in fact, hagbuts levelled and pointing directly at them; and that the group up on the belfry-tower had drawn swords in their hands. The consternation, almost indignation, developing below thereupon, was quite dramatic.

But, through a kind of residual impetus and lack of any overall command to halt, the advance – if that it could be called – continued.

From the church-tower, Montrose rapped out an order. A volley of hagbut shots cracked out.

It was a distinctly ragged volley, not to say piecemeal, for the marksmen were less than expert. But its effect on the opposition was as great as though it had been fired by a crack regiment – and moreover, *at* them instead of well above their heads. All advance halted, some men fell on their faces, more turned back in haste, and confusion reigned everywhere.

'So that is the vaunted Gordon power!' the Earl of Kinghorne exclaimed. 'That pack of fools and cravens!'

'Do not judge too swiftly,' Montrose advised. 'They could be formidable enough, I swear, sufficiently bold, if well led. If indeed they were in fighting trim. Do not underestimate the Gordons, John. This but finds them unprepared. They would have served very well to capture your meeting – which was what they set out to do!'

Presently, when the noise abated, a voice could be heard shouting, 'Who dares to fire on Gordon? Who, I say!'

'James Graham of Montrose, Lieutenant-General of the Estates!' was thrown back. 'What rabble is this?'

There was a pause, as of sheer disbelief. Then an incredulous voice called. 'James Graham? In person? The Earl ... ?'

'In person. Bearing the authority of the Estates of this realm. Who are you?' Obviously this was not Huntly himself.

'Straloch. Gordon of Straloch. Chamberlain to Huntly. To my lord Marquis.'

Montrose sighed. He had rather liked Straloch at their previous meeting. 'Then, sir,' he answered, 'why come against me with this great host? I mislike it.'

There was a pause again, as the spokesman consulted his fellows. 'My lord Marquis of Huntly,' was shouted back, at length, 'is appointed the King's Lieutenant of the North. No gathering may be held lacking my lord's permission.'

'Who says so? To the Earl of Montrose, Lieutenant-General of the realm?'

That was in the nature of stalemate. All perceived it. There was another interval.

'Montrose ended it. 'Come up higher, sir,' he commanded. 'I also mislike shouting, like fishwives at a market!' And when Straloch and a group of Gordon lairds had part-climbed the hillock obediently, 'That will serve. Where is my lord of Huntly?'

'He is at the Ford of Towie, my lord. Two miles . . .'

'Why is he not here? I do not deal with intermediaries!'

'He did not know, my lord. That you were here. We believed you . . . in Angus. We did not conceive it . . .'

'Then go and fetch your master, Straloch. Tell him that I await his explanation for this display of force against an assembly under the authority of the Estates of Scotland. Go tell him, sir.'

Strangely, this arrogant assumption of authority, so contrary to Montrose's courteous habit, well served its turn. Returning to the main body, after a little delay Straloch and his group of lairds, leaving the multitude to its own devices, turned and rode away south-westwards.

It was an hour before they were back – with the Gordon host meantime settling down to wait, variously but scarcely warlikely employed, more like a fair than ever. Montrose improved the impression of disciplined strength on the higher ground by having Black Pate and his troopers move out from the manse garden, mount, and station themselves in two long lines of a hundred, on either side of the kirkyard, sitting their horses motionless and looking threatening.

A great blowing of bulls' horns heralded Huntly's arrival on the scene – what he had been doing at Ford of Towie unexplained. With his colourful entourage, and a loping pack of deer-hounds, and to the cheers of his multitude he came riding up the brae, dressed as for the hunt, but with tall eagles' feathers sprouting from his bonnet.

Montrose let him come close – although the hagbuts remained levelled and swords drawn. 'My lord Marquis,' he called, 'do you come in peace or war? This great company would seem to offer me threat – me, Lieutenant-General of the Estates! I have borne with them, in your absence, with such patience as I might. I trust that you will now remove them.'

Huntly puffed, frowning. 'In this land, my lord, none speaks Gordon so. Even you! You are holding an unlawful assembly, it seems, so that . . .'

'By what laws, sir? Not the laws of Scotland!'

'*I* administer and declare the laws here, my lord of Montrose – I, Gordon! I am Justiciar of the North. And now King's Lieutenant of the North likewise. From Esk to Caithness. Perhaps you had not heard?'

'And does the King command you to interfere with the Earl of Montrose, contrary to the law of Scotland?'

'No-o-o. But meetings, assemblies of . . . of the King's enemies are forbidden.'

'You dare to name *me*, Montrose, the King's enemy, sir? He has no more loyal subject. All here are the King's loyal subjects. I urge that you remember it!'

Huntly changed his stance a little. 'This meeting? What is its purpose?'

'Its purpose is the lawful conferring together of the King's lieges. Under my authority. If you deny that authority, my lord, and that of the Convention of Estates, then *you* are an enemy of this realm, and must abide the consequences. Do you?'

The Gordon took time to consider that.

Recognising hesitation, and gauging the other's character, Montrose pressed his point. 'If you do, sir, I have many armed and trained men here, to argue that authority, as Lieutenant-General, if you so desire. If you desire a decision by arms, declare it now. Or leave us to our lawful occasions.'

While not a few deep breaths were drawn around him, at this over-bold challenge, Huntly took it seriously. He bent in his saddle, to confer with Straloch.

Encouraged, the Graham added, 'We have wasted much time over this, my lord. Hours. We grow impatient. My hagbutters. My cavalry in especial.' He waved his sword right and left. 'Do I order attack? Or is it peace?'

Huntly cleared his throat. 'I could, should, punish your insolence, Montrose – here in my Gordon country. But I am

149

the King's Lieutenant. And I have His Grace's express command to engage in no armed warfare until . . . until my lord Hamilton comes. Or until King Charles crosses the Border. His Grace is merciful. I do not conceive you to deserve it. But I do not controvert my lord the King. These orders – I must abide by them.'

'Ha! Excellent and wise orders, my lord! Would all were so wise, used such discretion! So it is peace – until my lord Hamilton arrives?'

Stiffly the other inclined his handsome head.

'So be it. I bid you good-day, my lord Marquis. And hope that when we next meet it will be in happier circumstances.' Montrose made a gesture of sheathing his sword, and doffed his feathered hat with a flourish.

For moments the Gordon stood, biting the ends of his luxuriant moustache. Then abruptly he reined his splendid stallion around, and rode off down the brae. In some confusion his close supporters hurried after him. He drove on right through the ranks of his host, without pause, unspeaking, men drawing hastily aside for the Cock o' the North. On he went, in the direction from which he had so recently come, nor once did he look behind him.

'There goes a lamb in lion's skin!' Montrose observed, almost sadly. 'That the Gordon should have come to this! And that it fell to me to act skinner – before all his people.'

'George Gordon will never recover from this,' the Lord Pitsligo said. 'Kinder, I think, to have shot him with one of these hagbuts!'

The Graham turned away, wordless, to descend the tower stairway.

Left leaderless, uncertain, it took some time for the great host to disperse. And all the while the Graham troopers sat their mounts, still as statues – though most were half-asleep in their saddles – and the hagbutters remained leaning against the kirkyard wall, weapons levelled. The minister of Turriff came to announce that his wife had supper prepared for their lordships.

So ended the first confrontation of the Bishops' War.

12

JAMES GRAHAM WAS NOT LONG BACK AT OLD MONTROSE –
having crossed all Aberdeenshire openly and unchallenged
– when Field-Marshal Alexander Leslie arrived. Rothes
came, briefly, to introduce him, with 1000 men, mainly foot,
recruited from Fife; which, added to the nearly 3000 Montrose already had mustered in Angus, made a sizeable force,
much too large to maintain in or around Old Montrose. He
decided to move to Stonehaven, twenty-three miles north,
in the Earl Marischal's country, where the Keiths were
solidly pro-Covenant, and the impregnable castle of Dunnottar offered a secure base. Moreover, Stonehaven was
only fifteen miles south of Aberdeen, and it was important
to keep an eye on that city, and its harbour – where Hamilton's expeditionary force was expected to make a landing.
So Old Montrose was once again shut up, Magdalen electing
to take the children back to Kinnaird.

Sandy Leslie was a little, wizened, wiry man, sour and
with few graces, but shrewd, decisive, with a jaw like a rat-
trap. He was not a man Montrose could take to; but there
was no question but that he was an enormous asset to the
Covenant cause, and to be accepted accordingly. The position meantime was difficult, however; for though Leslie was
to be Commander-in-Chief, for some reason his appointment
did not commence until May. In the interim he was to serve
under Montrose in an advisory capacity. If the little veteran
felt resentment at being thus presently under the command
of an inexperienced amateur of less than half his own age,
however highly born, he had to swallow it for the time being
– though such was his jerky and ungracious manner, that it
was hard to tell if he did.

At Dunnottar, with no sign of Hamilton or his fleet, a
strange verbal message reached Montrose, stressed as most

secret by its bearer, a Forbes laird from the Garioch. It was from Huntly himself, requesting a private meeting, as soon as possible. No reasons were given, no other suggestions made; merely the request.

The Graham pondered it awhile, while, under Leslie's keen eyes, training of the raw troops went on. Did Huntly seek an accommodation? Did he reckon the King's cause to be hopeless? Was he preparing to resile, with Hamilton's non-appearance? Or was he just seeking to lull Montrose into a false sense of security, seeking to gain time?

Other word of Huntly came from Aberdeen spies. Rumours were rife therein that the Gordons were preparing to descend upon it, with the co-operation of the magistrates and the University authorities. Certainly earthworks and other fortifications for the defence of the city were being constructed. Montrose's advisers – and now he had a-plenty – were strong that he take the town and hold it against Hamilton's arrival; but he did not wish to add to his responsibilities thus, and restrict his essential mobility. The Tables, in Edinburgh, now apparently more and more dominated by Argyll, had issued a fiat appointing Military Committees for all counties and all commands, on which the Kirk was strongly represented; and these committees had to be taken into consultation on all matters of policy. The Graham discovered that a great crowd of divines, chaplains and other long-faced gentry had descended upon his camp at Stonehaven, all claiming the authority of the Tables as advisers. Vociferously they demanded the taking of Aberdeen immediately. Whether from conviction or policy, Leslie backed them up.

Reluctantly, at the end of March, Montrose marched on the city.

There was no resistance – and no signs of the Gordons. Some of the city fathers fled by sea, as did the University professors and doctors. The citizens did not welcome the Covenanting army, nor did they provoke it. Black-robed divines descended on the erring town from near and far – like black crows on carrion, as Montrose asserted privately to Pate Graham – and did not confine themselves to monopolising the city pulpits. It was becoming most evident that many of the Kirk's ministers and supporters considered that a theocracy was now the rule in Scotland, the voice of God's ordained servants to be supreme in law and governance, and all soldiers, like other citizens, however lofty, to be subject to their guidance. Montrose, of course, saw it otherwise, and there were clashes. It was strange that Sandy Leslie should so consistently take their side – a Field-Marshall might have been expected to be the first to resent any ministerial interference in matters military. But, of course, they were in effect his paymasters.

Deciding that he did not like the atmosphere developing in Aberdeen, the Graham drew up orders for its good administration, strict but fair, appointed the Earl of Kinghorne as Lieutenant-Governor, ordered all Covenanting troops to wear a blue ribbon, as identification, imposed a fine of 10,000 merks – as advised by his Military Committee – as suitable contribution from a community which hitherto had failed to support the cause, and announced his own departure. He declared that he was going to keep an eye on Huntly and the Gordons. On the pretext that Hamilton's fleet might arrive off the harbour at any time, and coping with his reception require a skilled and experienced hand, he managed to leave the Field-Marshal behind, with his 1000 from Fife. And most of the ministers. Breathing more freely than he had done for a while, James Graham rode sixteen miles north-west, to Inverurie, a small and ancient royal burgh at the confluence of Urie and Don, and camped there.

All along, there had been stories of the Gordons mobilising their admittedly enormous war potential, in earnest. The air was thick with their reported numbers – 5000, 8000, 10,000. Oddly enough, Huntly's personal credit having suffered grievously at Turriff, the semi-legendary renown of his house had become transferred meantime to his sons. The eldest, Lord Gordon, was not much mentioned; but his next brother, the Viscount Aboyne, was said to have been so disgusted with his father's inactivity that he had run off, and sailed in a fishing-craft, south to join the King in the North of England; while the Lord Lewis, though only thirteen, was ranging round the Gordon country with a banner and a drawn sword, whipping up forces.

Inverurie, a grey-stone town amongst low green hills, with a great, green isolated mound which had supported a former royal castle – where the mighty Bruce had lain ill, before rising from his sick-bed to win a battle against the Comyns

– was an ideal spot to keep watch and ward on the vast
sprawling area of rural Aberdeenshire, strategically sited
not only at the junction of rivers but where the Bourtie,
Benachie, Corrennie and Correen hill-masses forced road
communications into a fairly tight bottleneck. If a wary eye
was to be kept on the mighty Clan Gordon, this was the
place to do it.

Montrose had scarcely expected, however, that his first
sure word of the Gordons should be from such an authoritative level. On only his second day at Inverurie, a nondescript
traveller from the north came seeking his presence – and
turned out to be none other than Gordon of Straloch,
Huntly's Chamberlain, though very much incognito. His
master had sent him, he said, to arrange the private and
secret meeting with Montrose, with a view to a possibly
mutually beneficial arrangement.

Seeking to hide his astonishment, the Graham enquired
further, as though this was perfectly normal procedure
between rival commanders.

Huntly proposed, it seemed, that they should meet secretly,
each to have only ten companions and armed only with
swords, at an inconspicuous place mid-way between Strathbogie and Inverurie, each side to send forward three of their
number to inspect the other, before meeting, to ensure that
these conditions were scrupulously complied with.

'Does my lord of Huntly not trust my word?' Montrose
interrupted warmly, at this stage. 'If I agree to the meeting,
there is no need for such inspection, sir.'

'Your pardon, my lord. I said as much. But my master
insisted upon it. He believes that your ministers might seek
to deceive him. Not yourself, to be sure . . .'

'He wrongs them. But I will bring no ministers, I assure
you . . .'

So, despite warnings of a possible trap, from Kilpont and
others, two days later Montrose and Huntly did meet, at a
hidden waterside hamlet under the steep slopes of Benachie.
It was a strange encounter, with the Gordon strained,
nervous, almost furtive, apparently wary even of his own
companions – amongst whom James Graham was surprised
to find the young Lord Gordon, as unimportant- and un-
distinguished-seeming as ever, but calmly alert and detached,
in contrast to the others who presented a picture of corporate

discomfort. Huntly insisted on drawing Montrose well aside, and out of ear-shot, for a start, and conducting the subsequent conversation in whispers – unlikely behaviour for the man at whose least word all the North-East was supposed to quake. The other, as a consequence, was the cooler, more off-hand.

Huntly's troubled discourse went thus. He had been deceived, shamefully deceived. Word had reached him from his son, Aboyne, now at Newcastle, that Hamilton was not in fact coming to Aberdeen at all. His force was to sail for the Forth, not the Dee. Probably he never had intended to come to the North-East. It was but a ruse to encourage the Gordons to rise. Yet now the King was criticising him for not acting more strongly. When he had His Grace's own commands to mobilise only, to await reinforcement. It was most unfair.

Montrose sympathised, distantly, agreeing that the King could be difficult, and was in most matters ill-advised. Probably it was Hamilton's fault. The man was a puffed-up bull-frog. But how did this concern himself?

An armistice, Huntly suggested, so far below his breath as to be almost inaudible. An end to this folly, in the North-East at least. An agreement – secret, of course. That there be no foolish fighting, no wasting of good lands, that Aberdeen should be left in peace, that grown men might get on with more important matters than playing soldiers.

Seeking to keep his voice level, the other agreed soberly that the situation was unsatisfactory. He would be glad to be able to call off hostilities. But what assurance had he that if he pulled back his forces, the great Gordon power would not once more resume an anti-Covenant attitude?

'You have my word,' Huntly said. 'Gordon's word!'

This was a little awkward for the man who had insisted that *his* word was sufficient guarantee for the security of this meeting. '*I* would accept your word, my lord,' he said. 'But others, I fear, might be less sure. Matters are decided, not by one man but by many, under the Estates. I am Lieutenant-General, and in the field I command. But I have the Field-Marshal Leslie to consider. And my Committee. This that you suggest is policy, not tactics. And for such I must carry a council. Such, I fear, would require more than just your word.'

Huntly tugged at his pointed beard. 'What? What would these require?'

Montrose took his time. 'I think, my lord, that nothing but your signature on the Covenant itself would satisfy them!'

Oddly enough, Huntly was clearly less shaken by this proposal than the other anticipated. He declared that he could not do such thing, of course; that he could by no means put his name to a Band against the King – but all less vehemently than might have been expected. And he listened to Montrose's disclaimers that it was nothing such, patiently enough. The other offered, as he had done once before, to endorse a copy of the document especially to cover the Gordon's loyal scruples. When Huntly questioned him on detailed wording for this, he elatedly perceived the battle won. The Gordon was going to sign.

There was a copy of the Covenant in the camp at Inverurie, he informed. If the Marquis would ride with him there – under his personal protection, of course – all could be done without delay, and the peace they both sought put in train forthwith.

After some suitable hesitation, Huntly agreed.

Unfortunately, back at Inverurie, a party of divines had arrived from Aberdeen in the interim, in their mission to the soldiery, and these reacted to Huntly and his son as they might have done to the Devil in person. There was a notable scene, with the Gordon losing his temper, and the Graham under fire from both sides. It was with difficulty that Montrose eventually got the precious signature, to a Covenant copy duly endorsed to the effect that the subscriber was binding himself in it to maintain the King's authority together with both the liberties of Church and State, Religion and Laws – an endorsement which the ministers at least were far from happy about, muttering darkly anent Papists, heretics, idolators and suchlike.

Assuring Huntly that the main step towards peace in the North-East had hereby been taken, and the King's best interests thereby advanced, just a little hurriedly Montrose saw the Gordons off, back to Strathbogie. The young lord, it was, who had the last word.

'You, my lord of Montrose, I think, are on the wrong side

156

in this conflict. You and the Covenant, both!' And he rode after his father.

Brows puckered, the Graham stared after them.

The Lieutenant-General's return to Aberdeen with Huntly's signature to the National Covenant, and the news that Hamilton was now likely to descend on the Forth, not the Dee, was received differently from his anticipation. The folk of the city rejoiced, of course, as did many others. But not the Covenant leadership there. The ministers, with one accord, condemned the Gordon move as a mere ruse, a snare, to trap the godly. And even if it was not, they should have no truck with the papistical horde. Huntly was nothing better than a deceitful limb of Satan, fit only for the consuming fires of Hell. And Montrose was at fault, at grievous fault, in having agreed to have any dealings with him – and, having done so, to have treated him so gently. Vipers should be stamped upon, not nurtured, by God's servants.

In vain Montrose argued before his Military Committee – which was as unmilitary a body as might be imagined. In a military situation, he declared, other matters than ethics, dogma and theology fell to be considered. Numbers of armed man-power, for instance, a hostile population, available resources, supplies, sheer tactics. Of such, as commander, *he* had to be the judge. He appealed to Alexander Leslie, but got no help from that hard-bitten individual, who declared that in his experience war was fought with wits, swords and powder, until one side was defeated – not by gentlemanly private converse between noblemen. Had he been in Montrose's place, Huntly would now be on his way to stand trial as rebel, in Edinburgh!

Coldly Montrose observed that, fortunately for the good name of the Covenant, treachery was not yet an acceptable method of gaining their ends – a statement which, it is to be feared, turned Leslie from somewhat contemptuous observance into implacable enmity. But the Graham's attitude gained little support. Kinghorne backed him, and the Earl Marischal; but most of his closer colleagues were away commanding units of the army, and the preponderance of ministers on his Committee were wholly lined up against him. They insisted that Montrose's agreement with Huntly, Covenant-signature notwithstanding, could not be ratified until the Gordon had appeared in person before them, for questioning and instruction. Moreover, declaring that Scotland was now godly and democratically governed, they demanded that the matter be put to the vote – and Montrose was overwhelmingly defeated. Announcing that he had never heard of armies and campaigns being commanded thus, the Graham all but stormed out – being persuaded to stay only by the thought that he still might exert influence if not control. When it was passed that Huntly and his son be summoned before the Committee forthwith, he announced, amid uproar, that he would personally advise the Gordons not to appear unless their safe-conduct was assured. Leslie intervened to say that the Earl of Montrose's personal safe-conduct was surely sufficient for any man. It was agreed that the Marquis and son be asked to compear, at Aberdeen, to elucidate details of the proposed armistice, on the 13th day of April.

Surprisingly, on that day, the Gordons did come, again secretly, with Straloch and his son, the Laird of Rothiemay.

That was a sorry day for James Graham, one of the bitterest in his life. Much stemmed from it; indeed nothing was ever quite the same after it. Here he tasted humiliation, of quite another sort than had been offered him at the Palace of Whitehall three years before, a shame such as had never come his way hitherto. Huntly had been enticed into a trap, baited with the Graham's given word. From the first, the Gordon chief and his heir were treated like prisoners, their interview with the Military Committee as appearance at the bar – but for sentence rather than for trial. Accusations were hurled at them, contumely, diatribes. Montrose did what he could, protested, sought to temper the blast, appealed, raged. But it was all most evidently arranged, organised, and he was consistently not only out-voted but shouted down. Time and again he was on the point of marching out. He even contemplated bringing in troops to silence these insolent preachers and orators – but recognised in time not only that this would assuredly end his influence in the cause to which he had set his hand, but that in fact almost all the troops now in Aberdeen were Leslie's Fifers, and Leslie himself was now clearly in command. All pretence of deferring to the younger man was gone. The Field-Marshall now was Commander-in-Chief indeed, and not concerned to hide it. More, Montrose gained the distinct impression that this whole affair was being staged by Leslie largely to humiliate himself.

Be that as it may, it was very much Leslie's, and the ministers' day. Huntly, conjuring up a strange dignity in the face of ranting, was harried and lambasted unmercifully, the younger George Gordon listening to all with his quiet detachment. Finally, he was told by Leslie that, having raised his forces against the realm, he was a traitor and without rights. That he had cost the realm dear, and must therefore pay a large sum in recompense. That he must bring in a number of Gordon notables as prisoners. And that he must accompany Leslie to Edinburgh the next day.

'I shall do none of these,' the Gordon answered, simply.

'I say that you shall!' the Field-Marshal declared. 'We ride tomorrow.'

'I ride, then, only as your prisoner! And I remind you that I am here under the safe-conduct of my lord of Montrose.'

'That is a matter for his lordship, not this Military Committee.'

'I protest! Most strongly I protest!' James Graham cried. 'I have listened to enough! My word stands. My lord of Huntly goes as freely as he came!'

'I care not how he goes, free or other! But he comes to Edinburgh with me, the morn. That I put to this Committee. Do you wish a vote to be taken upon it, my lord Montrose?'

The roar of approval left no doubts as to how the vote would go.

'The matter is decided. The officers will conduct the Marquis of Huntly and the Lord Gordon to their quarters. And attend on them well! My lord of Montrose – as *Lieutenant*-General, you will return to your force at Inverurie, to prosecute your campaign with all address. And with increased vigour.'

'So – you have assumed the command, sir?'

'I have assumed the chief command, yes. On the instructions of the Tables. And no' before time, I swear!'

'On the instructions of my lord of Argyll, rather than the Tables, I think.'

That remarks, injudicious perhaps, fell like a stone into a sudden pool of silence.

After a significant pause, Leslie rapped out, 'I declare this meeting adjourned,' and rose to his feet.

Before the Gordons were hustled away, the young lord caught Montrose's eye. Gravely the youngster inclined his dark head.

13

DESPITE THE NEW COMMANDER-IN-CHIEF'S ORDERS, IT WAS not long before James Graham followed Leslie south, instead of prosecuting his campaigns in the North-East with the required address. He was in a strange state of mind for that man, uncertain, perplexed, unsure of himself, and with no heart for his appointed task. He had, in fact, been struck where it hurt most – in his pride and his honour. All men know now, he felt, that Montrose's word was worthless – since a committee of divines and a fifty-eight-year-old mercenary soldier could invalidate it at their will. And all men must see him as ineffectual, Lieutenant-General in name, but harassed and thwarted by anyone wearing ministerial black. Perhaps it was the pride, more than the honour, that was the principal casualty.

But his distress was for the cause also, to which he had set his hand, at cost. Both in the long and the short term. It was going awry, falling into the wrong hands, becoming an oligarchy with menacing potential. While he was stranded up here in Aberdeenshire, far from the centre of decision. And even here matters were in reverse, with the entire Clan Gordon now raised to fury over the insult and treachery to their chief. There were uprisings and outbreaks of anarchy everywhere, even in Aberdeen city itself. Montrose found himself spending much of his time hurrying about the county putting down small conflagrations; acting the repressive policeman, in fact – a role for which he had by no means entered the cause of liberty and religious freedom.

So, leaving Aberdeen and his command temporarily to the Earls Marischal and Kinghorne, he rode south, with Black Pate and a small escort.

On the last day of April he arrived to find Edinburgh in a state of much excitement. King Charles had issued a proclamation, declaring his Scots subjects in treasonable rebellion and due to be punished by his royal self in person. He was marching north with his large force. Moreover, gallopers from Berwickshire had just brought word that a great fleet was beating slowly northwards along that coast, in the face of north-westerly winds – no doubt the Marquis of Hamilton, at last. Leslie had taken over the main Coven-anting army, and was now encamped, with it, on the links at Leith, the seaport of Edinburgh, preparing to repel in-vasion by sea. Huntly and his son, summoned before the Tables, had been told that he must sign another and un-endorsed Covenant, and make sundry other drastic con-cessions; and, having refused, with his heir was promptly confined prisoner in Edinburgh Castle. To some extent, it seemed, he had redeemed his Turriff-tarnished reputation, by making a resounding valedictory speech, before incarcera-tion, which ended thus : '. . . I am in your power, and resolved not to leave the foul title of traitor upon my posterity. You may take my head from my shoulders, but not my heart from my sovereign !'

The Gordon seemed to be a hero, at last.

Repairing to Archie Napier at Merchiston Castle, Mont-rose learned all this, and more, and communicated his own indignation, disappointment and apprehensions for the future to his brother-in-law. The older man was sympathetic, and had like doubts and fears; but he declared that this was hardly an auspicious moment to seek remedial action and changes in policy, with armed invasion and conflict immi-nent. Edinburgh was in a fever of military preparedness, and all hopes pinned on their renowned and experienced Field-Marshal. He would scarcely find the Tables in a mood to listen heedfully or patiently. Especially as, more and more, they were tending to come under the sway of Archibald Campbell of Argyll.

Demanding to know how Argyll had achieved this sudden pre-eminence in a cause he had so long held aloof from, Montrose learned that the Campbell could act swiftly and decisively enough, in all conscience, when he saw fit. Given the wardenship of the West, as the Graham the North-East, with the especial task of containing the threatened invasions by Strafford in the Clyde area and Antrim's Irish on the West Highland seaboard, he had swiftly mobilised much of his great Campbell man-power, and garrisoned particularly all the landing-places on the long Kintyre peninsula, where, if Antrim was to try to link up with Strafford, he must make his short crossing from Ulster. Then, with another force of Campbells, he had descended upon the Isle of Arran in the Clyde estuary, taken the main strength, Brodick Castle, by surprise, and won the entire island without having to fight – a brilliant stroke, in more ways than one. For with Loudoun, Eglinton and other Covenant lords controlling the Ayrshire coast opposite, Arran was the key to the Clyde approaches, and Argyll could now control any invasion attempt therein; not only that, but Arran was the Marquis of Hamilton's property – he was also Earl of Arran – and the Campbells had long coveted that great island, with their lands all around. Now they had gained it, and from a man whom none would stand up for, in Scotland – a shrewd move indeed. Argyll, it appeared, would serve the Covenant and himself equally well.

Thus, Napier explained, the Campbell had made a great and swift impression, at no cost but only gain to himself – for the twin Western invasions never materialised. Vastly relieved, the Tables and the Covenanters generally welcomed him back to Edinburgh with open arms. But he was discreet, modest, on the surface, a humble, self-effacing and pious man. He did not have to beat the big drum; for the Earl of Loudoun was also a Campbell, and as Convener of the Joint Tables' Standing Council, was in a position largely to control all for his chief.

But what about Alexander Henderson? And Rothes? And others, Montrose demanded? Surely these were the true leaders of the cause, with Loudoun a mere figure-head, something of a dolt indeed!

A strategically placed dolt, now with a very shrewd and cunning brain behind him, the other pointed out. As for Henderson, he was still the true moral leader; but he had the whole uprising Kirk to manage nowadays – and a difficult and unruly horse that was to ride, puffed with its victory

over the bishops. Clearly Henderson found Argyll a useful
ally; more useful than Montrose, it seemed! And Rothes
was less than well, a man sickening. Always he had eaten
and drunk too much; and the excitements and journeyings
of these days had been taxing for a man of his habits. He
appeared less and less at the Tables, or in Edinburgh at all.

Depressed by all this, Montrose nevertheless decided to
tackle Henderson, Sir Thomas Hope, and others, on the
morrow.

On the morrow, however, the 1st of May, Hamilton's
fleet, with a change of wind, sailed up the Forth, and city and
port were agog. The Marquis was said to have some 5000
men aboard – much less than Leslie – but also much artillery,
of which the Covenanters had little or none. The great
squadron of nineteen ships made an impressive, a daunting
sight, as it dropped anchor in Leith roads. The port and the
army of the Covenant prepared for a one-sided bombardment, while glancing back over its shoulder towards the
Border and the King's main invasion.

But no bombardment eventuated. And, oddly enough,
after two days lying off Leith, the fleet up-anchored and
sailed off to the other side of the Forth. There were many
more harbours on that side than on the south, although all
smaller than Leith; but Fife was Leslie and Lindsay country,
and neither the Field-Marshal nor Rothes his chief had
neglected to have these defended. Easily seen from the south
shore, at most times, the invasion fleet sailed up and down
the north, found no unguarded landing-places, and seemingly decided against doing anything rash. For, presently,
with the easterly wind rising somewhat, the fleet split up,
groups of ships seeking shelter in the lee of the undefended
Forth islets – Inchkeith, Inchcolm and Inchmickery – and
there remained.

Although a descent by open boats on open beaches, by
night, was anticipated thereafter, and forces sent out to keep
watch on a long coastline, gravely weakening the main
Covenant strength, nothing such developed. Hamilton
appeared to be no more successful as warrior than he was as
statesman or ambassador. Perhaps it was his old mother who
worried him, a dragon if ever there was one. Ann of Glencairn, Countess-Dowager and strong Presbyterian, who
turned up at Leith pier, from Lanarkshire, with two drawn

and loaded pistols, declaring that one was for her son Hamilton and the other for her son Lanark, if they dared to set foot on honest Scots soil.

At all events, invasion by sea remained only a threat. And King Charles's 40,000 moved but slowly, being still somewhere between Newcastle and Berwick.

Meanwhile Montrose made many calls and saw many people – although he avoided any actual confrontation with Leslie, whose authority as Commander-in-Chief might well have been turned to awkward account. This was no time for a trial of strength. He learned that not a few, especially amongst the nobility, were almost as anxious as he was about the way matters were trending in the Covenant leadership. There was much agreement that something must be done – but not at this difficult moment. Even Alexander Henderson admitted privately, guardedly, that a deal that went on was not to his liking, and would fall to be rectified. But certainly not just yet. Many in the ministry were proving over-zealous, yes. The Earl of Argyll was working himself into a position of great power, yes. But he was an able as well as an influential man, and now wholly committed to the Covenant cause. General Leslie could be harsh, difficult; but he was absolutely essential to Scotland in this pass. They must be patient, and await more convenient time for reform. Especially, he added, would patience become the Earl of Montrose! Had he not deserted his army, against the authority of the Tables who appointed him? Entered into private arrangement with Huntly, the enemy commander? Rejected the advice of his own Military Committee, with contumely? And spoken hard words publicly against the Covenant's friends and for the Covenant's enemies? Henderson was at his upright sternest, in making these charges, however quietly.

James Graham sought to be as calmly objective. He refuted the charges, explained – and added some of his own – ending by demanding Huntly's and his son's release. The other declared this to be impossible, save on the orders of the Tables who had commanded the imprisonment. And it was not practicable to summon the members thereof from their respective commands and duties, in this crisis, just to debate again on such matter. Moreover, the Tables once in session, might well take a serious view of one of their generals absenting himself from his post at such time, to come south on this mission. Henderson strongly advised his lordship to return to his northern army forthwith, and make any representations by letter from there.

On that note they parted, civil but strained.

By first light next morning, Montrose was indeed on his way north again. But not wholly on account of Henderson's advice. Late the night before, a messenger came from the Earl Marischal. The Master of Forbes had been surprised and driven out of Turriff with his small garrison, by a combined force of anti-Covenant Ogilvies, Setons and Urquharts. This little victory had heartened the leaderless Gordons, who had now joined these others in force, and together they had marched on Aberdeen, gathering numbers all the way. The city had risen to welcome them – even the women were tying blue Covenant ribbons round their dogs' necks, as insult and provocation – and he and Kinghorne had had no option but to retire on Stonehaven, Dunnottar and the Keith country. He urged Montrose's return, and sought guidance, instructions.

The Earl of Marischal was aged nineteen, the Earl of Kinghorne twenty-two.

Their twenty-six year-old general cursed them, the whole Covenant leadership, the folly of men – but, above all, himself – as he raced northwards.

Even by Queen Margaret's Ferry over Forth, Glen Farg, Perth, Gowrie and Strathmore, it was 130 miles to Stonehaven. Montrose rode at his vehement hardest, but it was still two days before, with Pate and his faithful Grahams, he pounded up the steep defensive way to the gun-looped gatehouse of Dunnottar Castle, on its great thrusting rock promontory, amongst the sea-spray and the screaming, wheeling gulls. It was, however, to find the situation less bad than he had feared. The Gordons, many of them from the upland glens, had, after the fashion of hillmen, discovered the city to be a place meet for pillage rather than rescue, and Aberdeen had endured what amounted to a rape, with no single strong hand to command. As a result there had been battles between the indignant citizenry and their saviours, and more looting. Thereafter, well laden with their spoil, most of the Gordons had headed back for their glens. So the Marischal and Kinghorne had, the day previously, marched back, and retaken the town with only sporadic opposition, the Gordon, Ogilvie, Seton and Urquhart lairds and cavalry retiring before them in some confusion. The dogs of Aberdeen were now minus their blue bows again – not a few minus their lives.

The Grahams rode on into the city, tired as they were.

Montrose, deciding that Aberdeen obviously required a lesson as to where its best interests lay, imposed a much stricter regime than heretofore, a curfew, and requisitioning. Also another severe corporate fine. In war, especially civil war, the price for facing both ways – or neither – can be high.

Scouts trailing the retiring Gordon allies sent back reports that they had made, not for Strathbogie but for Gight, a strong castle of a branch of the Gordons, on the Ythan, near Fyvie, much more centrally placed. That they had settled here, rather than retired to their remoter fastnesses, seemed to indicate that this was only a reforming, a gathering of strength for further hostilities. The young Lord Lewis, the thirteen-year-old fire-eater, was said to be there.

Montrose had sent out urgent commands, on his way north, for more men to be mustered to his banner. Waiting three more days for these levies to accumulate, on the 30th of May, with a force of almost 4000, he marched north for Gight.

He found the castle a tough nut to crack, a strong place crowning a tall and rocky eminence amongst the Formartine braes, with the valley-floors around it deliberately flooded and boggy, so that the castle-crowned bluff was but the summit of a sort of island, an island only reachable by a causeway, crooked and gapped, through the marsh, and easily defended. Moreover the swamp-enclosed area was sufficiently large to offer temporary support to considerable numbers of men and horses; there were even cattle grazing there – so it would be difficult to starve out the defenders. Only by artillery could the place be fairly swiftly reduced – and Montrose had no artillery. There was little that they could do but sit down and besiege the place; but at least it would keep the enemy leadership immobilised and out of further mischief meantime. It was inglorious warfare – but anything else would inevitably have produced heavy casualties, with no certainty of success. The thought that he was facing a thirteen-year-old opponent did not help the Graham much, either.

So passed two frustrating, mosquito-haunted days and nights, as May turned to June, and the cuckoos mocked the Covenant's Lieutenant-General from every braeside. Then, almost relievedly, he received news, sent hot-foot from Edinburgh and by Henderson himself, of all people, that the young Viscount Aboyne, with Hamilton's invasion fleet, had persuaded that reluctant warrior to switch plans, leave the unrewarding Firth of Forth, and sail for Aberdeen. All the King's ships had not left, but a sizeable proportion had sailed away, allegedly with much artillery. It was the Tables' urgent commands, therefore, that a landing should be prevented if at all possible, and the city held at all costs.

So the siege of Gight was raised forthwith, and Montrose, feeling distinctly foolish, hurried the twenty-five miles back to Aberdeen. There he found no enemy force, but rumours that there had been a landing farther south – indeed in his own Montrose area. Concerned, he passed on to Stonehaven, recognising that this might be a move to cut his communications with the Covenant forces in the south. He waited at his old headquarters at Dunnottar, while probing squadrons rode off to gain firm news.

The firm news, when it materialised however, came from a different airt. No fleet, but a single small ship flying the King's flag, had made a secret landing *north* of Aberdeen, disembarking a tiny but quite illustrious company – not Hamilton admittedly, but young Aboyne, with the Earls of Tullibardine and Glencairn – the latter Hamilton's cousin – and a well-known mercenary-soldier named Colonel Gunn; also two field-pieces. Where the rest of Hamilton's fleet might be, was not clear; but the present information seemed definite and detailed enough.

Montrose was in something of a quandary. This new leadership clearly indicated a stepping up of enemy activity – especially as it was said that the King had transferred Huntly's Lieutenancy of the North to his second son, Aboyne, only seventeen years of age as he was. On the other hand, where was Hamilton himself, and the main invasion fleet? The rumours that there had been a major landing somewhere farther south, might still have some foundation – and this could have more immediate danger than the arrival of

167

the little group farther north. No word of it came from his scouts or local informants; but it still might be a projected rather than an actual landing. Hamilton had apparently left the Forth; he must be somewhere.

So the Graham waited at Dunnottar, ready to move either way. He utilised the time further to train his forces; and was probably fortunate in having the services of one more of the mercenaries, one Major John Middleton, son of a local Mearns laird, a loud-mouthed, swaggering, uncouth soldier, but experienced and efficient at his trade.

In the event, it was from the north that the trouble developed – and more swiftly than might have been anticipated – while still there was no word of Hamilton. Aboyne made a quick link-up with his brother Lewis, and the enheartened Gordons flocked to their joint standard. They had as many as 4000 clansmen and allies at their backs in a couple of days, determined to avenge the insult to their chief. In brave style they dashed south, and once again Aberdeen fell. The young Gordons had all the traditional fighting spirit missed out of their father. Without delaying in the city, most of their host pushed on southwards for Stonehaven and a decision. Not only so, but they commandeered two Aberdeen vessels, to add to their single King's ship, and put aboard these three a collection of cannon raped from various castles in the area, heavy, rusted and antiquated pieces, as well as the two fine field-pieces brought from the South. The ships were to sail parallel with the Gordon advance, and to bombard the Covenant forces from the sea.

This bold strategy was rather spoiled by strong off-shore winds and driving rain, which kept the vessels out to sea, far out of range, and shrouded the land in dull grey curtaining. Montrose took fullest advantage of the weather – which he reckoned would be apt to unsettle and depress hastily mustered irregulars more than his better-trained and disciplined force – and moved north to take up a strong position at Megray Hill, just inland from Garron Point, two miles north of Stonehaven, where the road from Aberdeen ran through a fairly steep wooded ravine. In the circumstances, since Aboyne was so keen, he would let the Gordons take the initiative.

Whether it was the weather that indeed depressed them, a recognition that Megray was no place to fight a battle, or good advice from the veteran Colonel Gunn, the royalist army ground to a halt. There was no way round Montrose's positions, which he could not block. Artillery could have blasted him out of that ravine and its flanks – but the Gordons' artillery was at sea and nowhere in evidence. It was either a frontal assault against an entrenched foe, with most certain heavy slaughter; or retiral, with Montrose content to sit tight. It took a while to convince the Gordon fire-eaters, a wet and gloomy interval in the rain. They then turned round and retired in good order for Aberdeen again – although taking the elementary precaution of leaving a strong rearguard to continue to bottle up the mouth of the ravine until they were safely withdrawn.

Scarcely a shot had been fired.

Montrose, still concerned about his rear and Hamilton's main army, did not attempt to rush the Gordon retiral, as he might have done. He waited there in the rain, until in the early afternoon Kilpont arrived back from a three-day survey of the coast-line as far south as Arbroath, to declare that there was no single sign of Hamilton or his army. Whatever Henderson and the Tables said, it seemed that the elusive Marquis could be forgotten meantime.

Relieved, Montrose gave the order to advance on Aberdeen.

The weather cleared a little, and a pale sun was gleaming fitfully when, towards early evening, they approached the Dee, the great river which bounded the city to the south. Not unexpectedly they found the Brig o' Dee held against them, the ancient narrow bridge of seven arches, 350 feet long, endowed by the good Bishop Elphinstone, founder of the University, in the days when bishops were more to Scotland's taste. This had been an obvious point of hold-up; but what Montrose had not allowed for was the high spate in which the river was running. Presumably the rain had been even worse in the high Monadh Ruadh mountains to the west where the Dee rose. It was now a wide and raging torrent, and all ideas of fording it could be abandoned. And there was no other bridge.

Nor was it merely that the Brig o' Dee was held against them. The Gordons had stopped there, drawn up their entire army across the river, Highland foot in front, Lowland cavalry behind, flanking the bridge for half a mile on either side, with a strong party of musketeers on the bridge itself.

Montrose took counsel of his only professional. 'What think you, Middleton? Are they safe from us?'

'No force is ever safe from another, of similar strength, my lord. And we are not far off equal strength, I think. If you are sufficiently determined, you can have them.'

'By that, you mean prepared to lose sufficient men, sir?'

'War is not possible without losing men.'

'But wits and generalship may save many lives, sir. And every life a soul before God.'

'I never yet went into battle to save souls, my lord!'

'Perhaps not. But *I* do not forget it. What do you suggest, in this pass, Major?'

'To wear them down. Where they are weakest. A time-honoured maxim, my lord. And where are these like to be weakest? Not in numbers. Not in spirit, I think. Not in broadswords, or even cavalry. But – ammunition, now? For their muskets and hagbuts. I jalouse they'll have no great supplies of powder and shot. We have not, ourselves, by God – and they are like to have less. Have them to use it up, then, without us using our own.'

'Sound, yes. But how?'

'Make cavalry charges. At the bridge-head. A squadron at a time. Many charges. Always drawing off just before coming into musket range. Musketeers and hagbutters, I'll vow, will not sit close under charging horse, without firing well before they are in range.'

'Mm. That is well thought of . . .'

So the Covenant horse, of which Montrose had about 1000, were formed up in their squadrons, and sent in charging, banners waving, trumpets blowing, 200 or so at a time, to the bridge-end, time and again, always to swing away left and right, just out of musket-shot of their target. And each time the ragged rattle and crack of fire rang out. It looked, of course, as though it was the fire which consistently turned the cavalry back – though few men fell. The odd stray or spent shot at times did wound or bring down man or beast; but the losses were very small. Between charges, the enemy were given plenty of opportunity to reload and wait anxiously. In time it probably dawned on the Gordon command that they were being led grievously to waste powder and shot; but it would be an unusual commander who could prevail upon his infantry to sit tight, in an exposed position, under repeated cavalry charging, and to reserve their fire until it could be fully effective. The men, of course, never could tell whether or not this time the riders would indeed thunder down upon them, with no swinging away, and mangled death under slashing swords and horses' hooves be their lot.

Although this manoeuvre, therefore, was successful, so far as it went, and great quantities of Gordon ammunition was expended at little cost to the Covenanters, while the two main armies stood by all but inactive, the time-factor told against the one side as well as the other. The clouds had come down again, and it was going to be early dark for a June night. Admittedly the night might offer new opportunities – but that applied to both almost equally matched sides.

The Gordon command, for their part, had not been just idly watching. Much activity had been going on in the rear; and it was now seen that at least some of this was the bringing up of timber, from near and far, as fuel for great bonfires, placed all along the riverside, and even on the bridge itself. There was to be no darkness for surprise attacks. This, of course, applied equally to the Gordons, and seemed to indicate a purely defensive strategy.

Montrose, who had been bewailing his lack of artillery, decided that he might utilise the hours of darkness with profit. They were still only fourteen miles from Dunnottar; and at Dunnottar and Marischal had a number of old cannon. These were not field-pieces, but fixed and immobile features of the defence. If they could be transported here, first by boat to Covehaven, and then slung between pairs or teams of horses, they might attain a notable surprise with them, and change in the situation.

He gave the Earl Marischal himself the task, since he best knew the country and coast.

It was a wet night, which was both uncomfortable and disappointing – for it meant that the river's level would not sink, as hoped for, to permit fording at selected points.

A grey and chill daybreak, with the Gordon fires flickering low, saw four heavy cannon in position and assembled, with some ball and barrels of powder therefor – though a weary Montrose kept them well hidden meantime. Two more were on the way, but he ordered their arrival delayed unless they could be kept out of the enemy's sight. The Gordons still held to their former positions, the bridge as strongly guarded as ever – however short the defenders might be of ammunition.

James Graham, who had had plenty of time to think of it during that comfortless night, now staged a show, a play-acting, for the opposition's benefit. He sent off a small detachment to ride up the riverside, in full view, westwards. With little delay, a similar picket of horsemen moved off parallel, at the other side, to keep them under observation. They went for some three miles up, to Ardoe, where the river widened, in green levels, and there was a mid-stream island and double ford. The Dee was running as high as ever, but the party proceeded elaborately to make test of it, for depth and current. The thing was barely possible, and really out of the question for an opposed crossing – but still, leaving some of their number still prospecting there, the rest spurred back to Brig o' Dee, as though with news. Thereafter, Montrose made a great display of mounting, parading and inspecting the main mass of his cavalry, before duly despatching them off, squadron after squadron, in the direction of the ford. And, as he had hoped and prayed, almost at once the Gordon cavalry were off, likewise, to deny any crossing. Both mounted hosts disappeared westwards, up-river.

But there was a difference in the topography of the respective banks. The south side was fairly level land, and wooded; while the north was open and sloping upwards after a belt of marshy water-meadows. In consequence, the Gordons' progress was visible along the terraced roadway, whereas the Covenant horsemen were largely hidden in woodland. Moreover, beyond Banchory-Devenick's thicker forest, over a mile up, a wide bend in the river northwards pressed back the road on the far side still farther, and here was the village of Cults. The enemy commander could by no means see what was going on on the south road for well over a mile.

So, whenever all his cavalry was in this thicker woodland, Kilpont, in command, halted the main body. He sent on a small number of horsemen, with all their flags and banners, with orders to show themselves progressing westwards as much as possible. Then, with the Gordon horse well past on the other side, he turned his main body and went spurring back to Brig o' Dee.

Montrose waited long enough for Kilpont's returning host to come into sight, before ordering the cannon to be uncovered and the bombardment begun.

It was complete surprise. The densely massed Highland foot on the other side, quite unprepared for artillery-fire, and unable to hit back, fell into panic – as who would blame them? The cannon were aimed well behind the bridge – since its destruction was the last thing desired – and the defenders on the bridge itself found themselves isolated, as their main force retired precipitately and in confusion, to get out of range.

The returning Covenant cavalry was immediately switched back to charging the bridge-end, as before. And quickly, the musket-fire, fierce, almost hectic, at first, lessened. Yesterday's tactics were proving their worth. Montrose gave the order for a general advance.

It was all over in a brief half-hour. After ragged, scattered musket-fire from the bridge, the holders thereof retreated hurriedly. The cannon increased their range somewhat, and though most of their balls went wide, they made some lucky shots, especially amongst a group of Gordon lairds. The enemy command, hastily seeking to re-form and reorganise their alarmed infantry, and without cavalry support, were unable to do so before the Covenanters were surging across the bridge. Once Montrose's cavalry were over, of course, the thing was decided. One or two counter-attacks were thrown in, especially a determined one led by the new Provost of Aberdeen's own son, one Colonel Johnston; and many clansmen fought bravely. But against a thousand horse, in open country, they had no chance. Aboyne and his brother Lewis, under their father's great banner, were amongst the last to flee – but flee they did; and before there was any sign of Colonel Gunn, who had led the cavalry off, returning from the Fords of Ardoe.

When the issue at Brig o' Dee was clear. Montrose pulled out most of his horse – for a running slaughter was no part of his design, whatever Middleton vociferously advised – and sent them off westwards to deal with the unfortunate Gunn. But, in fact, no mounted battle developed, that veteran knowing at least when further fighting was useless. The royalist cavalry did not wait to make gallant gestures, but galloped off northwards for the Gordon country with all speed.

Aberdeen lay open once again, unhappy city.

There was something like mutiny, even anarchy, in the grey northern town that night. Victorious soldiery like to celebrate, especially when all the facilities lie so conveniently to hand. And when most of their officers are of the same turn of mind. For not only Major Middleton, but the Earls Marischal and Kinghorne – and, of course, all the ministers – were in favour of this wretched city being taught a lesson which would prevent it from ever again ranging itself against the Covenant. But Montrose was adamant. Without the handicap of having to defer to Leslie as overall commander, he was not hesitant about asserting his fullest authority, Military Committee or none. There was to be no sacking of the city. He had to use his own Graham troopers to impose that fiat in the narrow streets that night, and with little help from his leading colleagues – and was not entirely successful, inevitably. And next day, in a tense situation, there were hard words and threats. It was the first military victory of the Civil War – but its consequences were less than wholly happy.

Then, suddenly, unexpectedly, all was changed. Messengers arrived from the South. The war, scarcely begun, was over. Two days previously, King Charles had more or less capitulated. The Pacification of Berwick had been signed. All hostilities were to cease forthwith.

Details emerged. The King's forces, having reached Berwick-on-Tweed, and Hamilton having removed himself from the Forth, Leslie had moved his Covenant army south into Berwickshire, carefully sending word before him that they were coming in all loyalty to welcome the monarch to his Scottish realm. The host had taken up its stance at Duns Law – which could not be called a threatening position but which effectively blocked any royal advance towards Edinburgh. So the two armies glared at each other across the green levels of the Merse, neither side willing to take the first step in hostilities – the King because he was worried about reports from his inimical English parliamentarians in London, and lack of word from Hamilton and the Gordons; and the Covenanters anxious to postpone outright and treasonable attack on their lawful monarch, and concerned lest such should involve them in war with England itself. So Henderson sent secret messages and tentative terms to Berwick – and to the surprise of all, Charles accepted them. Possibly the timely arrival of Hamilton there, without having struck a blow in this peculiar war, was the last straw. A conference followed, at Birks near Berwick, and at it the King agreed that in future all ecclesiastical questions should be dealt with by free General Assemblies of the Kirk; and civil affairs should be put before duly called and regular parliaments. Charles Stewart was at his most courteous, reasonable, sadly noble. Bishops, Liturgies and the like would no more be imposed upon an unwilling people. As sovereign, he was concerned only that peace should prevail, the rule of law, and the wellbeing of his leal subjects. It was accepted that both armies should be disbanded, and all warlike behaviour cease. There were to be no reprisals, on either side, and all prisoners were to be freed.

So sanity and goodwill, belatedly, prevailed. Aberdeen in especial heaved a great and corporate sigh of relief.

Montrose was summoned south to deliver up his commission as Lieutenant-General, to attend a full meeting of the Tables to homologate all this, and in due course take part in another General Assembly and subsequent parliament. Winding up affairs in Aberdeen, he handed the place back to its Provost and magistrates, sent civil word to Aboyne and the Gordons regretting any inconvenience caused, dismissed his lieutenants, sent his army home, and said a thankful goodbye to his Military Committee – which now seemed somewhat dejected and at a loss. He took the road for Edinburgh.

It did not fail to occur to him, as he rode, that the Battle of the Brig o' Dee, the only real armed clash of the entire affair, had been fought and won after peace had been declared.

14

DESPITE ALL THEIR TRIUMPHS, THEIR CONVICTION, EVEN their talents, it was a strangely uneasy, even diffident group that waited in the Great Hall of Berwick Castle, perched high on its bluff above the town and the silver Tweed, six men who eyed each other a little askance and fidgeted rather. Yet these represented the true rulers of Scotland, their power and activities the reason for their presence here – while the man they waited to see represented weakness, failure, ineffectiveness. All were very much aware of the fact – yet achieved little confidence therefore. Bearding archbishops, high commissioners and ambassadors was one thing; facing the King in person was something quite other. That they had been *summoned* here, and had come, was indicative of their state – even though only six had come, where fourteen had been summoned, and by name; and of the six, Alexander Henderson had come without being summoned. Rothes, Loudoun, Lothian, Dunfermline and Montrose, all earls of Scotland, knew that they were in the right, held all the cards – but shuffled nevertheless.

An elegant young Gentleman of the Bedchamber, Will Murray by name, son only of a minister of Dysart in Fife but high in the King's favour, opened a door.

'His Majesty will receive you now, my lords,' he said. 'Come.'

In the end, Montrose went first, as the others all held back, it not being in his nature to insist on deferring to anyone. They were ushered into a small and simple chamber in a flanking-tower, without display or formality. Here was no chair-of-state, no heralds or trumpeters, no ranks of dignitaries – only Charles Stewart, dignity itself, sitting at a small table by the window, with an inoffensive-looking cleric in episcopal garb standing near by. Montrose bowed low, at his second sighting of his monarch, as did those behind him, the black-robed Henderson at the rear noticeably less low than the others.

The King seemed to have aged a little in those three years since the Graham had last seen him, but the process made him look only the more noble. Calm, a little sad, his great lustrous Stewart eyes so deeply full of patient understanding and care, he looked every inch a king. Bare-headed, hair falling in natural waves to his shoulders, he was dressed simply enough in the royal blue that he favoured, with deep lace collar and ruffles at slender wrists. He had been writing, a quill still in his hand.

'My lord of Montrose!' he said – and his voice was kind, almost warm. 'I rejoice to see you once more. A captain of renown now, I am told. My lord of Dunfermline. My lord of Rothes.' The smile was a little less warm. 'My lord of Loudoun . . .' He paused, fine brows raised. 'But five, six, of you? These only? Where are your friends? Whom I summoned. My good lord of Argyll? My lord of Eglinton? Of Wemyss? Of Cassillis?'

It had been agreed that Rothes, the oldest, should act spokesman; but since he said no word, Montrose made answer.

'All send their loyal devotion and greeting, Sire. But all could not leave their duties at one time. And some were at too great a distance.' In fact, Argyll had flatly refused to attend, and the Tables had forbidden others. 'But we six have full authority to speak on behalf of all, Your Grace.'

'The King's Highness prefers Majesty to Grace, my lords.' Will Murray said quietly, at their backs.

'Their attendance was a summons, my lord – not an invitation,' the King mentioned, but more in mild reproach than anger. 'I must not blame you, however, for the failings of others – you who *have* come. Forgive me, my friends. And this gentleman, whom it has not been my pleasure to have met hitherto?'

'The Reverend Master Alexander Henderson, formerly of Leuchars, now of Edinburgh's High Kirk, Sire. Moderator of the General Assembly.'

'Ah, yes. The General Assembly. I have heard of Mr Henderson. He has even honoured us with letters. I greet you, sir.'

177

Stiffly the minister bowed. 'Your Grace is kind,' he said. 'I came unbidden – but for good reason.'

'Majesty,' Murray jerked again.

'Your reasons, sir, I hope, for your breaking of our compact and treaty, the so-called Pacification of this Berwick? This has much grieved me, my friends.'

'*We* break the treaty!' Rothes burst out. 'Of a truth, Your Grace – Your Majesty, the boot is on the other leg! You have called the bishops to the new Assembly! After all that has been done and said! It is beyond all belief! Bishops again!' He glared at the prelate at the King's side.

'Control yourself, my lord,' that cleric said. 'Here is no way to speak in His Majesty's presence.'

'Sir – I do not require any English clerk to tell me how I should speak with my liege lord! It is my duty as an earl of the Scots realm to advise His Grace. And I do so advise him that in this of the bishops he has made grievous error. To call them to another Assembly is beyond all in folly. Against all that was decided here at Berwick. The Kirk of Scotland, in Assembly, has abolished bishops.'

'You say so, my lord of Rothes?' Charles's voice was sorrowful but restrained, reasonable. They had never been on good terms, these two. 'Did your Assembly *appoint* the bishops? No. Then how may it abolish them? But, even allowing it jurisdiction in the matter, surely the bishops had the right to appear before the Assembly that sought to depose them, to speak for themselves, to present their case? You call your Assembly the high court of the Church. It is the veriest, simplest, right of any subject of mine, in any of my realms, to appear before the court that tries him, to answer charges before judgment. You are all holders of jurisdictions, my lords. Is it not so?'

There was a pause, since none could gainsay that. Henderson, not being any sort of magistrate or judge, did his best. 'The bishops could have attended the Glasgow Assembly, Sire. None forbad them. But they chose otherwise.'

'Scarce the same thing, Mr Henderson.' That was said with a sigh, not harshly.

'To summon the bishops to attend this Edinburgh Assembly, in August, is an affront to the Kirk and people of Scotland,' Rothes went on, bluntly. 'Your Majesty must see it.'

'I see, my lord, other things. That your Tables continue to meet and to exercise authority – the authority of *my* Privy Council. Your Covenant army is not disbanded, nor your General Leslie dismissed. My Treasurer, the Earl of Traquair, is attacked and ill-used in Edinburgh streets. Others of my loyal servants likewise. These things I see, my lord – and require your explanations. And apologies. Do I have them?'

'We did not come here to make apologies, Sire,' Rothes declared grimly out of a tense silence. 'The time is past for such bairn's play.'

'Then why did you come, my lord? For I cannot believe that it was but in humble obedience to my royal summons!'

'We came to inform and advise Your Majesty. Inform that by this calling of the bishops again, you have set back the cause of peace in Scotland in marked degree. And to advise that you seek to undo some of the harm done by recalling the former bishops forthwith. Preferably to England – where they might be better thought of!'

'And if I choose to disregard such unsought advice, my lord?'

'Then Your Majesty must bear the consequences. Renewed warfare in Scotland. And the possibility that the Scots might join forces with your English Puritans – who do not love bishops any more than do we!'

That brought gasps even from Rothes' fellow Covenanters. And a hand upraised in horror from the cleric.

'How . . . how dare you speak the King so!' he cried.

'Who is this English clerk?' Rothes demanded.

Murray answered him. 'No Englishman, my lord. But Dr Balcanquhal, from my own Fife. And yours. Dean of Durham.'

'So much the worse for him!'

Charles spoke, quietly. 'Are you making a threat, my lord? To me – the King! In this of the Puritans?'

'I would name it advice, and warning, Sire.'

Charles rose from his chair. 'I cannot accept such threats from any subject of mine,' he said, head shaking. 'I find your manner and behaviour unsuitable and unsupportable, my lord. Were you not here on my royal summons, and therefore presently secure from the consequences of my displeasure, you would discover how ill-advised are your words. You have my permission to retire, sir.'

Curtly Rothes bowed, and turned away. The others, glancing at each other in doubt, began to move after him.

Not so Montrose. He had been shocked at Rothes' tone. The man was obviously not well, and all his bonhomie and shrewd canniness seemed to have disappeared with his health – like his Doric speech. His attitude in the monarch's presence was not only deplorable, but damaging to the Covenant cause. They had not come all this way deliberately to offend the King and add to their problems. Today, whatever the rights and wrongs of the conflict, Charles had become the injured party.

'Sire,' he exclaimed, 'of your royal clemency, hear me. My lord of Rothes has not spoken so by our prior agreement. He is a sick man – not himself. He and we all, are loyal subjects of Your Majesty. We did not come here to threaten nor to distress Your Highness. But to discuss with you the better-ment of your Scots realm's affairs.'

'Then, my lord of Montrose, I think that you chose but an unfortunate spokesman !'

'Perhaps, Sire. But the Earl of Rothes is senior as to age. We crave your royal indulgence.'

'Very well.' The King sat down again. Rothes went out, slamming the door behind him. But the others lingered.

'We believe, Sire, that mistakes, errors, on both sides of this controversy, might have been avoided had we been able to speak face to face. Instead of through intermediaries who have proved by no means reliable. This of the bishops and the next Assembly, for instance. If Your Majesty had been advised to ask that they attend a special hearing, to answer and speak to their deposition at the previous Assembly, instead of summoning them as of their right to take part, no clash need have occurred.'

There was a stir and murmur behind him, but no outright denial of that from the others.

'You would have me submit the bishops, the lords spiritual of my Church, to your trial, my lord ?'

'Such was Your Majesty's own figure, a trial and judg-ment. Speaking before a court. But my contention is that if we could but consult together, from time to time, much distress, misunderstanding, might be spared all. Your Highness's advice on matters Scots has, I fear, been but poor. And the first that we are apt to hear of your policies is their implementation.'

'And you conceive this to be improper, my lord? I have a Scots Privy Council to advise me.'

'Of whom the former bishops still comprise the majority, Sire!' That was Loudoun's first contribution.

'You would wish me to turn your Tables into my Privy Council, sir?'

'Not so. But your present Council has served you but ill. We urge that your interests would be better served by keeping in touch with the Tables, Sire,' Montrose suggested, moderate of voice.

'Very well. Your urgings I have heard and will consider, my lord.' There was a pause.

'And the bishops, Sire?' Henderson asked. 'Do they attend, or do they not?'

'That is for my decision, sir. But . . . they will not attend to be insulted. Nor, I think, will I.'

Quickly the Covenanters glanced at each other.

'Were you . . did Your Majesty think to attend? To attend the General Assembly in person?' Seton, Earl of Dunfermline, put their question.

'I did. That is why I am still here, at Berwick.'

'But . . . Traquair? We understood that the Earl of Traquair, the Treasurer, was now your High Commissioner?'

'My Commissioner in Scotland, yes. When I am not present. And my lord of Hamilton . . . otherwise occupied. Had I come, he would of course have stood down. But, after today, I fear, that is not possible. I can by no means attend an Assembly where the Crown is like to be insulted. As it has been today. This you must perceive.'

Montrose spoke. 'Sire – I pray that you reconsider. We knew nothing of your possible royal attendance. It would greatly rejoice and encourage your loyal Scots subjects. If . . . if . . .'

'If Your Majesty acted somewhat other than did your Lord High Commissioner at the last!' Henderson ended for him, grimly.

King Charles rose to his feet, once more. 'My lords, gentlemen – I cannot, will not, be harried and assailed thus. I think that you perhaps forget yourselves, in your pride. I counsel you to beware of that sin, that deadly sin. You, my lord of Montrose, at least I thank for your courtesy. I bid you all God-speed. You may retire. This audience is now ended.'

Bowing, they backed out – although Montrose would have waited to say more, if he might. But such royal dismissal was not to be questioned.

His colleagues eyed him not a little askance, and less than kindly, as they left the presence.

PART TWO

15

IT WAS ALMOST A YEAR LATER, AND IN VERY DIFFERENT circumstances, before Montrose was near Berwick again. He alone of the party of six who had so displeased King Charles now considered the fast-flowing Tweed and wondered. His companions now were soldiers, not great nobles and emissaries and churchmen; and although he was much more at ease in their company, still he wondered. Indeed this wondering, doubt, questioning of self and of others, so unlike the man's basic character, had become ever more part of James Graham's life these many months. He seemed to be forever being carried along on a tide, a flood, so much more dark, swift and daunting than this Tweed, carried where he would not, questioning the direction, fearing the outcome, suspicious of others and himself suspect. Quite gone were the days of enthusiasm, faith, hope. He was still a Lieutenant-General of the Covenant forces – but more, he imagined, that he and his Grahams and friends might be kept under the keen and stern eye of the Commander-in-Chief, Alexander Leslie, than for any trust in himself.

For it was war again, of a sort. The Covenant army was remustered and encamped at Duns Law once more, with actual invasion of England imminent. And crazily, Montrose and his 2500 personally raised men, Grahams, vassals, allies and friends from Strathearn, Stirlingshire and the Mearns, were to form the van, to lead the way in an exercise of which he disapproved. To invade England – how could that be called necessary for the freedom of worship in Scotland? Which was his concern, all that he had joined this cause to achieve. Even though the main object of the expedition was not battle, but to arouse the dissident English, the Puritans and parliamentarians, to rise and so bring pressure to bear on the King.

This invasion, however, was only one of a long line of Montrose's disagreements with the main Covenant leadership. The Edinburgh Assembly of the Kirk had taken place last August. No bishops had dared to show their faces, despite the King's refusal to withdraw his summons to them to appear. But, under David Dickson's Moderatorship this time, the proceedings had degenerated into little more than an anti-King demonstration of snarling vehemence. Charles had held to his decision not to attend, appointing Traquair, a weak man, as his Commissioner; but he had sent a statement of his case, written by the same Dr Balcanquhal, Dean of Durham – and this was read amidst hootings, and rejected with a violence and contumely most derogatory to the monarch. And it was ordered that every citizen of Scotland *must* sign the Covenant. Montrose had objected to much, especially the arrogant declaration that episcopacy, even in England, was unlawful and to be rooted out.

Thereafter a parliament, the first in Scotland for many a year, had been held. And here the Earl of Argyll at last moved out into the open, dominating the proceedings, not so much by his strangely shrinking presence as by his influence, his cunning manipulation of the more extreme elements, his willingness now to become the focus and centre of the anti-Charles forces which were becoming ever more vociferous. That parliament of 1640, in effect, reduced the monarch, in Scotland, to a mere symbol, a name, without power. Montrose had fought against the whole trend of it, but without avail. Whispers had begun to circulate in Scotland; one, that Argyll was seeking the Scots throne for himself – he could claim descent from Bruce's sister; and the other, that Montrose had been seduced by the King from his allegiance to Covenant and Kirk.

And that was not the worst. The Tables were reconstituted by parliament a more official Committee of the Estates; and though Montrose still sat upon it he was in a permanent minority now. Argyll, oddly enough, did not let himself be nominated a member; but he had a faithful group of supporters thereon, led by Loudoun, who served him well. The Campbell had had himself appointed to Montrose's own previous duty of ensuring that the Gordons and other North-East clans did not trouble the Covenant's rear in any future activities; and very differently from the Graham he went about his task. With 5000 of his own clansmen, he proceeded in person on what was nothing more than an old-fashioned and savage clan-feuding foray against his hereditary enemies, leaving a terrible trail of ferocity, slain and tortured men, burned homes and domestic disaster, right across Scotland's North, from Argyll, through Atholl and Lochaber, to the Angus glens. The Ogilvys of Airlie were long-standing foes of the Campbells; and concerned to prevent further savagery, Montrose had persuaded the young Lord Ogilvy – his father, the Earl of Airlie, was in England with the King – to hand over Airlie Castle to local Covenanters, "in the public interest"; and had sent urgent message of the fact to the advancing Argyll. But the Campbell was not to be balked of his prey. He descended upon the Airlie country with redoubled fury of fire and sword, and burned not only Airlie Castle but the lesser and more remote castle of Forter, in which Lady Airlie had taken refuge, with unrelenting ferocity, driving the Countess into the hills, a pathetic refugee.

All this while Montrose was raising his regiments in Stirlingshire and Strathearn.

So now the Graham was prospecting the fords of Tweed, over which, in due course, he would lead the van of the Scots army into England – and doing so a prey to doubts indeed. Even the river was adding to his problems. It had been another deplorably wet season, and all the waters were running high, the mighty Tweed no exception. Royal forces still held the bridge at Berwick – although the King, of course, no longer was there. There was no other bridge. Montrose had decided on the Coldstream area, some fifteen miles from Berwick. Not that there was much choice; fords were few and far between on that wide, swift-running stream; and even hereabouts, unless the weather much improved, any crossing was going to be difficult for cavalry and impossible for foot.

Black Pate came spurring back from an investigation farther upstream, having discerned no improvement. So Coldstream it must be – where King James the Fourth had crossed, 127 years earlier, before Flodden. Might that be no ill omen.

Returning to Duns, twelve miles to the north, Montrose

found the great camp in a stir. The Earl of Argyll had arrived, from the North.

The inevitable clash was not long in coming. When Montrose repaired to the Commander-in-Chief's tent, to report his findings, it was to find the Campbell closeted with Leslie.

The older soldier pinched his bony chin, looking from one to the other. 'Here's a pleasant meeting, my lords,' he said, grinning. 'Convenient, is it no'?'

'I do not esteem it either pleasant or convenient,' the Graham answered, stiffly for him. 'My business is with yourself. I interrupt. I will return, with word of the fords, at a better moment.'

'Tush, man – not so hasty! My lord of Argyll and yourself will have much to discuss. The entire fate o' this Scotland, belike! Say on, say on!'

'My lord of Montrose will be weary with travel,' Argyll said in the softly lisping yet grating voice. 'After refreshment, no doubt, we can speak together more kindly.'

'I am not weary. And I cannot conceive of converse between us as being kindly, in this pass!'

The Campbell spread his hands, wordless.

'Come, come, my lord! *MacCailean Mor* has come all this road of set purpose to see you. Here's no way to greet him.'

'To see me? I cannot conceive why!'

'You are too modest, my lord,' Argyll said thinly. 'I have a paper, which requires your signature. Yours, and Master Henderson's. His I have obtained.'

'Ah. Then it must be important. To bring you, in person.'

'The Committee conceives it to be so. The Committee of the Estates. Requiring signature before you leave for England.'

'To what end?'

'A matter of administration. During the absence of yourselves and the army. The country will be much . . . impoverished. It is the appointment of myself, my unworthy self, as responsible for the peace of part of the country.'

'The peace? You! What part? Other than your own Argyll?'

'That part, my lord, lying north of the Rivers Forth and Clyde.'

'Dear God! Forth and Clyde? That is . . . that is more than half Scotland!'

'The stony half!' Argyll agreed dryly.

'I'll not believe it! This – this would make you, one man, master of half the land!'

'Not master – servant. My task to preserve the peace and see to good governance. At your backs, gentlemen. In the name of the Committee of the Estates. Its servant.'

'As you have just kept the peace in Angus! In Atholl. In Badenoch and Lochaber!'

'As you say, my lord. As I did, on the authority and the behalf of the said Committee.'

'Did the Committee authorise you to burn Airlie Castle? After it had surrendered to the said Committee, on my command?'

'I had full authority to take all steps as appeared to be necessary. As had you, my lord Montrose, when you were Lieutenant-General amongst that nest of vipers!' The Campbell raised his consistently down-bent, diffident gaze for a moment, to shoot a venomous glance at the younger man. Of that glance there could be no doubt – although most of the time it was hard to say just where Argyll looked, on account of his squint.

'I did not use *my* commission as excuse for rapine, torture, slaughter, war against women and bairns! I will not sign such paper, delivering thousands of my fellow countrymen into your hands, sir!'

There was a long silence. Leslie coughed, scratched a leg, and appeared to be grinning to himself.

'Your words, unbecoming in a Christian gentleman who has set his hand to the Lord's work, pain me,' Argyll said, at length, apparently considering the floor of trampled grass. 'But perhaps I should remind your lordship that this is a decision of the Committee of the Estates. Not mine. All members signed it, save Master Henderson and yourself, here with the army. Henderson has now signed. Your signature is requested. But nowhere have I heard that it is *essential*. That my commission is invalid lacking one signature. I am Lieutenant and Justiciar of the North, whatever you may say, sir. As well to recognise the fact.'

Montrose took a deep breath. Here it was again – he was faced with the damnable decision of those who committed themselves to a cause; whether to abandon it when things went wrong, or to compound, stay on, in a position where better influence might still be exercised. How many times he had put this grim choice to himself of late? To gain a little time, and aiming perhaps to shake the Campbell's hypocritical pained righteousness, he went on, slowly.

'Perhaps there is some truth in the tale that men tell, in the North? That your men, in Atholl and Angus, slew and burned to the slogan "In the name of King Campbell, not King Stewart!"'

Argyll licked his thin lips. 'I charge you, watch your tongue, Graham!' he rasped.

'My tongue is still my own. As is my signature!'

'Then take heed lest they become otherwise!'

'None will make them so, I think.'

'Be not so sure. There are powers which even the Graham must bow to.'

'To be sure. God's. And the King's.'

'And the Committee of the Estates'!'

'That Committee I lend my service to. Not my honour nor and yet my conscience.'

'Remember that, when it comes to question you!'

'Question? Me? Why should the Committee question me, my lord? One of its own members. Who has served it only well. Better, and longer, than most!'

'Served it well? Some say different. When you encourage and nurture the Committee's enemies.'

'Have I done so?'

'What of Huntly? Of Aboyne? Ogilvy? Others without number. Aye, old Southesk himself, and Carnegie likewise. All enemies of the Covenant and Christ's Kirk. Your whole campaign in the North-East has been stained with lenience to God's foes, comfort to those who oppose Him.'

'Lenience? So that is it! None will accuse *you* of that, at least!'

'God's enemies are Campbell's enemies,' the other said. In anyone else, that would have sounded as ridiculous as it was objectionable. But not in this man. He might even believe it.

Shaken a little, Montrose glanced at Leslie. That hard-bitten veteran looked as though he might be enjoying himself. He probably found them both equally absurd.

'Do you sign my commission, my lord? Or do you not?'

Argyll's voice was back to the sibilant West Highland normal.

'Let me see it.'

Scanning the paper he was handed, James Graham saw that it was a typical commission, only unusual in that it gave Archibald Campbell complete powers over the largest if not the most populous area of Scotland. He drummed fingers on it for a moment. Then spoke. 'Have you a pen, sir?'

Leslie emitted a gleeful little croak of a laugh, and pushed over a quill and ink-horn from the clutter on his table. Argyll said nothing.

Montrose dipped the pen, and smoothed out the paper. He applied one to the other. But he wrote more than just the single word at the foot. He wrote quite a number of words, indeed. Then he signed it, in the space left for him at the top of the list, next to Loudoun's, and pushed it from him.

Argyll grabbed it, and held it close, to peer. Then he stammered something explosive, undoubtedly a Gaelic curse, rising to his feet and slamming down a clenched fist on the document.

'For the peace and good governance of that part of the realm, my lord,' Montrose observed. 'Do you believe only yourself fit to ensure it?'

'This – this is outrage!' The other was almost choking. 'Not to be tolerated . . .'

'You have what you came for. My signature.'

'These . . . these others! Time-servers. Toadies of your own!'

'Earls of Scotland, sir. With as good a right as Argyll to serve the Committee while others of us are furth the country. They are men of experience in affairs. They will but strengthen your hand!'

Leslie reached out, to claw the paper to him. He tee-heed a high-pitched, sniggering laugh. 'So – that's it! Mar! Home! Cassillis! Kinnoull! These put in to share! Share your commission. God – here's a ploy! S'wounds – here's a tod amongst the poults!' His glance at the younger man was almost admiring.

'It will not stand – it will not stand, I say!' Argyll exclaimed. 'The Committee will not have it. All the signatures made null. By this . . . this insolent addition! They will not have it. I shall see that they do not.'

'Indeed, my lord? As yet you are not a member of the

Committee. Whereas I am. It will stand – until another commission comes, requiring my signature. In England!'

The Campbell glared, just where was hard to say. But there was no doubt as to its quality.

Montrose turned back to Leslie. 'Sir – I have to report that the Tweed is still impassable. I will ford it, with the van, at Coldstream. But not for days yet. The people there tell me that the river will take three days to drop, after wet weather. And still it rains. Cavalry might cross before, but not foot.'

'Aye. As I feared. So be it . . .'

Montrose was not one to allow physical weariness to dictate his actions. Within two hours of the return to camp, he and Pate Graham were spurring northwards through the Lammermuir Hills, the rain and dusk notwithstanding.

At Edinburgh, forty miles north, they went straight to Merchiston Castle, where they got Archie Napier out of his bed, for urgent discussion. From him they learned enough to know that further riding was ahead of them. Borrowing fresh horses, and rousing some of Napier's men there and then, as messengers, they set out once more through the July night, this time almost due westwards.

Dawn found them thirty-five miles on, and half-way to Glasgow, clattering spent mounts up the steep brae to Cumbernauld Castle, in the skirts of the Kilsyth Hills. This was the house of John Fleming, Earl of Wigtown, Montrose's friend and distant kinsman. More important perhaps, here visiting was the Lord Almond, heir to the Livingstone Earl of Callander, who was another Lieutenant-General to Leslie, indeed second-in-command since Montrose himself only had charge of the van.

With more messengers sent out, the two weary horsemen retired to sleep.

When they were awakened, in the early afternoon, most of the men summoned to Cumbernauld had arrived, an illustrious company. There were the Earls of Home and Mar, whose names Montrose had inserted into Argyll's commission. Also Kinghorne, Seaforth, Atholl and the Marischal, plus the Lords Boyd, Erskine and Ker. The Earls of Perth and Kellie, and the Lord Drummond arrived soon thereafter. With Wigtown and Almond, they represented a

good cross-section of the moderate Covenanting nobility.
And the Graham believed that he could trust them all. None
were members of the ruling Committee of the Estates, save
himself. Others he would have called; but they were too far
afield to be brought here in time. He was fortunate to have
caught his two previous lieutenants, Kinghorne and the
Marischal, who had been training their new regiments near
Edinburgh.

When all were assembled, Montrose addressed them. 'My
friends,' he said, 'some of you know why I have had the
temerity to bring you here; some may not know all my mind,
I think – if I know it myself. But most have come at some
inconvenience – for which I crave your pardon. But I would
not have asked you, nor myself come all the way from my
regiments at Duns, in haste – nor prevented my lord Almond
from returning this morning to the army there – had I not
deemed it sufficiently important.'

There was a stir of anticipation.

'For long I have been concerned at the manner in which
the Covenant cause, which we have all embraced, has
become spoiled and misdirected. There are times, now, when
I scarce recognise it for the noble cause to which we set our
hands. You all know it. I need not labour it. But you will
forgive me if I trace the beginnings of the ill to that day
when the Earl of Argyll announced his adherence to the
Covenant, at the Glasgow Assembly.'

There was a growl of agreement from all present.

'Argyll is no friend of mine, and therefore I must, and do,
take heed against my own prejudice. But it is proven fact
that the Campbell controls much of the Committee of the
Estates today, encourages the fiercer Presbyterian factions
for his own ends, and increasingly has his way in this realm.
To its hurt, I say. He has gained altogether overmuch power,
to soil a fair cause. And you all know how he has exercised
that power, in the North, this last month!'

Atholl and Mar, whose lands had been overrun by the
Campbell horde on its way to Angus, led the chorus of
assent.

'Last night, my friends, Argyll brought to me at Duns, for
my signature as member of the Committee, his new commission therefrom to have sole authority in all Scotland north
of the Forth and Clyde. Argyll alone ...'

He got no further, in the uproar of dismay and anger.

When he gained quiet, Montrose went on to describe what he had done, and the probable consequences. It was time to call a halt, he declared. 'At Argyll's instigation, the Covenant cause is fast becoming not a cause to free religion but a cause to pull down the King and raise the Campbell ! King Charles has been foolish, ill-advised, obstinate; but he is still our King and liege lord. Our cause puts itself ever more in the wrong, in this. And I, for one, will not stand by and see Charles Stewart replaced by Archibald Campbell !'

'Nor I !'

'Nor I !'

'A plague on that ill-favoured fox !'

'Fox, yes. But foxes are cunning. It behoves us not to forget it. Argyll is a clever man – make no mistake. If he is to be countered, it must be by shrewd means. And unity amongst the right-minded. He will divide us if he may. We here are all loyal to the King, however mistaken he may be. He is *Ard Righ,* the High King of Scots – and we, his earls, are the lesser kings. This has always been our status in this ancient realm, from beyond history. A status that has its duties. We have the duty to advise, warn and guide the King, when he is wrong – not to pull him down. Is that agreed?'

All admitted it.

'Then I say that we should make a compact. A bond, if you like. To bind ourselves, each and all, to resist the schemings and savageries of Argyll, to uphold the true Covenant cause and freedom of worship, and to maintain the King on his throne, better advised. See you – the Campbell has his friends and bought men, who will support his every move. We must prove as united, as ready to act. Others will adhere to us, later. The Lord Napier sent his fullest support. But here we have a resounding company to begin the climbing of Argyll's wings ! How say you?'

There was no dissentient voice in the loud and long acclaim.

They thereupon thrashed out a statement which would cover their intentions without specifically naming Argyll or the extreme left-wing ministers. They proclaimed their loyalty to the King, their adherence to the National Covenant, and how they had joined themselves together for the maintenance and defence of freedom. But that, by the practices of a few, their country was now suffering; so that now the undersigned bound themselves to hazard, if need be, their lives, their fortunes and estates, to see that these objectives were not controverted by any soever; and to act together in so far as might consist with the good and weal of the realm and the public interest.

All signed.

Copies were made, and subscribed; and with the ink barely dry, Montrose and Black Pate, with Almond in company now, were off again, on the long road back to Berwickshire and the army.

In the end, it was many days, weeks later, in that deplorable summer, before Leslie was able to set his force of 23,000 foot and 3000 horse in motion. The delay was not all in the high state of the Tweed, and the presence of royalist forces patrolling the far bank. The Committee had decided, sensibly, that proclamations should be sent before the army, into England, emphasising that this was no invasion, that the Scots had no quarrel with the English people nor desire to make war against them, but that it was only a means of convincing King Charles and his assembled forces in the North that they must come to terms with the dissidents on on both sides of the Border.

The river was still a formidable obstacle for men on foot. To encourage the doubtful infantry, and to set the right tone for the proceedings, Montrose himself waded in and across, alone, fully clad and armed as he was, and then back again. Where such happily uncomplicated matters were concerned he was in his cheerful element; indeed, he had been looking forward to the actual campaigning, as distinct from the politics thereof, almost more than he would have admitted. This gesture he made under the eyes of a troop of English horse which had been watching them at a discreet distance on the other shore, but prudently vanished once the real crossing began. Montrose ordered a squadron of cavalry to move into the water and there to stand, in close order, to act as a breakwater for the current and had his foot move across, arm in arm, just below them. All got safely over.

By-passing Berwick entirely, they headed southwards, un-opposed, through central Northumberland, two regiments of 1000 horse and 1500 foot. This was very much Montrose's personal force, largely drawn from his own clan and estates, the cavalry Lowland lairds and their tenants, the foot mainly hillmen from Strathearn, the Highland Line and the Lennox, some of the fastest-moving infantry in the land, lightly armed, fleet of foot. It was an ideal force for the van of a great army, the horse deployed in depth, ranging the countryside on either flank, the foot pressing straight ahead, at speed, eating up the miles, clearing the way but leaving the main force behind to consolidate.

Not that a deal of clearing or consolidation proved to be necessary. Certainly, English videttes from Berwick kept them company and under observation, but at maximum range and carefully avoiding any clash. And the local people showed not the slighest concern. Clearly the Northumbrians accepted the proclamation's terms to the effect that they were not being invaded. A less rousing Scots affray over the Border had never been mounted. It was the 20th of August.

Montrose chose a camp-site for the main army at Millfield, ten miles from Tweed, in the Till valley, and pressed on with his own force another five miles nearly to Wooler. There they spent an undisturbed night, with scouts posted over a wide perimeter.

Next day was equally uneventful. Riders from Leslie informed that the King's Berwick army of about 5000 was retiring fast down the coast towards Newcastle, definitely not concerned with giving fight at this stage. Orders were to press on to the Tyne, west of Newcastle, and there halt.

That they did, without interference, avoiding all centres of population such as Wooler and Alnwick and Morpeth. Driving fast, Montrose reached the Tyne at Newburn, some five miles upstream from Newcastle, in three more days, and there had to wait for another three while the main army came up – acting now as wary bait for Leslie's trap.

But the mouse would not nibble. The Lord Conway was the King's Major-General at Newcastle, a cautious individual with a restive and ill-assorted force which, he complained, was only fit for Bedlam and the Bridewell. Probably he was wise to hold back. Strafford was his senior officer, based at York, and he made no move to advance to his subordinate's aid, declaring that the King himself had left

London on the day the Scots crossed Tweed, to take personal command, so that, meantime, a holding action was advisable.

Montrose, at Newburn, learned off this swiftly; for the English Puritans, Presbyterians and dissenters generally, conceiving the Scots cause their own, were quick at sending information. The Graham was no less swift at passing it back to Leslie, with his own comments. The last thing they wanted was for King Charles to be personally involved. So long as he was not there, they could make use of the fiction that they were not in arms against their monarch, but against his advisers. But if he led his forces in person any attack thereon must rank as treason, and would gravely tie the Scots' hands. Montrose advised an immediate assault on Conway before the King could put in an appearance. Moreover, spies in Newcastle reported that the townspeople were mainly of dissenting mind, and also smarting from the outrages of Conway's unruly soldiery. He suggested letters be sent to the Mayor and local leaders declaring that the city would be left unharmed if co-operation with the Scots was forthcoming.

It was. Newcastle gave Conway notice to quit; and that sensible man, deciding that King Charles was the best man to direct his own strategy, commenced a retiral on York. However, Montrose now commanded both sides of the Tyne, astride the fords at Newburn; and Leslie, coming up with his cannon, was able to cut Conway's line of retreat in the most dramatic fashion by sustained artillery-fire. There was no real opposition. The English cavalry fled headlong for Durham, abandoning the foot – which turned and raced back to unwelcoming Newcastle in complete disorder, abruptly a horde of refugees instead of an army. It was all quite shameful. There were one or two local scuffles, but nothing worth calling even a skirmish. Total casualties on the royal side amounted to less than sixty; on the Scots side they did not reach a dozen. Yet this was the main part of the King's army, destroyed almost without a blow.

Charles reached York, and stayed there. He had little hope of raising another army, meantime. The Short Parliament had refused to finance this one – hence its quality; and certainly it would not finance another. The tide of Puritanism was rising. There was ever-growing disaffection in the South, with even parliamentary demands for the abolition of episcopacy. Charles was obstinate and no craven, but even he could not fail to read the signs. With the Scots beginning to settle in at Newcastle, most evidently for a long stay, he called for negotiations with his loyal Scots subjects.

The Second Bishops' War had ended even more swiftly and ingloriously than the first.

From Newcastle James Graham wrote a letter to Charles Stewart at York. It was written in sympathy and loyal duty, assuring the King that, like himself, the great majority of the Scots people were loyal, and that if His Majesty would finally dispose of the bishops' question and accept the Covenant, he would find that he had no more devoted subjects. It was a simple letter, the gesture of a warm-hearted man to one to whom he owed allegiance and who was bound to be in a sorely distressed state of mind.

It was, in effect, to change the course of history.

16

IN NOVEMBER, STILL WITH THE ARMY OF OCCUPATION IN England, Montrose received a summons to attend a meeting of the Committee of the Estates, in Edinburgh. He was nothing loth, for Newcastle had its limitations as a wintering place for a Scots nobleman. Perhaps, however, he should have perceived some significance in the fact that Almond, the second-in-command, and two colonels of regiments, Kinghorne and the Marischal, travelled with him 'for consultation'.

At all events, when they reached the capital, it was to discover that Montrose was called to appear *before* the Committee, not on it – and the others with him. Not only that, but all the remaining signatories of the Cumbernauld Bond were here likewise – with the exception of Lord Boyd, who was dead, and whose demise was partly responsible for their presence here. Taken suddenly ill, on his death-bed Boyd had remembered his copy of the Bond, and had given it to a trusted servitor to burn; but the trusted servitor had served other masters. The Bond was now in the Committee's hands – and, no doubt, a facsimile in Argyll's.

This probably would not have been sufficient to give the Campbell the lever he looked for. But further unsavoury behaviour provided it. One of the King's gentlemen-of-the-bedchamber found Montrose's letter in the royal apartments, and recognised that here was merchandise for which some-one might be prepared to pay. He had no difficulty in finding a market in 1640 Scotland. Now this also was in the Com-mittee's hands – with the Earl of Argyll's explicit instruc-tions.

Montrose and his friends were not exactly arrested; their enemies could hardly go so far against two of the Covenant's Lieutenant-Generals, two serving colonels of regiments, and nine other peers of Scotland, seven of them earls. They could not even summon them to a trial – since all could claim to be tried by their peers; and the majority of other peers would find for them, undoubtedly. So they were requested to appear before an enquiry of the Committee – or at least the others were summoned, while Montrose was asked more politely. This was the tactic throughout, to drive a wedge between the Graham and his associates. Montrose perceived it quickly, and insisted on aligning himself with the others, accepting no special treatment.

The enquiry was as clearly intended as a warning only, to scare influential men away from forming any sort of party or alliance with Montrose, which might challenge the party of Argyll. It could not claim that the Cumbernauld Bond was in any way either unlawful or contrary to the Covenant and the realm's weal; but the implication was that it might be a secret conspiracy, with its true terms other than those written down. Montrose, as spokesman, poured scorn on that, declaring that the same might be alleged of any written agreement – including the National Covenant itself. He had signed the one as he had signed the other – the first name on both documents – for the freedom of worship and the good of the King's realm. As to the suggestion that his letter to King Charles was intelligence with the enemy, and some-how treasonable, he pointed out that such charge was laugh-able. Every liege had a right to communicate with his

monarch, a *duty* if he was one of the earls of Scotland and
had advice to offer. Moreover, the King was still head of
this realm, not the enemy; and communication with him
could not possibly be so styled. Indeed any assertion that it
was, itself could better be termed treason, as an unwarrant-
able attack on the rights of the Crown. Let the Committee
consider its own position in that respect, and that of those
who sought to manipulate it, he counter-charged.

The enquiry ended abruptly, with its witnesses dismissed,
and a copy of the Bond ceremoniously burned, to appease
certain of the left-wing fanatic ministers. But it served at
least to alarm some of the Cumbernauld signatories, to let
them see that connexion with Montrose might have its
dangers. Not all were proof against this sort of pressure.
Argyll's name was not so much as mentioned throughout.

Montrose and his military colleagues returned to the
army at Newcastle.

If Argyll and the Committee thought that by this proceeding they had warned off James Graham himself, they were
far wrong. Warned he was – but in the other direction. It was
clear to him now that, not only could the Campbell and he
not work together for the Covenant or Scotland's wellbeing;
but that the one must in the end put down the other. And
since he conceived Argyll's policies, like his nature, to be
against all that he himself believed in, there was no question
as to what simple duty demanded of him. He owed it to his
conscience, and to his country and his monarch, to see Argyll
reduced from his dominant position. And not being of a
secretive nature, nor seeing any advantage in secrecy anyway
now that the Cumbernauld association was known to all, he
went about it openly, in effect proclaiming himself focus and
axis for all to rally round who hated the Campbell and all
his works, as well as the rule of the zealot preachers. He even
wrote to the King again, this time a long and carefully
worded letter outlining a well-thought-out programme which
he urged Charles seriously to consider. He advised, as vital,
that the requirements of the original Covenant, regarding
religion and liberties, should be granted forthwith, clearly
and finally; and that thereafter His Majesty should come
to Scotland in person, the realm over which his forebears had
ruled for a thousand years, and which would rally to and
love a monarch whom it could see and greet. Let him trust

his cause no more to commissioners and the like, men of straw, who could neither give nor gain contentment in the mighty distemper that afflicted the ancient kingdom. And let him hereafter trust, as public servants only those of known integrity and sufficiency, choosing them carefully and not on mere credit or recommendation; while avoiding absoluteness, which would only stir up further trouble.

This letter Montrose sent openly, by the hand of official couriers carrying documents to the Covenant delegation now negotiating with Charles in London.

Alexander Henderson and Johnstone of Warriston, now Procurator of the Kirk of Scotland, led this Covenant commission in London, negotiating, in the event, more with the English parliamentarians than with the monarch. This began by being a necessary fiction, for in theory the King could not treat with his rebellious subjects; but in time it was apparent that more was to be gained from parliament than from Charles. But the proceedings were delicate and long-drawn; for not only were the Scots in theory rebels, but equally they were not in theory invading England at all – yet the removing of the occupying army back to Scotland was the main item that they had to offer – at a price – with Leslie's force sitting firmly at Newcastle dominating the North of England and cutting off all coal traffic – and £50,000 of royal revenue therefrom – out of the great mining area there. London was having a cold winter, in consequence. The Long Parliament was now sitting there, and causing King Charles more anxiety than were the Scots, with Pym and the Puritans and malcontents proving their power, and the Huntingdonshire squire and grazier, Cromwell, beginning to make his mark.

The seething cauldron that was seventeenth-century politics, in England as in Scotland, was coming to the boil.

Montrose was arrested on the 11th of June 1641, by order of the Committee of the Estates. He was arrested at Merchiston Castle. He, along with much of the army, had at last returned to Scotland, most of their objectives at Newcastle satisfactorily achieved – to the tune of £300,000 paid by the English parliament, plus £850 per day 'occupation costs' for the long period in Northumberland; there can have been few more profitable and less bloody interludes in Scotland's long association with her neighbour. King Charles, at his wits' end, and now looking for Scots support rathen than enmity, in his obviously coming struggle with his English malcontents, had given in to the Covenant negotiators all along the line – had indeed promised to come to Scotland in the near future. So Leslie retained only a token portion of his army at Newcastle, as a sort of insurance, and the rest was not so much disbanded as stood down on a temporary basis. The Graham had sent his own troops back to Strathearn, Stirlingshire and the Mearns, relinquished his commission as Lieutenant-General, and was settling up sundry affairs at Archie Napier's house preparatory to heading north to Magdalen and his children at Kinnaird, when a troop of Loudoun's men came, without warning, to take him into custody. Clearly they would not have dared do this a couple of weeks before, when he still had two regiments of Grahams at his back. Napier was arrested with him; also Sir George Stirling of Keir, Napier's nephew, and the latter's brother-in-law Sir Archibald Stewart of Blackhall, who were likewise staying at Merchiston. They were escorted to the great fortress of Edinburgh Castle, on its towering rock, and there locked up in separate cells.

The charge was the vague and unspecified one of treason. Montrose, at least, had no doubts as to the real reason for it all. Argyll had been biding his time. Just as soon as the Graham was no longer part of the army, with his own protecting units and Lieutenant-Generalship, he had acted. But there must be a pretext; something more than the Cumbernauld Bond and the letter to King Charles. The arrest of Napier and the others provided the clue. It must be connected, he thought, with the business of Argyll and the alleged deposition threats to the King – although one might have imagined any treason therein to be on the other foot.

His jailers would give him no information. They were civil, and he was not maltreated, though denied his own servants; indeed he was kept incommunicado and in a small semi-subterranean room, an intolerable affront and constraint to a man of his standing and temperament. His demands to see the rest of the Committee fell on deaf ears; his letters to Rothes – now said to be mortally ill – Henderson, Eglinton and others, remained unanswered, if ever they were delivered.

So the hot summer days passed in that eagle's nest of a prison – and like a caged eagle indeed the Graham beat at his bars. Fiercely he disciplined himself to accept, to wait, to swallow his rage, forcing a proud, free spirit to steely restraint, if scarcely patience.

For six long weeks he was held there, alone, without explanation or detailed charges – and however illustrious his friends might be, none won through the barriers to visit him. Perhaps Argyll's strategy over the Cumbernauld Bond had been more effective than realised, and wise men recognised Montrose as someone too dangerous to associate with. Black Pate, Kilpont, Morphie and others of his close associates, would be seeking to move heaven and earth – that could be accepted; but what were they against the Campbell and the Committee?

Then, on the 27th of July, at last, he was taken from his cell, out of the castle, and down the Lawnmarket of Edinburgh, the sun dazzling his eyes unbearably after the long half-light of confinement. He walked between close files of an armed guard of at least one hundred, his captors taking no chances of a rescue. They brought him to Parliament House, behind St Giles. He had expected to be taken before a sitting of the Committee; but this proved to be a full session of parliament – or at least, scarcely full, for at the most cursory glance it was obvious that there were large and significant gaps in the attendance, gaps where his friends should have been. Argyll was there, however, on the notably sparsely filled earls' seats – which, of course, he could not have been at a Committee meeting.

The hush as Montrose was brought into the great chamber was absolute, the atmosphere electric. He was led to stand beside Napier, Stirling and Stewart at a central table usually reserved for clerks, as though in a dock at court. Napier looked pale and drawn, showing his years, but kept his grey head high. Sir George and his brother-in-law, much younger men, appeared nervous, unhappy and, most of all, bewildered. All showed, as no doubt did Montrose himself, the effects of their incarceration. Smiling briefly to them, Montrose bowed stiffly to Traquair, the Commissioner, and took prompt initiative.

'I wish to know, my lord High Commissioner, since this seems to be a parliament why I am not sitting in it, of right, as an earl of this realm? Why I have been held captive, without trial, for six weeks in Edinburgh Castle? And on whose authority this has been done?'

Helplessly Traquair spread his hands, in the throne. 'That is not for me to answer, my lord of Montrose. Perhaps – my lord of Argyll . . . ?'

Argyll sat still, head bent, silent, as though he had not heard.

In the Lords of Parliament benches behind that of the earls, a swarthy middle-aged man stood, John Livingstone, second Lord Balmerino, a friend of the Campbell. 'May I speak to this matter – with your permission, my lord President? The Earl of Montrose stands accused, with these others, the Lord Napier, Sir George Stirling of Keir and Sir Archibald Stewart of Blackhall, of grievous offence against the realm. For which reason he, and they, were put in ward by the Committee of these Estates, for the better weal of the same realm. And now appear before this parliament to answer questions, preparatory to trial hereafter.'

'This parliament cannot accept that statement,' Montrose answered strongly, authoritatively. 'Lord Balmerino, as a peer of this realm, knows full well that I, and the Lord Napier, have the right to trial by our peers, and by them only. That right I claim.'

A murmur ran through the assembly. Balmerino coughed. 'This is an enquiry. A questioning. Trial is not yet.'

'I will answer no questions, sir. Save to a properly constituted court of my peers. And I demand that I, and these my friends, be released forthwith.'

Amidst much stirring on the benches, Balmerino, looking flustered, glanced at the Earl of Loudoun, chairman of the Committee.

'The Committee of the Estates, which ordered your arrest, my lord, alone can order your release. It will be considered,' the Campbell rasped.

'That Committee, of which Lord Napier, Sir George Stirling and myself are all members, yet were not informed, is a committee of this parliament,' Montrose gave back. 'Therefore this parliament can and must overrule it. I request that parliament does so. Now. Orders our immediate release.'

'That request is out of order,' Balmerino said. 'Since the

Earl of Montrose is here not as a member of the parliament, but as a prisoner and witness.'

'A prisoner of whom, sir? Not of the King. Not of this parliament. Not of my peers. While parliament is not sitting, the Committee has its full powers. But when it is, the Committee is powerless in law. The greater cannot be bound by the lesser. As an earl of Scotland, prisoner or none, I am a member of this parliament. And demand a decision.'

Johnston of Warriston, that white-faced, strained and nervous young advocate, now a great man in Scotland, Clerk to the Assembly and Procurator of the Kirk, rose. 'My lord President,' he stammered. 'May I speak? This parliament cannot make any decision, save after heaving the facts. Those facts have not been laid before it. What are those facts?'

Montrose opened his mouth to challenge that, since the decision that he requested was not on the facts of any alleged offence, but on the right of a committee of parliament to overrule the parliament that appointed it. But he paused. For he, as much as any, required to know with what he was charged – otherwise he was the more hampered in his defence.

Balmerino was not slow to take up Warriston's point. 'My lord President – the facts are these. The Earl of Montrose has declared, before witnesses, that the Earl of Argyll did seek the deposition of our liege lord King Charles, on three counts – that of desertion of his ancient kingdom; of invasion thereof with English soldiers; and of vendition and bribery. My lord of Argyll entirely denies ever having said anything such. Yet one of my lord of Montrose's creatures, Stewart of Ladywell, Commissary of Dunkeld, now admits that the accusation was false, and that he aided in the forgery thereof. Nevertheless, the Earl of Montrose did cause him to send word of the said damnable forgery and traducement, which he knew to be false, to the King's Majesty in England. To His Majesty's misleading, and to the hurt of my lord of Argyll and this realm.'

There was a great uproar in the chamber now. When he could make himself heard, Balmerino asked, 'Does the Earl of Montrose deny this? We have full supporting testimony.'

'I neither deny nor confirm it, sir. I have no need. I answer no questions, save before a due court of my peers.'

After a pause, Robert, Lord Balfour of Burleigh, President

of the parliament, spoke. 'My lord of Montrose seems to have the right of this.' He was a cautious, scholarly man, occupying a curious position, one which had no precedent. The chairman of the Scots parliament was always the Chancellor. But since the Archbishop Spottiswoode was in theory still Chancellor, and the King had appointed no other, parliament had elected its own president. All knew that, hereafter, the whole proceedings might well be declared null and void, in that they were unconstitutional, without the Chancellor's presence, even though the Lord High Commissioner attended.

'My lord President – may I suggest that the Lord Balmerino puts his question to those who can claim no such right as trial before their peers?' That was Johnston of Warriston again. 'Namely the accused Sir George Stirling and Sir Archibald Stewart.'

'Ah, yes. Well said. Lord Balmerino?'

'Aye, my lord. So be it. You then, Sir George Stirling of Keir, I require you to answer before this high court of parliament, as you value your life. First – did you hear the Earl of Montrose make this slander upon the Earl of Argyll's honour?'

Agonisingly, Stirling looked at Montrose. That man nodded, smiling a little. 'Answer, George,' he said calmly. 'As you value your life! And your honour. This is no trial of mine. You can harm me nothing here.'

'Silence!' Burleigh exclaimed.

Stirling swallowed. 'I heard my lord say that he had been told it by Stewart of Ladywell,' he faltered.

'In what circumstances?'

'During the Earl of Argyll's punitive raiding on Atholl and Lochaber, last year. Ladywell, Commissary of Dunkeld, was taken into custody, along with his master, the Earl of Atholl. He heard the Earl of Argyll make the statement that King Charles should be deposed, in the Earl's own tent at Bridge of Lyon.'

'Fool! Think you that the Earl of Argyll – a wise lord who knows how to keep his tongue if anyone does! – would speak such traitorous things before any soever? Even if he thought so – as he does not. In especial before this Commissary of Atholl's?'

'I do not know, my lord. Who knows what any man will

206

say, on occasion? But I do know that, on that campaign, the Earl of Argyll acted so as to astonish many. Who would not have believed him capable of it. As the burning of Airlie Castle. And the harrying of the Lady Airlie!'

'Silence! Silence, I say! How dare you, sir! Answer the questions asked only – do you hear?'

'Well said, George,' Montrose remarked genially, loud enough for all to hear. 'My lord of Argyll will no doubt wish to explain that, himself!'

There was a deathly hush, as all looked expectantly at the dark-clad Campbell. But that strange man did not so much as blink an eyelid. He had a great gift for silence.

Balmerino, frowning, went on – but it was now at Sir Archibald Stewart that he looked. 'Blackhall,' he said, 'answer this, and truthfully, as you would before Almighty God. You also heard the Earl of Montrose repeat this slander? You, and others not here present?'

'I heard my lord say that he had heard Ladywell declare it as truth.'

'But Ladywell has admitted that it was untruth, a wicked forgery.'

'Of that I know nothing, my lord.'

'I think that you do. That you all, with others, contrived this with Ladywell. At the Earl of Montrose's instigation. To injure my lord of Argyll.'

'No, my lord.'

'And in concert persuaded the perfidious Ladywell to write this slander to the King, in London?'

'No. I know nothing of any letter to the King.'

'Nor I, my lord,' Stirling added.

'You lie, I say – both of you! For Ladywell has confessed to it.'

'Under torture, perhaps?' That was Archie Napier's first contribution.

'Will you inform us where the Laird of Ladywell is now, my lord?'

Balmerino glared, and glanced round for guidance. Argyll offered none. But his fellow Campbell came to his aid.

'It ill becomes the Lord Napier to make question of this matter,' Loudoun declared, rising. 'As an extra Lord of Session, former Treasurer of the realm, Privy Councillor and member of the Committee of the Estates, he was offered absolution from these charges, and his freedom. He rejected it, declaring that if any were guilty, he was guilty. Who is he to speak of torture and ill-using ... ?'

Montrose reached over to press his friend's arm.

'My lord President – I asked a question, as I have a right to do as a Lord of Parliament,' Napier went on firmly. 'Like my lord of Montrose, if trial there is, I require it of my peers. But these friends of mine, having no such right, have at least the right to know how such testimony against them was obtained – since Stewart of Ladywell is not here present, and therefore his evidence is mere hearsay. I would remind all that I am a lord of Session, a judge, and know the law. I require to be informed – where is Stewart of Ladywell? And was the alleged retraction obtained by means of torture?'

There was complete silence in the great hall.

'Very well, my lord President. Since this parliament is not to be supplied with the evidence it requires to make any decision in this matter, I move that it proceeds to the next business.'

The Earl of Dunfermline stood. 'I second that motion,' he said.

There were not a few cries of agreement from around the hall.

The President glanced at the Lord High Commissioner, and nodded. 'Very well. I so rule. Remove the Committee's prisoners. The next business ... ?'

Amidst some tumult, all four captives were hustled out, and marched back to their cells in the Castle.

Seventeen weary days later, on the 13th of August, Montrose was again taken to a renewed sitting of the parliament – alone, this time, his enemies at least having learned that the captives gained strength by supporting one another. Now, although still close guarded, he was treated more courteously. This was no trial, he was informed; merely an enquiry by parliament, which had taken the matter out of the Committee's hands; but which, as the Lord Napier cogently had pointed out at the last sitting, required information before it could come to any decision. Would the Earl of Montrose, therefore, answer certain relevant questions?

'No, my lord President. As a prisoner, I will not,' the Graham said, but courteously also. 'I accept the right of this parliament to ask questions. But I stand on my own right, as a prisoner, wrongfully or rightfully held, not to prejudice his trial before his peers by any reply to questions material to the issue. Free me, as you can do, with assurance of no re-arrest, and I will answer gladly.'

'But that is impossible, my lord,' Johnston jumped up to protest. 'It is to prejudge any trial, lacking the evidence. Parliament cannot release the Earl of Montrose with promise of protection, *before* it hears his defence. That is the negation of justice.'

'The negation of justice is that I, and my friends, have been held close prisoners without trial for two months, sir, on an alleged confession of one man, whom this parliament does not, or cannot, produce to substantiate it. I will answer no relevant question before my due and proper trial. But I request that Thomas Stewart of Ladywell, Commissary of Dunkeld, be produced forthwith, to inform this parliament.'

'That will not be possible,' Lord Balmerino said in a cilpped voice. 'Ladywell is dead.'

'Ha-a-a!' Montrose looked slowly round the assembly. He noted that Argyll was nowhere in evidence today. 'Dead? Convenient! Is it permitted to ask, my lord President, how this unfortunate man so fortunately met his death?'

'I understand that he was hanged, my lord of Montrose,' the President said thinly.

'Hanged! for retracting a statement?'

'For the felony and crime of leasing-making,' Johnston of Warriston amplified.

'Leasing-making! Lying! Lying in public! Dear God – if this is a hanging offence still, how many here are safe? I could myself witness to the offence of fifty! A hundred! How long since a man died under that barbarous ancient law?'

'Barbarous my lord of Montrose may call it, but it is no less the law of this land. The penalty of hanging was asked for by Sir Thomes Hope, the King's Advocate,' Johnston declared.

That gave Montrose pause. He could not be sure that Hope was his true friend; but he certainly was Archie Napier's. Even though, in his search for a strong man to rule Scotland, Hope had decided that Argyll was the answer, he would surely never sacrifice Archie Napier callously by getting rid of the witness who could save him, equally with

Montrose himself. Perhaps then, there was more to it? Perhaps Hope had conceived Ladywell to be a *hostile* witness, a danger to them, so broken by torture or other pressure as to give false evidence which could condemn them? Hope was undoubtedly the cleverest lawyer in Scotland. Whose side was he on?

Montrose looked at the President. 'My lord – if Ladywell was so notorious a liar that he was adjudged by the courts worthy to die for it, is his alleged evidence of any value to convict myself and my friends?'

'The point, I am sure, is taken,' the other nodded gravely.

'Then I request immediate release, for them and myself, sir.'

'It is less simple than this!' Balmerino cried, jumping up. 'My lord of Argyll has been most grievously injured, in his name and repute. He demands due recompense. Whether or not Stewart of Ladywell forged and invented this slander – and on whose instigation – my lord of Montrose conveyed the slander to the King. That is sufficient offence in itself. It could result in a charge of treason against my lord of Argyll.'

'Who says that I sent this information to the King? Ladywell again?'

'We have supporting evidence. A courier from the King was intercepted. One Captain Walter Stewart. Amongst others he carried a letter from King Charles to the Earl of Montrose, acknowledging receipt of a letter received by His Majesty *from* the Earl.'

'What of it? I wrote to His Grace from Newcastle, urging compliance with the terms of the Covenant, the end of the bishops, and His Grace's presence in his Scottish realm. If this is offence, then all the Committee of the Estates should be charged likewise – for that is its policy. Is it not also the policy of my lord of Argyll?'

'There was another letter. Secret. In a code of special meaning . . .'

'Saying what, my lord? And to whom addressed?'

'I say it was encoded. Clearly secret instructions . . .'

'You do not know what it contained, nor to whom it was written? My lord President – must we suffer more of this folly? Wasting the time of this parliament? And I would seek your ruling on this question. Is not interception of the

King's courier, receiving from him the King's sealed letters, and reading them thereafter – is not this treason? And lese-majestie also?'

Into the stir of excitement this aroused, the President declared that he would require time to consider that. They would take it to avisandum. Perhaps the King's Grace himself could best answer it. Perhaps those concerned would put it to him, in person? For His Grace was on his way to Scotland, and would attend the next sitting of this parliament in a few days' time. Meantime, with the situation unclear, and no further progress apparently possible on this vexed issue, with the Lord High Commissioner's permission he would adjourn this sitting . . .

Montrose was taken back to Edinburgh Castle, with a great deal to think about.

On the 14th of August, James Graham was brought face to face with Charles Stewart for the third time. And it was no more satisfactory an interview than were the other two. The four prisoners were led again to a special sitting of parliament; and it was only when they came to make their formal bows to the throne that they perceived that its occupant was now the monarch himself, and not Traquair.

Charles nodded in friendly fashion to his old servant Napier, but made no such gesture towards Montrose. He was looking at his most regal, gracious, dignified, the only man in that great assemblage wearing a hat – not his crown – and dressed in blue satin with the sash of the Garter, and over his shoulder the cloak of the Order with its large star. Just behind him Traquair stood, to whisper in his ear occasionally, and keep him right as to procedure – for the Scots parliament was very differently composed and conducted from the English model. Here the monarch or his representative personally presided, entitled to take part, although the actual conduct of the sittings, the chairmanship, was in the hands of the Chancellor; and of course, there was only the one house, peers and commons and burghs sitting together; though now, since the Glasgow General Assembly, no ministers and clerics attended save as spectators.

A debate was in progress when the prisoners were brought in; and listening, Montrose learned from it, to his astonishment, that the question at issue was whether or not the King should have the use of the Scots army still mustered under Leslie at Newcastle, against his recalcitrant English parliament, in return for sweeping reforms and concessions in Scotland. That such should be even considered, on either side, seemed almost beyond belief, but clearly this was so. When, presently, Hamilton of all men, rose from the earls' benches to commend the project, the Graham decided that he was seeing the ultimate in political cynicism, as well as in hypocrisy. Hamilton was, of course, a peer of Scotland and entitled to speak and vote; but when the man next to him rose, patting the other's padded and beribboned shoulder as he sat down, and proceeded in a sibilant Highland voice to welcome the King's royal presence in most flattering terms and then to indicate possible conditions for such a use of the Covenant army, Montrose had much ado to believe his own ears and eyes and keep from crying out. No final decision should be taken at this sitting, Argyll suggested, if his humble advice was of value to any. But the matter was infinitely worth exploring further, as the excellent and most noble Marquis of Hamilton had made clear.

While Montrose still sought to understand – and to stomach – this, the parliament moved on to discuss a motion by Loudoun that for the better governance of the realm, with the monarch apt to live furth of it, the judges and other officers of state should be appointed by the King only on the advice of parliament – powers far in advance of anything put forward even by the most left-wing English parliamentarians. Argyll rose again, briefly to commend this to the company, making it clear that it was the Committee's considered policy, and therefore his own. The King, for whom this must have been a bitter pill indeed, nevertheless sat silent, calm, unprotesting. He was apparently prepared to pay a high price for the Scots army. The motion was passed with little question.

Even then it was not the turn of the prisoners. Undoubtedly they had been brought in early just to be made to wait and so proclaim to the King and all others their captive and helpless status. More than once Montrose all but made intervention and protest, demanding his rights; but refrained, for the King's sake. If Charles was stomaching all this, he must be more than anxious to placate the present Scots leadership. For himself, Montrose, to upset this precarious balance, in the circumstances, would be unsuitable. It was part of the code that there should be no unseemly bickering in the presence of the monarch. Again, any hopes he might cherish that the King might obtain his release, could be jeopardised – and Charles had not acknowledged him at their entry as he had done Napier. He held his tongue.

Still another item of business was introduced, and by Loudoun again. All who held office in Scotland, any jurisdiction, hereditary or appointed, if they had not already done so, must sign the Covenant or forfeit such office. Was it agreed?

Since this involved every noble in the kingdom, all holding hereditary jurisdictions, barons' rights, sheriffships and the like, there was a tense hush. All looked at the King expectantly.

Charles sat his throne, impassive.

Argyll's nudge of Hamilton's arm was blatant, undisguised. The Marquis rose.

'I gladly undertake to sign the said National Covenant, my lord President,' he said. 'And therefore do second the motion.'

'And I so agree,' Traquair added, from behind the throne.

'And I,' the Earl of Roxburgh acceded.

So all was obviously arranged. Argyll, in unholy alliance with Hamilton, was as obviously in process of becoming at least uncrowned king in Scotland. Tom Hope had known what he was talking about.

Only then was broached the matter of the four patient prisoners. Loudoun declared that they appeared before parliament to answer questions, which two of their number had refused to do on previous occasions. Were the Earl of Montrose and the Lord Napier still obdurate and contumacious, even in the presence of their liege lord?

The Graham bowed deeply to the throne, but addressed the President, as parliamentary custom required. 'My lord – is this a trial? he asked. 'We are entitled to know.'

Balmerino replied, 'No, sir. Parliament still makes enquiry as to the need for a trial.'

'But not into the need for holding the King's loyal servants and subjects, let alone peers of Scotland, in close ward for eight weeks without trial or charge?' That was said as courteously as Montrose could make it.

'Silence, sir! *I* will put the questions, not you.'

'Then I, uncharged, and a member of this parliament, will reserve my answers, as do you, my lord.'

'You refuse, then, to answer the lawful questions of your realm's parliament, sitting in the monarch's presence?'

'No, sir. I but reserve my undoubted right to refuse answer to any question which I conceive might prejudice any subsequent trial before my peers. We are both sheriffs of counties, my lord – and well know the law in such matters.'

'You quibble, sir. You fence. How dare you!'

'Not so. I have, so far, refused to answer no question. If you are at a loss to know which to ask, try me. You might commence, my lord Balmerino, by asking the same that you asked before. Did I write to His Majesty of the Earl of Argyll's alleged declaration that His Majesty be deposed?'

There was an appalled silence at this bold turning of the tables on his enemies, in the very face of King Charles. Balmerino moistened his lips.

'This . . . this is an outrage!' he gasped.

'The question was asked, at the last sitting. If it was not outrage then, how is it so now? The only difference is that His Majesty is present. Who can, if he so wishes, inform this parliament that no such letter was sent by myself, or any friend of mine.'

'You dare, sir, to bring His Majesty into this?'

'*You* did that, my lord, when you intercepted His Majesty's royal courier, and took from him His Majesty's own letter to me, and read it. As you declared at the last sitting.'

That halted even Balmerino. Anyway, every eye was on the King.

Charles sat his throne as though sculptured therein, a picture of royal and dispassionate authority. But he did not speak.

When it was clear that he was not going to intervene, Balmerino whispered to Loudoun, and then straightened up. 'My lord President – it is intolerable that the Earl of Montrose should act thus, mocking this parliament and seeking to embroil the Crown in his villainies. I move that he be returned to ward forthwith. And the questions continued with the other accused.'

'Seconded,' Loudoun said.

'I move that the questions continue,' Montrose declared.

'Seconded,' Napier backed him, although not hopefully.

In the upheaval, Burleigh beat with his gavel. 'I rule that it is not in order for the Earl of Montrose and the Lord Napier, as prisoners and witnesses, to make such submission to parliament. I accept the motion. The two lords named to be removed from this sitting.'

Montrose bowed to the President, more deeply to his liege lord, and followed his guards out. The entire interlude had been merely a demonstration, he perceived, the object of which was to let the King see that he need place no confidence in himself, Montrose, or any other party, to support him. The monarch was to be isolated. Even Hamilton, Traquair and Roxburgh, his former toadies, had obviously been suborned, detached, and now danced to Argyll's tune. It was all very clear. Unfortunately, what was equally clear to the Graham, was that Charles Stewart was not going to raise hand nor voice in the matter. Argyll had calculated aright, in this also.

In the desperately slow, frustrating, lonely weeks that followed, James Graham came near to despair. Denied all contact with the outside world, a man of action, he was a prey to alternate helpless furies and deep depressions. To be utterly unable in any way to affect or influence his own fate was probably the most grievous affliction he had to bear.

Yet, despite himself, he could not but turn his mind towards the King, for aid. Charles, however circumscribed, still had powers, and could assist if he would. So he wrote letters to the Palace of Holyroodhouse – but had no way of knowing whether they ever reached their destination, however much he offered his jailers as bribes. He requested interviews with those in authority, Henderson, Loudoun, Johnston – but not with Argyll himself, never Argyll. And was vouchsafed no answer from any. He might have been already a dead man – as he would be, he knew well, if ultimately Archibald Campbell had his way – for all the notice the rest of Scotland took now of James Graham, *An Greumach Mor,* first signatory of the Covenant and Lieutenant-General. Had Magdalen and her father been right? Had he dabbled in things too great for him, and now must bear the consequences? Should he have stayed at home, tending his own wide acres, playing only the family man? He, the Graham?

It was nearly mid-October before he obtained his first gleam of hope, his first contact with other than his jailers – and also a personal blow. A new captain of the guard proved venal, and one night handed Montrose a letter from Kilpont. This began with the sad news that little David, the second youngest son, had died. He had been a weakly child from the first, and his father hardly knew him; but it was a blow, and poor Magdalen's heart would be sore. After this the letter declared the urgent loyalty of his friends, their horror at what was being done, and their constant efforts on their chief's behalf. Kilpont informed that they were ever pressing the King to act; and His Grace had assured them that he was concerned, and indeed would not leave Scotland until Montrose was freed – since he, with them, believed that the Graham's life hung on it. Charles was more sympathetic and understanding than might seem – but he was surrounded by traitors, spies and creatures of Argyll and Hamilton. These two were now inseparable. The King was desperate for an army, any army, to teach his English parliament a lesson – and only the Scots could provide one, mustered and equipped. All was subordinate to that, Leslie and his force the trump card. Edinburgh was full of Campbells and Hamiltons, in unholy alliance – it was said that Argyll had 5000 of his clan in and around the city – in name more volunteers for the King's army, but in fact . . . who knew? It seemed more like Campbell's kingdom. Much of the country, and probably most of the nobles, were now alarmed at the way things were going. But they were leaderless, and Argyll was careful to keep the Kirk behind him. But Montrose must not despair. He, Kilpont, believed the King when he said he would not leave Scotland until the Graham was freed – the only man who could stand against Argyll. The Campbell would never dare move against his life while the King was present. Kilpont ended by informing that the Earl of Rothes had died.

This very doubtfully encouraging letter was as a ray of light into the dim grey cell, nevertheless. Montrose had an objective again, not only hope but something to work for. There and then he sat down and wrote an acknowledgment to Kilpont, with sundry instructions, and another letter enclosed, to be handed, somehow or another, personally and secretly to the King. Means must be found. In it he warned Charles Stewart that there was no reason to believe that the deposition story was a forgery. He did not specifically accuse Argyll of being behind it, but he had known of it, and spoken of it – that was sure; for Ladywell was not a man who could or would have invented such a tale. Moreover there had been circumstantial rumours circulating, before his own arrest, that plans were being formulated to set up a Commonwealth embracing both kingdoms of Scotland and England, with the Crown put down and government by the parliaments only.

This letter sent, he could only wait, and hope.

He had to wait for a full month more. Then, on the night of the 17th of November, late in the evening, he was quite unceremoniously taken from his cell, conducted to the castle gatehouse by a junior officer, and told that he was free to go where he would. No explanations, no instructions, certainly no apology, was offered. *An Greumach Mor* now might have been some petty felon who had served his time in jail, casually released.

It was a wet night, and dark. In the Grassmarket below the castle, Montrose managed to hire a broken-down nag, all he could get, and made his way to Merchiston. There he found Archie Napier and the two knights, each having been freed earlier and separately, also without explanation. But from the servants at Merchiston, Napier had pieced together a strange story.

It seemed that the King was due to leave Holyroodhouse for the South first thing in the morning – hence their release at the last moment previous to the royal departure, when it would be too late for them to make any arrangements for an audience with Charles, who was, of course, kept most watchfully surrounded. But at least the monarch had not forgotten his promise.

It seemed that the royal departure was sudden and urgent. Rebellion had broken out in Ireland, and the English parliament had discovered that it required the King's authority to take the necessary steps to deal with the crisis. Charles apparently had hopes that this situation would benefit his position, proving to his malcontents in the South that they were less potent than they thought. With Leslie's Scots army to threaten them in the North, the King believed

that he might bring Pym, Hampden, Cromwell and the rest
to their senses. To this end he had hurriedly granted everything the Covenanters wanted; and had added a positive
shower of honours and appointments of office and profit,
quite fantastic to contemplate. Argyll himself had been
made Scotland's third marquis – it was said that he had
accepted only because there was an ancient West Highland
prophecy that the Argyll earldom would end with a squint-
ing, red-haired holder, and here was an ingenious way of
averting the curse, commentary indeed on the Campbell's
mind. Loudoun had been made Chancellor of Scotland.
Sandy Leslie, astonishingly, had been created Earl of Leven.
Alexander Henderson was now Dean of the Chapel Royal
and so King's personal minister in Scotland. And that strange
young man, Johnston of Warriston, although just thirty, had
actually been knighted, given a liberal pension, and made a
Lord of Session, the first of the new judges. If all this was
almost as laughable as it was shameful, the shame at least
looked like being extended and perpetuated. For there was
word from usually knowledgeable sources that the reason
behind it all, Charles's buying of the Scots army, had never
really been even remotely considered, in the first place, by
the said recipients of the largesse and titles. The information
was that, the moment the King was out of Scotland, the
new Earl of Leven was to bring his army home and disband
it. Here was Campbell diplomacy with a vengeance.

Even while Montrose all but wept for his duped and unfortunate monarch, he was told of still another and scarcely
more believable story – and one which might more closely
affect the late four prisoners. Scotland, it seemed, was ringing
– however little of it had reached the cells of Edinburgh
Castle – with a new sensation, which was being called the
Incident for want of any more credible description. A plot,
it was alleged, had been unearthed against Argyll and Hamilton, of all directions, to discredit them with the King – and
there were inspired rumours that Montrose was behind it
all. It was difficult to unravel the details and any real sense
of it, but the gist seemed to be that though Edinburgh had
been packed tight as a drum with thousands of Campbell
clansmen and Hamilton retainers, to discourage other lords
from questioning Argyll's hegemony, nevertheless the said
pair of nobles put it about that their lives were in danger,

and that they were being traduced to the King. So serious
the threat, these two wronged and distressed statesmen had
thereupon retired from unsafe Edinburgh to Hamilton's
Kinneil Palace in West Lothian – from whence they could
be back in an hour – in high dudgeon and deep sorrow.
Nobody could make head nor tail of it all – save perhaps
Napier, who, when he heard of Montrose's smuggled letter
to the monarch with its specific information regarding the
Commonwealth idea, declared that Argyll's devious mind
had probably concocted the whole thing, to get him out of
the King's presence until the royal departure, and to have
every pulpit in the land ringing with his wrongs as a godly
man endangered, hunted for his life; and to sow suspicion
and mystification amongst his enemies.

At all events, whatever the rights of it, fairly obviously
Charles would not be over the Border before his two
marquises would be back in Edinburgh, and far from inactive. In the circumstances, it would be the most elementary
precaution for the four ex-prisoners to get out of the city,
and much farther away than Merchiston, before that happened, if they valued their new-found liberty. Deep in the
Graham lands, Montrose declared, was the place for them,
in this pass. He had never liked Edinburgh; now it stank in
his nostrils.

That very November night, in thin drizzling rain, the
horses were saddled and all four set out for the North with
as minimal delay as disturbance.

There were times when discretion was not merely wise but
the only course.

17

STRANGELY ENOUGH, THAT WINTER AND THE FOLLOWING
months of 1642, James Graham came almost to give thanks
to Archibald Campbell and his machinations, for so effec-

tively cutting him adrift from all Covenant and national affairs. His name undoubtedly stank in the nostrils of the militant Covenanters and the fanatical ministers – who now, under Argyll, ruled Scotland unchallenged; but, secure within his own domains, it would have been a bold man who actually sought to lay hands on Montrose. While he had been held prisoner, Argyll had ordered the Lord Sinclair to go and harry the Mugdock estate, and pull down its castle – a piece of typical Campbell ferocity; but Mugdock was an isolated property as far as the Graham clan was concerned, only seven miles north of Glasgow. It was noticeable that there had been no attacks on Kincardine or other Strathearn lands, nor on Old Montrose, deep in traditional Graham territory.

So, for the first time in five years – indeed, for that matter, in his adult life – Montrose, unwanted by either his country or his king, could be himself and lead the normal life of a Scots nobleman, chief and landowner. And he had had enough of the alternative to appreciate it. Not that he did not frequently fret and fume with himself at Argyll's complete triumph, and his own helplessness to do anything about it – even, meantime, to avenge burned Mugdock. But the long months in Edinburgh Castle had taught him his lesson, he assured himself. He knew now when he was fortunate. After all, *he* never had had any wish to rule, to dominate. He had taken up the cause because he conceived it to be right; and if it had gone sour, and into wrong hands, he had reason to be glad that it had no further use for him. Thus James Graham in 1642.

More truly he rejoiced to become a family man – not again, for in fact he had never been one. On this score he did not have to convince himself. He went back to Kinnaird, to pick up Magdalen and the children, to take them to Kincardine Castle; and perhaps because he was so obviously defeated, perhaps because he had brought Archie Napier with him for the latter's safety, old Southesk was almost welcoming. He had been proved right – which is an excellent thing for any man; and he was able to emphasise, and to go on emphasising, the nobility of his beloved liege lord Charles, who despite all James Graham's sins against him, had vouchsafed to save the prodigal at cost to himself. Montrose, clearly, would have to listen to variations on this theme for the rest of his father-in-law's life; but at least they could live with each other again – for short periods.

As for Magdalen, she discovered that she could be sorry for her so splendid husband – and the experience was as a balm to her troubled soul. Undoubtedly she was a better mother than she was a wife; and now James Graham qualified in some measure for mothering, and she felt better able to cope with him. Perceiving something of it, however ruefully, the man also perceived that, while not really solving any problems for him, it would make life a deal easier, and certainly pleasanter for the woman he had married and whom by any standards he had grievously neglected. He suffered the mothering and sympathy, like he suffered Southesk's sermons and the periodic frustrations that boiled up within him. He was learning forbearance.

His children were his true joy. John, now twelve, was a sturdy lad, dark, keen, strong-minded, a son of whom any father might be proud – although undoubtedly he needed the said father's hand occasionally. James, with some of his mother's diffidence, was a little delicate and of less independent spirit, but a thinker, an asker of questions, interminable questions, intelligent enough for two, but not yet so much so as to be a trouble. Any fears their father might have entertained that his sons might look at him askance were quickly dissipated. Magdalen had done better by him, in this, than perhaps he deserved, bringing them up to look on their sire, not as one part of herself did – or as did their grandfather so obviously – but as gallant gentleman, cavalier, almost hero. His splendid good looks, noble bearing yet essential easy friendliness, did the rest. Unfairly, perhaps, within a day or two of his return, his sons were doting on him, and he could do no wrong.

Montrose remained no longer than he decently must, at Kinnaird. Magdalen made no objections to removing to Strathearn, and at Kincardine Castle most evidently sought to make the best of it. Almost it seemed that her recent troubles, the death of their third son, and her husband's imprisonment and fall from popularity, had bred a new strength in her, an increase in independence. And she was now preoccupied, not with living up to her husband so much as with retaining him at home and contented. So life at the little castle by the Ruthven Water was much improved on previously, for all concerned. Inchbrakie was only a few miles away; and Black Pate's wife Jean, a daughter of the Lord Drummond, was almost as much at Kincardine, with her children, as at home. Kilpont was not much farther away, on the other side; and Stirling of Keir closer still. Other friends, clansmen and supporters lived all around. Frequently Montrose asked himself why he had ever left this his own place. Archie Napier's continued presence with them helped likewise.

Not, however, that James Graham abandoned all concern for his country and its fate. He kept himself informed of what went on; and many were the discussions and arguments in Kincardine's hall, that winter and spring, on what was to be the outcome, and what ought to be done. But, more or less, by mutual consent, these were conversations, not councils, with no suggestion that any there must again involve himself.

Leaving Edinburgh, King Charles had gone back to London, to authorise the necessary steps against the rebellion in Ireland. But that done, promptly the parliamentarians had resumed their campaign against him, producing the Grand Remonstrance, a detailed indictment of his rule, and which demanded supreme powers for parliament. All his hopes of betterment were shattered – like his hopes of a Scots army. With disaster and massacre in Ireland, and the mob shouting for the blood of his Queen Henrietta Maria – whom it blamed, along with Strafford and Archbishop Laud, for most of his English policies – too late as always, Charles acted. He sacrificed Laud and Strafford, who were arrested. But to no purpose. Parliament continued to defy him; and on the 4th of January, 1642 the King took the ill-advised step of going in person to the Houses of Parliament, to arrest the men whom he considered the leaders. The gesture failed. Defeated and humiliated, Charles was forced to retire. Indeed, a week later he retired from London altogether, wiping its dust from his royal feet, and heading northwards.

But the English dissidents were not confined to the South. On the 23rd of April, Sir John Hotham shut the gates of Hull in his monarch's face. It was the final, unforgivable affront. There could be no more compromising. It was war, civil war, in England, with the King summoning all loyal subjects to arms.

Both sides wooed the Scots. The Earls of Lothian and

Lindsay were sent south, ostensibly to mediate, actually to discover which side was most likely to win, and which offered the best terms. By May, it seemed evident that the Committee of the Estates, at least, were likely to plump for the parliamentarians.

It was at this stage, reluctantly indeed, and greatly against Magdalen's urgings, that Montrose agreed to take a hand, a very modest hand, once more. The blame could be laid at Napier's door. During the long winter's evenings, he had advised his friend to put pen to paper and set down his theory of government, the art and ethics of it as he saw it, to clear his own mind and to instruct his companions. It was a change from the poetry and lyrics which the Graham had been penning, and though without enthusiasm at first, he had warmed to the task. He discovered in the process that he had indeed certain strong convictions which, set out, formulated a sort of creed. This, much acclaimed by others, presently began to nag at his conscience. Was it possible for a man of integrity to know all this, to construe it and believe in it, and yet to do nothing about it when he saw what he believed in set at naught and mocked, his country and his king at need? There was no use in telling himself that he no longer had the power to influence matters. He might not be wanted by either side – but he still could raise 1000 armed Grahams to back his word. Not that he had any intention of so doing; but he could not hide behind the screen of helplessness.

In May, Napier, who was still a member of the Privy Council, received a summons from Loudoun, now Chancellor, to attend a meeting thereof at Edinburgh, to decide on policy anent the King and his English parliament. Needless to say, he was in doubts as to whether to venture into the lion's den again. Montrose said that he should – for his voice was honoured and respected by many, and somebody must advocate the right. His friend's safety would be vouched for by the provision of a close escort of some hundreds of Graham troopers. His brother-in-law, in return, countered by advising that, in such case, Montrose himself should go to the capital with the escort – and not only he, but other like-minded nobles, to be present in Edinburgh during the period of the Council meeting, to press their views on the Councillors, in private, and to let the people see that all Scotland was not yet Argyll's.

So, towards the end of that month, a large company rode to Edinburgh – Grahams, Drummonds, Murrays and Ogilvys – not too aggressively armed, as escort for the Lord Napier, Privy Councillor, Montrose and his friends accompanying it, not exactly incognito but not parading their presence, and very much in a private capacity, their objective certainly not to provoke any clash with the Covenant leadership.

It was strange to be back in the city from which James Graham had all but fled, in darkness, six months before. He went nowhere unguarded, naturally, and so was scarcely able to test the true temper and opinion of the citizens. But he could sense the tension and unease of the place, the suspicion and fear in men's faces, the feeling that tyranny was not far away. The Kirk might be ruling here, rather than the Crown – but men's hearts were none the lighter.

Argyll was in town, attending the Council; but the two men made sure that they did not meet. They both were active, however. Montrose sought to impress on all Privy Councillors whom he might influence that so long as Charles Stewart was King of Scots they could not lawfully or morally take the side of the English parliamentarians against him. They had to accept that the King and his people were indivisible; and that monarch and parliament together ruled the state, not one or the other. His 'creed' now clear in his mind, he was the better able to convince others; though what effect he might have against Argyll's contrary influence, he could not tell, and was scarcely optimistic. For his part, the Campbell went to work in a different direction, sending out minions to rouse Fife and the Lothians to the threat of an armed bid for power on the part of the malignant Earl of Montrose and other royalists, Papists and traitors. In the event, Argyll had much the best of the exercise, the Covenanting gentry and ministers, with their retainers, flocking into Edinburgh from a wide area, intent on rescuing the Lord's faithful servants from the bloody hands of wicked men; so that to avert armed clash and bloodshed, which would serve no good purpose, the Grahams and their friends had to withdraw from the city, back to Strathearn, taking Napier with them, and leaving the Privy Council to make a carefully non-committal decision – which, in fact, had the effect of giving Argyll and the Committee all the powers they desired to make common cause with the English parliamentarians and Presbyterians.

More frustrated than ever, Montrose admitted that the non-success of this venture had been on a par with all his other recent activities, and that he was in fact beating the air. Magdalen did not fail to confirm that point of view.

The summer of 1642 stretched itself out in disquiet and tension. Another General Assembly was held, at St Andrews, now openly under Argyll's thumb – Montrose, of course, and none of his like, being summoned. Its main decision was that aid should be accorded to the English parliament if it would abolish episcopacy in England. To maintain the fiction of impartiality, it urged King Charles, in loyal duty, to see to this also. That this was shameless interference in the rights and affairs of another country, the very thing that the Covenant had stood out against for themselves, seemed to trouble few. And, almost unbelievably, the thing was accepted. The English parliament thereafter voted unanimously to abolish the episcopate, the bishops were driven from the Upper House, and the Church of England was instructed to turn itself into a Presbyterian body. For his part, King Charles did not reply to the Scots dictation.

Argyll was triumphant. He not only ruled Scotland, but was in a position largely to impose his will on England also, owing to the need of both sides for Scots aid. Oddly enough, he celebrated his ascendancy by betrothing his son, the Lord Lorne, to Hamilton's eldest daughter.

On the 22nd of August King Charles, joined by his nephews the Princes Rupert and Maurice of the Rhine, sons of his sister Elizabeth, Queen of Bohemia, set up his standard at Nottingham, the Earl of Essex moving against him, on behalf of parliament. There were a number of small, indecisive engagements, and then, on the 23rd of October, was fought the Battle of Edgehill, in Warwickshire. It was more of a drawn fight than a great victory; but the circumstances turned the result much to the advantage of the King. The parliamentarians went into retreat, and sent urgent appeals to Scotland for help.

Suddenly all was changed. It was come time for acting, not scheming, manoeuvre and diplomacy. And Archibald Campbell was less expert at this.

Late in that year of trembling balance, Alexander Henderson arrived, alone, at Kincardine Castle, for a second visit exactly six years after his first, looking tired, drawn and much more than those six years older. But still strong, stern, upright. He came, he told the younger man, at the behest of the Committee of the Estates, to seek the aid of the Earl of Montrose, and to offer him the Lieutenant-Generalship of the Scots forces about to proceed on active service.

James Graham stared at his visitor. 'Can it be true? Can you be serious, man?' he cried. 'After all that is past, you can come here to me again! In heaven's bright name – why? Why, I say?'

'For the same reason that I came before, my lord,' the other said evenly. 'Because I, and others, believe that this realm needs you, in this pass. And conceive you to love your country, despite all.'

'Despite all! Aye, well may you say it. And you? You conceive yourself, you and your like, to represent that country?'

Henderson raised dark, bushy brows. 'If not we – who? The duly elected representatives of parliament and the Assembly. If not we – who then? However unworthy.'

'And the Campbell? Your master?'

'I have only one Master, sir. But . . . my lord Marquis assents.'

'He assents!' Montrose took grip of himself, so that his knuckles gleamed white. 'Master Henderson – for you I retain some respect. Although I mislike much of the company you keep! Argyll has taken and soiled a noble cause. And few therein have sought to counter him. I have not seen yourself prominent in this! You who brought Argyll into it.'

'As I brought you, my lord. With the Earl of Rothes.'

'As you brought me, to my cost! And now the Campbell rules Scotland, and stains its honour. And you come to me?'

'I come to you, yes.'

Helplessly the Graham shook his head. 'I cannot understand you, sir. That you should conceive it possible that I should once again put my neck into the noose. Or take up a cause which I believe to have gone far wrong.'

'The cause is not wholly wrong yet – and can be righted.

Must be righted. And I never conceived you to be so fearful for your neck, my lord!'

'The cause, the Covenant, is dead. Murdered by Archibald Campbell. You have sold your king, and mine – gained all that you wished from him, and then sold him! With such cause I will have no truck.'

'You judge too harshly. The King only gave us what we sought, and what Scotland required, because we forced him to it. Though weak, he is the most stubborn of men. Think you that he will let us keep what we have gained, our liberty to worship as we will, if we do not still press him? He is a man consumed with the knowledge that he is right, that all others are wrong. If he wins this battle with his English parliament, then we in Scotland will feel the weight of his hand. And where will our won freedom be then?'

'You call this freedom? I'd mind you, sir, that I tasted five months of it, in Edinburgh Castle!'

'That was ill done, yes. I, and others, sought to undo that wrong. But your enemies were too strong for us . . .'

'Argyll and Hamilton, you mean. Can you not say their names, man? Though indeed, Hamilton is but a jackal in the coils of a snake! He could do nothing, without the Campbell. I have no enemy in this realm that I need cast a glance at, save *MacCailean Mor*. He whom you have raised on high.'

'A national cause, my lord, cannot be over-nice in the props it uses to support it. My lord Marquis is a great noble, as are you. Entitled to take a hand in the affairs of this realm – as are you. You may not love each other, but you are nevertheless both powerful peers of Scotland whom the realm must look to in its needs. Do you blame the realm, or me, for your quality?'

'By God, sir – now you speak plain! And I will do likewise. Since Argyll is so much to your liking, appoint *him* Lieutenant-General! Yet him lead the army into England. I gladly defer the command!'

Henderson changed neither his grave expression nor his even, calm speech. 'Not so, my lord. In this, *you* can serve Scotland the better. The King has won certain victories, and the tide of war seems set in his favour meantime. The English parliament demands the aid our parliament promised them in their fight against the bishops. Such aid we must send.

But clearly such army must be most carefully led. Not to fight against the King. Not to fight at all, if it is possible. The position is delicate. It could find itself in dire straits. If the parliament cause were to go down swiftly, and the King thought to turn on it. It must therefore be led by more than a mere soldier. You understand? The Earl of Leven is a good soldier. But ...'

'To be sure, sir – I understand very well. You and your friends are concerned lest you support the wrong side, the *losing* side! You are not concerned with right and wrong, you are concerned with expediency. The Scots army is to smite its own monarch, if he is losing; but not if he is winning! That would be inexpedient. And you cannot trust old Leslie with the delicate business. Too blunt a man.'

'You judge too harshly, my lord. We – that is, the Scots parliament and the General Assembly – are committed to aid our English brethren in *their* struggle for freedom of worship and the reform of government – as we have gained for ourselves. As is only right and proper. But we are not in rebellion against the King. Our true function is to mediate, to use our army for that good purpose. Not to fight battles and shed blood. Leslie is a soldier, and nothing more. But you – you have shown yourself to have both a gift for strategy, for soldiering, and also for statecraft. Moreover, the King is disposed in your favour ...'

'And there you have it! The King is disposed in my favour. If the King's cause prospers, you may want that favour – so you turn to me. But if it fails, where would Montrose be then? Like as not Argyll's prisoner once again, with Leslie resuming fullest command! Think you I am a child, Master Henderson? Not to see it?'

'I think that you see it amiss. The position is delicate, as all must admit. It must be delicately handled, for Scotland's sake. This you cannot deny, my lord. And we conceive that *you* can handle it delicately.'

'Amiss or none, what I see is that you would have me play turncoat and trimmer, prepared to sail with the most convenient wind. That, I promise you, I will not do. Go back to our King's new marquis, better qualified than am I to so sail, and tell *him* to go south with Leslie. The Commander-in-Chief will heed *his* voice, never fear! The King chose to honour Argyll – not Montrose. Will he not be disposed further to favour him?'

'My lord Marquis conceives it is his duty to remain in Scotland . . .'

'Do you tell me so? Then, what of that other royal favourite, Hamilton? Would he not serve very well, for this delicate mission? And him so close to the Campbell.'

'My lord of Hamilton is scarce suited to it . . .'

'And, on my soul, nor am I, sir! I am a loyal subject of King Charles, one of those whom he should be able to trust. He is our liege lord, however many his mistakes. I say that he has been shamefully used by those who rule in Scotland today. I will by no means aid them in it, further.'

'So, my lord – you choose the King, in the end? Not the Covenant.'

'I chose the Covenant while still I could be loyal to the King in it. But now that Covenant is dead, trampled by self-seekers and by fanatic preachers. Aye – I choose the King!'

There was a long pause. Then Alexander Henderson sighed. 'I am sorry, my lord of Montrose. Truly sorry.' And stiffly he bowed himself out.

Slowly, heavily, Montrose climbed the narrow turnpike stair to his private chamber at the tower-head. Unlocking a drawer there, he took from it a letter, much scuffed and battered. It was headed from Nottingham, and dated the 22nd of August, the day that the King raised the royal standard there – although it had only reached Montrose recently, and by devious means, having certainly been opened, read and considered by his enemies on route, Will Murray being Will Murray. It went:

My good lord and traist Cousin,
I send Will Murray to Scotland to inform my friends of the state of my affairs and to require both their advice and assistance. You are one whom I have found most faithful, and in whom I repose greatest trust. Therefore I address him chiefly to you. You may credit him in what he shall say, both in relation to my business and to your own; and you must be content with words until I be able to act. I will say no more but that I am your loving friend,
                                                            CHARLES R.

*   *   *

229

He read that through again, even though he knew every word of it by heart. And then, throwing it down on the table, he slammed down his clenched fist upon it, decision taken. It was necessary. He could no longer put off, procrastinate. Magdalen was wrong, as was her father. And others. A man must do what he was born to do. Especially when he was born the Graham.

Turning, he ran down those same twisting stairs, back straighter, shoulders braced. Near the stair-foot he began shouting for Black Pate of Inchbrakie.

18

SIX WEEKS LATER, IN COLD AND WINDY FEBRUARY WEATHER, Montrose was back near his former winter quarters at Newcastle, this time not with an army but with a squadron of 120 Graham troopers, and the lordlings Ogilvy and Aboyne – the latter with him as his father's representative, to vouch for the swords of 5000 Gordons. Black Pate and Kilpont were also of the company. Montrose's numbers were carefully chosen – enough to provide a safe escort for a great noble in dangerous days, but not enough to be seen as a threat to any faction or as part of an army. And it was a company which could move fast, for they had a long way to go. They were making for Oxford and the royal Court – so close was the King to London again.

But at Newcastle Montrose heard news which changed his direction somewhat. The Queen, Henrietta Maria, had gone to France and the Continent less than a year before, to raise foreign support for her husband, taking the crown jewels and other treasure to sell, for the purchase of munitions of war. She had, it seemed, just arrived back, disembarking at Bridlington with artillery and warlike stores. Henrietta Maria was said by many to have more influence on the King's decisions even than had Archbishop Laud;

indeed it was she who had been sent to the Continent largely to get her out of England because parliament was proposing to impeach even the Queen for having undue and hostile influence on the monarch in matters of state. Montrose wanted to influence Charles Stewart in no small fashion. He decided to see Henrietta first.

The Graham company bore away slightly east of south, for Bridlington.

They found the Queen, with her artillery train assembled, on the point of setting out for York on her way to Oxford. She was a slight, pretty woman, wearing well, vivacious, hot-tempered and wilful, alleged to be much interested in good-looking young men. If so, Montrose and his young friends caught her on one of her off-days. She was, of course, scarcely at her best. A poor traveller, she had suffered much on the February seas, and was not yet recovered. Moreover her welcome back to England had been a cannon-ball, fired from one of the parliament fleet, into her own chamber in the harbour-side house; indeed the town was still under occasional fire. Enough to upset any lady. She was, it appeared, prepared to distrust most Englishmen, and all Scots. She greeted the Graham coldly, and had it not been that his 120 troopers made a valuable addition to the guard for her baggage-train, he might have got little further with her. She would by no means grant him the private inter-view he sought, and he had to make do with snatches of conversation as they rode, amidst the chatter of her bevy of courtiers and the fears of armed attack.

'Madam,' he urged, at an open stretch of country, as they left the village of Burton Agnes behind them, 'I pray that you hear me. In this situation, His Majesty sorely needs the help of Scotland. More, that it should be denied to his enemies. Of this none can be in doubt. But the present Scots leaders incline towards the English parliament – whatever their words. I know. So long as the King appears to be winning, they will be most careful. They intend to send an army across the Border. But not to aid His Majesty. To threaten him, rather. The moment parliament seems to get the upper hand, they will turn against the King.'

'So? Was it not ever so? The Scots are a treacherous race, my lord.'

'Not so, Madam. The Scots are amongst the loyalest folk

on this earth. But they have been betrayed, neglected, abandoned. Ever since His Majesty's father left Scotland for London, in 1603, on the death of Elizabeth, the canker has been eating in. They are a people who cherish and love their chiefs, grouped in their clans and families, a patriarchal people. They require a chief of chiefs – their King. All the system, the direction, of the Scots depends on this. But their kings have left them, to live 400 miles away, and in another land with other customs. Their loyalty, then, lacks focus, lacks its true centre. So it spends itself on the lesser chiefs, on the chieftains of clans and heads of houses. Who, lacking a master, often turn and rend each other. So we have feud, clan warfare, while he who should be ruling us, rules instead another people, differently spirited, who know him not.'

The Queen, it is to be feared, was paying little attention to this disquisition. 'I care not *why* they are treacherous, sir, so long as they are,' she told him. '*Parbleu* – what would you have? For His Majesty to give up his great English throne and return to beggarly Scotland?'

The man was patient. 'That I do not ask. Although His Majesty might do worse, I think! But in this present case, I say, he would be wiser to return to his own people, there to put his ancient house in order, first. Scotland. He cannot bend both England and Scotland to his will, at one time.'

'He came to Scotland, did he not, my lord? And was received with contumely and insult.'

'He came on a brief visit. With all the bishops trouble at his back. He chose to uphold the very men who were his enemies . . .'

'Enough, sir! Enough. *Mon Dieu* – must I listen to this, this *calomnie,* this *médisance* of my husband! It is too much!'

'Your pardon, Madam. But His Grace's situation is parlous. And demands plain speaking.'

'No. No more. Sir Peter – here come, ride by me. I have finished speaking with the lord of Montrose . . .'

Late that afternoon they were in a brush with a small force of parliamentary cavalry near Great Driffield, and the Queen had good reason to be grateful to the Graham squadron for seeing them off in gallant style. In consequence, she was rather more gracious to Montrose when they halted for the night. Loth as he was to be subjected to another rejection, he did not spare her, or himself – for to this end had been his journey.

'Your Majesty will, I hope, forgive me if I offended by my plain speaking,' he said. 'It is only out of my love for the King's Grace. All along he has suffered much from ill advice as to Scotland. He wrote to me, in August, seeking my advice in this pass. It is to offer him it that I ride south now. But . . . he is surrounded by men who give him bad counsel – as, dear God, has been more than amply proved! But you, Madam, he will heed. You can greatly move him. If I could make *you* understand . . .'

'What is it that you want, my lord? What is your petition? But make it short, of a mercy! For I am tired.'

'No petition, Majesty. Only the advice he asked. Briefly this. Scotland is being mustered *against* the King. By his enemies. Argyll in especial. Hamilton aiding . . .'

'That I will not believe, sir. *Monsieur le Marquis* is the King's good friend. And mine.'

'Not a true friend, Madam – that I swear. By his acts . . .'

'Stop, sir! I will hear no more of this. If you insist on speaking evil of my friends, as also my husband!'

'Very well. I shall say no more of persons. But – Scotland *is* being mustered against the King. But the people do not hate him, despite the preachings of some divines. The people could be raised against the King's enemies, instead. I know it well. If His Majesty struck first.'

'How can he so strike? He has no army in Scotland. The Scots army is in his foes' hands. You say it yourself.'

'*I* could find him an army, quickly. Let His Majesty give me a commission to raise Scotland for him, and I will have 10,000 men in two weeks, 20,000 in six! Young Lord Aboyne, here, is empowered to promise 5000 Gordons. But give me the authority, and I will win Scotland for the King. Let him come north himself, when I have mustered his army, and all the land will fall to him. Come in strength, as a king should, not in weakness, and the Scots people will prove their loyalty.'

'You are most sure of yourself.'

'I am most sure of my countrymen, Madam.'

'Others say differently.'

'Others may not wish the King so well as do I.'

233

'Yet you are one of those of this Covenant, are you not? One of the most strong, sir?'

'I was. Still I believe in what I signed then. But that battle is won. And I walk no more with those who misuse the power it won.'

'In France, we have a saying how if a man changes sides once, he may do so again!'

'And in Scotland we say, Majesty, that it is only a fool who holds to a road past his destination! What I have said is true. Will you so advise the King? To his great good?'

'I will think of it, sir. I do not know. I will tell you, at York . . .'

But at York, next evening, they discovered more travellers awaiting them – Hamilton and Traquair, of all people, with quite a large entourage. It seemed that Loudoun, Henderson and Warriston, with themselves, were forming a deputation to Oxford, to urge on the King that he accept the concept of Presbyterian uniformity of worship throughout his dominions, banning episcopacy entirely – obviously only a time-filling device while forces were raised in Scotland, since Charles would certainly never agree to it. Hearing of the Queen's coming, these two practised courtiers had waited, letting the others go ahead. No doubt they were as sensible of the lady's influence on her husband as was Montrose.

They reacted towards the Graham as might have been expected, and quickly the predictable took place. They worked upon the Queen and, old friends of hers, were not long in convincing her that Montrose was both unreliable and dangerous. They assured her that there was no cause for alarm over Scotland, that her present leaders sincerely desired only to mediate – indeed were here in England to that end – and that no threat need be looked for from Leslie's army. They suggested that the Graham mischief-maker be sent packing.

Since this advice matched Henrietta Maria's own inclinations, she took it. Montrose was told that his representations would be put before the King, but that there was no need for him to proceed farther south in person. It was not exactly a royal command not to go to Oxford, but it was a dismissal. And what point was there in going on, in defiance of the Queen? It would scarcely endear him to the monarch, who positively doted on his Frenchwoman. Moreover, Henderson,

Loudoun and the others were already ahead of him, it seemed, and would deny all that he had to say, even if he was permitted to say it.

He wrote a letter to his liege lord, then, far from optimistically, and entrusted it to Ogilvy, who, with Aboyne, elected to go on southwards. And grim-faced he turned back for Scotland, with Pate and Kilpont, a man with all the talents but whom the fates did not appear to love.

Argyll saw to it that all Scotland soon was ringing with Montrose's discomfiture. The Graham had thought to cozen and delude the King, by working on the Queen; but she had snubbed him, and sent him home – thanks largely to the Marquis of Hamilton's wise counsel. Their Majesties were happy in having true and wise servants in Scotland, to warn them against such as this trouble-maker, who would divide the country in civil war for their own ends. And as though to emphasise how right was the Marquis of Argyll, word came that on the 23rd of April King Charles had taken the almost unprecedented step of raising his good servant Hamilton to the rank and status of duke.

There was no reply to Montrose's letter to the monarch.

Everywhere, that summer, recruiting was in progress in Scotland – the more so as Charles's forces, under Rupert of the Rhine, the Earl of Newcastle and Sir Ralph Hopton, were making headway almost everywhere. John Hampden was slain, and Bristol, England's second largest port, about to fall into the King's hands. A Scots parliament was demanded – and although the King postponed a decision on this, Argyll thereupon demonstrated his complete power by calling it himself, for the 22nd of June. Lacking the royal authority, he had to call it a Convention of the Estates – but the result was the same. A General Assembly was to succeed it. The theme of both was to be the same, the unification of a parliamentary commonwealth in a Presbyterian United Kingdom, with all that this entailed.

Montrose was not invited to either Convention or Assembly, not were many other moderates and loyalists.

During those bitter months, however, James Graham was by no means idle. He accepted now that the King was unlikely to seek his services. And to muster men on his own accord, on any large scale and lacking the royal authority, would be technical treason – for in theory it was still the

King's government that ruled in Scotland, with the trappings of legality. But he also accepted that his conscience would give him no rest if he did nothing, and abandoned the royal cause – which he saw as equally his country's. He therefore sought, quietly, to form a coalition of powerful nobles, moderates, royalists, Episcopalians, even Catholics – since Huntly was so important in man-power; but he was less successful than he had hoped, lacking any commission; indeed under a cloud of royal disapproval, according to general rumour. The great lords could not be brought to agree amongst themselves, so diverse a crew. Huntly would have nothing to do with the Earl Marischal. Airlie said Kinghorne had stolen lands of his. The Lords Fraser and Forbes were at ancient and deadly feud. Crichton, Viscount Frendraught declared that nothing would make him associate with Papists. Montrose could have licked them into shape had he possessed any sort of commission; but they were mainly older men than he, and without it he was hamstrung.

Unexpectedly, in June, two events proclaimed to him that perhaps he was less ignored and ineffective than he assumed, however. He had a letter, dated the 31st of May, from the Queen, of all correspondents, declaring that she had heard a rumour that he, Montrose, was keeping ill company, was in touch with the King's enemies, the men he had warned her of, who were offering him high position, and money to pay his debts. She hoped that this was untrue, and said that arms were arriving from Denmark shortly, which might be diverted to Scotland if he was in a position to use them effectively in the King's cause; and ended by assuring him of her continuing confidence.

Utterly at a loss to understand this strange communication – or to what debts she referred – Montrose had still deferred any answer when he had an unusual visitor. Sir James Rollo, elder son of the Laird of Duncrub, was actually a brother-in-law, for he had been married to the Lady Dorothea Graham; but on her death he had wed Argyll's half-sister, the Lady Mary Campbell. He was now accepted to be in the opposite camp – although his brother, Sir William Rollo, remained faithful to Montrose. Duncrub was only a few miles from Kincardine, but Sir James's visit was rare enough to be significant. He came, confidentially, to invite the Graham to a secret meeting with Master Alexander Henderson.

'Save us – what next!' the other exclaimed. 'I saw Henderson seven months past. Has aught changed? And why secret? He came here to Kincardine before, openly enough. If he wishes to see me, why not again?'

'I do not know, James. All I was told was that this time none must know of it. And that it is important.'

'What will it serve? What that is new can we say to each other?'

But, because he still believed that Henderson was the best of the churchmen and not yet wholly Argyll's man, in mid-month he saw the Moderator and Dean of the Chapel Royal again. They met dramatically in a meadow amongst the windings of the Forth, near Stirling, Henderson's odd choice, between Highlands and Lowlands, North and South. This time, lest there be any trap, Montrose brought Napier, Ogilvy and George Stirling with him; but there was only Henderson and Rollo waiting for them.

'Why this strange meeting, Master Henderson?' he asked, without preamble. 'I gave you my sure answer last time. I chose the King, you will recollect.'

'But the King, it seems, has not chosen *you*, my lord.'

'No matter. Nothing is changed.'

'I say that much is changed, my friend. The two realms are now agreed to be done with bishops. This war in England is hateful and unnecessary. There is no need for further conflict. Only the King's obduracy. To encourage that obduracy is evil, against God's will and purpose!'

'As interpreted by Alexander Henderson and Archibald Campbell!'

'As interpreted by all lovers of peace and religion,' the other insisted patiently. 'You, my lord, do not *desire* war?'

'No.'

'Yet you prepare for war. Seek to join with other lords. In a confederation.'

'As do you.'

'*We* act in the name and on behalf of the realm.'

'But against the head of that realm. Against his express desires and commands.'

'The King acts the autocrat, beyond his due powers. And you encourage him in it. You lead him to believe that much of Scotland will fight for him, against its appointed representatives. This is to the injury of peace, to make war more likely.'

'You fight what you believe to be wrong, Master Henderson, calling it sin. You do not knuckle to the Devil, for the sake of peace. Should I?'

'I say that you should reconsider your position, my lord. If you showed a true and fitting solidarity, now, with your fellow signatories of the National Covenant, then undoubtedly the King would perceive that Scotland is not to be divided. He will be forced to heed our mediation, our mission for peace. At this Convention of the Estates that is to be, and the General Assembly to follow, a new Covenant is to be put forward. To include our English brethren. A noble document ensuring freedom of worship hereafter, and the putting down of idolatry and episcopacy in both realms. A testament of lasting peace between England and Scotland. We think to name it the Solemn League and Covenant. It is an affirmation of Christian unity and faith which will ring down the centuries to come. It would give me the greatest satisfaction, my lord, to see your name thereon. More still, if it was the first name – as it was on the other!'

'Mine! On my soul – you cannot mean it? Have you and your like not been calling me traitor, malignant, back-slider? You would have *my* name first on your new paper?'

'I would, joyfully. That is why I am here.'

'To what end?'

'To show that Scotland can unite for a worthy cause. Nothing could more powerfully convince the King that he cannot use Scotland against England. But must come to terms with both realms. For his own good.'

'For his own downfall!'

'Not so. His better state, and well-being. Only so will he regain peaceful rule over his kingdoms. You must believe me that it is so, my lord. I am as much a King's man as are you . . .'

'And as Archibald Campbell?'

'You are consumed with hate for that man. Can you not forget him . . . ?'

'I doubt if he will allow me to! For yourself, Master Henderson, I advise that you cease to blind yourself as to that same man. You I conceive to be honest. But working with him becomes you little. He is evil. And such as associate with him cannot but become corrupted, I think.'

The other said nothing for a few moments, looking across the meadows of Forth to the soaring rock of Stirling Castle.

At length he spoke. 'Supposing that you are right, my lord, should it not be your duty, as you love your country, to seek counter the works of this man you believe so harmful? By any means in your power? And will you not do this the better, more surely, within the cause than without? You chose the King. But at this moment you are rejected of King and Covenant both. You can do but little for Scotland as one man, alone. Yet Sir Thomas Hope says that you only in this realm can match the Marquis of Argyll. I accept that. Therefore I am here.'

'Ha! So that is why it is so secret? At last you are having doubts as to the Campbell?'

Henderson glanced over at Rollo, Argyll's brother-in-law. 'Have I said so? You it is who say it, my lord, not I. But – if so you believe, come back into this noble cause and make it the nobler. Take on the Lieutenant-Generalship of the army. Mediate, from that position, with the King. Sign the Solemn League and Covenant. And put Scotland and England both in your debt. You will find both parliaments not ungrateful, I warrant you. Restitution will be made for your shameful imprisonment. Your debts will be paid in full . . .'

'So-o-o! Debts, eh?' Keenly James Graham searched the other's stern face. 'This of debts interests me. I heard tell of these from . . . elsewhere. What debts, sir?'

The minister raised his bushy brows. 'Why, my lord – I have no knowledge of what they are. But the word is that you are much indebted. The costs of raising and arming your Graham soldiery, perhaps? I know not . . .'

'Nor do I, Master Henderson. In moneys, I am not a rich man. But I am not yet in debt. Even although it suits some man to say that I am! Some man who much advertises the matter. Why?'

'I am sorry if in this I offend. I but follow my instructions . . .'

'*Whose* instructions, sir?'

'That I am not at liberty to say.'

'I think that you are. Must be. This meeting you would

239

wish to keep secret. I should know what is behind it. To know how much I trust I may put in what you offer me.'

'Let it suffice to say that you may have the fullest confidence in it.'

'Does the Committee of the Estates send you to me, then?'

Henderson did not answer. Rollo it was who spoke, stepping closer.

'I say that Master Henderson speaks with the full authority of the Committee.'

'No,' the minister declared. 'I cannot so say. What I do say is that the Convention to open in a few days' time will undoubtedly confirm what I offer.'

'Which can only mean that Argyll himself sent you!'

'None sent me, my lord. I came. Believing that nothing is more earnestly to be desired, in this pass, than that you should join with your peers, and the other Estates of the realm, and by your example bring over the few, if any, who still respect merely the empty shadow of royalty. To your profit, yes. But also, I do aver, to your honour. I came, and will heartily thank God, if He but makes me the minister and mediator of so great a good.' There was no doubting the sincerity of the man. 'Will you accept, my lord?'

'No,' Montrose said quietly, simply.

Obviously Alexander Henderson was quite shattered by that reply. For long moments he could find no words.

'I am sorry,' the other went on. 'But it is not to be. I respect you, Master Henderson, and accept that you mean me well. But I believe you mistaken. Grievously so. And in the cunning hands of evil men. I will not tamper with my conscience. My debts, such as they are, I will pay myself!'

Scotland's foremost divine, in his sixtieth year, looked an old man as he stumbled away, head bowed. These two were never to see each other again.

The Convention of the Estates met at the end of the month, with the new Duke of Hamilton acting as the King's unofficial representative. It heard a declaration from Charles solemnly assuring all of his acceptance, now and in the future, of the liberties and freedoms in worship and government gained by his Scottish subjects. These assurances, however, were not accepted or believed in by the Convention, which proceeded to legislate for war. It promised the English parliamentary delegation which attended armed aid to the tune of 18,000 foot, 2000 light horse, and 1000 dragoons, on condition that their leaders signed the Solemn League and Covenant. But not without payment. £30,000 per month was the price decided upon for this support, the first monthly instalment to be paid before a man or a horse or a cannon moved across the Border. Argyll was not the man to give anything for nothing. It was astounding that the Englishmen agreed to this without a murmur – or none loud enough to affect the issue – and the whole thing was signed and sealed, the King's new duke benignly presiding. The Great Seal of Scotland could not be used on this document, since this was not a true parliament; but the Royal Signet was available, Lanark, Hamilton's brother, being its Keeper. He appended it apparently without hesitation, the King's seal to authorise the King's subjects to fight against the King.

The issue was thereafter referred to the General Assembly of the Kirk for divine blessing. More especially, the new Covenant fell to be ratified, this being very much the Kirk's business. A resounding declaration, it made it clear beyond all question that Presbyterianism was, and always had been God's own choice for the governance of His Church and creation; and that English conformity in this divine pattern was a prerequisite for any advancement in faith as in works. Moreover it showed that religious uniformity alone would produce political harmony such as all honest men desired, and peace between the King's realms. All was done in the King's name, as was right and proper.

If one man saw fit to reject all this, in his obdurate blindness, and that man happened to be the present occupant of the throne, it was unfortunate, but invalidated nothing. No man born of woman should, or could, hold up God's will and purpose. The Solemn League and Covenant was ratified – and God save the King !

Before this highly intricate and ingenious exercise in metaphysics – which probably only Scots divines could have worked out to such satisfactory conclusion – reached its happy finalisation, James Graham had seen the writing on the wall. Despite the appeals of his wife – although this time actually with the blessing of her father – he had kissed her goodbye and shaken his sons gravely by the hand. He was

241

on his way to join his unfortunate liege lord – and this time he did not intend to come back until it was to place himself at the head of a Scots army with which honest men could link the King's name without blushing.

PART THREE

19

IT WAS OXFORD AND NOT LONDON, THE HALL OF CHRIST
Church, not the Palace of Whitehall; but otherwise there
was an uncanny similarity between this and that other occasion when Montrose had waited amongst the courtiers for
King Charles – an ominous thought that did not fail to
occur to him. There was the vast chamber full of the same
inane, high-pitched chatter, the same exaggerated gestures
and costume, the same hothouse atmosphere and strident
insincerity, many of the same people. There were differences,
to be sure. If anything, the women were even more extravagantly dressed, there were more contrasting colours, more
ribbons and bows and jewellery, more bosoms displayed,
more paint and powder, more elaborate hair-styles – for that
is the way in wartime, especially well away from where the
fighting takes place. The men, too, were affected; swords
were not permitted in the royal presence, but military-style
clothing was *de rigueur,* thigh-length riding-boots worn
turned-down were all the rage, and some wore even half-
armour, breastplates – though admittedly richly chased or
gold-inlaid. Spurs clanked and rattled, and the general impression was one of instant readiness for the battlefield –
though few indeed of the cavaliers present had ever heard
a shot fired in anger. Montrose, clad again in his accustomed
black-and-silver best, looked the more elegant by contrast –
but most unfashionably, almost treasonably, unwarlike.

Once again only Kilpont was at his side, with most of the
company eyeing him even more doubtfully than on the last
occasion, a man whose name almost inevitably spelt trouble.
As before, his toe was apt to tap the floor, however serene
and clear his brow and assured his carriage.

The usual fanfare of trumpets preceded the throwing
open of the Hall doors, and all began to dip and bow. It

proved to herald the Queen alone, come from her own Court at Merton College – or, at least, without her husband, for she was by no means alone, a gallant bevy in attendance, chiefest of whom was none other than the Duke of Hamilton, gorgeous in orange and scarlet, become an inveterate traveller between Scotland and the South.

Henrietta Maria came forward into the great room at quite a pace, with little of pause and chatter, seemingly more interested in the brown-and-white spaniel in her arms than in the curtsyings and genuflections. She did however incline her ringleted head here and there – a head down to which Hamilton frequently bent to murmur. Opposite Montrose, the Duke bent lower and spoke for longer.

'Ah, yes – the Lord Montrose!' the Queen said into the hush, clearly. 'Still with us.' And she passed on, eyebrows raised.

Straitening up, James Graham bit his lip. It was not unexpected, but none the more pleasant to endure. He had been weeks now, endeavouring to see the King, unsuccessfully, and had gained no single advantage with the Queen, or with any who might influence her. Charles had been away, first at the Siege of Gloucester – where Montrose had followed him, but failed to achieve contact – and then making a tour of royalist strongholds in the West Country. Henrietta Maria's coolness was no good augury – presumably she had forgotten what she had written earlier about the Graham retaining her confidence; but it was the King whom he had come to see, and see him he would. So he had not withdrawn from Oxford in despair. Now, with Charles only arrived back the previous night, was his opportunity. He had sent in a request for an audience, but received no reply. This was his only way to achieve an interview.

Charles was long in coming, and the Graham foot was tap-tapping again, the more so as loud laughter rang out from up around the Queen's chair-of-state at the head of the room, with Hamilton's bray predominant. It was by no means necessarily concerned with himself, but glances did tend to flicker in Montrose's direction.

Then, at last, the trumpets sounded again, and the King made his entry. This time he had only a small group in attendance, five men – and the sight of two of them lifted the Graham's heart, the young lords Aboyne and Ogilvy.

Of the other three, one, on whose arm the King's hand rested, was a dark, sardonically handsome and tall young man, with a carriage and assurance to match Montrose's own, who looked around him with a sort of grinning fierceness strange to see. Another was a paler, more stolid edition of the same, less dark and piratical. The third was a floridly good-looking man of early middle years, with twisted mouth, beaked nose and stooping wide shoulders – something of an eagle about him, but perhaps a slightly moulting eagle.

'These – who are they?' Montrose murmured, as they bent low.

'That is Rupert, with the King's hand,' Kilpont informed. 'His brother Maurice at the other side. And behind, Antrim.'

'Ah! So-o-o! The MacDonnell. Rupert, I think, I like.'

The Graham, in those moments, knew a further uplift of spirits. Here, at last, was Charles Stewart in the company of real men – not clerics, or painted popinjays or shifty, time-serving politicians, but soldiers. Rupert of the Rhine was one of the finest cavalry-leaders in Europe, despite being no more than twenty-four years. Maurice was not so brilliant, but an able and reliable commander, already experienced though younger still. And Randal MacDonnell, second Earl of Antrim, whatever else he might be, was a warrior, a noted captain of gallowglasses, descended from the Lords of the Isles though planted in Ulster; many looked on him as a Catholic monster of savagery, but he had survived in that blood-soaked land. The fact that the two Scots lordlings, developing fighters both, were included with these others round the King was itself significant.

Charles himself was looking better, less worn. Dashing about even a rebellious country appeared to agree with him. There was more vigour in his step, even in the dignified entry to this audience-chamber. His nephews, on either side of him, were no saunterers, of course.

This time, when they were opposite the Graham, Ogilvy came closer, to touch Prince Rupert's free arm. But there was no need to draw the royal attention. The King turned and paused, of his own accord.

'My lord of Montrose – welcome to my Court,' he said. 'I rejoice to see you in happier case than when last we saw one another.' And he held out his hand.

'Thanks, I am assured, to Your Majesty's gracious intervention on my behalf.' Montrose bowed low, to kiss the royal fingers. 'I am the more your most devoted servant, Sire.'

'So say many, my lord, who act otherwise! But you, I think, do mean it truly. I will speak with you later.' He nodded to Kilpont. 'My lord – I greet you.'

As Majesty passed on, Prince Rupert's glance caught and held James Graham's for a long moment.

'That was better, a deal better,' Kilpont murmured, thereafter. 'At last, perhaps, he will hear you, heed you.'

'Hear, perhaps, yes. But heed? How much influence with the King has Rupert, do you know?'

'Much, they say. More, now, even than the Queen. After all, most victories gained have been won by Rupert.'

One or two courtiers, quick to notice any change in the royal favour, now condescended to notice Montrose – and were received civilly but coolly. The King, with his wife and two nephews, at the head of the Hall, were naturally the focus of attention, accepting or summoning many to their presence. No such call came for the Graham – and he was the last man to push his way to the forefront there, as reminder. The courtiers drifted away.

When, at length, a herald announced that an acting of Will Shakespeare's play entitled *Much Ado About Nothing* would be held presently in the Hall at Merton College, at Her Majesty's gracious command, and all present were invited to attend forthwith. Montrose's patience became more obviously strained. As the company began to follow the King and Queen from Christ Church Hall and through the leaf-strewn and mist-hung gardens to near-by Merton, James Graham had to steel himself to move in their wake.

But, in an alley of dripping clipped-yew, the pair were approached by a resplendent figure, the new Earl of Dysart. This was none other than the ineffable and utterly untrustworthy Will Murray, former whipping-boy to the King, son of the minister of Dysart in Fife, and now Lord in Waiting. Charles was very free with his earldoms – or, at least, with the titles of such; for no lands went with them, and it was all a travesty of nobility to such as Montrose, for whom an earldom meant ancient lineage, great authority, vast territories and patriarchal responsibilities. This man in especial he looked upon as no more than a dangerous mountebank, and knew to be a creature of Hamilton's.

'His Majesty will see you in the Master's Room at Merton, my lord of Montrose,' he announced, almost as though he had personally arranged it. 'Ah . . . no doubt you will be able to inform His Majesty that the position in Scotland is by no means so ill against him as some ill-wishers seek to convince him? That most with any power there are loyal, and only seek the King's good.'

'What I say to the King, sir, is between myself and His Grace,' the other returned briefly.

'Undoubtedly. But there are those who, for their own purposes, seek to delude the King that the Scots are rising in arms against His Majesty. You, I am sure, know this to be untrue, and like my lord Duke of Hamilton can assure King Charles that such rising will only be against the King's enemies. If such indeed is the burden of your message, the Duke is convinced that His Majesty will be much relieved, and that you will have cause to rejoice in a successful outcome of your visit to Court.'

'Indeed? And what would constitute such success, sir, in the eyes of the Duke of Hamilton?'

'Who knows, my lord? Advancement of your personal cause and circumstances in Scotland, no doubt. The Privy Council, perhaps? The Duke is very influential. A marquisate, even, might conceivably be . . .'

'I see, sir. I shall not forget the Duke of Hamilton's interest in my concerns. Nor your own!'

'That is only fitting. And wise,' the other said, as he led the Graham past an armed guard and into a handsomely panelled chamber of Merton.

King Charles sat at a table spread with refreshments, and in the company of the five men who had attended him earlier, plus two others; one nearing middle-age, one youngish, whom Montrose recognised as Sir Edward Hyde, the Chancellor, and the Lord Digby, heir to the Earl of Bristol, and one of Charles's favourites and commanders. There was no sign of Hamilton, or of his brother and shadow, Lanark.

'Come, my lord of Montrose,' the King said, in friendly fashion. 'Let us hope that we will not long detain you from Her Majesty's entertainment. Drink a glass of wine with us. Will – conduct the Lord Kilpont to Her Majesty, and request her to proceed with the play-acting. We shall join

249

her later.' Prince Rupert murmured in his uncle's ear. The King shrugged, and added, 'And, Will – you need not return.'

That further commended the Prince to Montrose.

'Sire, I am grateful to you for this audience,' he announced. 'I have been seeking it for weeks. I rejoice also in the company which attends you here.' He glanced particularly at Rupert. 'In what I have to say, I believe that their guidance will be invaluable.'

'Indeed, my lord? Invaluable to *my* cause, or yours?'

'Yours, Sire. And that of your Scots realm. I seek none of my own. If I did, I think I would not seek it in Oxford!'

Rupert laughed, though none other did so.

'Mm. You are frank, my lord, at least,' the King said, warily.

'I came to be frank, Sire. Only that. There has been too little of frankness to Your Majesty, in matters Scottish, I believe. I trust that I have your royal permission to be so, entirely?'

'I can scarcely say you nay. But – do you say then, that my other advisers in or on Scotland are less than frank?'

'I do. Especially the most highly placed of them, the Duke of Hamilton.'

At the general gasp, Rupert slapped his thigh, while his uncle stroked his pointed beard.

'There can be over-frankness, I think, my lord of Montrose. Especially in matters of personal opinion.'

'No doubt, Sire. But not in matters of state. As is this. I declare to you, before these many witnesses, that the Duke of Hamilton has long deceived you. To what purpose I know not, but with grievous hurt to your realm and royal cause. Others likewise. But he to your most injury.'

'I think that you forget yourself, my lord. The Duke is my friend.'

Rupert spoke, his English perfect but his voice husky, guttural. 'Sire – no man makes such charges before witnesses unless he is convinced of their truth. Or is a great fool. Does any here conceive the Earl of Montrose to be that?'

'*We* would be the fools not to hear what my lord has to say in this matter, Your Majesty,' Edward Hyde said. He looked like a shrewd cherub.

'You have never loved James Hamilton, Sir Edward. Nor

has Rupert,' the King complained. He shrugged. 'But – say on, my lord.'

'The Duke of Hamilton, Sire, I do assure you, is wholly in the pocket of the Marquis of Argyll. Than whom, I believe, you have no greater enemy. Argyll now rules Scotland, and Hamilton chooses to aid him in it. However much against your royal interests.'

'Or yours, perhaps?' Digby put in. He was a good-looking, fair-haired and blue-eyed young man, impetuous but not unintelligent, though with a petulant mouth.

Montrose nodded. 'Or mine, indeed. Or those of any loyal and honest man.'

'The Marquis of Argyll is your enemy, my lord – as all know.'

'And yours, sir, I hope! And every man's here – since he is the King's enemy. He would take the King's Scottish realm from him – has all but done so. And now seeks to aid those who would take his English one also.'

'The Duke of Hamilton assures me that the Marquis of Argyll's only intention is to mediate,' Charles said.

'Argyll's intention, Sire, is to set up a Commonwealth, in which you have no part. And in which he rules Scotland – and has much say in the rule of England.'

'This I cannot believe. This new Covenant, this Solemn League, is mistaken. But not disloyal.'

'That is not Argyll's work, but Henderson's. Henderson is honest. Argyll but uses him. And Hamilton aids him in it.'

'What proof have you of what you assert, my lord?' Digby demanded.

'Ample. Would the English parliament pay £30,000 per month for the services of a mediator? That is what they have agreed to pay for the aid of the Scots army. From the day it crosses the Border. Indeed a month's payment is already made!'

Clearly all were shaken by this revelation, staring at the speaker.

'It appears that my lord Duke has not informed you of this? Yet he was present and assenting when the compact was made.'

None spoke.

'Further to this. Your English subjects, Sire, as deputation to Scotland, were concerned that the Scots should indeed fulfil their part of the bargain – which was to be 18,000 foot, 2000 light horse, and 1000 dragoons . . .'

'Christ God – over 20,000 men !' Rupert burst out.

'Yes, Your Highness – over 20,000. Large mediation! I was offered the Lieutenant-Generalship of it, under old Leslie. Indeed, it was much pressed on me. But that the English commissioners should be convinced that Argyll would fulfil what he was being paid to do, the compact was sealed with your own Royal Signet. Of which the Earl of Lanark, Hamilton's brother, is the Keeper. He sealed it in person.'

Charles Stewart gazed great-eyed past them all to the panelled wall, showing no emotion; but his long, delicate fingers beat a tattoo on the table-top.

'It gives me no pleasure to declare this shame to Your Majesty,' Montrose went on. 'But that you should know of it there is no doubt.'

'You say, my lord, that you were made offer of the Lieutenant-Generalship?' Rupert asked. 'This seems scarcely believable.'

'So thought I, Highness – until I discovered what my duties were to be! They were quite clear. If the English parliament forces were to lose, and the Scots army found itself in a difficult position deep in England, facing Your victorious Majesty, I was to be there, to mediate indeed, my known love of Your Majesty to prove that Leslie's army meant you no ill. On the other hand, if your enemies were winning, I was but *Lieutenant*-General, junior to Leslie, to do what I was ordered. I was to be, indeed, but a convenient warranty, if required, a safeguard and prudent discretion should matters go ill.' He paused for a moment. 'I think that Argyll and Hamilton overestimated my influence with Your Majesty!'

The Earl of Antrim guffawed.

Prince Maurice spoke, his voice thicker, more deliberate than his brother's. 'How many men has the Marquis of Newcastle, Sire? In Yorkshire?' he asked bluntly.

Hyde answered for him. 'No more than 6000, sir.'

'And the Lord Byron? In Lancashire?'

'He is now at Chester. With but 4000.'

Those around the King looked at each other. None appeared any longer to doubt Montrose's assertions, at least as regards the probability of a Scots invasion.

'How soon, my lord?' Rupert demanded.

'Who knows? They have been preparing, assembling, for long. I cannot think that Alexander Leslie will delay much longer.'

'Sir Alexander Leslie swore to me, when I created him Earl of Leven, that he would never again take the field against me,' Charles declared sadly.

None commented.

'Have you any suggestions, my lord of Montrose?' Hyde asked, pursing full lips.

'I have sir. What I came here to ask of the King. It were better that the Scots army, when it comes, be drawn back to Scotland than that you must needs fight it here. This I would seek to do. But, more than this – Scotland, I swear, can be saved for Your Majesty. Turned again from the evil courses of Argyll and his puppets. Most of the folk are still loyal. And the nobility much hate the rule of fanatic preachers. Give me authority to raise Scotland for the King, and I will restore Your Majesty's ancient realm to you. Or die in the attempt.'

There was a murmur of mixed admiration and doubt from his hearers. But Rupert raised his dark head abruptly, and stepping closer, thrust out his hand to the Graham, no word spoken.

The King looked troubled, nobly troubled, a man to whom decision-taking was agony. His glance at his nephew was almost reproachful.

'I esteem your courage, devotion, goodwill, my lord,' he said carefully. 'But have you sufficiently considered? You are a young man yet. Head of a notable house. But single-handed, how could you raise a whole nation? Which is already in arms against me.'

'My lord is not single-handed, Sire.' That was young Aboyne, making a first contribution. 'Clan Gordon will join with the Grahams. And where Gordon goes, will go many another.'

'As will Ogilvy,' the other lordling declared, as stoutly.

Montrose smiled at his two lieutenants, who scarcely numbered forty years between them.

Digby snorted. 'This is war, my lords – not game playing!' he declared. 'If what has been said is true, a deal more than this will be required to win Scotland from the Marquis of

Argyll and his Covenanters. I advise that Your Majesty thinks most carefully.'

'Can the King lose by it?' the Graham asked. 'I ask nothing but a commission to raise Scotland in his name. Authority. If I do not succeed, what have I cost him? A paper. And at least I will give Argyll and Leslie pause. That I promise. They will be less eager for adventures in England while I am recruiting at their backs.'

'Aye, Sire – here's a ploy!' the Scots-Irish MacDonnell, Earl of Antrim, broke in. '*I* can take a hand here, by God! I have never loved the Campbell. I will ship 10,000 gallowglasses across the Irish Sea into Argyll, by your leave. And see how your new Marquis likes the style of them!' Antrim apparently continued to cherish the age-old Clan Donald hatred for Clan Dairmid, even transplanted in Ulster. And undoubtedly he resented the Argyll marquisate.

'We have all heard of your 10,000 Irishry!' Digby said sourly. 'But even if we were to *see* them, for a change, they would be Catholics to a man! His Majesty would needs think twice before unleashing such on his Protestant realms. Even on Scotland!'

'Insolent puppy!' Antrim snarled. 'Think you the King's subjects must all be such as you? Mother of Christ forbid it! I . . .'

'Enough, my lords – enough!' Charles said, raising his hand. 'Restrain yourselves, at least in my presence, I charge you. My lord of Montrose – I will consider this matter. Consider it well. This is Scotland. Take sure advice. I thank you for your good will. Even if I cannot thank you for your tidings.' He sighed. 'Now, my friends – let us join Her Majesty.'

'And Hamilton, Sire?' Rupert demanded. 'What of the Duke?'

'This also I must consider. Make enquiry, painful enquiry. It may not be quite so ill as my lord believes. Who knows?'

'It may be *more* ill, Uncle! Cherishing a snake to your bosom can cost you dear! I say that you should arrest him forthwith. And his precious brother. And enquire thereafter.'

'That would be too hasty, Rupert. You are ever hasty. But we shall test the matter, never fear.' Charles rose. 'Her Majesty will look for us . . .'

Charles Stewart ran true to form. He delayed decision.

Hamilton and Lanark departed again for Scotland, unchallenged. And that he should not be badgered and harried in the meantime, the King arranged it so that impatient and importunate young men should be kept occupied and out of the way while he made up his mind. The Princes Rupert and Maurice were given a variety of urgent if minor military tasks to perform, from this Oxford base – since large-scale warfare was considered to be out of the question during the particularly severe winter conditions, by both sides, with armies and garrisons more or less sitting tight up and down England. And Montrose was instructed to accompany the young princes on these sallies, as schooling and experience – and was nothing loth, finding it infinitely to be preferred to the hothouse atmosphere of over-crowded Oxford, with its excesses, its drinking and gaming and brawling, its duels and back-stabbing, its promiscuity and vice, its everlasting play-acting, dancing, music and feasting – so strange a Court for a dedicated and religiously-minded monarch, who seemed indeed so other-worldly and high-minded as scarcely to be aware of what went on around him. Montrose found in Rupert especially a fellow being almost entirely after his own heart, and they were close friends more or less from first sight – even though the prince had a ruthlessness and violence in him which found no echo in the Graham. But particularly in matters military they made a pair, audacious, swift, artful, courageous, each with his own genius to complement the other's. Together during that bitter cold December and January, with small mobile forces, they dashed about the upper Thames area, relieving a castle here, and a village there, raiding in the Chilterns and Cotswolds, encouraging isolated commanders, threatening the communications of Fairfax's and Waller's armies, superintending the fortification of Towcester and other towns. Montrose found it all greatly to his taste; and had it not been for a preoccupation with the Scots situation, and a fretting that the King appeared to be incapable of positive action, it would have been one of the most satisfying periods of his life.

Then, on the 15th of January 1644, ignoring the winter conditions, Field-Marshal the Earl of Leven led the Scots army into England, and came fighting, not mediating, with the Marquis of Argyll acting colonel to his own Campbell regiment therein. Suddenly all was changed.

When the news reached Oxford, Charles was busy organising a parliament of his own, in opposition to that other sitting in London fifty-two miles away. His hurt was great. He actually wept. And when, presently, Montrose and Rupert got back from Towcester, Edward Hyde in person came to the former's quarters to conduct him to the King.

'I believe that His Majesty will grant your wishes now,' he said. 'He has just heard that all the North-East is falling to the Scots arms.'

'If I had been in Scotland these weeks past, instead of here, sir, Leslie might well not have marched.'

'I know it. But . . . you will be more likely to gain your ends with the King, my lord, if you refrain from mention of it!'

At Christ Church, the King had only his nephew Maurice with him when Hyde brought the Graham in. The younger men exchanged glances. Charles was looking drawn, unhappy, pouches under his fine eyes.

'You have heard the tidings from the North, my lord?' he asked wearily.

'I have, Sire, to my sorrow. If scarcely to my surprise. I grieve for your royal cause. But I believe that it is not yet too late to better it.'

'Ha – you say so? You still believe that you can win Scotland for me? Even now?'

'Even now, Sire. Although it will be the more difficult.'

'What do you need from me, to that end, my lord?'

'First of all, Your Majesty's faith and trust. If I am to imbue others with the spirit to rise and fight for you, I must convince them that Your Majesty is wholly behind me. Proof of such trust I do require.'

'You shall have it, sir. I shall appoint you my Governor and Commander-in-Chief in Scotland. Give you commission as my Captain-General and viceroy. And create you Marquis of Montrose. Will that serve to advertise my royal trust, my friend?' It was not often that Charles Stewart came out with decision at this rate.

'Hrm.' Montrose cleared his throat. 'I am deeply sensible of these high honours, appointments, Sire,' he said. 'They are altogether too much, I think. As well as undeserved. And not what I intended . . .'

'No? Then what, my lord? What more can I do for you?'

'Not for *me*, Sire. It is for the folk in Scotland that I

require this proof, not for myself. That they may accept that I have now your entire confidence. And that, hm, others have not! For me to be Marquis of Montrose would be to my much honour. But would it convince my countrymen, who have seen other marquises created? Even dukes!'

Hyde coughed, and Charles looked almost shocked. Prince Maurice's smile was probably little help.

'I regret your attitude, my lord.' That was said with royalest dignity.

'Then I crave Your Majesty's forbearance. I acknowledge that I may be too frank. But the occasion warrants plain speaking, does it not?'

The noble head inclined, but only just. 'What is it you seek, then?'

'What would convince the Scots people that Your Majesty no longer trusted those who have ill-advised you for so long. Your dismissal of Hamilton and his brother.'

'That is in train, my lord. The Duke of Hamilton and the Earl of Lanark shamefully deceived me. They have been summoned from Scotland. They will learn of my royal displeasure.'

'If they come!' Maurice murmured.

'That is a step well taken, Sire. It will please many in Scotland, and ease my path.'

'What else do you require of me?'

'Nothing, Sire – but your blessing.'

'That you have in full measure. But you have more. As Governor as well as Captain-General, you will have my *authority*. To act in my royal name. To levy and requisition as you need. To appoint to office, and demote. To bring to trial, to judge, to execute if need be. A grave responsibility for so young a man. But you will require all such powers, I think.'

'No, Sire. Humbly and with respect – no.' Montrose shook his head. 'Such powers and state I do not desire. More, I conceive it to be harmful to your cause. See you, Sire – Scotland is a proud country. And as you say, I am a young man. Offence must not be given to any who have the power to fight for you. We are a people of clans and great families, jealous each of our name and standing. I am one of the earls of Scotland, the *old* earls – that is sufficient. Your Grace alone is *Ard Righ*, the High King. None must fail to flock to your royal standard because *I* seem to set myself too high.

As many would, Sire, were I to be your viceroy. I know my own people. I will not even be Captain-General. Not at this time. Lieutenant only. Under some other. With Your Majesty's permission.'

'You are a strange man, my lord of Montrose. But it appears that you well know your own mind. And I accept that you know your strange countrymen – and mine. But . . . if you are to be only Lieutenant, who is to be Captain? Who, in Scotland, would you have me make Captain-General, master over Montrose?'

James Graham found a smile. 'None that I may think of, Sire. Since it must needs be a soldier. Rather it should be someone here, I think, in England. Close to your royal person. But someone whom the Scots will accept. Not – not an Englishman!' He paused. 'Prince Rupert you have made Master of the Horse and Duke of Cumberland. Might not Your Majesty make His Highness Prince Maurice Captain-General for Scotland?'

The King looked from one to the other, and then to Hyde. 'I cannot spare my nephew to Scotland, my lord. Not in this pass. Once the campaigning season starts, there is too much for him, for us all, to do here.'

'I did not think that you could, Sire. I will gladly send reports to my Captain-General – at Oxford!'

Maurice emitted his throaty chuckle, unoffended. 'He desires only my shadow, Sire – not my substance,' he said. 'And I shall be able to rule all the Scots at your Court here – who have until now ignored me!'

'These I intend to take back to Scotland!' Montrose countered.

Charles, who was not a man of humour, looked slightly dis-approving of this levity in his presence. But he glanced at Hyde, who nodded. 'Very well, my lord. It shall be so. Lieutenant-General you shall be, under Captain-General the Prince Maurice of Bohemia. Yet in Scotland you will have the complete command. Over all who fight for me. Including my lord of Antrim's Irish. It is agreed.'

'Mm. Sire – Lord Antrim's Irish . . . ? Is this wise? Lord Digby spoke of it, before – and I saw point to his fears. To loose a large number of Catholic Irish on Protestant Scotland might but ill serve your cause. They might make my task the harder.'

Charles frowned. None of his commanders wanted the Catholic Irish, even Lord Herbert, himself a Catholic. 'My lord – I will forgo the use of thousands of loyal troops because of unsuitable religious prejudice. We are all Christians, I would remind you! Lord Antrim's levies can best be used in Scotland. It will give you a core of experienced fighters. You cannot go to Scotland alone, single-handed, to conquer a country. You will delay your return until the Irish force is ready to join you there.'

'With respect, Your Majesty, I would prefer to find my way secretly back to Scotland, and forthwith. Once in my own place, I swear I should not be long in raising an army to fight for you – and to force Argyll and Leslie to look anxiously behind them. Without calling in the Irish . . .'

'No, my lord. That is not how it will best be done. This, from the first, must be seen to be the King's answer to rebellion. Not a further rebellion taking place behind the invading Scots army. I have spoken of it to certain of my commanders and advisers, and on this we are agreed. You must invade Scotland in *my* name – not foster a rising within Scotland on your own. The difference is important. I will send you to my lord of Newcastle, at York, and request that he supply you with a body of horse to serve as kernel of your new army. Also arms and ammunition – these are expected from Denmark any day. I will give you a commission to raise certain levies in Cumberland and Westmorland. With these, you can make entry to Scotland, in force. In the west, since the Scots army it seems controls the east. Carlisle, perhaps. When my lord of Antrim's force is ready to meet you, from Ireland. Thus you will come to Scotland as my Lieutenant-General indeed – not as a private nobleman seeking to stir up petty insurrection behind the Scots government. You understand?'

Montrose sought to keep his voice level. 'This will take valuable time, Sire. And for me to lead Englishmen and Irishmen into Scotland will not endear me to many Scots. I had rather rouse themselves to put their house in order.'

'*My* house, my lord of Montrose, I'd remind you! If you go as my representative to my Scottish realm, you will do so as *I* decide.'

The Graham bowed. 'As Your Majesty commands . . .'

20

It was, in fact, fourteen weeks later, on the 13th of April, that Montrose left English soil and crossed the River Esk into Scotland as royal Lieutenant. And, despite the delay, and the King's desire that he should do so at the head of an impressive force, he forded the river with only a few hundred ill-assorted men, many of them already disgruntled. The Earl of Newcastle, commander in the North of England, already short of men, with only 8000 at grips with Leslie's 21,000 on the Durham border, was in no mood, or case, to obey his monarch's command and detach precious cavalry for the Scots venture. And the royalists of Cumberland and Westmorland, seeing the way that things were going, with Leslie winning over a wide front, were much more concerned to stay at home and protect their own hearthstones from the barbarian invaders than to volunteer for a hazardous wild-goose chase into Scotland. As for Antrim's 10,000 Irish, there was still neither hint nor hair of them, although the MacDonnell had promised to deliver them in force before the end of April. Not desiring the complications that such a Catholic host might produce in the Presbyterian Lowlands, Montrose had managed to persuade the King that these should land only in Argyll and the West Highlands, where Catholicism was still the prevalent religion, there to menace the Campbells in their own country.

Montrose's company, therefore, was an almost farcical host with which to invade a warlike and already warned country – for, of course, it had all been the talk of Oxford for months, and few in Scotland had not heard that the Earl of Montrose was coming, with a ravening horde of Catholic savages from Ireland; so much so that Archibald Campbell had hurriedly withdrawn himself and his regiment from Leslie's army and sped northwards to defend his West Highland patrimony. The Graham had 1300 altogether, consisting of 800 Cumberland and Westmorland militia foot, and 500 assorted horse – very assorted, consisting of 100 ill-spared and poorly mounted troopers from Lord Newcastle, three troops of local yeomanry, and the rest gentry, Scots exiles, North Country royalist squires, and a few paid professional officers from the foreign wars. As a fighting force it was unbalanced, undisciplined, formless, and would have been laughable had it been any laughing matter. James Graham felt more like weeping. This was the last way that he would have chosen to return to his country and commence his campaign – a campaign which, even with the best of conditions and good fortune, would be a colossal gamble, all but a forlorn hope. To attempt it in these circumstances was little short of madness.

And yet, even so, the King's new Lieutenant-General could not but rejoice, in some measure, could not prevent his spirits from soaring, as he set foot once again on his native soil, with possibly the greatest venture of his life ahead of him, an endeavour which only he could make, a challenge to dwarf all others. None was better aware than he was of the difficulties and heartbreaks which must inevitably lie ahead. Yet he rode through the spring morning, amongst the blazing gorse and broom, the shouting of the larks, the long-lying snow-wreaths and the clamour of tumbling waters, with a lightness of heart – however heavy might be some of the thoughts at the back of his head.

Crossing the green plain of Gretna and the mouth of Annandale, field of battles innumerable, they worked round the wide-spreading Solway estuary and the wildfowl-haunted reaches of the Lochar Moss, to the great castle of Caerlaverock within its marshland moats. This presented no challenge, for its lord was in fact with Montrose – Robert Maxwell, head of that turbulent clan and Earl of Nithsdale. But he was a Catholic, and the Graham was loth indeed to burden his campaign with any further alleged Popish bias such as it already was being given. He got over the difficulty, meantime, by sending the Earl off into Galloway, to find and try to control a fellow-religionist, the Viscount Kenmure, who for some time had been terrorising these remote counties, all in the King's name, roaming the country with a brandy-barrel on a pole as his standard, indiscriminately pillaging, burning, raping.

Unfortunately this judicious detachment of Lord Niths- dale was promptly followed by another, neither ordered nor anticipated. Most of the Cumberland and Westmorland militia suddenly took fright, declaring that they had not enlisted for adventures in Scotland. They wanted to go home. Montrose might have taken a stern line with these, threatening them with the penalties of mutiny; but on a desperate attempt such as this, he saw no advantage in clinging to a reluctant crew. They were foot, anyway, and as a born horseman he tended to see such as more of a delaying factor to his preferred swift movement than any- thing else. He sent them home.

That he was immediately thereafter joined by a squadron of well-armed horse under the Lord Herries, was a doubtful compensation – for Herries was another Maxwell and Catholic.

A rather more welcome encouragement met them when they pressed on the few miles to Dumfries, still without opposition, in the person of Provost John Corsan and some of his magistrates and townsfolk, come out to greet them. Dumfries, where Nith joined Solway, was the first sizeable town on this west side of Scotland, and this adherence was heartening. Montrose decided that here he would take the significant step of raising the royal standard of King Charles.

So, on a cold and showery afternoon, the 14th of April 1644, in the Market Place of the trim red-stone burgh of Dumfries, trumpets shrilled and the red-and-gold Lion Rampant banner of the Kings of Scots was unfurled, to flap in the breeze, while James Graham, fifth Earl of Montrose, read out his commission as the King's Lieutenant-General – under Captain-General the Prince Maurice – with all necessary powers and authority to restore the King's rule and governance to his ancient realm. To ringing cheers he then read out a proclamation of his own composing, calling on the people of Scotland to join him for the defence of the true Portestant religion, His Majesty's just and sacred authority, the fundamental laws and privileges of Parlia- ment, and the peace and freedom of all oppressed and en- thralled subjects. God Save the King.

It was a stirring moment, long awaited. The Earls of

Kinnoull and Wigtown, supported by the Lords Herries, Aboyne, Ogilvy and Kilpont, led the cheering; but the occasion was rather spoiled by another earl of Scotland – or at least by a message which reached Montrose only a few minutes previously, to the effect that Lieutenant-General the Earl of Callander was making forced marches from Edinburgh south-westwards, to intercept him with 7000 men. This was none other than his old colleague the Lord Almond, fellow lieutenant to old Leslie and co-signatory of the Cumbernauld Bond, who had now succeeded his late brother as Earl of Callander, and moved firmly into Argyll's camp. But whatever his loyalties and politics, he was an able soldier; and the thought of him and his 7000 only three or four days' march away, was dampening to enthusiasm.

Montrose, however, gave a scratch banquet for the Provost and leading citizens of Dumfries that evening, and thereafter even danced with Mrs Corsan, the Lady Maxwell of Munches and other ladies. But however attentive he seemed, his mind was in fact filled with assessings and calculations other than such partners might have considered suitable. How fast could a host of that number, mainly foot, travel through hill country still largely snow-bound after a particularly severe winter? By what route would they come, using which passes through the Lowther Hills especially? Was there any point where a few hundred horsemen might successfully ambush such thousands? Could, in fact, such determined horsemen reach the passes in time? And if they failed, would that be the end of the King's cause in Scotland before it had even begun?

Such cogitations tended to fairly consistently depressing conclusions – which no doubt was hard on the ladies. And unfortunately James Graham perforce took the cogitations to bed with him that night – which was hard on himself. Moreover, it did not fail to occur to him that if he could think along these lines, others could do likewise. Others whom he was hopefully summoning to the royal standard. In the circumstances, with no sizeable increase in the King's force meantime, would *any* in fact, in their sane sense, rally to himself at Dumfries? It seemed improbable.

The next day and the next Montrose waited by the Nith, and learned that his fears were well founded. A few lairds, mainly Maxwells and Catholics, brought small groups and contingents. But their enemies, the Johnstons of Annandale, under the new Earl of Hartfell, though nominally royalist, kept their distance; as did the Douglasses, Murrays, Armstrongs, Elliots, Jardines and other West March clans. And Callander drew closer apace.

On the third day, James Graham accepted the bitter reality. Dumfries and Galloway are separated from the rest of Scotland by great ranges of hills and wide empty uplands. There was not another town of any size for fifty miles, no populous area where he might look for major support. And thereafter, the lowlands of Ayrshire and the uplands of Lanarkshire were both strongly Covenant, dominated by Loudoun, Cassillis, Eglinton and Hamilton. This was no country to invade from the south in small numbers. He had told the King and his advisers so; but they had known best. With under 1000 men all told, he was in no position to press on against an army seven times his size. Dumfries was not a walled town, and impossible to defend; besides, for him to be cooped up, besieged, only a mile or two into Scotland, would look pathetic, and do no service to the royal cause. There was nothing for it but to retire whence he had come – and quickly.

But one duty he had, and must attend to, first. The local volunteers must be dispersed and sent home, however much they might protest. Since obviously he could not adequately make use of them, they must at least be spared the reprisals that Callander's army would be almost certain to visit upon them.

To a man of his temperament and pride, the entire business was an agony. And, almost, he left the final withdrawal too late. Callander sent most of his horse ahead of the main body, and they came dashing down Nith only a few miles to the north of the town at the same time as Montrose was riding out to the south. It became practically a race for the Border, and Carlisle city walls. They even had to abandon some of the heavier cannon, which were severely holding them up. It was debacle, complete and shameful. Probably only because Callander's cavalry had no instructions about crossing into England and confronting the fortress of Carlisle, did the royalist force make good its escape, without loss. Its leader, set-faced, drank deep of the draught of humiliation. Only one credit was to be salvaged from the entire sorry affair. He was being taught a valuable lesson. Never again must he allow himself to be forced into commanding a military adventure which he knew to be mistaken, even by his liege lord. His duty was to serve the King – but with his mind and will, not merely with his blind obedience. James Graham was a man who did not spare himself. He blamed himself now – not for this fiasco of an invasion, but for not having refused utterly to countenance it from the beginning, when he knew it folly.

Never did a general less relish his safety as the gate of Carlisle, an English citadel, clanged shut behind him and in the face of his compatriots.

Strangely enough, this deplorable withdrawal by no means produced the storm of contumely and derision from the royalist camp which might have been expected. The English commanders cared little for the situation in Scotland; and the Earl of Newcastle in especial saw Montrose's return as admirable, heaven-sent indeed. Instead of being blamed, he found himself being treated as a wise man who had seen the better course, accepted as the sorely tried Newcastle's deputy in the North-West, and given urgent commands to raise all Cumberland and Westmorland and North Lancashire, and to assail Leslie's right flank. The impression given was almost that he had forgone pressing on into Scotland in order to return to the greater danger in England. If there was some slight balm to a young man's wounded pride in this, there was also another salutary lesson. The English, unlike the Scots, had the priceless gift of single-mindedness, of seeing matters always and entirely from their own point of view; nothing extraneous really mattered – unlike the metaphysical Scots to whom everything mattered, and too much. Here was understanding vital to any student of statecraft, any commander likely to handle troops of both nations.

Montrose, rather to his further surprise, found the Cumbrians and Westmorlanders, whom he had tended to dismiss as craven, far from it. On their own ground, fighting for something they approved of, they were both keen and valiant. Recruiting for the Scots venture had been grim; now it went with a swing. Soon the King's Lieutenant for Scotland under his new hat as royalist general in the North-West had an army of nearly 6000 under his command, mainly foot admittedly, and untrained, raw. But then, so were most of those who would be opposed to them, in civil warfare. With these he was able, not only to force Callander to keep well back on his own side of the Border, but to harry Leslie's right by making repeated brief sorties through the Pennine passes. He also formed something of a barrier diagonally across the country, to deter the parliamentary army based on Chester from moving north-east to link up with Leslie. If this was not what James Graham had left Kincardine Castle to do, at least it had the effect of salvaging his reputation as a commander – indeed enhancing it – and of giving his bevy of young Scots aristocrats, now willy-nilly officering North Country English levies, valuable experience in mobile warfare.

The strategic situation, that spring of 1644, was complex, with the centre of gravity moving distinctly into the North of England. Or at least, into Yorkshire, for the Scots were steadily pressing Newcastle southwards on that city, after being held up by the snows of a phenomenally hard winter. England was now a bewildering patchwork of loyalties, with basically, the parliament strong in London, the South and East, the King in the North and West, and the Midlands a chaos. With the Scots wholly altering the balance in the North, the Midlands and Eastern parliamentarians decided to try to join up with Leslie and take the Earl of Newcastle from the rear. To this end the two Fairfaxes moved up their central army into South Yorkshire and the Earl of Manchester commanding the Eastern Association, headed north-west. Newcastle called urgently for help.

The King ordered Rupert, building a new army at Shrewsbury and the Welsh marches, to hasten to Newcastle's aid with all speed. And he sent the hot-tempered Earl of Crawford to Montrose at Carlisle.

'You are to assail Leslie's rear,' that fiery-headed, red-bearded nobleman declared. 'Forget Scotland and Callander, meantime. Newcastle and the North must be saved at all costs.'

James Graham frowned at this chief of the Lindsays, sixteenth Earl, who had spent much of his life at the Court in England and had latterly been colonel of a regiment of royalist horse. 'Does His Majesty realise what he asks?' he demanded. 'I have here a motley crew of Westmorland squires, Cumbrian farmers and Scots gentry. Take most of them twenty miles from their homes and they mutiny! With these, the King asks me to assail the rear of an army five times as large, the best led and best trained and disciplined in three kingdoms. With another at my back, led by a man I know to be a most able soldier...'

'His Majesty does not ask – he commands!' Crawford said brusquely. 'But, look not so glum, man. Being cautious is no way to win battles. The King has sent me to strengthen your hand. We will tickle old Leslie's backside the way I tickled Waller's at Alton! Never fear!'

Montrose, with sad experience both of His Majesty's military commands and judgment of character, considered the dashingly picturesque but arrogant figure before him – who had lost 600 men at Alton in a grandiloquent gesture that gained precisely nothing. He could have done without the Lindsay – especially as he had not brought his regiment with him. But royal commands or none, he was the general here, not Crawford; and he was not going to make the same mistake twice. He had no faith in the royalist Northern forces, or in their leadership – indeed in any of Charles's generals other than Rupert and Maurice; nor had he any wish to involve himself seriously in the English civil war, when Scotland was tugging at him all the time. But he had to do something in the circumstances. He would interpret the King's orders in his own fashion – and endeavour, tactfully if possible, to keep the sixteenth Earl in his place.

On the 9th of May, then, leaving the unreliable and slow infantry behind to offer some sort of threat both to Callander's army over the Border and to the Lancastrian parliamentarians, with all the horse he could raise, 400 of his own and 600 Cumbrian yeomanry under Colonel Clavering, a distinctly cynical professional soldier, Montrose set out eastwards from Carlisle at speed, the fire-eating Crawford in attendance. Sparing neither men nor horses, he drove through and across the spinal heights of Cumberland and Northumberland all day, by the valleys of the Irthing and South Tyne, by Brampton, Naworth and Haltwhistle, thirty-five miles to Hexham. There, although already many of his men were complaining, he turned northwards up North Tyne, and in the long May evening half-light climbed out of the valley and over the bare empty moors, by Chollerton and Kirkheaton to the valley of the Wansbeck. Here, at Hartburn, he relented, and allowed his weary and outraged troopers a few hours' rest, not for their sake so much as that of the horses. Crawford, though eloquent on the military art for the first half of the day, had been silent now for some time; but Clavering at last was beginning to look less disillusioned. They halted in woodland, but no cooking fires were to be lit. Seven miles ahead, down this twisting vale, the main highway from Scotland to the south ran through the fortified town of Morpeth. A vital point on Leslie's lines of communication, it was held by a Scots garrison. Montrose proposed to assault it as soon after daybreak as might be.

Of a still misty early morning, divided into four squadrons under Crawford, Clavering, Aboyne and Ogilvy, they trotted on quietly down Wansbeck towards the sleeping town. Morpeth lay in the valley-floor, at a wide hairpin bend where the Colling Burn joined the Wansbeck, with gentle slopes to north, east and south, but steep banks to the west, on top of one of which perched its castle and citadel. This was, of course, the key to the place, and though not exceptionally strong in itself, nor very large, was very strongly sited. Montrose had been here during his winter with Leslie's army at Newcastle three years before, and knew the position.

At this hour of the morning the town gates would all be shut; and any attempt to storm them would inevitably arouse the castle and dissipate any advantage of surprise. Leaving his force hidden in the scrub woodland around the ruins of Newminster Abbey, Montrose went quietly forward with Clavering, to prospect.

They were able to get within 300 yards of the town gates, in cover. Neither gates nor walls looked very serious barriers, Clavering pointed out.

The other would have none of it. 'We could get ourselves into the town, yes. But what will that serve, if the castle is warned? We do not know the numbers of the garrison. And they had cannon in that citadel when last I was here. It is a Scots garrison. They might not hesitate to fire down into the town, an *English* town. Either we take that castle by surprise, or we do not take it at all, since we have no cannon. So – we await the opening of these gates. And pray that it may not be long delayed. It is market-day – for so I chose. The countryfolk will come early with their produce.'

'And if they delay?'

'Then we withdraw. Go elsewhere. The Shields, perhaps. Sunderland. Lesser prizes, but with no castles to defend them.'

Back at the main body, presently scouts watching the highway to the north reported that a party of folk were approaching, men and women, even children, with pannier-ponies. Still a mile off.

Montrose nodded in decision, and issued his orders. Crawford to take his squadron and circle the town and castle west-about by Morpeth Common, well hidden amongst its banks and braes, to as near the *south* gates of the town as possible, remaining secret. When the gates opened, to move into the lower parts of the town from that side, and to meet up with Clavering, who would be doing the same from the north. Aboyne and Ogilvy's squadrons would come with himself, and the moment the north gates were open, rush through and make a swift dash for the castle, heeding nothing else. From this side they could do so without being seen until the last moment. Was it understood?

All his commanders agreed, and Crawford led his party off south-westwards. The others mounted, and moved quietly forward to the edge of cover, to wait with what patience they could muster for the approaching countryfolk to gain their admittance, dismounted scouts out to send information.

It seemed a long wait, with every minute lessening the chances of catching the castle garrison asleep. Even with the market people at the gate, it remained unopened. More people joined these, the scouts reported. Presently, even round the river's bend, the hiding men could hear derisive shouts to the porters to waken and open up. Montrose was in a further fret now lest other early-rising locals should come down from the village of Mitford and stumble on them in this woodland – although there seemed no reason why any should leave the road to enter it. But 750 horsemen take a deal of hiding. He was at least thankful for the new May flourish and foliage.

Then, with a clanking creak they heard the gates open – no need to await the scouts' announcement. Spurring his mount, Montrose waved them on.

He was first through those gates, scattering astonished folk right and left, his squadrons thundering behind. Sleepy gatekeepers and burdened market-goers alike stared open-mouthed – and none were foolish enough to seek to halt such intruders. Down the narrow main street they clattered.

Without waiting for any marshalling and splitting of forces behind him, James Graham swung off right-handed at the Tolbooth, down a side-street, to splash dramatically across a ford of the river. Then, slithering and striking sparks from the cobblestones, he drove on through a huddle of houses, in steps and stairs, and set his mount to the steep grassy banks beyond, in the most direct route to the castle. Looking back, half-way up, he could see young Aboyne leading his squadron across the ford in a shower of spray. The castle's gatehouse-tower entrance was at the other side, facing south, which meant a half-circuit of the curtain-walls on a steeply sloping bank. But at least there was cover here. Concerned not to show himself before the gatehouse until he had enough men with him to risk rushing it, he slowed down, in a fever of impatience.

Then, the noise of his horse's hooves and snorting breath lessening, suddenly he was aware of disturbance ahead, uproar, though the bulk of the high castle outer walling blanketed it to some extent.

Cursing, he kicked his mount onward again, rounding those walls. And as the bank levelled off southwards to a wide grassy platform, the situation was revealed. The Earl of Crawford and his squadron were milling around on the greensward, shouting challenges and hurrahing for the King, before the square gatehouse-tower with its archway – an archway in process of being blocked by the rising drawbridge. Even as Montrose stared, angrily, the bridge clanked into the up position, and the portcullis went down with a rattle. And at the same time, a few musket shots began to crack out from the battlements.

Groaning despite himself, and caring nothing for flying ball, James Graham rode across to the sword-flourishing, martial Crawford. 'My lord – what is this?' he demanded hotly.

'Devilish ill-fortune !' Ludovic Lindsay called. 'I near had them. But a minute or two more and the place would have been mine. Marshalling my men for the assault. The Devil's own luck !'

'I am not concerned with your luck, sir!' Montrose's voice quivered. 'Why are you here?'

'The town gate, to the south, was open. We could ride in. I perceived that I could reach the castle before you – for the south gate is closer.'

Montrose held out an arm and pointing finger that shook, indicative of the effort with which he held himself in. 'Nearer, yes. But see there, my lord – visible of approach most of the way from the lower town.' He was pointing down the wide Castlegate. 'Only a guard asleep could have failed to see you approach thus. Why think you I planned to approach from the north? And commanded that you capture the lower town, making cause with Clavering?'

Gulping, he stopped. This would not do. Crawford was chief of a great family, sixteenth Earl, next to Mar the most senior of all the earls of Scotland. And an older man than he was. It was not suitable to berate him thus, to berate any commander in front of his men. Besides, musket-balls were coming thick and fast.

'I advise that you get your men down into the town swiftly, my lord,' he went on, even-voiced. 'Clavering may need your aid. And when I last was here, there were cannon in this fort . . . !'

He did not finish that, as a musket-ball screamed between them, setting their horses dancing.

Furiously the other earl reined around, and waved his squadron to retire whence it had come. Aboyne's people were advancing round the perimeter wall now. Gesturing to them to turn back, Montrose saw the first flash, and mushroom of smoke, from the keep's platform-roof, and the crash of the cannon coincided with his own urgent departure from that place.

The capture of the town itself was not difficult, with surprise, and the full thousand cavalry to devote to it. But the failure to gain the castle left Montrose in a serious quandary. Any siege of the citadel demanded cannon, of which he had none. It might be best to abandon Morpeth altogether, and concentrate on spreading alarm and confusion behind Leslie's lines by assaulting other Tyneside towns. On the other hand, Morpeth was astride the main north-south road, supply and retreat line with Scotland. Holding it would more effectively embarrass the Scots army than would any other. Yet he could not just sit in it, under the threat of the castle's own artillery and garrison. If only he could lay hands on some cannon . . .

It was this line of thinking that moulded his subsequent strategy. The city of Newcastle lay only fifteen miles to the south – and there would be cannon therein. It was still in royalist hands, but being contained rather than besieged by a rearguard of Leslie's force, neutralised. If the containing force could be lured away, even for a short time . . .

James Graham did not delay. Within hours of the castle disappointment, and before the word could spread around the countryside, Crawford and Clavering were sent off south-eastwards, with their squadrons, openly, to make for North Shields, thirteen miles away. It was an unimportant place at the mouth of the Tyne estuary; but a ferry plied to South Shields across the river, with its small fort that had once been Roman. A force which could capture both North and South Shields could bottle up the Tyne, prevent supply by sea to Leslie's thousands, and bypass Newcastle's bridge as access to a wide area. No commander sitting outside Newcastle could ignore such.

Montrose waited until dusk, when a rider from Clavering arrived with news that they had taken North Shields without difficulty – likewise Seaton Delaval and Earsdon on the way – and all were now burning, to draw attention to the fact. They were making great play with the ferry-boats, and the fort at South Shields, less than a mile across the estuary, could not but assume an attempt against it. They would retire northwards during the night, but leave a fire-tending party to keep the blazes bright.

Leaving Kilpont in command at Morpeth, with Ogilvy's squadron, Montrose with Aboyne's remaining 250 horsemen, set out through the quiet May night for Newcastle.

A mile short of the city, and an hour short of midnight, scouts waited to inform them that there was a fairly large military encampment outside the northern gate but that few men appeared to be there. It looked as though the Scots containing force, at least on this north side of Tyne, had been drawn off, as planned.

Montrose had to be satisfied with that. At a brisk trot they advanced on encampment and city gates.

They encountered no trouble at the first. The guard, a

picket of Fifers, obviously assumed them to be part of their own army – as who would blame them? When Montrose called out to them in his broadest Angus Doric, the squadron was allowed to trot on without hindrance. It was a scattered camp, really a staging post for supply convoys. There might well be trouble here later, but meantime it was child's play.

Not so when they reached the high city wall and the Scots Gate, however. They reared dark, blacker than the May night, the doors solidly closed against all comers. No answer was accorded to fairly low-pitched calls and summonses, and Montrose was loth to bellow demands for entry such as would resound back in the camp and arouse immediate suspicion.

In a fever of frustration they waited, while various members of the company took turns at whispered shouting, as it were, to gain some response from within; all to no effect. It was, eventually, that lively youth James Gordon, Viscount Aboyne's suggestion that bore fruit. They tied together some of the horses' tethering-ropes, with breastplates, helmets, even swords at one end, to throw up and over the walls as improvised scaling-ladders. If sentinels there were, they could scarcely ignore such a gesture. And if the walls were indeed unguarded, then they might be able to get men up the ropes, to open the doors themselves.

This ingenious challenge was successful. The first clattering rope, after two false throws, was tossed back at the throwers even before the second was up, with some good, thick Tyneside objurgation.

'Guard, there!' Montrose called. 'Hear me. I am the Earl of Montrose, the King's Lieutenant-General. I may not shout louder, or blow trumpet, for fear of arousing the Scots camp behind. I am come to speak with the King's governor of Newcastle.'

That produced little more than a snort of disbelief.

'Quickly, man. Open the gates for us. We dare not stand waiting here.'

'D'ye think us right fools?' a hoarse voice answered. 'To let in your murdering Scots!'

'I tell you, I am the King's Lieutenant. Montrose. Fetch the guard-commander, man.'

'Ho ho! He'd thank me for that, at this time o' night! Your lord-generalship had better come back at a decent hour!'

'Fool! We cannot wait. Fetch someone, anyone in authority. With whom I may speak. In the King's name. Or when I get in, I will have you hanged, see you – also in the King's name!'

That seemed to give the spokesman pause. There was some muttered talk.

A thought occurred to James Graham. 'Guard – can you see North Shields ablaze, from up there?'

'Aye.'

'That is my doing. To draw off the Scots. You would see them ride off?'

'Aye.'

'Devil take you, fellow – have you no wits? Hanging will be too good for you. Get your officer.'

After a wait, wherein Montrose, cursing the guard's stupidity, had to admit, in fairness, that the man was only right to be suspicious, an officer did arrive above; who after some further parleying, announced that he had seen the Earl of Montrose when he had been captured by the Scots at Newburn, as one of Conway's force. If his lordship would light up his face in some fashion . . . ?

So flint and steel was struck, tinder ignited, and a letter from Montrose's pocket burned before his upturned, hatless features. The captain declared himself satisfied, and at long last the gates were opened – and closed again almost before the last of the squadron was inside.

Using all his inborn and acquired authority now to obtain swift action, Montrose spurred through the empty streets to the castle, grim, stark and strong at the riverside, where were both the governor, Sir John Marley and the wanted cannon, according to the watch-captain. Marley, who was middle-aged and portly, and mayor as well as governor, despite being put about by being found in bed with a shrilly angry wife, was only to glad to get rid of his untimely visitor by authorising the removal from the citadel of whatsoever cannon were required – since he had little ammunition for them anyway.

Montrose had less choice of artillery than he had hoped. The heavy pieces which he would have preferred would be too difficult to transport; and the light, mainly naval guns would make no real impact on Morpeth Castle walls. He took six medium cannon, but was able to collect precious few balls to go with them.

Quickly he had the weapons disjoined, and their barrels, wheels, axles and carriages tied into fishnets to be slung between four horsemen each. The few casks of powder and heavy ball likewise. Then, wasting no time in leave-taking, he wished the governor well on all counts, and hastened back to the Scots Gate, some hundred of his troopers reluctantly acting carrier.

The guard at the gate declared that there had been some stir in the Scots encampment meantime, but not any large-scale return from down the estuary, they thought; probably only curiosity as to what had become of the visitors.

Montrose formed his people up into three companies now – a fighting spearhead of 100, the transporting 100 who would inevitably be less fast-moving, and the remaining fifty as rearguard. Then he ordered the gates to be opened.

A fairly sedate trot was all the pact that his cannon-bearers could muster, with their heavy and awkward loads. At this decent rate they headed for the camp and the road.

Now there was question, opposition, it having been realised that the newcomers had gained admission to the beleaguered city; therefore they could not be what they seemed. Somebody had gathered together a fair number of men to block the way. But even in the semi-darkness they could be seen to be only a mass, a mob rather than any disciplined formation. Montrose whipped out his sword, and gave the order to his advance-guard to charge.

It was the first true charge, in anger, which many of these present had made. But led by the dashing Scots lords, they drew steel, levelled lances and spurred mounts. 'A Graham! A Graham!' Montrose cried – and some even took up that strange refrain.

They went through the mob as though it was chaff, with little or no swordery required, or indeed possible. A pistol or two cracked, men shouted, some screamed as they went down under trampling hooves, horses whinnied, and they were through.

Montrose and Aboyne tried to wheel them round, right and left, in true cavalry style, to drive back again; but of this they made a notable botch, ending up in a confused tangle, lances menacing each other. In fact, the return was not

275

required. Seeing more cavalry coming behind, the camp orderlies, cooks and odds and ends of an army perceived no point in further interference in what seemed to be no business of theirs. Prudently they drew aside, and the transporters and rearguard trotted through, swords out but unchallenged.

After that it was merely a matter of following the winding road through the night northwards, keeping the rearguard well behind and watching keenly for pursuit. Also seeing that all took turns at the miserable duty of carrying artillery. They reached Morpeth exactly twenty-four hours after their first arrival.

Crawford and Clavering were already back from North Shields.

That afternoon, rested and refreshed, Montrose tried out the reassembled cannon. He had them dragged to the top of the Ha' Hill, the best vantage point, and from there fired a few trial shots. Unfortunately no trained nor born artillerymen showed themselves amongst his force, and their trial-and-error education in the science was grievously wasteful of the small store of ammunition. Moreover, the castle's own cannon promptly fired back, and with rather better aim and much greater prodigality. He set his men to dig trenches for shelter – but even so there were casualties, largely due to splinters from trees and rocks. As an artillery duel it was scarcely a success; but, with one good hit they did demolish a turret of the gatehouse-tower – proof that, given time and ball, they could batter their way into the place.

Accepting that patience was the quality required now, Montrose gave orders that every smith in and around Morpeth was to be set to the manufacture of cannon-balls of the required calibre. Lead and iron must be gleaned from near and far. Gunpowder was less difficult, for most mansions and manors had stocks for small-arms and sporting use.

All this took a lot of time, and Montrose used the waiting period to good effect. The fact that the Scots force left to contain Newcastle was making no move to attack him, despite the provocation, seemed to indicate its poor quality and leadership. He was emboldened, therefore, to initiate a hit-and-run cavalry campaign from this base at Morpeth, both to north and south-east. His flying columns took Amble, Rothbury and Alnwick in quick succession, from small Scots garrisons. Clavering, after burning North Shields, had declared that he believed South Shields could be taken, without too much difficulty, from across the river. This Montrose now gave him permission to attempt. Quickly the place fell – and for the meantime at least, Montrose held the mouth of the Tyne. He could not retain it for long, of course, with only cavalry; but his objective was to create maximum confusion behind Leslie's lines, not to occupy territory.

Clavering and Crawford went on to assault Sunderland.

Then, at last, Leslie reacted. Eight hundred first-class cavalry were detached from the main Scots army before York, and sent north hot-foot, to be followed by a larger body of infantry. This was success – even though it gave the besiegers of Sunderland a fright when the Scots horse was reported at the other side of the town, and they had to beat a hasty retreat, via the Shields South and North, sinking the ferry-boats behind them. That evening the Graham recognised that his time at Morpeth was probably short. He did not intend himself to be besieged.

He had now assembled a sizeable supply of cannon-balls and powder. Deciding that little was to be gained by waiting for daylight, with the target the size it was and the marksmanship erratic anyway, to say the least, he had the guns dragged up to a point of vantage on the Ha' Hill, there and then, and bombardment opened, darkness or none.

He made an awesome night of the 28th of May, with the town shaken by the thunder of explosions, the lurid flashes of the charges, the fires started in castle and town, the billowing acrid smoke-clouds. The garrison fired back, of course, but less vigorously than heretofore; perhaps they themselves were running short of ammunition. The besiegers suffered a few casualties, but not many – for the defenders' aim was poor in the darkness, with nothing so large as a castle to fire at. The town itself suffered more. It was difficult to assess just what impact their own cannon made.

Some time during that hideous night, after the castle guns had been silent for a notable period, Montrose called a halt. In the relative quiet he went forward with a trumpeter, to near the battered gatehouse-tower. After a fanfare which even to his own ears sounded crazy in all that smoke, he shouted, coughing a little.

'Guard, ho! Guard, I say. Bring the governor of this

castle. I, James Earl of Montrose, would speak with the governor.'

Almost immediately the reply came, quite clearly. 'You would, would you, James Graham – a plague on you!' In these nightmarish conditions the casually conversational tones taxed credibility. 'My compliments, James – frae Sandy Somerville o' Drum. Here's no way to spend a night, man!'

'Dear God – is it yourself, Sandy!' Montrose cried. 'Sandy Somerville, by all that is wonderful! Are you . . . are you well?' Even the speaker all but choked at that ridiculous question. The Master of Somerville, heir to the ninth Lord thereof, was an old friend from St Andrews University days.

'Never better, James – never better. Save for an empty belly. You caught us with the larder empty. What can I do for you?'

'You can come out of that Englishman's house and let me shake you by the hand, Sandy. And be done with this folly.'

'Ooh, aye. We'd have to think about that, James. Shaking an excommunicate by the hand, man, may no' be allowed! It's an ill thought.'

'Eh? What did you say . . . ?'

'Don't tell me . . . don't say nobody has told you, James? That you are excommunicate? Utterly damned! Hech, aye – bell, book but nae candle!'

Into the pause which succeeded that announcement, the Master of Somerville shouted again, 'Have they not told you?'

Even then it took James Graham moments to answer, 'No.'

'Och, well – never heed. You're no' the only one,' the other called. 'What terms will you offer me, James?'

Montrose pulled himself together. 'This shouting. We could talk the better face to face. Come out, man, under safe conduct, and we'll discuss it.'

'I'll send a depute, James. Myself, I'll bide, and have a bit look round this auld rickle o' stanes you've been battering. To see if we can hold out a mite longer! Till auld crooked Sandy Leslie sends a wheen stout lads to our aid, may be.'

'I have still much ball and powder, Sandy. Must I batter on?'

'We'll see. I'll send you Jock MacGulloch to discuss the matter . . .'

So presently Captain MacCulloch, a Galloway mercenary, came out under a flag of truce, and after a certain amount of formal parleying, informed Montrose privately that the Master of Somerville was indeed anxious to yield, if he could so honourably, for they had had no food for three days, and all their powder was exhausted. But he did not wish to seem to do so precipitately. Let them wait until daylight . . .

Soon after a misty sunrise, on the 29th, Montrose formally slammed another couple of cannon-balls at the drunken-looking gatehouse-tower; and thereafter, almost at once, the white flag was run up from Morpeth Castle keep and all was over. Presently the governor and garrison of some hundreds – more than anticipated – marched out to tuck of drum, and James Graham shook hands with his friend and offered a short speech of congratulation to all concerned. Somerville and his officers retained their swords, his men laid down their arms, and thereafter all marched down to the town, where Montrose had been having a large meal prepared, out of his own pocket paying for oxen, poultry, ale and bread in abundance. In courteous style he entertained the Master, the enemy officers and his own, to dinner in the Tolbooth, while the men feasted cheerfully in the streets.

It was a rousing and pleasant occasion – and it would have been more so had Montrose himself been in a happier frame of mind. But this news of his excommunication weighed heavily upon him. It had come as a great shock, such a thing never having occurred to him as possible. Though not intensely religious, and less than patient with fanatical divines, he always had been a God-fearing man, and for years had carried everywhere with him a pocket-Bible, well-worn and much annotated with his own hand-writing. His Presbyterianism was no mere outward form. That the Kirk of Scotland should officially declare him excommunicate, expelled from salvation, was scarcely believable, and bore sorely on him. It had been done, according to Somerville, when he had invaded Dumfriesshire at the head of 'a foreign host.'

His banquet guests, however, had other tidings, by no means all of it more cheerful. Sir John Gordon of Haddo, impatient at his chief Huntly's failure to rise again on the King's behalf, had led a raid on Aberdeen, kidnapped the Provost, and ridden off triumphantly. This had made a great impact, but had split Clan Gordon – for though Huntly had tentatively emerged from Strathbogie to occupy Aberdeen thereafter, his eldest son, the Lord Gordon, had declared this to be folly and had actually elected to join the Covenant side – the fruits presumably of Montrose's own influence on that serious young man. Argyll had sent a force north to deal with this – and Huntly, much alarmed again, had handed over the city and its keys to his son, and decamped northwards at speed, not stopping it was said until he reached the Pentland Firth at Strathnaver. The young Lord Gordon was now, to all intents, chief of the clan, and co-operating with Argyll – a serious situation and strange end-product of James Graham's association with him. His brother, Aboyne, all but exploded at the news. Argyll had executed Gordon of Haddo, out of hand, for treason – and, sadly, also hanged the Provost of Dumfries who had been rash enough to welcome Montrose.

Coping with these indigestible tidings, Montrose was a little heartened to learn that Hamilton and Lanark, at least and at last, had met their deserts. They had been summoned south to Oxford from Scotland, by royal command, had come, and had been arrested and tried before a commission of enquiry. Found guilty of deliberately misleading the King and aiding the King's enemies, they were condemned to imprisonment – despite strong pressure from a powerful party, led by the Queen, on their behalf. On the way to ward in Cornwall, somehow Lanark had made good his escape and was now with the Covenant army. The Duke, it seemed, was held secure at Pendennis Castle.

It was perhaps typical of King Charles's Court and methods that news of this should reach his Lieutenant-General only from the enemy.

Montrose, sending Somerville and his people back to Scotland, was faced with the question whether to get out of Morpeth and back to Carlisle while the going was good, having created a sufficient diversion behind Leslie's lines; or to stay where he was, further to fortify the town, and seek to hold it in the face of the larger force Leslie must inevitably send north from York when he heard the news. It was tidings from York, indeed, which eventually decided the issue – but not from Leslie. A letter arrived from there – but by a messenger of Prince Rupert's. That dashing commander had hastened north to the Earl of Newcastle's aid, had reached York and pushed Leslie back somewhat. But he was now threatened by the Fairfaxes' northern army, and Manchester's Eastern Association, as well as by the Scots – and with only 15,000 men was much outnumbered. He ordered Montrose to leave whatever he was doing, and march south to join him immediately. As a sort of postscript the Prince added that His Majesty had, on the 6th of May, signed a warrant creating his well-beloved James Graham, Marquis of Montrose, in recognition of services rendered.

Heavy at heart, and filled with foreboding, the new marquis – who had no particular desire to exchange his proud and ancient style as an earl of Scotland – wound up his affairs in Morpeth, and set out with his very reluctant force, first westwards into the Northumbrian hills and then southwards, by devious ways, to avoid Leslie's army. It beat in his mind that he, the King's Lieutenant for Scotland, was proceeding deeper and deeper into England, to involve himself ever more inextricably in the affairs of another country when his own was crying aloud for his return. Although, he had to admit, that cry was so far of his own will and imagining.

On the 3rd of July, at the Durham-York border near Middleton in Teesdale, a group of fleeing North Lancashire troopers gave Montrose the dire tidings. There had been a great battle, the day before, on the Marston Moor west of York. Prince Rupert and the royal army had been completely defeated, with great slaughter. All was lost. It was every man for himself. No, they did not know how fared the Prince, or where he was – nor greatly cared, it seemed. But some of the royalist officers, it was said, were seeking to rally at Richmond. Much good it might do them . . .

Montrose, distressed, was again placed in a dilemma. Every impulse tugged at him to turn back. His thousand far-from-eager warriors could not effectively alter the situation, and were most likely merely to run their heads into a noose. And behind him, Scotland pulled. Yet, his orders had been to join Rupert. And to seem to desert the Prince now, in his hour of need, was unthinkable. Yet he might be dead, a prisoner, or fleeing far.

Contrary to the advice of most of his colleagues, he

decided to go on, warily, at least as far as Richmond, another twenty miles.

They found Richmond an armed camp, in a touchy state of alarm but Rupert himself in command. Weary, slightly wounded and harassed, he was by no means despondent, and greeted Montrose warmly. Indeed their arrival seemed to give him an accession of vigour and hope. The Graham found that, once again, his own reputation had outgrown his deeds. His taking of Morpeth and cannon-ball raid on Newcastle was being looked on as a great victory, and the belief here was that all the North of England was in his sure hands.

Rupert had nearly 6000 of the royal troops collected at Richmond – which meant, of course, that 10,000 at least were lost, 4000 said to be dead. More might come in, and he had sent far and wide for new levies. But he dare not wait here much longer. That devil-damned Cromwell was coming – indeed had allegedly sworn to take him, Rupert, and hang him!

Montrose had heard of Oliver Cromwell, a Huntingdon-shire squire who had been making a name for himself in the English parliament as a stern opponent of the King. But now, it appeared, he had changed to a military role, and the defeat at Marston Moor seemed to be largely of his making. He had raised and trained and disciplined a body of heavy cavalry, almost as fanatical religious zealots as the Scots divines, and used them with diabolical, almost unbelievable skill. Rupert had been caught between Leslie's veterans and Cromwell's horse. Newcastle's army had collapsed on his flank, and the day had been lost. But it had been this Cromwell's tactics that had turned the scale late in the day. And he was now heading west, by Skipton and the Ribble, to Wensleydale no doubt, to approach this Richmond from the rear, while Leslie circled the Cleveland Hills to make a frontal attack.

That evening, in the inn in which the Prince had taken up his quarters, his surviving commanders urged on him differ-ing courses – to head west and then south, in front of Cromwell, for Oxford and the King; to retire north-east, to Marley and Newcastle; to do what would be least expected, disperse the foot and make a dash back to York with the cavalry and surprise the Fairfaxes denuded of Cromwell and

Leslie. Montrose urged his own old and favoured theme. Use Scotland. Move up over the Border with this 7000. Callander would not hold them. That land was basically loyal to its King, in a way England was not – a Scots-born king. Rouse it by a show of strength. Lacking Leslie's army, Argyll would be lost. He was no soldier. Then, strong, turn back to England.

When even Rupert shook almost pitying head at this totally unacceptable suggestion, the Graham changed his plea. Give him just 1000 crack cavalry, to replace his hotch-potch of a force. Give him these, and he would cut his way through south Scotland like a sickle through corn, to his own territories, and there raise Scotland for the King. He asked no other help than that – he, the King's Lieutenant for Scotland.

But again Rupert shook his dark head. He needed every man he could raise – and crack cavalry were more precious than fine gold. He needed five times his present numbers. He could afford to detach not one. They would ride north, yes – but not to Scotland. To Carlisle, where they would be protected by hills and sea. The North-West had scarcely been touched by war. There they would re-form and renew their strength. To turn again in a month or so – and teach the King's rebels who was master in England.

James Graham sighed.

But next morning he was more cheerful. At least they were moving northwards, not south.

21

IT WAS SIX WEEKS LATER BEFORE JAMES GRAHAM HAD finally had enough of England, the English, even of Rupert of the Rhine, six weary weeks on the very verge of Scotland, yet all the time with their backs to it, considering only the South. Earlier he had sent Ogilvy and his connection by marriage, lame Sir William Rollo, secretly into Scotland disguised as pedlars, and after three weeks they had returned, their news not such as to ease Montrose's mind in any way. The proposed Irish landing had at last taken place, months late, but in a half-cocked fashion and anyway up on the Ardnamurchan coast of Argyll; and not 10,000 men, not Antrim himself – only 1600 commanded by a Scots Mac-Donald chieftain, Alastair, son of MacDonald of Colonsay, commonly known as Colkitto and a kinsman of Antrim's. This character was said to be busy ravaging the Argyll sea-board with fire and sword, from Mingary Castle on Loch Sunart; but so far none of the clans had risen to aid him in what looked like merely a typical incident in the unending MacDonald-Campbell feud. And elsewhere in Scotland the royalists were completely inactive, having lost all hope under Argyll's savagely repressive regime. Even the most moderate nobles were kneeling to the Campbell. The two emissaries' report amounted to this – that if the King's Lieutenant-General for Scotland was ever going to achieve anything in that unhappy land, it had better be soon.

But any such move had now no sort of priority with the King or the royalist command in England. Rupert was sympathetic, but wholly concerned with his all too serious problems in the South. Not only were not troops available to lend for a Scots adventure, but the new Marquis's own ser-vices were required for more immediate campaigning. All were to move towards Oxford, with the new levies.

So Montrose came to a decision, a dramatic one. He duly set out for the South, with the rest. But a short distance from Carlisle, leaving his own party and personal baggage under Ogilvy and Aboyne, he dropped to the rear, ostensibly for a word with William Rollo who had been deliberately delayed. With Rollo, and a Colonel Sibbald, a tough mer-cenary from the Swedish wars who had fought under him in the Bishops' War in Aberdeen and whom he had had his eye on for some time as a useful man, he trotted along at the very end of the long column for a little, dropping ever farther behind, a led horse with them. Then, in close timbered country in the Eden valley, all three quietly slipped away into the empty woodland, and turned their horses' heads northwards again.

In an hour's hard riding they were back on the Scots

border, but now in lonely country. Here they halted, and from their saddle-rolls drew out very different attire from their normal fine cavalier costume. Rollo and Sibbald produced and donned uniforms taken from captured Scots officers of Leslie's force, while Montrose himself dressed in the garb of a groom, tucking up his splendid curling hair under a rusty morion helmet. Thus, riding with the led horse decently behind his betters, Lieutenant-General the Marquis of Montrose forded Esk and rode back into his native land.

It was a curious and hazardous interlude – for inevitably they had to ride through parts of Callander's army which was holding all the passes of the South-West. They chose unfrequented and awkward routes, by Sark and Kirtle Waters, Wauchope and Ewes; but even so could not avoid Callander's pickets. Rollo and Sibbald claimed to be wounded Scots officers returning from Yorkshire, and got away with it – although some rather odd glances were cast in the direction of their groom, who made only a poor job of looking like a menial, whatever his clothing. Disaster, indeed, came close on one occasion, when one of a party of Scots troopers, ignoring the officers, sidled his mount close to Montrose after some staring. He spoke low-voiced.

'The Earl o' Montrose, by a' that's holy! Here's a ploy!'

'You mistake, friend,' James Graham said stiffly. Then remembered his Angus Doric, 'Och, wheesht – dinna be daft, man!'

'Nae mistake,' the other asserted. 'D'you think I wouldna ken the Earl? Marquis noo, they say. I've seen you wi' my Lord Newcastle one time, at Durham. But . . . gang your way. And God go wi' you!' And, grinning, the man reined round, and away.

Montrose, catching his companions' glances, let out a sigh of relief. Presumably the fellow had been a deserter from Newcastle's army; or had been captured and changed his coat, but still retained some loyalties.

They rode on, for Eweswater and the North.

A devious journey they made of it, seeking to avoid all centres of population, especially where there were churches – for Montrose conceived the ministers to be his greatest hazard, keen-eyed divines who might have seen him at General Assemblies and the like. Obviously his disguise was less than effective. James Graham could hardly be expected to recognise that his whole bearing, carriage and the essential cleanness that always characterised his person, shouted aloud that he was no groom.

Putting up at lonely alehouses and remote hill farms, they were accepted as Leslie's and therefore Argyll's men, and feared accordingly. Clearly all Scotland now feared Argyll, who appeared to be exercising more arbitrary power and harsh authority than ever had any of her true monarchs. Although he used no style or title as yet, other than Marquis, Privy Councillor, Justiciar of the West and chief of his clan, professing to be merely the lowly servant of Christ's Kirk, the squint-eyed King Campbell nevertheless now held the fullest authority, and ordered matters as he would, and with a heavy hand. He was hated, yes – but cared not a snap of the fingers for it. His rule was not concerned with love, affection, even admiration. Effective power he wanted – and effective power he had.

The furtive travellers avoided Edinburgh like the plague, skirting well to the west much as Montrose would have liked to see and talk with Archie Napier at Merchiston. Stirling also fell to be by-passed, for the Graham was well known there. They crossed Forth by the little-used Fords of Frew, by dark, as many a hunted Graham had done before them – and thereafter slipped through unfrequented territory which he and Rollo knew like the back of their hands. *An Greumach Mor* was scarcely ready yet for his own country-side to know of his return.

On the fourth day – or, rather, night – of journeying, avoiding Perth by crossing Earn and Almond to the west they rode in the early dew-drenched August morning up through the birchwoods of little Strathordie, past the lonely little kirk of St Bride's, to the remote fortalice of Tullybelton on its shelf of the great Highland hills, looking southwards across the wide middle vale of Tay. To a great barking of deerhounds and shouting from tower-windows, they made their presence known, declaring true identity openly at last.

Black Pate Graham himself, bellowing incoherent delight and greeting, came hurtling down the turnpike stairway, to slide back the great drawbar with a crash, unbolt the iron yett and fling open the heavy oaken door, to throw himself bodily upon his chief and friend, still only in his shirt. Never before had James Graham seen that man sobbing. His grow-

ing and boisterous family had rather outgrown his ageing
father's castle of Inchbrakie in Strathearn, and for two years
they had been roosting here in more remote Tullybelton – a
place with its advantages for a man unsure of his popularity
with the powers-that-be.

'Man, Jamie! Jamie!' Pate cried. 'Yourself! It's yourself! At last – God be praised, at last! Och, James – you're
back? Look at you, man – look at you! Come chapping at
my door like, like any tinker! Christ God! I heard tell you
were the King's General. And a marquis, no less. But . . .'

'Empty names, Pate, meaning little. Yet! But we'll make
them mean something, you and I! Save us – it's good to see
you. Good to be back in my own place. It has been too
long . . .'

'Too long indeed. For us all. For Scotland. The Campbell,
God's everlasting curse upon him, has all at his feet. But,
now, you are back . . .'

'Back. With two men!'

'And one of them lame!' Rollo mentioned, from behind.

'Guidsakes! You . . . you're alone, man? No tail? No
army? You've come back empty-handed?'

'Alone, yes. But not quite empty-handed, old friend. I
have in my pouch the King's commission. To raise all Scotland for His Grace. With all and every power and authority
that Charles Stewart can give me. All the authority I needed
before, and did not have – if not the power. The power we
must forge, Pate. Forge, until it is tempered steel, to free
this land from shameful tyranny. No – I am not quite
empty-handed now, lad.'

'But no men . . . !'

'Scotland is full of men. Full of men who hate Argyll, I
have learned. And I am still the Graham. And you are Black
Pate of Inchbrakie, as good a recruiter-captain as any in the
land. You will raise the men for me. Starting with our own
good Grahams. How long till I present Scotland to King
Charles, Pate? Purged and free? How long?'

'God knows!'

'Give me a year,' James Graham said slowly, quietly. 'Give
me but one year . . .'

There was a moment's silence, there before the door of
Tullybelton House.

As its laird beckoned them within, Montrose's voice

changed. 'Now – your news, Pate? My wife? What of Magdalen? And the bairns? Have you heard? You will have watched out for them. What of my sons . . . ?'

Much as he would have liked to ride to Kinnaird, less than fifty miles as the crow flew, or even to Kincardine, nearer still, Montrose forbore to do so. Within a day or two, already somehow the rumour had got around that the Graham was back in Scotland. Perhaps that trooper near Langholm had talked; perhaps some other had recognised him, without immediately declaring it. At any rate, like wildfire the word spread – no bad thing, from one point of view, paving the way for his recruiters. But it did mean that certain places would be watched, for sure, Kinnaird where were the fugitive's family in especial. It might well be fatal for his chances, and no kindness to his dear ones, to approach there. Letters he risked – but not a visit. The same even applied to Tullybelton itself, for Pate Graham was well known as his close friend and lieutenant, and his house a likely refuge and venue. So, after that first day, Montrose kept away from its close vicinity, hiding in the spreading woodland and secret deans and valleys of central Perthshire.

But this was no idle skulking. James Graham was like a spider at the centre of its secret and ever-shifting web, now, sending out emissaries, messengers, scouts, to lairds and lords and chieftains, receiving reports, replies, secret visits. It was a risky business, for even some of his own Grahams, despairing of their chief's and the King's cause, had compounded with circumstances and were now, for their very necks' sake, toeing the Covenant line. The dangers of betrayal were serious. For the answers and accounts that reached Tullybelton told a sorry story. Clearly the morale of the country was low, seldom had been lower. None saw salvation from Argyll and the Kirk Militant as likely, even possible. The King seemed to be no longer concerned with Scotland, the ministers had taken over the entire parish system and purged it of anti-Covenant and moderate elements, and no sane man saw any future in revolt, with the entire nobility now truckling to the Campbell. Montrose's name might mean much still; but what could one man do?

After days of consistent temporising, foot-dragging and sheer refusal on the part of those to whom he looked for support, even James Graham grew depressed. A few rallied to his call, or to Black Pate's bullying mainly young Graham lairdlings and Drummond relatives of Pate's wife Jean; but, with their men, these did not make up so much as a squadron of horse. There were many more promises – but clearly these were unlikely to be fulfilled until it was evident that defeat was not inevitable.

A demonstration was needed, indubitably, some small victory which might serve as a beacon of hope for the many doubters. But how to achieve anything significant with so few? And not jeopardise all by courting early disaster?

It was at this juncture that, as Montrose declared to Pate, his prayers were answered – and in strange shape. It came in the form of a weary Irishman, a messenger on foot, hungry, tattered and demoralised, who arrived at Tully-belton, having been directed there from Inchbrakie, seeking help, food, if possible a horse, to aid him on his way to Carlisle. He carried a letter from his master, Alistair Colkitto MacDonald to the Marquis of Montrose, and he had been told that Inchbrakie would help him on his way.

Ever suspecting treachery, a trap, without informing the man that Montrose was within a mile of him, Pate fed him, promised a horse, and gave him a bed. Then, managing to extract the unaddressed letter from the Irishman's clothing, he took it to his friend in the birchwoods of Strathordie.

Under its blank outer cover, the missive was indeed addressed to Montrose, the King's General at Carlisle. And it was a cry for help, from Colkitto. It seemed that, after landing on the Ardnamurchan peninsula in early July, with 1600 gallowglasses and exiled Islesmen from Ulster, he had, as instructed by his kinsman the Earl of Antrim, harried the Campbell lands of North Argyll and called upon the Highland clans to rise for their King. This they had notably failed to do and the Campbells had rallied mightily against the invaders. He had had to fall back on his base at Mingary in Sunart. There he found his ships had been destroyed in an Argyll raid. Desperate, unable to get away by sea, he had decided to march right across Scotland to the only clan he believed he could rely on to rise – the Gordons. By Loch Eil and Lochaber he had trailed his ragged crew, reaching the fringe of Huntly's country at Badenoch. There he had discovered that the Gordons' revolt had fizzled out, and Huntly had fled to the North. Partly hoping to join him there, and partly in the hope that the Mackenzies under Seaforth, hereditary foes of the Campbells, would aid him, Colkitto had marched northwards. But he had found neither Mackenzie help, nor Huntly's elusive person. He marched south again, issuing on his own initiative a summons in the name of the Marquis of Huntly, for the loyal clans of the North-East to rise. Some 500 men, mainly outlying Gordons, did join him; but the Covenant clans of Grant and Fraser prevented him from reaching the true Gordon country. Argyll himself was now hot-foot on his tracks, and he had mutiny amongst the new Badenoch men, who did not like the Irish. Hungry, weary, short of everything needed for even a small Gaelic army, he did not know where to turn. Could and would the Lord Marquis of Montrose help him? Otherwise he feared complete disaster faced him. The letter was four days old, written from the Badenoch-Atholl border at Dalnaspidal.

'Dear God – hear this!' Montrose cried. 'To think that we knew nothing of it! This MacDonald stravaiging the Highlands in the King's name!'

'Achieving nothing,' Pate commented. 'Indeed, worse. Irishmen, barbarians, offending better men!'

'Tcha, Pate – use your wits! The Irish are Catholics, yes. But none so ill. And he says there are Islesmen, too. Properly led such are good fighters. Here is an army of 2000 men, but fifty miles across the hills! An army awaiting me, it's General!'

'An army, James? A rabble of starving, bog-trotting savages . . .'

'Armed men. Savages – who knows? But at least they will rise and fight for *something!* Which is more than most Scots will do this year of grace!' Montrose thumped fist on tartan-clad knee – for he was now dressed as a Highlander, in trews, doublet and plaid, to be less kenspeckle in this country. 'I'm for Atholl, Pate.'

'You could pay over-dear for that sort of army, James.' That was Sir William Rollo, looking grave. 'Scotland will never accept the Catholic Irish.'

'That is to be seen. Scotland will not accept *me,* in this pass. I think Scotland must be taught what things come first! I will see this messenger. Now.'

So the unfortunate courier was roused from his well-earned rest, given a Highland garron and sent off again forthwith northwards, with a letter for Colkitto. The Marquis of Montrose requested Alastair MacDonald, Younger of Colonsay, to meet him at Blair in Athol, in two days' time, for their mutual pleasure and conference.

At midday on the 18th of August, then, Montrose, alone save for Pate Graham, came by devious ways to Atholl, midway between Badenoch and Strathordie, that great mountain tract in the north of Perthshire, to find the Blair district in the wide vale of the Garry in a turmoil. Colkitto and the Irish, it seemed, had misinterpreted the message. Instead of coming quietly to a secret meeting here, the MacDonald had marched south with his whole ragged force, had taken forcible possession of Blair Castle, with the young Earl of Atholl – still a minor – within it, and had run up his banner at the tower-top. Promptly the Atholl Stewarts and Murrays, with their neighbouring Robertsons of Struan, had gathered to rescue the young earl, and take vengeance, and were still gathering. Battle appeared to be imminent.

'I told you!' Pate declared. 'Savages! And fools, forby. What good are such as these?'

'Wait, you,' his friend advised.

Quite openly. Montrose led the way, though anonymously through the ranks of the angry clansmen and towards the opposing crowd that surrounded the castle on its green terrace some 400 yards away, an alarming proceeding.

'Pray God they don't shoot us down like dogs!' Pate muttered.

'They will not do that. We present no threat to them. Keep your head up, man.'

Some distance off still, a rich and powerful voice hailed them. 'Who comes so bold, in the name of God?'

Montrose raised a hand in acknowledgment, but did not answer, and kept on walking. Perforce Pate did likewise.

'Stand you!' the great voice bellowed. 'You heard me – Alastair? Who walks so swack to his death?'

Even then the other took his time to answer. 'James Graham,' he called, at length. 'And I do not shout. At my friends. Or my foes.'

'Graham, d'you say? Graham? Stand you, then, Graham

– or you'll never shout again, I promise you! What Graham thinks he may outface Alastair?'

Pate could not restrain himself longer. 'Montrose, you fool!' he cried. 'Who did you come here to meet? The Marquis. The King's General.'

'Blessed Mary Mother o' God!' That was almost a howl. 'Montrose? Himself? By all the saints – if you lie . . . !' A giant of a man burst out from the ragged throng that faced them. Dressed in red-and-green short kilt and plaid, with ox-hide long sleeveless waistcoat, shoulder-belted broadsword at side and bristling with pistols and dirks, he was nearer seven feet than six and broad in proportion, with a shock of curling red hair and savage down-turning moustaches at strange variance with the almost boyish freckled face. A man of Montrose's own age, in his early thirties, he had hot blue eyes. He came forward, great-strided and grim-visaged.

But James Graham, for better or for worse, seldom managed to look other than he was, however dressed or circumstanced. The calm assurance was not to be mistaken. The big man, as he came close, slowed his stride and then halted, chewing his lip under those wicked drooping moustaches.

'Saviour Christ born of Mary,' he muttered. And then bowed, deeply. 'My lord Marquis – your servant. Alastair.'

'Not mine, Alastair – not mine. The King's only. We are both the King's servants. And here is another – Patrick Graham, Younger of Inchbrakie, my kinsman and friend.'

Those two sized each other up, stiff as suspicious dogs.

'I looked . . . I looked for you otherwise, my lord. I looked for the Captain-General. With an army . . .'

'And found only James Graham and his cousin! I fear that we are a grievous disappointment, Alastair. I am not even *Captain*-General. Prince Maurice is that. Only Lieutenant.'

The other swept that aside with a mighty arm, the shirt-sleeve of which was torn and far from clean. 'What are styles and titles?' he asked.

'What indeed? Do I call you Alastair MacDonald, Colkitto, Dunaverty . . . or my Major-General?'

The giant drew a quick breath. 'Major-General . . . ? Did I . . . hear aright?'

'To be sure. Mere style and title – but yours!' Montrose smiled wryly. 'I may have no army, no power – but I have all the authority that King Charles can give me. I am his royal voice and hand, in Scotland – God help me! So I make Alastair MacDonald of Dunaverty, son to Coll of the Left Hand, his Major-General and my second-in-command.'

For a long moment the other stared, perceiving what was here involved, the ramifications of that statement – or some of them. Then he inclined his red head, and held out a huge hand, large as a ham. '*Your* servant, my lord,' he said. 'At your commands.' He turned, and gestured sardonically. 'Your army!'

Montrose considered the fierce and motley throng of shaggy and unwashed Irish kerns and Highland caterans, armed to the teeth with steel but with hardly a musket, pistol, jack or helmet amongst them, and nodded gravely.

'Excellent,' he said, and there was no mockery in his voice. 'With these we shall do great things, you and I, Major-General. Now, bring to me your host, the Earl of Atholl, whose aid I seek. And make your officers known to me . . .'

The easy and quite unassuming assertion of command was accepted by the fiery Colkitto without a murmur. As was the later move, when with the boy Earl and Pate, Montrose walked back across the no-man's-land to the watchful, waiting ranks of Atholl and Robertson clansmen, to declare to them his identity and authority, and to announce that he had come, in the name of King Charles, to take charge of and discipline Colkitto's Irish and Islesmen host and to raise the Highlands for His Grace. With the Earl's, and Robertson of Struan's permission, he would request all to disperse to their homes forthwith, assured that there would be no further trouble; and thereafter, as many as loved their King and Scotland's cause and freedom, to rally to the royal standard, here in Atholl, next day. Let the Fiery Cross be sent out. Not for the first time the Highlands would teach the Lowlands their duty!

So, for the second time, and on a day of hazy August sunshine, with the heather glowing richly purple on all the Atholl braes, the Marquis of Montrose unfurled the banner of King Charles in Scotland. It was a very different occasion to that at Dumfries nearly five months before. Instead of a town square on the very southern edge of the land, the

293

ceremony took place in the wide green hazel-rimmed haughland where the foaming Tilt met the peat-brown Garry under the soaring mountains of the very heart and centre of Scotland. Instead of decent, hodden-clad burghers and mounted Border and Solway lairds and their levies, infinitely more fierce-looking Highlanders and Irishmen surrounded him, however softly musical their voices, most shooting suspicious if not downright hostile glances at each other, a sea of colourful if ragged tartans, flashing steel and brawny bare limbs. A big crowd was present, but it made a very small army. Colkitto had proved to have remaining only some 1100 men of his own, after his West Highland campaigning – if so it could be called – to which he had added another 500 or so from Badenoch, mainly outlying Gordons. He had no cavalry at all, nor ever had. A large number of Athollmen, Stewarts, Murrays and Robertsons, turned up for the occasion – but how many would remain as part of the fighting host remained to be seen. Summonses were sent out now, urgently, far and wide, for all who had promised aid, all who ought to have promised, to rally to the standard here in Atholl; but it would take time for any appreciable number to assemble from a distance. Montrose had only the boy Earl of Atholl, Donald Robertson, Tutor of Struan, Sir William Rollo, Colonel Sibbald, and a number of local lairds, with Colkitto and Black Pate, at his side.

'My friends,' James Graham said, in the Gaelic – since few there knew English – when horn-blowers had gained him silence, 'today we set our hands to a great and goodly venture. This land is most grievously oppressed by men, not all evil but most shamefully mistaken, and eaten up with the arrogance of spiritual pride. These men have risen against the King's Grace, to whom all owe allegiance and love – as do we. Tyranny reigns, imposed above all by Archibald Campbell of Argyll, *MacCailean Mor...*'

A great roar of execration interrupted him, at mention of that name.

He held up his hand. 'The Campbell rides high. But not so high that he cannot be pulled down. To that end have I come. Come with the King's command to save Scotland from such evil and disloyal men. And with his royal commission to do all that is necessary to that end, naming me Lieutenant-General and Governor in Scotland, with all powers as

Viceroy. In that name and authority, therefore, I, James Graham, call upon all loyal men soever to arms, to fight under my command, until Scotland is cleaned of the Campbell, of his minions, and of fanatic men who set themselves up as the very voice of Almighty God . . . !'

Again the bellow of approval. Deliberately, that was all he was going to say anent religion, with a host before him three-parts Catholic, and his own Covenanting background known to all.

'In the King's royal name, then, I unfurl the King's royal standard, the ancient emblem of this realm and kingdom, for which I am prepared to die. How many of you, my friends, do say as much?' And he tugged loose the cord which tied the great red-and-gold flag, and the Lion Rampant of Scotland streamed free in the breeze. He had carried that flag, rolled in his horse-blanket, since Dumfries.

Everywhere hands, swords, dirks were thrust up, bonnets soared into the air, and the uproar rose and maintained, echoing from the surrounding hills, in fierce, hoarse and continuing acclaim and assertion. Even the Irishmen joined in, affected by this heady draught.

When he could make himself heard, Montrose added, 'Your word I will test! And you, mine. Today we are not many. In a month, we shall be a great host. In our proud and sacred cause may we ask Almighty God to go with us, to strengthen our hearts and our arms, and to give us the victory. Amen. God save the King!'

Out of his own pocket thereafter, James Graham bought great quantities of beef and ale, whisky and victual, from the Earl of Atholl's steward, and fires were lit all over the grassy haughland to roast the meat, providing a rough-and-ready feast, with as much to eat as even the most starveling bog-trotter could desire. This while the necessary business of enrolment and forming into companies and commands proceeded. Montrose went round making himself known, speaking with the men, encouraging, questioning.

That late evening, with much good cheer in the camp, merriment, singing, story-telling, dancing – and some superficial fighting – all the well-fed relaxation of a Gaelic host, Montrose slipped away. Major-General Alastair MacDonald was roaring drunk and challenging all comers, three at a time, to wrestling bouts; so Black Pate was left in effective command. Borrowing a Highland garron from Atholl, James Graham gave himeslf twenty-four hours' leave of absence while they awaited the results of their widespread summonses, and rode off quietly, unescorted, south-eastwards.

He went down Garry, and into the mouth of the shadow-filled Pass of Killiecrankie. All night he rode, at a steady mile-devouring trot, bearing ever more into the east, by heather-tracks and drove roads, by mere footpaths and no paths at all, leaving the Garry near where Tummel joined it, to climb to Moulin, and up and up beyond, over the quiet, empty darkling mountains, by the Pass of Dalnacarn into Glen Brerachan, and so to the head of Strathardle. He knew the road well, having travelled it many times as a young man – but never by night. Down the long, long strath he went, barked at by the occasional dog but otherwise unchallenged. At its foot, where Ardle met the Blackwater of Glenshee, he forded that river to Strone, to start his climbing again, this time by the high Muir of Drimmie, eerie, strange, where the Stone Circles of the ancient people reared themselves out of the night like upraised fingers warning of the brevity and unimportance of all men's lives and activities.

In six hours of great riding he was looking down on Strathmore, or its grey vacancy, from the very lip of the Highland Line above Alyth, only level lands below him now, after over thirty miles of the mountains. It was two o'clock of a still August morning. This was Ogilvy country, where he cold feel reasonably secure; but he still went secretly, seeking to disturb none. In two more hours he had crossed the wide strath slantwise, almost due eastwards, by Glamis and Aberlemno, avoiding Forfar and Brechin, and could smell the sea in his nostrils as he rode down through the marshlands to the wide landlocked bay of Montrose. At the reedy head of it, on a little hillock amongst the cattle-strewn saltmarsh meadows, his tough garron going slowly, wearily, now, he halted at a low-browed, reed-thatched cot-house amongst the misty tidelands, where dwelt old Sim Mather, once his father's chief falconer, who had taught him that sport twenty years before. He had no need to rouse him – the old man's dogs had already done that – and his greeting, on identification, was heartfelt and heart-warming.

'Sim,' he said, after some account of his circumstances,

'you will serve me kindly by crossing the saltmarsh to Kinnaird. Does my lady still occupy the south-east flanking tower? Aye. With my sons, my children? Do you know?'

'Aye, lord. I saw the young lord but two days back.'

'Good. Go there then, Sim, secretly but swiftly. Tell my lady that I am here. Bid her, if she will, come to me, for a spell. As secretly. For an hour or two. With the boys. The baby, the girl, will be too young.' Eight months before Magdalen had given birth to a daughter, as yet unseen by the father. 'Bring them to me. Do not disturb the castle, or my lord of Southesk. There is a postern-gate. You will know it well . . . ?'

'Aye, lord. I will have them here within the hour.'

'Yes. She is well?'

'Well, and bonny. And the young lords fine lads. You will be proud o' them . . .'

Sim Mather was as good as his word. Montrose had dropped asleep on the settle by the smoored peat fire when, with the first hint of dawn beginning to whiten the coiling mist wraiths that rose from the saltings, the shack door burst open and his two eldest sons flung themselves in and upon him in a breathless flurry of exclamation.

'Save us – who are these!' their father cried. 'Robbers! Hielant caterans! Grown and ill-favoured men, for certain! Do not tell me you are Grahams of some kidney?' It was over a year since he had seen them.

They shouted with laughter, two tousle-headed, long-legged, good-looking youngsters, all knees and elbows, one fourteen, the other eleven years, bursting with excited questions and competing declarations.

The man's glance lifted from them. Magdalen stood in the low doorway, biting her lip, her youngest son Robert at her knee and a plaid-wrapped bundle in her arms, peering in.

The anxiety, uncertainty, implicit in her stance, her whole person, went to his heart. Life had been less than generous to Magdalen Carnegie – and he was no husband for her, no husband for any woman. He rose, and went to her, hands out.

She could find no words, only gazed at him from great eyes, holding out the baby a little way, as something which might have been part offering, part barrier and reproach.

Gently but firmly he took them both in his tartan-clad arms.

'My dear, my very dear,' he said, kissing her.

He felt her trembling. At first she did not, could not speak. But there was no doubting her emotion.

'So long, lass,' he said. 'So very long. Even since I returned. To Scotland. I could not, dare not, come to you. Even now, I come like a hunted beast. What a husband I have made for you, Magdalen!'

She nodded, and shook her head, in one.

'And this is Jean! Little Jean. We have a daughter.' He took the baby from her, easing the plaid back from the tiny wide-eyed face. 'A poppet. Like you, my dear – comely.' He kissed the child's brow. 'Jean Graham – deserving of a better father.'

The transference of attention to the infant seemed to loose Magdalen's tongue 'Oh, James – at last! How I have feared for you! Thank God you are back. Safe. All these weary months. Years. Waiting, hoping, praying.'

'Aye, lass. I know it. I can only beg that you forgive me. It seems to be my fate to fail you. But – at least I am in Scotland again. Not so far away. I can see you more often, God willing. This small one – to think that I have never seen our daughter till now. She looks well, well. As well as she is bonny. And these.' He turned to his eager sons. 'My dear, you have done well. So very well. I thank you.'

She shook her head. 'They need their father.'

'The *King* needs our father,' John said stoutly. 'All Scotland needs our father.' That 'our' was distinctly emphasised.

'He is the greatest man in all the realm,' young James declared. 'Tell us how you beat the English. At Newcastle. And at that other place. More . . . Morepath.'

'I did not beat the English, lad. I did not even *fight* the English. Only the King's enemies. And many of those are Scots, to their shame.'

'When can we come with you, my lord? *I*, at the least. To fight for the King,' John demanded. 'I am fourteen now. And can use a sword very well. As well as Tam Keith. And he is sixteen . . .'

'Hush, John!' his mother said. 'Do not talk so. I have told you . . .'

'But I am the Lord Graham, Mother! I must serve the King, too. I am old enough now. Tam Keith says . . .'

'You are a child still. Enough of such foolish chatter.'

'Lewis Gordon was fighting for the King when he was thirteen . . .' James declared – and then looked shocked as he realised that at that time his father had been on the opposite side.

'We will not talk about fighting now, for the King or other,' Montrose said gently. 'Time enough for that. Now let us talk of kinder things. For I have not long. I must leave here before most men are abroad. To get me into the hills of Glen Clova, just as quickly as may be, and so over the mountains to Glen Shee and Atholl again. I am too well known hereabouts to remain unrecognised for long. We have an hour, little more.'

'Oh, James – so little?'

'I am sorry, my dear. But I may not be away from my men – folly to call it an army yet – for longer. And I dare not risk capture, or the cause is lost. Kinnaird is bound to be watched. Argyll is no fool. There may be spies even in your own house.'

'If I found one, I would run him through! I swear I would!' John announced.

'You see! How they grow, without their father's hand. They see themselves as a hero's sons . . .'

'We are! We are!' the boys chorused. 'He *is* a hero. Everybody says so. Next to Prince Rupert he is the King's best general.'

'At the least, let me be a hero to my sons!' the man said, ruefully humorous. 'Now – enough, I said. And that is as good as a royal command. Let us talk of homelier things. Magdalen – how is it with your father?'

She smiled, despite herself. 'My father! Even he now reckons you hero. Since you chose the King's side! He but encourages these foolish children.'

'And you do not, my dear?'

'Oh, James – I cannot *afford* a hero for husband! Can you not see it? Understand? I want only an ordinary man. At home. A husband by my side, after all these years. I care nothing for heroes and battles and causes. Even for the King's Grace, I think! I want only my own, my husband and the father of my children. Is that too much to ask?'

Wordless himself now, he shook his head.

'But . . . I have but an hour with you, then? One hour!'

299

'I fear so, lass. Unless you would have me in one of Argyll's dungeons. He has a price on my head. Then, you would never see me again!'

'Oh, God!' she said, chokingly. 'Is that what we have come to?'

'I fear it is. But I *had* to see you. See you all. The Campbell does not scruple to fight women. Remember what he did to Airlie's wife.'

'*I* will see to Mother,' John assured. 'She will be quite safe.'

'Spoken like the Earl of Kincardine!' his father approved.

'Earl . . . who?'

'Earl of Kincardine. You are an earl now, Johnnie. Did you not know? Since the King made me a marquis. Earl of Kincardine. And you, Jamie, the Lord James Graham. How like you that, my lords? And your mother the Marchioness of Montrose.'

'Me! I am as little a marchioness as I was a countess! What do I care for such . . .'

'Quite so. Yet it does put you one step above, say, your stepmother! I conceive that might be to your satisfaction, on occasion! No? And two steps above your brother's wife! All folly – but if I guess aright, not wholly without advantage!'

Magdalen paused to consider that, while the boys yelled their new titles at each other excitedly. Sim Mather had discreetly made himself scarce.

Setting down the baby on the old man's pallet-bed of reed straw, Montrose took his wife in his arms again. He was no monk, and his need for a woman frequently was fierce – but he had never yet allowed himself to surrender to it. To that extent, at least, he had been a better husband than some. Now, with Magdalen's plumply rounded body under his hands, the urge to possess her, after so long, was all but overwhelming. But he could not possibly send his sons out of the shack; and they were still too young to recognise his need. Magdalen herself was tense within his embrace – although that might well have been her own frustration and necessity. With almost an unspoken curse, he put her away a little, and turned to pace the earthen floor.

'Can I come with you? With your army?' In a rush, she blurted it out. 'I could do it. Other women have done it.'

He stared at her, scarcely believing that he heard aright. 'Magdalen, lass . . . !'

'At least I would be with you. I could be a camp-follower – if soldier you must! I am none so delicate – only timorous! Take me with you, James.'

'My love – it is not possible. I thank you, with all my heart I thank you for saying it, offering it . . .'

'I am not offering. I am asking, praying.'

'No, lass. You do not know what you ask. It is not possible. What I go to do is too harsh, too hazardous, for anything such. You do not understand. How could you? I have no army – only some two thousand beggarly kerns and caterans. With that I must needs try to win Scotland. And I will do so, God willing. But for months, a year, it will be not warfare but skirmishing, banditry, ranging the land. No place for you, or any woman. Living in the heather, with never a roof or a bed. Moving all the time . . .' He went to take her hands again. 'No, Magdalen – it cannot be. But my heart goes out to you for saying it. Bless you!'

Her shoulders slumped. 'Am I never to have you, then? Never? Is it always to be . . . thus?'

'No. I swear it will not be. Give me this year, lass. I shall see you from time to time. But – give me a year to win the King his kingdom back. And then, on my oath and honour, I will come home to you.'

'If they do not kill you first,' she said flatly.

'That is in God's hands. But, never fear, I am none so easy killed. Now – tell me of yourself. Of your days, your life. How you spend your time. Of little Jean's birth. Of Ald Montrose. The lands, the folk – there is so much to hear. And so little time . . .'

They had their hour, and a little more, before the man could drag himself away.

'The parting,' he declared, then, in a strained voice. 'The parting again is damnable. Too high a price to pay. For us all. But this time it will not be for so long.' He put his arm around Magdalen's shoulders, and pointed to his sons. 'My Graham lords – look well after your lady-mother, I charge you. And these little ones. Grieve her nothing. It is the Lieutenant-General's command! This is *your* part. To hold my rear secure, in good order, while I advance. Else I cannot do so with a single mind. It is all part of the battle. And you, my dear, you hold so much that is precious to me beyond all telling, in these two hands. Do not fear that I will not come back to claim it. And soon. God keep you all.'

He left them there in that lowly hut, tears blurring their image, one lonely man to go and conquer Scotland. And he did not, dared not, look back.

The morning was further advanced than he had intended. He had to get into the empty hills as swiftly and as unobtrusively as possible, unable to return to Atholl by the shortest route, as he had come – and his garrison was tired. He rode west by north, by the Muir of Dun and the Muir of Pert, and by little Stracathro to the Catherthun hills, and so over into the quiet hidden valley of the West Water; and although he saw and was seen by a henwife or two, herds with their cattle, and some men with their sickles cutting the scanty oats, even raised his hand to them as a decent traveller should – while keeping his too-handsome head bent or averted – none challenged him. None of the quality, of course, were abroad at such hour.

Once the great rolling heather hills received him into their abiding quiet, the man relaxed somewhat. The chances of interception, of significant encounter, or any encounter, were now minimal. But instead of fifty miles to ride, he now had nearer seventy, and by rougher ways.

He elected to make one encounter. At the lonely Lindsay bonnet-lairdship of Craigendowie, where the rivers forked, instead of avoiding the house he turned in there, and exchanged his tired garron for another, plus a tankard of milk and some oatcakes, leaving a golden guinea as acknowledgment. He did not name his name, nor was it asked. And thereafter he had Scotland to himself.

At least he had time, and opportunity, to think, as he crossed the wide watersheds of Glen Clova, Glen Prosen, Glen Isla and Glen Shee, to Glen Tilt, in Atholl.

It was dusk again when James Graham rode down Tilt to the camp at Blair, heavy-eyed, drooping in the saddle, having covered a total of over 110 miles of mountain and moor in twenty-fours hours. The place was in an identical stir and clamour of singing, dancing and general uproar as when he had left it, almost as though it had never paused. But one change there was, to lift the droop from Montrose's shoulders. John, Lord Kilpont had arrived from Stirlingshire with

300 men – and these were trained in archery, an old-fashioned but especial interest of Kilpont's. They were mainly Menteith Grahams and their adherence, with the support of his friends, was an incalculable fillip.

Before he allowed himself to sleep that night, Montrose penned a formal letter to Archibald Campbell, Marquis of Argyll. As the King's Lieutenant he informed Argyll that he was in a state of armed and treasonable rebellion against the monarch, and that unless he withdrew immediately from this activity, and made full and suitable restitution and submission to His Grace, he would be proceeded against with all vigour forthwith by the King's forces, to his considerable and swift injury. An immediate submission was required. The letter-writer, tired as he was, smiled grimly to himself as he added his signature to this crazy if old-fashioned chivalric challenge.

22

THEY MARCHED AT DAWN ON FRIDAY THE 20TH OF AUGUST, 1644 – and from the very first, Montrose was at pains to show all concerned what manner of commander he was and what he expected of the troops under his command. He himself marched on foot, targe on arm, pike over shoulder, broadsword at side. He sang the lilting, fast-stepping Gaelic marching-songs with them, and laughed and joked with all. But he led at a fierce pace, and continued to do so, ignoring all roads and even tracks unless they took them directly or substantially in the direction he aimed to go. This was to be the fastest-moving force in Scotland, necessarily.

For that, of course, it was in fact ideally composed, cavalry or none. Lean and agile Highlanders and Irish kerns, lightly armed, carrying no more kit than their plaids, brogans of rawhide on feet hardened to roughest going, they were mobile light infantry par excellence, as far as swift movement was concerned – and could go where even garrons could not. Living off the country, with no bases to tie them, no communications to guard, a pouch of oatmeal each man's rations, they had no baggage-trains to hamper them, no cannon. Such as had firearms had in the main flintlock pistols and light sporting muskets, not the more ponderous military matchlocks which required V-topped supports and rolls of slow-burning fuse to fire. If the lack of ammunition for these was appalling – it was reckoned that the Irish contingent did not muster more than one ball apiece – at least it meant that they travelled the lighter.

There were some 2700, now, in all, 800 Athollmen and other North Perthshire clansmen having joined. They forded the Garry near Glackmore, waving goodbye to the young Earl of Atholl and his folk, and moving up-river to Invervack, climbed then straight up the long, long braeface, three miles and 1000 feet of ascent, to the heather ridge of Tulach which separated the valley of the Garry from that of Tummel, the men sweating out the effects of much beef and liquor of the last days. Over the lofty summit they spilled down to Loch Tummel-side at Tressait, without pause, nearly 3000 men brushing through the knee-high, dusty, scented heather of a golden August morning. At the loch-shore, Montrose swung right-handed, westwards, not left, as might have been expected.

His spies and scouts had informed him that the Lord Elcho, son to the Earl of Wemyss, was commanding the Covenant army being raised to deal with Colkitto's Irish, in co-operation with Argyll's Campbells. He was based on Perth, near his own castle of Elcho, and was estimated to have 7000 infantry and 700 horse, mainly from Fife and Angus. Whether he knew of Montrose's assumption of Alastair's command was uncertain; but at least he would not expect an immediate advance and attack by this beggarly host on his vastly larger and properly equipped army. The Graham, aiming at this stage for a gesture, a demonstration to arouse confidence, rather than any conventional battle, intended at least to surprise his former colleague – for Elcho had served with him in the Second Bishops' War.

Rounding the head of Loch Tummel, they crossed the river between it and Loch Rannoch to the west, and commenced to climb again, up and up under the mighty cone of shapely Schiehallion by the Braes of Foss. To the lofty, lonely small loch of Kinardochy they mounted, and so southwards beyond, down the green Strath of Appin, with the great valley of Tay beginning to yawn before them. By early evening they were down amongst the levels of Dull, where the ancient Celtic Church had once dispensed its urbane and genial faith. They had covered twenty-one miles – whereas the man Cromwell had recently declared that the utmost that even the best and most lightly armed infantry could achieve in any day was thirteen, and that not in mountainous country.

They were on the verge of Campbell lands here, filched from the MacGregors, and Montrose sought no conclusions with such, or any distractions at this stage. They turned eastwards down Tay – and soon found themselves in some trouble from Menzies clansmen, who sniped and skirmished – their chief, Sir Alexander Menzies, having Campbell connexions. Black Pate and a party were despatched to deal with these, and a few were slain, some roofs and corn-stacks burned – the first blood to be shed in this new campaign. Castle Menzies itself, above the haughs of Tay, was too strong to assail without cannon, so they attempted nothing. But, since he would assuredly have messengers off to Perth, to warn Elcho of this new danger, with the darkening, to keep such couriers delayed for at least a few hours, Montrose settled his men for a much-needed rest in a wide circle around the castle, lighting cooking-fires to roast Menzies beef and poultry. Neither welcome nor recognition came from the chief. When darkness fell the fires were fed anew, to keep them blazing for some time – although their lighters thereafter stole away quietly into the scrub woodland to cross Tay secretly by the ford west of Aberfeldy. With luck it might be long before Sir Alexander discovered that those fires were untended, morning even.

With even Alastair silent now, Montrose led his weary host up the steeply climbing drove road that lifted southwards out of the vale by the strung-out Falls of Moness, towards the next pass in that vast system of serried mountain-range and valley. But they were all now too tired for much more of this, and in a wide hollow by the shadowy Loch na Craige they threw themselves down in their plaids, to sleep in the heather. It was nearly midnight.

Even so, four hours only Montrose allowed them before they were on the move again – and men learned anew what sort of general the King had sent them. Down Glen Cochill and across the head of Strathbraan they hastened as the light grew on the mist-capped hills, by Amulree and another, lower, pass, and so down into the dramatic gut of the Sma' Glen and the rushing Almond. Nearing more settled lands now, Pate Graham was sent ahead with an advance-guard – and there was some excitement when he sent back word that a fairly large body of men was awaiting them at Buchanty, near the southern jaws of the defile, a strategic spot which the Romans themselves had recognised and fortified. However, a second courier came to say that the party was friendly; and on approach it proved to be 200 more mixed Menteith Grahams and Drummonds, under the Master of Madderty and Sir John Drummond, younger son of the Earl of Perth, on their devious way north to join Montrose at Atholl, in answer to his summons. All were much heartened by even this modest accession of strength – Montrose the more so in that he was desperately short of officers, and here he gained three of some experience. The Master of Madderty, son of the Drummond Lord thereof, was another of his own brothers-in-law, having married Jean, the youngest of the five Graham sisters, an impetuous young man but with the makings of leadership in him. Sir John Drummond, a kinsman, was actually brother to Black Pate's wife. And Major James Stewart of Ardvorlich, whose mother was also a Drummond, though strange, indeed known as the Mad Major, was a brilliant fighter. Almost forty of this party were mounted – the beginnings of a cavalry arm.

Thus reinforced in numbers and morale, they crossed the last of the intervening ranges, a comparatively small one, into Strathearn, with the Lowlands before them, by Fowlis Wester. This was all Drummond and Graham country, so that they could now go openly, and even gather up the odd extra adherent as they went. Montrose still marched on foot, dressed as a Highlander. They camped for the night just east of Fowlis, having covered exactly another twenty-one miles. For an infantry force to have marched almost forty-five miles in two days was next to unheard of.

During the night not much sleep was achieved by Montrose or his officers. Recruiters were out all around, seeking especially horses and ammunition; also food and money - partly Montrose's and Black Pate's rents, with Inchbrakie only two miles off. Scouts came in with reports – one being that Sir John's elder brother, the Lord Drummond, had gone to join Elcho at Perth, as had the Lord Murray of Gask, son to the Earl of Tullibardine, another of Montrose's former colleagues and kinsman of some of the Murrays in their own force. This was part of the heartbreak of civil war, with families shamefully divided. Elcho was also reported to have gained the support of a very experienced professional soldier of the Swedish wars, Sir James Scott of Rossie – a serious matter.

They were marching again by dawn, heading eastwards towards Methven. It was Montrose's aim to achieve a surprise by cutting off Perth from the south and east, and so confining Elcho's force in the city, unready, with only the mainly hostile north to retire on – for the Graham had many friends in Perth, and might expect considerable sympathy from the townsfolk. But, unfortunately, before they reached Methven, six miles down the strath, scouts brought word that Elcho, after early-morning devotions – it was Sunday, the 1st of September – had left Perth and was marching westwards by the Burgh Muir to meet them. Clearly, the Menzies chief had got his message through, by swift horsemen presumably, in time to reveal the secret advance.

It was a sore blow. The situation was wholly changed. Despite all their Homeric marching, Montrose's plan was now unworkable. He could not possibly work round to south of Perth now – Elcho's 700 cavalry could intercept any such attempt. They must either fight a battle, or turn back.

It made a dire choice. Outnumbered three to one, out-armed and out-classed, lacking cannon – Elcho was reported to have nine five-pounders – and cavalry, any head-on confrontation looked suicidal. Yet, to retreat now, at the first threat of action, could be nothing less than disastrous for the morale of his force, for his credit as the King's general, and for all royalist hopes in Scotland. Nothing could be worse than that.

In this cleft-stick, it was a strange chance which decided James Graham. Almost as an afterthought, the courier who had brought the news mentioned to Sir John Drummond that the city was ringing with the dread word that the ministers attendant on Elcho had decided, after due prayer and deliberation, that the slogan for the encounter should be 'Jesus, and no quarter!' Shocked, Drummond came to tell Montrose.

The Graham was utterly appalled, scarcely able to believe that any men calling themselves Christian, quite apart from being ministers of the gospel, could so blaspheme and traduce the name of their Saviour, who was Love personified. But when he had questioned the messenger, and satisfied himself that it was true, Montrose was a changed man.

'In the name of Almighty God,' he declared, voice trembling, 'I do swear before all that if He will give me strength, aid, this day, I will burn that infamous cry from the lips of damnable, ranting bigots who besmirch His Son's holy name! God help me, I will!'

His friends stared at him. Never had any of them seen the equable, calm and assured James Graham, the compassionate, the courteous, like this. None spoke as, white-faced, he turned away.

'Continue the advance!' he commanded, harshly.

When David, Master of Madderty, presently sought to ask tactics of his brother-in-law, Montrose cut him off short in a fashion hitherto unknown. Men repeated those awful four words to each other, throughout the host, and considered all that they implied, looking askance at the stiffly slender, tartan-clad back of their leader, as they marched, doubtfully now, on to Methven.

But though Montrose was more furiously angry than ever he had been in all his life, he was not wholly beside himself with rage and sick disgust. One part of his mind continued to work coolly, clearly. He saw in his mind's eye all the lay-out of the land between himself and Perth, knew it well, sought its advantages and problems. Much of it indeed belonged to Lord Madderty, and many a time he had hunted and hawked over Methven Moss and Tippermuir. The other side would know it equally well, of course, since what did not belong to Madderty was owned by Murray of Gask – Ruthven land given to the Murrays of Tullibardine by the late King James after the Gowrie Conspiracy of ill fame. But, if clash there was to be, the land itself must be made to fight for its king.

Since Elcho was coming by the Perth Burgh Muir, he was

obviously going to occupy the long, low ridge of Lamberkine, which lay to the south of this shallow side-vale of Strathearn, in which lay Madderty, Gask, Methven and eventually Perth itself. His own force was approaching along the northern flanks, also rising ground. Between lay the two-mile-wide soggy bottom-land of the sluggish Cowgask Burn, Methven Moss first and then the open levels of Tippermuir to the east. Neither force was to be expected to leave its secure higher ground to cross that low open waste; yet the advantage lay all with Elcho, for he could send his cavalry east-about, round by the lower Almond valley, to come in behind the royalist force – a manoeuvre Montrose himself could by no means attempt, first because he had no cavalry to do it, and secondly because the Almond fords would inevitably be guarded by the enemy. Any such move on the western side would be under observation all the way.

Catching up with Black Pate's scouting party on the Methven slope, Montrose could see the enemy already drawn up in position on the gentle north-facing Lamberkine braes opposite, less than two miles away, arms and armour glinting in the forenoon sun, banners flapping, all looking highly effective and frighteningly potent. Elcho clearly had his cavalry fairly equally divided between left and right wings, with his great mass of 7000 foot in the centre, a row of nine five-pounder cannon grouped ominously in front of them. That cavalry alone, sent in at once in two complementary thrusts, could so roll up and disorganise the royalist infantry as to leave them more or less helpless prey for the Covenanting foot – if they did not sweep them away entirely, without the foot's aid. To discourage any such early move, and to give time for his own dispositions – as well as to establish his constitutional position in proper fashion – Montrose sent forward the Master of Madderty under a flag of truce to inform the Lord Elcho that he was facing, in arms, the Marquis of Montrose, the King's Lieutenant-General and Viceroy, and that he was therefore in a posture of rebellion which could amount to treason. He conceived him, and his colleagues, to be essentially loyal subjects of King Charles, however; and therefore, looking on them as former comrades, for the good of all and to avoid shedding the blood of Scots fellow subjects, he required the Lord Elcho to disperse his forces forthwith, and come to make his due allegiance to the

King's Grace. Moreover, on the Sabbath Day, any such warlike posture was singularly unsuitable. If time was required to reconsider their duty to their undoubted liege lord, let them withdraw to Perth meantime and make submission on the morrow.

So soon as young Madderty rode off, his brother-in-law set about positioning his ragged host. Disaster could most easily and swiftly come by outflanking; therefore his main preoccupation at this stage was so to extend his line and make use of the terrain that this was impossible, or nearly so. His sheer lack of numbers told against him in this, forcing him to thin out his front in almost crazy fashion, so that, in the main, his men were ranked no more than three deep. On the other hand, his knowledge of the ground, plus the eye of a born tactician, enabled him to base the horns of his great semicircular front on marshland, the swampy Cowgask Burn where it emerged from Methven Moss, on the west, and the Tippermallo Myre on the east. It was a ridiculously long front for less than 3000 men; but it would be hard to outflank, at close range. Colkitto he put in command of his Irish, Islesmen and West Highlanders, in the centre; Kilpont, with the Graham bowmen, he placed on the left, overlooking the Tippermallo Myre; while he himself took the right wing, with the Athollmen and more local volunteers.

While these dispositions were hastily taking place, the Master of Madderty reached the enemy lines. Montrose could not actually see what then took place, but there arose a great shouting and hooting, and white flag and envoy both abruptly disappeared. Then, three horsemen came galloping from the Covenant centre, to rein up some two hundred yards away, across the Cowgask Burn and its reedy bed, there to shout that the Lord Elcho and the Military Committee held no truck with traitors and excommunicates of Christ's Kirk; that they had chosen the Lord's Day to do the Lord's work; and that the insolent envoy had been arrested, was being sent bound to Perth, and would be hanged just as soon as the Lord Elcho had leisure to arrange the matter. No quarter would be granted to traitors, in the name of Jesus Christ and His Holy Kirk.

The bold trio wheeled their mounts, and raced back whence they had come.

Even before they were back, to a great and fierce chanting of 'Jesus, and no quarter! Jesus, and no quarter!' from the

thousands of infantry, led by black-robed divines, the enemy
cavalry charged, the Lord Drummond's banner at their head.
It was the left-wing squadron, and no doubt was intended
partly as a feint, to force the royalist centre into a premature
break-up of formation, for it was aimed to right of centre.
Not for nothing, however, had Montrose placed Alastair
MacDonald and the most experienced fighters in the middle.
Although only in three ranks, they stood their ground stoutly
as the cavalry bore thundering down on them, the front rank
kneeling, to fire their single musket-shot from that position,
the second crouching, and the third standing – only these
last were mainly without muskets and had only stones to
throw, which their leaders had had them collect.

They waited until the charging horsemen were almost
upon them, so that even stones would have maximum effect.
But well before the clash, and just as soon as Montrose had
assured himself that the other squadron of enemy cavalry
were not immediately being thrown in in support, on the
right, he had a trumpet – borrowed from Atholl – blown
high and clear as signal to Kilpont, half a mile away. That
man promptly swung his bowmen down into the Tippermallo Myre, and from that wet and difficult stance faced
west to pour a shower of arrows into the flanks of the
advancing cavalry just as they reached Colkitto's front – at
extreme range but galling. At the same time, Montrose led
his own people down into the Cowgask bog, from which,
however uncomfortably, they also could discharge their
muskets against the left flank of the enemy horse.

The Lord Drummond, therefore, found himself under
fire from three sides – in a box, in fact. He could have
smashed his way, no doubt, through Colkitto's centre, though
at severe loss almost certainly; but then would as certainly
have found the royalist horns closing in behind him, between
him and his army, so that he would either have been out of
the battle for good or have to cut his way back through the
enemy. As probably most cavalry commanders would have
done in the circumstances, he chose to swing away to the
side, his feint not having worked. To swing to his right would
have brought him closer to those hundreds of archers, already
sorely harassing his flank. He swung left-handed, westwards,
for Montrose and the Athollmen, and out of the range of the
arrows.

Casting aside their useless muskets, the Atholl Stewarts and Robertsons drew swords and dirks, while those with pikes formed up into hasty hedgehogs, many of them up to their knees in mud and water. Drummond was no fool – and, after all, he knew this place as well as did Montrose, with his father's castle not a dozen miles away. He saw those fore-shortened legs, and knew that his horses would inevitably get much more seriously bogged down than men on foot, and that this mire was a trap for him. He yelled and gestured for what remained of his squadron to swing still farther round, and keep on swinging, so as to ride back to the main army.

But it is not so easy to control a cavalry charge gone wrong, with a third of its men down, riderless horses career-ing everywhere, men shouting and screaming. His Fife yeo-manry were far from highly trained, and yelling Highland-men darting out, bent low to avoid swinging cavalry swords from above, but dirks out to rip open horses' bellies, are apt to distract even the most stolid. The entire turning manoeuvre became little short of a shambles, which quickly developed into complete and disorganised flight.

Out of perhaps 350 horsemen, only some 120 were down. But the remainder, in fact, now offered Montrose a sudden and unexpected opportunity. They were fleeing back singly and in groups, anyhow, across the levels of Tippermuir, widespread, scattered. Taking an enormous risk, the Graham shouted to his trumpeter to sound the General Advance; and, in a fever of urgency, himself raced forward, broadsword on high, to lead his Athollmen out of their bog after the fleeing horse. Those 200-odd cavalrymen were wholly mask-ing their own cannon.

Alastair saw the situation and its possibilities, and swiftly flung his own three regiments forward at the run. It all meant abandoning their good positions, but he obeyed his com-mander's summons. Kilpont, farther away and less well placed to co-operate, lagged somewhat.

Yelling their clan slogans, the 2000 Highlanders and Irish-men charged, steel brandished, behind the fleeing cavalry, with half a mile to cover. And seeing them coming, a savage tide, and their own cannon unable to fire without shooting down their own folk, the prudent artillerymen did the sensible thing, and fled likewise.

Down – or rather up – on Elcho's waiting centre, then, pounded and flooded a host of men and horses, in flight and charge, in panic and pursuit, in chaos and yelling confusion. But the panic came first – and panic is perhaps the most infectious disease known to man. The thought that nine loaded cannon were now lost to them and could well be turned point-blank upon themselves, no doubt contributed. Despite the screaming, furious ministers urging death to the Philistines, and too full of the wrath of God to be frightened, the foot from Angus, Dundee and Fife wavered, appalled, gave ground involuntarily in anticipation, and then turned and bolted in a vast human flood.

It was not all fright and shame, of course. Elcho sought to rally those around him, and succeeded in forming at least an island in the rout. Sir James Scott, the mercenary veteran on the right wing, did not flee, but wheeled the second squadron of cavalry round to come up behind the advancing royalists – since he could not assail front or flanks without riding down his own folk; but now Kilpont was coming up fast on that flank, with his bowmen, and they paused to wing hundreds of vicious arrows at the circling horsemen at short range, to devastating effect. It was enough. Seeing all else disintegrating, all so suddenly lost, and no doubt worried also about those captured cannon, the cavalry, after a single ragged charge, rode off in the general direction of Perth.

Elcho and his lieutenants, recognising reality all too clearly, retired while still they could, and hurriedly.

Montrose himself was quite dumbfounded at the speed and scale of his unexpected success. But despite his continuing anger over the shameful 'Jesus, and no quarter' sacrilege, he by no means lost his head in triumphant glee. He perceived very well that this was not a true victory, but something of an accident, a fortunate chance for him and a mere superficial defeat for his enemies. Excellent for morale and prestige though it would be, he had not really vanquished the Covenanting army, only dispersed it in panic. At the end of the day it would recover itself, and be still twice as large and many times as powerful as his own – and that much wiser. In *his* circumstances, he needed much more than that.

Panting then, at a lull in the flailing, stumbling swordery, he gasped to Black Pate who never left his side, 'On! On!

Smite! Tell Alastair. Pursue. To the . . . very gates . . . of
Perth! No let-up. Tell all – on!'

'Aye. God, aye! Trumpeter? Sound Advance again . . . ?'
The other nodded, and plunged on.

And so took place, along the Lamberkine ridge, over it on
to the Aberdalgie side, and on across the east-facing slopes of
the Burgh Muir and the braes of Friarton and Craigie, what
was nothing less than a running and interminable slaughter.
And deliberately, torturing himself, the man who had
ordained it, and who hated bloodshed, steeled his heart to it
all, and pressed on and on towards the outskirts of Perth.
This army, this impious army that chose to pervert the very
name of the Saviour in its arrogant savagery, must be destroyed. Destroyed, not just scattered. The cavalry could get
clear, and did; but the foot, the staggering, stumbling, frantic
foot was their prey. Some stood and fought, of course, some
few grouped together and cut their way to safety, some
managed to outrun their pursuers; but the great majority
not only just ran, but threw away arms and armour to run
the faster – and were in consequence cut down by the hundred. Included in the shambles were not a few citizens of
Perth who had elected to spend their Sabbath watching the
sport of the Host of the Lord destroying the Midianites hip
and thigh. When Montrose discovered this and perceived
what they were, he sought to command that all such should
be spared. Also any of the ministers fleeing. But to control
Irish and Highland fighting-men in the heat of victory, and
over a wide area, was wellnigh impossible. Many non-
combatants fell with the rest, undoubtedly.

It was a long, bloody and vastly exhausting business for all
concerned – save the cavalry – despite the brevity of the
actual battle, a four-mile carnage over a great expanse of
moorland, rough pasture, and latterly quite steep scrub-
covered braesides down around Pitheavlis and Craigie.
Weary, hoarse, mud- and blood-spattered, but unhurt, Montrose at length found himself at the very southern walls of
the city – indeed exactly at the place which he had originally
hoped to reach by surprise. Under-officered as his host was,
he sought at last to hold on, to draw up and take a firm grip
of his fevered, excited horde, his trumpeter blowing and
blowing, big Alastair's bull-like voice bellowing, hunting-
horns winding. Long before there was any real semblance of

order, and with running fights still going on over a wide area, a deputation of magistrates and leading citizens of Perth came hurrying out under a positive forest of white flags, evidently believing that the trumpeting represented a summons to surrender, shouting aloud for mercy, forbearance, peace, declaring complete submission. Their Provost was amissing, none knew where; but the city was the Lord Marquis's, and all therein. If he would but spare it, and them . . .

A little dazed by the suddenness of it all, as well as by sheer physical fatigue, Montrose drew strongly upon his reserves of wits, discernment, even courtesy, and switched from playing the guerilla leader to playing the King's representative and responsible governor. He accepted the city's surrender, the third greatest in the land, declared that he had no quarrel with its leaders, promised order and good treatment for all, so long as his needs were supplied, his orders obeyed and his men well treated and catered for; but demanded that all arms and ammunition, and all horses, should be brought and handed over to his officers before nightfall. All fugitives who had taken part in the late treasonable fighting must render themselves to him as prisoners; and if they did so without delay and further resistance, there would be mercy and no more slaughter. Let the magistrates and bailies take fullest charge of their city; he would require a good accounting. But he hoped that there would be no need to make examples. God save the King!

And so, that night of the 1st of September, the man who had started the day as little more than an outlawed fugitive with a price on his head – £1600 sterling – and only the stars for a roof, ended it as master of the third largest city in Scotland, and complete victor over the country's second-line army. Admittedly this was a poor affair compared with Leslie's great professional force in England; but it had represented the largest assembly of armed men mobilised north of the Border, and had been well equipped. To all this equipment, arms, ammunition, commissariat, tentage and some horses, as well as the nine cannon, Montrose fell heir – as well as whatever Perth could supply to him. By the most abrupt change of fortune, he who could lay hands on little or nothing, now had a superabundance at his disposal; and for the moment, undisputed sway over a large area. It was exactly fourteen days since the victor had crossed the Border disguised as a groom.

Before he slept that night, between sheets for the first time for long, in the house of one Mistress Donaldson, he was concerned to send out invitations to all the ministers of Perth to dine with him next day. The diplomat and statesman was in control again. Not that this precluded him from sending a messenger hot-foot to Kinnaird Castle.

23

THREE DAYS LATER, THE ARMY OF KING CHARLES WAS ON the move again – they were daring to call it that, now, though perhaps still a little ambitiously. Certainly it looked, and was, a very different host from that which had fought the Battle of Tippermuir. It was no larger – for though some Perthshire lairds had rediscovered their courage and duty to the King, and some numbers of Elcho's men had elected to change sides, nevertheless most of the Athollmen, not to mention the Highlanders recruited by Colkitto earlier in Badenoch and Lochaber, were no longer present. This was not desertion, but the normal pattern of Highland military service. These clansmen were nobody's servants, crofters, cattle-herds, drovers, fishermen, hunters, supporting a chief but not employed by him or by any man. They would gladly wield their swords in his cause, unpaid; but when the battle was over, they went home, to get on with the business of living and keeping their families alive. Moreover, this was harvest-time in the Highlands, and their cattle stock, the basis of the whole Highland economy, could not survive the long winter without the oats now waiting to be gathered in from a thousand glens. They would fight for the Lord Marquis another time, and for this King Charles perhaps, to a lesser extent – but meantime they were going home, with the booty of their victory.

Montrose knew all this too well to seek to dissuade them. And he saw that they went adequately rewarded.

So there were large changes in personnel. And those who remained *looked* different – the Irish, the Islesmen, the Grahams, Kilpont's bowmen and some Gordons. They were no longer ragged and ill-equipped. Now all who wanted them had breastplates, helmets, good Lowland clothing and boots, and were armed comprehensively with firearms, and ample ammunition therefor – for, after all, they had captured over 5000 stands of arms. Most of the Gaelic warriors would by no means wear Lowland gear, so Montrose had demanded a vast amount of cloth, tartan where possible, from the Perth merchants, to renew kilts, plaids and jerkins. Apart from that, the horses, and a £50 levy – to give Alastair, who had not a penny-piece left in his war-chest – James Graham had imposed no further penalty upon the city, and had kept his troops from any excesses, with a stern hand. It was important, since he could by no means remain there to hold the place, that Perth should thereafter look fairly kindly on him and on the royal cause.

For he had to move. Static warfare was not for him and his – and Perth no place to be besieged in even if it had been. Already there were reports that the Estates were mobilising feverishly in Edinburgh, Glasgow and Dundee; and they said that Callander, with Leslie's reserve army on the Border, had been called home. More immediately threatening, Argyll himself was known to be hastening eastwards from his own Highland territories with a large force of Campbells and their allies, and demanding reinforcements from all sides in the name of the Privy Council and Estates. And there was said to be a sizeable Covenant force in the North-East, based on Aberdeen – although who was its general was not clear, the young Lord Graham adhering but presumably not in command.

Above all things, the royalist force must not be trapped between three converging armies – or two, for that matter. Montrose decided to move north by east, partly because the opposition in that direction was the least specific, and with the Gordon element in it liable perhaps to change allegiance again; and partly because he wanted to recruit men in Angus and the Mearns, Graham and Ogilvy territory. Even the Carnegies might now be persuaded to join forces with him,

317

on the King's behalf. But few would risk it, he believed, if the city of Dundee remained hostile, so close at hand. Therefore he would make for Dundee first of all, where he had hopes that the ruling party might be dislodged without too much difficulty – the Graham lairdships of Claverhouse, Claypotts, Fintry, Strathdichty and Mains circling the place on north and east.

So, on Wednesday the 4th of September, they marched away from Perth, crossing the Tay and up its eastern bank, making for the wide mouth of Strathmore in the first instance, and the Ogilvy country. They made quite a gallant show, for they had cavalry now, to the number of 200 – Grahams, Drummonds and 100 Hays under George, Lord Dupplin, the old Earl of Kinnoull's heir, the only new recruit of any note. Most of the officers were mounted – although Alastair MacDonald scornfully refused a horse, preferring to march with his men. As indeed Montrose would have done, had he not had occasion to ride escort. For this day, trotting at his side, were his Marchioness and his eldest two sons, the Earl of Kincardine and the Lord James Graham.

On the Sunday night, after victory, Montrose's messenger to Kinnaird, as well as informing Magdalen of success, had also invited her to join him for a day or two at Perth, with John and Jamie. None would hinder or assail the Graham's family, within a fair radius of Perth, in the meantime – so it would be safe enough. They had come the next day, to a joyful reunion – even though Magdalen did not fail to declare her continued fears for the future, and her loathing of all warfare, victorious or otherwise. The boys, of course, were in a seventh heaven of delight, sons of a manifest hero now, for all to acknowledge. Two nights and a day they had had together – and at least the nights had been their own.

Now they rode, and marched, up the wide pastoral vale of fair Strathmore, between the Sidlaws and the Tay, through the pleasant settled land of North Gowrie and the Stormont. At the junction of Isla and Tay, they swung eastwards for Coupar-Angus, the slow cannon already left far behind. And near where the Romans had once made their great camp, at Lintrose, Montrose halted likewise, and sent out probing parties southwards through the Sidlaw passes of Balshando and Glack of Newtyle, to discover the state of affairs at

Dundee, and to make contact with the Grahams of that area, while he waited for the slow cannon to catch up. Meanwhile, he sent to the Earl of Airlie, at Cortachy Castle, and to the Earl of Kinghorne at Glamis, for reinforcements, mounted if possible.

He gained little joy at Coupar-Angus – save for what he obtained from his wife and sons. Airlie was loyal King's man enough, and answered the call personally, bringing his sons Sir Thomas and Sir David Ogilvy with him – but only forty-five men. This was a grievous disappointment, even though they were all horsed, from one of the most powerful lords in the East of Scotland. Montrose had looked for many times that number. And Kinghorne sent only his regrets. He did not actually declare that he was not so agile at changing sides as was James Graham – but he indicated that he still adhered to the Covenant which he had signed, and did not feel that he could rise against it in arms, with a clear conscience. Nor was he in the best of health . . .

Only a comparatively few other recruits joined them at Coupar-Angus.

Old Airlie brought sad news as well as few men. His eldest son, Montrose's faithful lieutenant, the Lord Ogilvy, with most of the rest of the Scots whom James Graham had left so dramatically and secretly south of Carlisle, had fallen into an ambush on the way to the King at Oxford, at Ribble Bridge, and were now the English parliamentarians' prisoners. Aboyne had apparently escaped, for it was had sent the word from Carlisle; but many others were taken. Airlie may not actually have blamed Montrose for desertion of his son; but undoubtedly it still rankled that he had failed to save the Ogilvy castles of Airlie and Forter, and the Countess herself, from Argyll's savagery, when he was still Covenant Lieutenant-General in these parts. Probably this accounted for the merely token force of Ogilvys he brought with him.

On the second night at Coupar, while still they awaited firm news of Dundee, Montrose was aroused in the tent he was sharing with Magdalen by the agitated captain of the guard. Not attack, no. But trouble. Great shameful trouble. Murder . . . !

Hastily seeking to quieten and reassure his alarmed wife, James Graham ran, half-naked, through the drizzling night and the slumbering camp, to another tent, where three men lay dead, horribly contorted in a sea of blood – his friend, John, Lord Kilpont, and two sentries, all stabbed with savage, multiple wounds. By the light of a flickering lamp, he starred, appalled.

'John! Johnnie!' he choked. 'God in heaven – what is this? Dead? Dead? All dead . . . ?'

'Dead, my lord. When I got to him. The sentries gave the alarm. Then these two slain likewise. Another wounded . . .'

'But . . . why? Who? How came this . . . ?'

'Ardvorlich, my lord. Major Stewart of Ardvorlich. He did it. Him they call the Mad Major.'

'But . . . but Kilpont was Ardvorlich's friend. His closest friend, in this host. Some mistake, here . . .'

'No, my lord Marquis – none. They were together in this tent all the night. Playing at the cards. See.' He pointed to the overturned ammunition-box, the scattered cards and the fallen wine-flagon and tankards. 'The wounded sentry is one of my lord Kilpont's bowmen. He heard shouting, and came running. He saw his lordship on the grass, and the Major stabbing at him, stabbing and stabbing with his dirk. He ran for aid. Fetched these two others, and went back. Ardvorlich was a man crazed. He knifed them all. He shouted "Mac-Gregor!" at them. MacGregor – though they were none of MacGregor. Then he bolted. I heard noise at the horse-lines. He is gone. And . . . these are dead. All dead.'

'Sweet Jesu – MacGregor! That old story! Of a mercy – so sore a sin, so ancient a sin!'

'But there were no MacGregors in it, my lord . . .'

Montrose did not explain what he meant to the captain of the guard, but knelt down beside his friend, head bowed, to take the limp hand and try to pray. Pray also for the souls of the two innocent sentries, who had all unwittingly paid the price of a thirty-year-old enormity. He knew the story well. All who dwelt in Strathearn knew it. How Ardvorlich on the south shore of Loch Earn had been a Drummond property, and how the son of Stewart of Glenbuckie in Balquhidder had wed the daughter of Drummond-Earnoch, Keeper of the royal forest of Glen Artney, and had been given this Ardvorlich as her tocher. Dying, Drummond had been succeeded by his son, as Keeper, and one day a marauding band of MacGregors, poaching the forest, and who had a grudge against the father, chanced upon the son in Glen Artney, and slew him there and then. Satan-inspired, they cut off the dead man's head, and took it across the hills and down to Ardvorlich House. Stewart was from home, but his lady only temporarily out-of-doors. When she came back, it was to find the MacGregors sitting round her kitchen-table, feeding themselves and her brother's severed head bread and cheese. In screaming horror she had run away, away and away, up into the empty hills, a crazed and preg-nant woman alone, wandering, out of her mind. And there, by a lonely lochan, still known as the Loch of the Woman, her child had been born – James Stewart. He had survived, and indeed had grown up strong, handsome but with a strange look to his eye, renowned for strength, temper and courage, utter disregard for danger, waging ruthless and un-relenting war on all MacGregors. Whenever he saw one, he killed him if he could, as he would a fly; and all such learned to keep their distance from Loch Earnside. Half a Drum-mond, he had joined Montrose with that party, and had been given a company of the Athollmen. None had fought more bravely or fiercely, or wrought more havoc, at Tipper-muir, than the Mad Major. And now – this.

Montrose took the business hard – harder than many deemed was necessary. Kilpont had been his especial friend and loyalest lieutenant. Save for Black Pate, there was none closer to him. And had it not been that he had brought his wife to share his tent with him, this would never have happened – for Kilpont and Pate and he had always been together hitherto, and only Magdalen's coming had caused his friends to tent elsewhere. Had his lust, his need for his wife's woman's body and softness, been the cause of his friend's death? The thought of it would not leave his grieving mind.

James Stewart did not return. Where he had gone, none knew.

Next morning, Pate Graham, as ever master of scouts, brought the waited news from Dundee. Any assault on the city was out of the question, he advised. To it had gravitated all the Covenant zealots and friends of Argyll from a wide area. Heavy cannon had been gathered in, from Broughty Castle and elsewhere. Three shiploads of arms and ammuni-tion had just arrived from Leith. The place was like an armed camp, and no amount of Graham lairdships round about would avail against it.

Montrose was in no mind to disagree with his friend's counsel. Siegery was foreign to his temperament anyway; and though the cannon he had captured from Elcho would be useful on a battlefield, they were far too light for use against a walled town. It was not by sitting down and seeking to starve out cities that he would conquer Scotland.

They would move north for Aberdeenshire and the Gordon country. Angus would never rise wholeheartedly for the King with Dundee secure on the other side.

So, in a strangely remote, self-critical, almost harsh mood for that man, the King's Lieutenant turned his face to the North-East. Magdalen, troubled, had never known him like this, he who was usually so courteously sure of himself, so unfailingly master of the situation. His sons took it all in their stride, of course.

It was no more than an easy two days' march to Kinnaird and Old Montrose, achieved without opposition – but also without any influx of support from the Angus gentry, worth mentioning. One battle obviously did not constitute any sure foundation for success. Approaching Kinnaird, where Magdalen and the boys were to be dropped, his elder son John made shift to speak with his father, apart from the others.

'My lord Marquis,' he declared stiffly, jerkily, in most formal style. 'Request permission to speak with the King's Lieutenant-General.'

Brows raised, his father eyed him. 'To be sure, Johnnie. But – you have never sought such permission before! Is aught amiss?'

'No, sir.' The boy coughed, but went woodenly on. 'I have never so spoken you before, my lord. As . . . as the Lord Graham. I would rather not be named the Earl of Kincardine, if it please you. I need not be, need I? The Lord Graham is . . . better.'

Surprised, Montrose looked at him with a new interest. 'Indeed, you are probably right . . . my lord! There have been Lords Graham for centuries. Yes, I think you have the rights of it, lad. The Lord Graham you shall remain.'

'Yes, sir. The Lord Graham means more. Always meant a deal, in Scotland. It must do, yet. Permission, my lord

Marquis, for the Lord Graham to remain with His Grace's army.' That came out in a breathless rush.

'Mm. So that's it! Laddie – you are only fourteen.'

'The Lord Lewis Gordon was only *thirteen* when he raised the Gordons! I will be fifteen soon. And I am the Lord Graham! I have learned all that they can teach me at Kinnaird, see you ...'

'You say so? But – your mother needs her eldest son to look after her, Johnnie. Jamie is only eleven and Robert four – too young.'

'Mother, and my lord of Southesk, my grandfather, say that I must go to St Andrews. To the University. So that I will not be with my mother. And I could not study at the University when you were fighting for the King in Scotland. I *could* not! Father – take me!'

Montrose stroked his tiny beard. 'You think of war as glory, adventure, lad. It is not so, believe me. In especial, civil war. It is blood and bestiality and cruelty. Aye, and treachery too. Do not see it as a thing fine, splendid ...'

'*You* are not cruel. Nor treacherous. You are noble – all say so. And you make war, for the King. I am the Lord Graham, sir. I have ... I have been too long at Kinnaird, my lord. With women. With old men. And I do not want to go to St Andrews. If they send me there, I swear that I shall run away! To fight for the King. As a common soldier.' The boy was flushed now, stammering, but determined.

'So! You would threaten, Johnnie?'

'No. No – never that. But – I cannot stay at Kinnaird. Do you not understand? I ... I *hate* the Carnegies, I think! They think only of lands and properties and marriages. My grandfather is already seeking a wife for me! I heard him telling Mother so ...'

'He is, is he! We must see about that, must we not?' Unwittingly, the boy had struck the right note, now. 'Hm. Your mother would not thank me for taking you, Johnnie.'

'My mother knows my intention, sir. I have told her, often.'

James Graham pondered. Magdalen had said nothing of this to him. Nor of any going to University. And certainly not of possible marriage contracts or betrothal. Was the boy indeed being smothered at Kinnaird? By Carnegies? He was right, in that, indeed; the Carnegies were concerned with the Carnegies, to be sure! But this boy was the heir to Graham.

Young he was, but conceivably he might have the rights of it.

'I will think of it, Johnnie,' he said.

One night at Kinnaird, with the army camped at Old Montrose near by – one night of his father-in-law and his brothers-in-law and their women, decided James Graham. The Carnegies and the Grahams just did not look at life from the same standpoint. Which might be right, the dear God knew. They might even both be right. But their all too evident difference of outlook must not be allowed to damage and distress his spirited sons, at a significant and impressionable age. Magdalen had been too long at Kinnaird. If Kincardine was too far away, and too vulnerable in present conditions, at least she should keep her own house again, and his, here at Old Montrose. This he would insist upon. With separate schooling for James, Robert and little Jean, free of the crowd of Carnegie children. And Johnnie, the Lord Graham, would come with him, at least meantime.

Surprisingly enough Magdalen did not take nearly so much objection to this programme as her husband anticipated. Perhaps she had been getting a little tired of being under the thumbs of her father, brothers and step-mother, not being mistress of her own house; perhaps she had been reconciled for some time to losing the spirited Johnnie; perhaps Tippermuir, and her husband's suddenly increased stature, had even affected herself, however little she was likely to admit it. At any rate, her opposition was half-hearted and brief. Montrose promised that he would look after Johnnie like a hen with one chick, and see that he was kept out of danger, as far as in him lay. And when the campaigning was over, he should certainly go to St Andrews University.

On that note they allowed the matter to rest, and permitted the more personal concerns of their last night together to possess them.

In the morning, the Ensign Lord Graham rode proudly northwards, as aide-de-camp to the King's Lieutenant-General, while the Lord James swallowed the tears which would have branded him as unfit to do likewise. Biting her lip, the Marchioness of Montrose watched them go.

24

Two days later, on the 11th of September, they had crossed the Mounth and were descending the empty uplands to the Dee valley near Banchory, with all Aberdeenshire and the Gordon lands before them, when at the same time riders approached the long-strung-out host from front and rear. The first was a hard-riding, gallant group, Nathaniel Gordon of the Ardlogie sept, with thirty mounted men; and the second was none other than the Master of Madderty, who had escaped from his captors and come hastening after his friends. Both brought news, and both Montrose was glad to see – even though their tidings furrowed his brow.

Nathaniel Gordon's adherence, even with only thirty men, was at least an augury for the future. Montrose had been looking for large-scale Gordon support for days. This was the very modest first of it. Nathaniel of Ardlogie was hardly influential, however notorious. He was in fact a wild character, even spoiling for a fight and seldom out of trouble; but if kept under control – such as Huntly had never found possible – he was a daring and seasoned fighter. It was not so much his presence as the news he brought that was important. It appeared that the Covenant army of the North-East was near by, on the outskirts of Aberdeen itself, only some fifteen miles away. It was under the command of the Lord Balfour of Burleigh, and he had as lieutenants the Lords Fraser and Frendraught – old Covenant colleagues of Montrose at Turiff – and the younger Lord Gordon with his brother, the still younger Lord Lewis. According to Nathaniel, the young chief was unhappy about the entire situation, his father having sent orders from the far North that he was not to involve the clan in fighting on either side; in consequence he was looked on with suspicion by practically everyone, especially Burleigh, Fraser and the other leaders.

The Covenant force was some 3000 infantry and over 600 horse – much of the latter Gordon.

This was significant news. Balfour of Burleigh was the man who had acted President of the parliament which had sought to try Montrose, in King Charles's presence, a creature of Argyll's. The Graham had no high opinion of him as a soldier or anything else. Fraser and Frendraught had not proved themselves masters of the military art at Turiff or thereafter – and they were at permanent feud with the Gordons. Any army, with such leadership, was unlikely to be at its best – especially with the man who controlled most of the cavalry already harbouring doubts and resentment.

The Master of Madderty's tidings clinched the matter. He brought word that Argyll himself, with 2500 foot and over 1500 cavalry, plus a number of large cannon, was only three or four days' march behind, at the western end of Strathmore and thought to be going to advance up Glen Shee from Blairgowrie and into Deeside from the west. He added that Stewart of Ardvorlich had fled to join Argyll, and now was being fêted as a hero for his slaying of one of Montrose's principal lieutenants. Indeed, Argyll was offering £12,000 Scots to anyone who would do the same for Montrose, payment to be made on production of the Graham's head at the Mercat Cross of Edinburgh.

Montrose, forcing himself to swallow meantime his anger and revulsion at this second part of the report, concentrated on the more important item – Argyll's 1500 cavalry and large cannon. Here was menace indeed. He must not allow these to get within striking distance of his own force, or all would be lost. Nor, if he could help it, must he allow Argyll's army to join up with Balfour of Burleigh's, or to sandwich his own between them. Aberdeen city, unlike Dundee, had been on the side of the King, and anti-Covenant, formerly. Argyll would change all that.

So James Graham altered his plans there and then. Instead of going recruiting in the Gordon lands of Central Aberdeenshire, he would seek to strike an immediate blow at Burleigh, the weakest link in the chain threatening to encircle him – even though it seemed to be considerably stronger than his own force. Aberdeen must be shown, at all costs, that the King's cause was far from lost. After a word with Alastair, he ordered a change of direction in the march, to the east.

They crossed the Dee, near Durris, where there was a mid-stream island which permitted fording. There was no sign of opposition. They camped for the night at Crathes, to whose hospitable castle Sir Thomas Burnett of Leys made Montrose welcome. He was that rare character for Scotland, a quiet inoffensive man, who took no sides; and although he was a good Protestant and Presbyterian, he acknowledged his duty to his monarch. He had no armed men, but he offered the King's Lieutenant a sum of money – which Montrose courteously refused. He said that Aberdeen, fifteen miles away, was in a great stir, having heard that Argyll was coming, and was tending to believe that the Covenant must win.

By sunrise they were on their way down Deeside, on the north bank. Montrose, held back by the infantry and slow-moving cannon, sent his few cavalry ahead now, with orders not only to scout and clear the way, but to secure the vital Bridge of Dee. He had vivid memories of its military significance heretofore. Riders presently came back to declare that they were not meeting with resistance, but that their arrival was expected. Not that they could have hoped for surprise, with such slow-moving force. Balfour of Burleigh had moved out from the city and taken up a strong defensive situation on the slopes of a gentle hill, between the How Burn and the Craibstone, just two miles south-west of the centre of Aberdeen, the Covenant forces flanking a climbing lane, with houses and walled gardens and orchards on either side. These were being held by parties of forward troops, so that the entire position resembled a quite extensive and elaborate strong-point. Balfour was known to have some heavy cannon from the citadel, and had high ground on which to site them. This could be no easy contest. He had made no move to hold the Bridge of Dee, however, which had fallen without trouble.

Montrose's instinct was to start his attack with the least possible delay, giving Balfour no time to lay plans and perhaps call up reinforcements from the city. The man was no firebrand, deliberate, stolid, the sort to be put off by his stride by sudden, swift, unexpected moves. Also, there was Argyll pressing up behind from the south-west. But James Graham, despite the black mood which had gripped him since the terrible revelation of his enemies' attitude in the 'Jesus and no quarter' slogan, deepened by the murder of

Kilpont and the murderer's welcome from the other side, would not abandon his principles. Aberdeen must be given the opportunity to declare for the monarch. He was in Scotland not merely as the King's General but as Viceroy. His first duty was to win over his fellow citizens to their due allegiance rather than to make war on them. Therefore he disappointed Alastair MacDonald, Black Pate and other impatient warriors – including the Lord Graham, aide-de-camp – by ordering camp to be set up on the other side of the shallow valley, in view of the enemy but just out of cannon range, between the Lower Justice Mills and the Ferry Hill Mills. It was late in the day, anyway, with thirteen miles covered since Crathes.

Now that hostilities were imminent, he rather wished that he did not have Johnnie with him, hero-worshipping, itching for splendid action.

In the morning, he sent Sir William Rollo, under a white flag and with an Irish drummer-boy of Colkitto's to beat a rat-tatting way for him, through the enemy lines and into the city, to proclaim the King's greetings to his royal burgh of Aberdeen, to require its due allegiance and support for the King's forces, and to expel any obdurate enemies of His Grace and minions of the rebellious Marquis of Argyll. If, however, the magistrates and townsfolk refused loyally so to do, Rollo was to inform them to send out of the city to a place of safety all old and infirm, all women and children – for the Marquis of Montrose, the King's Lieutenant, would surely put such rebellious and disloyal town to the sack, and those who remained could expect no quarter, as the Covenant leaders were proclaiming no quarter to the royal forces. He hoped that this would have the desired effect of avoiding bloodshed and preventing the citizens from aiding Balfour.

While they awaited the return of this embassage, Montrose deployed his force. As at Tippermuir, he gave the centre to Colkitto's Irish and Islesmen. The right wing, of Perthshire men, he placed under a veteran of the foreign wars, Colonel James Hay, with Rollo to aid him if he returned empty-handed. And the left, taking a chance, he allotted to Nathaniel Gordon who, coming from the country, knew the area like the palm of his hand, having conducted nefarious private ploys of his own hereabouts. The few cavalry he split into two groups, stiffened with Kilpont's bowmen and some lightly armed Highlanders, who could race with the horses, clutching a stirrup, an employment only for the boldest and most agile, but which could yield notable dividends.

Montrose was returning from making these dispositions, almost at noon, when he heard uproar in the main camp, the Irish in particular yelling in anger. Rollo was back – but alone. The magistrates and leaders of Aberdeen had received him warily, coolly, and returned an equivocal answer to the Lieutenant-General's summons, committing themselves to nothing and most evidently playing for time. They sought elucidation of the Lord Marquis's terms, particularly his threats of no quarter. They gave the drummer-boy a silver piece and sent Rollo away. And as they had come back, fire had been opened upon them, flag of truce or none, and the boy had been killed.

The news touched off a highly unusual outburst of sheer fury in Montrose. He was not a man of violent passions, and though he could be roused, was able to keep his temper under stern control. But now he was suddenly and excessively enraged. Or, perhaps, it was no so sudden, in fact, and the anger had been boiling up in him for days – at the savage hatred of his opponents, the price on his head, the shocking slaying of his friend, the reluctance of those who should be aiding him to rise in support of their King. Also, there is no doubt that the fact of the drummer-boy being of a like age and size to Johnnie affected him strongly. He burst out in a storm of cursing – and when an outraged and red-faced Colkitto came demanding vengeance for the lad and declaring that he could not promise to control his Irish if any order was given to spare Aberdeen, as Perth had been spared, the Graham grimly assured him that no such order would be forthcoming. If they won this battle, Aberdeen should pay the price. He sent Alastair back to his post, and commanded the trumpets to sound for action.

Although very much the weaker force, it was the royalists who now set the pace. Colkitto was ordered to move individual parties forward, to clear the houses and gardens flanking the lane, which must inevitably be the main axis of advance – fairly certain that Balfour would not train his cannon on this area where his own people were hiding. Also, because of the slope of hill, it would be difficult to depress the gun-barrels sufficiently; this must be a central point in Montrose's strategy.

The clearing of the orchards and houses was achieved without too much difficulty, although it took time, place by place. Prisoners sent back informed that the Gordon cavalry on the enemy left was under the command of young Lord Lewis, his elder brother having apparently returned to Strathbogie in disgust with the ministers who dominated the Covenant host. Fraser and Frendraught were on the same left wing, with the infantry; while the right was commanded by Sir William Forbes of Craigievar, a man of some stature. The main body, in the centre, was under Balfour of Burleigh himself, with the cannon.

Presently, there was a counter-attack on the enemy left. A sudden wild charge down the hill by Gordon cavalry led by Lord Lewis took everybody by surprise, since it was un-supported by any other, infantry or artillery, and was not in great force. More surprising still, this attack was not pressed home against Hay's and Rollo's Perth men, the Gordons dashing only to within range, discharging their pistols, and then wheeling round in fine style and galloping back. When this odd performance was followed by a tentative advance of left-wing infantry which sent forward relays of ranks, each to fire muskets and then hastily retire out of range again, Montrose recognised that it could only mean one thing – a distraction. The enemy centre was strongly dug-in, and therefore unlikely to move out at this stage; so it must be on the right. Hastily he sent word to Nathaniel Gordon to be ready for surprises, and also to Rollo to be prepared to switch to their aid.

It was only just in time. Down a sunken and hidden lane between the Upper and Lower Justice Mills, well to the west, some 400 Covenant foot and 100 horse suddenly erupted upon the royalist left flank. Nathaniel Gordon, who had been raring to make some spectacular advance in typical dashing fashion was hardly in a posture or frame of mind for dogged and effective defence. Recognising the danger, Montrose sent in half of his cavalry in support, and called Rollo's foot to make swift transfer behind the centre lines.

It was then that Sir William Forbes charged, with the main body of Covenant horse on the now cavalry-denuded royalist centre, a full-scale and determined attack and no mere

demonstration like Lewis Gordon's. It was as well that
Colkitto's men were veterans, the survivors of long and
bloody campaigning; other infantry might well have
panicked. But they had experienced cavalry charges before
this. They stood their ground, waiting to fire their muskets
until the horsemen were almost upon them – and then shooting at the mounts rather than the riders. Hastily darting
aside, to open ranks and let the horsemen through, dodging
swinging sabres, they closed in again behind, and turned to
attack the cavalry's rear. It took strong nerves – but whatever
else these kerns and Islesmen lacked, they had these. Forbes's
horse, disorganised, suffering heavy casualties, and now
detached from their own forces, were then faced with a
furious charge by the other half of Montrose's scanty
cavalry, under Madderty, Black Pate and Dupplin. They
broke and scattered.

Rollo had succeeded in rescuing Nathaniel Gordon, so that
now the advantage on both wings lay with the royalists. No
artillery had so far fired, on either side; nor had Montrose
so much as drawn sword, but sat his horse on a vantage-
point, young Johnnie at his side, where he could oversee all
and direct, a general's stance, however frustrating for an
excited youth – and for that matter for his father likewise,
who always itched to take the active role. Now he ordered
a general advance, with Nathaniel Gordon to make a swift
encircling move to the west. The trumpets shrilled.

Strangely, the two centres never really came in contact.
Those trumpets, in fact, sounded the real end of the Battle of
Aberdeen, without a cannon-ball fired – for Balfour and his
main body, seeing what had happened to their flanks and
alarmed at the obvious flanking move on the west, did not
wait for some specific defeat. Led by their mounted leaders,
they fled – though the ministers with them, shaking fists upraised to heaven, called down the wrath of God on weak-
kneed back-sliders and craven sons of Belial, some still
screaming that 'Jesus and no quarter' cry. These were the
last to go – and the Irish made short work of such as left it
too late, cloth or none.

So now there was another running fight, like that after
Tippermuir – only the distance to run was much shorter and
soon the fighting was taking place in the streets of Aberdeen.
This time, of a set and harsh purpose, Montrose made no

attempt to call off the dogs of war. It is doubtful indeed whether he could have done so effectively, if he would. The Irish had Colkitto's promise that on this occasion they should have their way. Aberdeen required, and had asked for, a lesson. It should have it. James Graham deliberately turned his back on the city which had opposed him four times, and returned to his camp with his disappointed son. Major-General Alastair MacDonald should show Aberdeen who was King in Scotland.

The night Montrose paced the dusty floor of the mill granary he had taken over as headquarters, in no mood for sleep, handsome features set, fine eyes bleak, with none of the victor's triumph, no sense of duty well done. For once, none of his lieutenants dared seek his company, even Pate Graham keeping his distance. He went through the hell of his own deliberate choice, steeling himself to do no more than this dire pacing, when every inch of him, every nerve, screamed to him to go, go back to Aberdeen and halt what he knew must be taking place therein, the terror and horror of a great city sacked. He won that savage fight with himself and his better, or weaker, nature – but at a price, a terrible price. He would never be quite the same man again, and knew it. But . . . he was the King's Lieutenant, no private individual. And Scotland, as well as Aberdeen itself, required, demanded a demonstration of unmistakable vehemence and proportions. An infinity of lives might well be spared, years of warfare saved, by this stern decision. Somewhere, some-time, someone must take it. It had to be he, and it had to be here.

The recurrent thought that Archibald Campbell would have taken it without a second thought, and slept sound thereafter, was no least help to him.

Hollow-eyed and still awake, he watched the new day dawn. He did not wait to see his son John, felt that he could by no means face him. Thus early he rode into the city.

Bodies still littered the route of the fleeing Covenant army – in the main naked bodies for, it seemed, the Irish were particular about this, stripping their victims before finally despatching them so that good clothing might not be spoiled. In the city streets it was the same – although here not a few of the bodies wore tartan and lay about drunk rather than dead. Smoke billowed from burning buildings, blood was

splashed on walls and cobbles, furnishings lay smashed everywhere, warehouses spilled their contents. Sickened, Montrose
rode to the Town House and Tolbooth, where he unceremoniously roused his snoring Major-General out of drunken
slumber on the Council-table with an unclothed lady, and
ordered him to get his men rounded up and out of the city
as quickly as might be, without further licence. They, and
Aberdeen, had had their night. At Colkitto's incoherent
protests, he rounded on him with a harsh vehemence hitherto
unknown, eyes blazing. Muttering, the giant MacDonald
stumbled off, dragging his bewildered bedfellow with him.

All morning James Graham sat in the Town House
receiving complainants, petitioners, protestations, of individuals and deputations, magistrates, ministers, merchants,
prominent citizens. Stony-faced he heard their woes, their
pleas, their charges. From these assertions there could
scarcely be a citizen who had escaped death, injury, rape,
pillage or outrage. Considering that Colkitto's total force
was now less than 1200, and that the population was nearly
ten times that, this seemed less than probable. He demanded
details, numbers, specific instances. He did not get them –
only allegations that men, women and children had been
slaughtered indiscriminately by the hundred, and things
done which it was not lawful even to mention. That it was
heathen Papists who had committed these enormities was
the prime complaint, especially of the ministers; a woman
raped by a good Protestant seemed to be another matter.
Montrose dismissed them all, refused to see more, sent out
a fact-finding team under Black Pate, and himself rode out
of town northwards, unaccompanied, to be alone with his
thoughts.

If it was peace of mind that he sought, he did not find it so
easily. Nor was it so easy to impose the discipline and order
he had commanded – even for Colkitto to round up his
Irishry and Highlanders. Many of them had gone to ground,
with women and drink, all over the city, making up for long
months of privation, danger, hardships. Covenant soldiers
too had likewise gone to ground and were equally beyond
discipline. From the ordinary Aberdonians' point of view,
there was probably not much to choose from between them.

That night was only a little better than the last.

Pate Graham's team reported to Montrose, back at his

headquarters, such facts as they had been able to uncover. The city had had a bad time of it, undoubtedly, and many were dead, there had been much looting and a deal of rape and assault likewise. But there had been no wholesale slaughter of the citizenry, nor yet of women and children, as some alleged. So far as they could ascertain, out of a total of about 200 dead within the city, only nine women were included, these apparently slain in drunken brawls. Most of the others were Covenant soldiers who had got as far as the streets, and to whom Colkitto's men had given no quarter admittedly. A few houses had been fired, undoubtedly much gear stolen and warehouses rifled. Also a number of women were missing – but some of such who had been run to earth proved to have gone with the newcomers voluntarily and quite happily. All in all, Newcastle had suffered much worse from Leslie's army, and even Cromwell's Puritans made greater havoc in conquered towns.

Nevertheless, James Graham was sick at heart. God willing, never again would he allow himself to be manoeuvred into a position where such a decision and responsibility was demanded of him.

Meantime, he was determined to get away from Aberdeen at the earliest possible moment. Argyll was drawing near – and if he sent any large proportion of his 1500 cavalry on in advance, they could be here in a day or so. In the present drunken and demoralised state of his force, this could spell disaster. They would move out tomorrow, for the north.

But the morrow saw Colkitto still 300 men short of total, and angrily refusing to move without them. They were the backbone of the royalist army, and both men knew it. Montrose could only fret, and send out search-parties and wait.

It was next day before the blear-eyed, jaundiced, grumbling, overladen, over-dressed horde straggled out of Aberdeen northwards, up the Don valley, everyone out-of-temper. Despite Montrose's objections and offence a long tail of women now accompanied them. Colkitto informed him that they were part of the price he had to pay for his veterans – and he could have the choice of any one of them any night! Argyll was reported to be only twenty miles away, coming down the Dee – but from all accounts going very warily, and certainly not rushing his cavalry ahead of him. Presumably he had heard of Balfour's defeat, and was more impressed by it than was the victor. Indeed Montrose had to remind himself more than once that he *had* just won his second major victory. He had no least feelings of triumph – quite the reverse.

They made slow progress, slower than ever, for now they had the heavy cannon captured from Balfour, as well as the lighter Tippermuir pieces, to hold them back. And, of course, the women and the lengthy, untidy train of booty. It was a humiliation and a disgrace for James Graham to trail this sorry spectacle through the Aberdeenshire countryside; but he was not in a position to take strong action with the Irish and Islesmen. He needed them too much. Also, he was feeling less than well. Not only his mental state was depressed. He had seldom felt less lively.

But at Kintore, where they camped that first night, amidst an uproar of drunkenness, skirling women, and general indiscipline, he wrote a despatch to King Charles, at Oxford, in determinedly cheerful note, announcing victory and sending all encouragement – so much more than in his present frame of mind he felt. Duty has many facets. Right away, in the September dusk, Sir William Rollo was sent off with it, on the long road south, before Argyll could block the way.

In one way, in his present angry mood, a trial of strength with Archibald Campbell, a once-and-for-all set-to, would have appealed to Montrose, even lacking his accustomed energy. But the other's 1500 horse precluded anything of the sort. Until he himself could build up a powerful cavalry wing, or arrange it so that any clash took place on terrain where the advantage lay with the foot, he dare not come to conclusions with Argyll, galling as it was to seem to flee before him.

They were in Gordon country now, however, and would be for days. At Kildrummy, two days later, farther up Donside, he sent off Nathaniel Gordon to Strathbogie, with a message to his young chief, urging that he join him and give command to his clan to do likewise. The Gordon lairds could produce horsemen by the hundred, the thousand almost, basis of the cavalry force he so greatly needed. He would have gone himself so important was the requirement; but Colkitto was still resentful over the Aberdeen business and his men must on no account be allowed to get more out-of-hand

335

than they were already, in this Gordon country, or all hopes
of co-operation could be forgotten. He sent his son with
Nathaniel however, as of equal rank to the Lord Graham –
his first duty in the King's cause.

Aberdeenshire is a vast county, and progress was painfully
slow. On the 20th, they heard that Argyll had entered Aberdeen city the day before – his first act to levy heavy contri-
butions on the already outraged citizens. But so far there
was no sign of pursuit. It looked as though the Campbell
was little more anxious to come to blows, meantime, than
was his foe.

Nevertheless, always concerned about the enemy's great
preponderance in cavalry, which could so rapidly catch up
with his cumbered and crawling host, Montrose pressed on
farther into the west, following Don up into the mountains
of its birth, by Glenbuchat and Inverernan, Forbes country
with no friendliness shown to the visitors. And when
Nathaniel Gordon and young Johnnie caught up with them
again, he pressed on farther and faster. For they brought
word that he was not going to get his much-needed cavalry
from the Gordons. The Lord Gordon had listened to them
courteously enough, and admitted that he was at a loss to
where his allegiance lay. But his father, Huntly, had sent
categorical commands from his hide-out in Caithness, that
there were to be no Gordon levies lent to Montrose, King's
commission or none. Was not he himself King's Lieutenant
of the North? If King Charles was so foolish as to trust the
wrong man, and to choose such as Montrose to represent
him, instead of his old and tried friends, so much the worse
for His Grace. George Gordon had an excellent memory,
however lacking he might be in leadership. And he was still
chief.

If the Gordons would not rise for the King, none of the
lesser North-East clans were likely to do so, the low-country
clans, from whom Montrose might have looked for cavalry.
The Highlands were different – but they did not produce
horse-soldiers. He might be the winner of two battles – but
he was no nearer winning Scotland for Charles Stewart than
when he had crossed the Border. Or so he told himself.

Dispirited and now feeling physically sick – no doubt the
result of too continuous strain and fatigue – he decided that
it was the Highland fastnesses, now, for him and his dis-

tempered horde. Scouts informed that Argyll was slowly following him up through Central Aberdeenshire. In the mountains, those cannon which so grievously delayed them, would be no more than a useless impediment; so reluctantly he buried them, with all the heavy ball and powder, in a riverside haugh near Corgarff. Then, lightened at least, though now encumbered with large herds of hill-cattle which he was buying from scowling Forbes farmers, and which were going to be a deal more valuable than artillery where they were going, he turned away from Don at last, to climb up into the heather, into the outliers of the mighty Cairngorm mountains, by remote Tomintoul and the lonely desolations of Stratha'an. He did not think that Argyll would follow them there.

25

JOHN GRAHAM SAT ON A LOG OF PINE BESIDE HIS FATHER'S couch of horse-blankets, biting his lips, great-eyed. This was nothing like the going to war, to fight for the King, that he had visualised. He was worried, frightened, and rather disappointed. Nothing was as he had imagined. He would have admitted to none, not even to himself, that he was even a little disappointed in his hero-father, who had won a battle, true enough – although he himself had been allowed no part in it – but had been leading a retreat ever since. And now he was ill, tossing and muttering on this bed in the forest, while his lieutenants quarrelled and bickered amongst themselves, and that great bull of a man. Alastair MacDonald, strutted, shouted at everybody, and got drunk. Not that he blamed his father for being ill; but surely they should not be in this ridiculous Rothiemurchus Forest, hiding like beaten fugitives – the King's army, led by the King's Lieutenant-General! And a heathenish Papish Irishman, or Highlander or whatever he was, ordering about good Scots lairds, even earls like Airlie. John Graham rather wished that he was at home with Jamie.

His father was mumbling again. The boy leant forward to listen. It was very hard to make out what he said – and what words were distinguishable did not seem to make sense, anyway. It was very frightening. Could his fine father, the great Montrose, the King's and Scotland's hope, be going to die? Pate said no, that it was just a fever, that he would be right again soon, with rest and quiet. But Pate was not a physician. They had no physician with the army – except one of the Papist Irish who called himself a doctor, but whom nobody would allow near his father, naturally. Pate, indeed, was allowing practically nobody into this tent, he or one of his men standing guard like a watchdog at the door, by day, and sleeping across it by night. Pate was good. So was Lord Airlie. And his sons. He didn't like Dupplin very much – he should now call him Earl of Kinnoull he supposed, since his old father had evidently just died. And the Master of Madderty, whom he *did* like, was away on a deer-hunting expedition. It was daft, surely, that so many of the King's soldiers should spend their time hunting deer in this outlandish forest, when all Scotland was waiting to be won for the King. Though, at least, the forest was a good place for deer.

They had been here for three days.

Suddenly Montrose sat up, peering straight ahead of him out of strangely vacant eyes, a trembling hand out, finger pointing. A flood of words spilled from his lips, disjointed, harsh, utterly unlike his normal calmly assured, almost musical speech. Campbell and Henderson and Rothes and other names, the boy could make out; but though his father seemed to be asking questions, he had not the least idea how to answer him. It seemed terribly important, too. He did not know whether Pate was still outside the tent. He called for him, urgently.

Only a sentry looked inside, a Graham admittedly, but only one of the bowmen. 'Get Inchbrakie,' John cried. 'My father – my lord wants something. Quickly – get Major Pate.'

But Montrose had fallen back again, and was staring at the tent roof, lips moving but without words. But when presently Black Pate came running in, and the boy began to explain, a weak voice from the couch interrupted.

'What's to do?' it asked, flatly, a little querulously, but quite sanely. 'Pate? Johnnie? What's to do?'

Surprised, they both turned to stare. These were the first lucid words for three nights and two days.

'Glory be, man – you are yourself again!' Inchbrakie exclaimed. 'Thank God!'

'Father! You are well? Can you see me now? Hear me? You have not known me. All these days.'

'Days? Days, you say?'

'Yes, many days. You have lain there . . .'

'This is the third day, Jamie,' Pate amended. 'We . . . we feared for you.'

'I have been . . . on a journey, I think. A strange journey.' That was said slowly. 'Far. Where all was very different.' His eyes travelled round the tent, seeing eyes now. 'I doubt . . . if I am very glad . . . to be back.'

'*I* am glad – and that's God's truth!' his friend declared. 'You were strange, yes – sick, Jamie. Sick. Knowing nothing. And this camp has been in a stour while you lay. They are all crazy-mad, I swear. That Alastair . . .'

Montrose was not listening. 'This Scotland,' he said, his voice ruminative. 'I saw it all. As in a picture. A fair realm. All this goodly land. But doomed. Fated. Betrayed by a fatal disease. You hear? Doomed.'

They stared.

'Betrayed. By disunity. And treachery. This Scotland. Every man a law unto himself. So that he will unite truly with none. Each esteeming his own freedom above all else. Above the realm's freedom. To think. To speak. To act. As each will. And so distrusting all other. It is our curse . . .'

'Aye. Maybe.' A little askance Inchbrakie eyed him, unsure whether or not he still might be wandering in his mind. 'But, Jamie – there's closer trouble than that. Here, in the camp. High words. My lords Airlie and Kinnoull cannot get on with your Alastair. Nor he with them. Or any, save his own barbarians. There's been near to bloodshed. Here is no army, any more . . .'

'I say this Scotland is torn apart,' the other went on, in the same quiet, withdrawn voice. 'Torn by ravening wolves, while the shepherds tear each the other. I saw an army. An army of dead men. All dead. Weeping for this Scotland. The King led it . . .'

'The King? Dead!' John cried. 'Never that! It was but an ill dream. Father, you but dreamed . . .'

Montrose turned his head to look thoughtfully at the boy. 'I saw other in that army,' he said. Then he turned away again. He did not say that he had seen himself and his son, both, behind the King.

Pate fidgeted uneasily. He did not like such talk. Montrose's mother, the Lady Margaret Ruthven, was reputed to have had 'the sight', even to have dabbled in witchcraft. The Ruthvens were that way inclined. Abruptly he changed the subject.

'You will be hungry, Jamie? No food has passed your lips these three days. Nor drink. I will bring you something . . .'

There was a commotion at the tent-door. Stooping, the huge person of Alastair MacDonald came striding in. He was a little unsteady on his feet – but that was nothing unusual.

'So you *have* come to your wits, my lord Marquis!' he said. 'The whisper is round the camp. Not before time, 'fore God! I was near away, your warrant or none.'

Not very interestedly, Montrose eyed his Major-General. He inclined his head, but did not speak.

'Mary-Mother – are you yourself, man? In your right senses?' the big man demanded, raising his voice.

'I can hear you very well, Alastair.' That was quiet.

'You can? Then hear this, my lord. I have had enough of lurking and idling. As have my men, whatever! It is time that we were off, by God! About our own affairs. It is October now. Soon the snows will block the passes. No time for campaigning in these mountains. I am for off, my lord Marquis.'

The other moistened his lips, but said nothing.

'We serve no good end here.' Colkitto's great voice was rising again. 'My men are fighters, see you – not dodgers and sitters! This idling and scuttling mislikes them. They are less than the men they should be. We must be off.'

'Where, Alastair? Whither?'

'To the West. To the Western Sea. Where we came from. To winter there. Where there are no snows. I go to my castle of Mingary, in Ardnamurchan. My lord Antrim was to send me supply ships. More men. Provisioning. Arms. From Ulster. They may be there now. We go winter on that western seaboard.'

340

'But not as . . . scuttlers? Idlers?' That was mild, gentle almost.

'God's wounds – no! All the Campbell lands lie south of Ardnamurchan. We shall not spend our winter idly!'

'Scotland will not be won for King Charles from Ardnamurchan, Alastair, I think.'

'Is it being won here? Thus?'

'If I can coax Argyll into these mountains, where his cavalry are little use to him, much may be won.'

'He was leaving Castle Gight, on the Ythan, last word to come in, my lord Marquis,' Pate interpolated. 'Turning westwards towards the Spey. Still following. But slowly.'

'A cat to your mouse!' the MacDonald snorted, scornfully. 'You will not win Scotland so, either! I am for the West.'

'Even if I am not, Major-General?'

The giant frowned. 'Aye,' he said. 'You are a sick man, my lord. I, and mine, cannot dance attendance on a sick man, who prefers to skulk than to fight. Through a Highland winter. My sorrow – but that is the truth of it. I am for Ardnamurchan.'

'You have not forgiven me for Aberdeen, I think? That I called in your dogs of war.'

Colkitto said nothing.

'I cannot hold you, Alastair,' Montrose said, with a sigh. 'You will do as you must. Who am I to *command* you to stay. But . . . I ask you.'

The other shook his red head. 'There is much to be done in the West. Nothing to be done here. I go. Tomorrow. Come with me, my lord – if you will.'

'No, sir.' Sir James Graham's voice was weak now, only a whisper – but lacking nothing in decision. 'If I go . . . to the West . . . Argyll will follow me. Where he is stronger than ever. And Lowland Scotland . . . will lose what heart . . . it has. I bide.'

Shrugging, the big man turned, and stalked out.

'Hielant barbarian!' Pate growled. 'Papist scum! I told you they were not to be trusted. Any of them. Treacherous dogs!'

Sinking back, staring at the tent-roof again, Montrose shook his head. 'Not treacherous,' he murmured. 'They fight a different war. That is all.'

341

So, next morning, weak and leaning against the gnarled trunk of an ancient pine, but on his feet again, the King's Lieutenant-General watched two-thirds of his force march away from the tree-clad shores of Loch-an-Eilean in Rothiemurchus – with bickering and vituperation between the Gaelic and the Lowland contingents right to the end. At least they took their pathetic trail of women with them – the cause of much of the strife. Montrose himself had carefully refrained from acrimony; but he could not hide his sadness at the occasion, nor his awareness of the blow this was to the King's cause. He had asked God, the King, his friends, even Magdalen, for a year, one year to win Scotland – and he had been given five weeks. In this time he had won two battles, taken two cities, covered a deal of Scotland, countenanced a great evil, besmirched his name – and lost his army. Only O'Cahan and a party of 120, out foraging, were left him of Colkitto's force. With the last bagpipe notes of the Gaelic host fading away amongst the pines, James Graham, refusing all company, even his son's, but accepting a stick Johnnie found for him as support, moved shakily down to the water's edge and along the loch-shore. His mind was still bemused, woolly, far from incisive; but he had to think clearly.

Gazing out across the lapping waters to the little castle on its island, built by that shameful royal brigand, Alexander Stewart, Earl of Buchan and Wolf of Badenoch, two centuries before, he sought to concentrate his thoughts. His strange illness had affected him as strangely, causing him to see things from a different standpoint. That it was a more philosophical perhaps fatalistic standpoint, he was aware. For too long he had been fretting, anxious, harassed by great matters and small, of national import or merely personal. And alone – always and essentially alone in it all. Now, it seemed that somehow his body and mind together had called a halt, taken their own steps to relieve the strain he had long been under. He was still weak, of course, and this might be partly responsible; but the fact was that in his mind he now felt strangely at peace, unconcerned with what had so worried and frustrated him hitherto – or perhaps resigned might better describe it. The pressure, somehow, was relaxed. By some means or other, in those past three days and nights of wanderings in far places, he had reached and emerged from a crisis. And now, on the other side of it, he was, he knew, a slightly different man. He believed that he would never be quite the same again.

Which was all very well – but obviously such relaxation, such resigned attitude, held drastic dangers for a commander of men. In his new frame of mind, was he no longer fit to be the King's Lieutenant-General? Even of so small a host as was left to him? It might be so. But he certainly could not be relieved of his command for a considerable time to come; and he owed it to his men, and to Charles Stewart, to be at least as good a general as he had been hitherto, if not better. No change in his outlook, or state of mind, however attained, altered his simple duty.

Eyes lifting to the great heather mountains behind the loch, above the dark green sea of the pine forest, already turning to the ochres and sepias that spoke of coming winter, James Graham considered what he could and must, do for Scotland and King Charles, with 500 men. First of all, he must try to keep alight the flame of hope which he might have lit in loyal hearts, hope that the cause was far from lost – this above all. So it meant gestures again, devices, continuing tokens, constant activity to make men talk and wonder, even to chuckle. To do that, he had to continue to keep Argyll involved, winter or no winter. He could not now hope to engage the Campbell in battle; but he could trail him endlessly across Scotland, harass and weary him, make a fool of him for all the land to see, show the King's flag here, there and everywhere, to set tongues wagging. Pin-pricks perhaps – but if these were persistent enough they could have cumulative effect far beyond their actual worth. The Campbell had shown himself to be a slow and cautious campaigner in the field. He must be baited, outstretched, mocked. So would his name, and the menace of it, sink in Scotland. It was the only way . . .

His mind made up, Montrose returned to the camp.

The following day, therefore, with the early morning frost making diadems of all the myriad spiders' webs that decked the juniper-bushes of the great forest, weak still but determined, James Graham hoisted himself into the saddle and led the way out of Rothiemurchus, southwards. Argyll, scouts said, was three days' march behind, down Spey.

*　　　*　　　*

As a programme of attrition it was not unsuccessful. But attrition is a double-edged weapon, and not without effect on both sides. Fighting men do not take kindly to continual retreat and coat-trailing – especially when they see no end to it. And when they have lands, farms, crofts, with wives and bairns at home, all calling them. Alastair and his Irish were not the only ones affected.

Seeking to keep no more than three days ahead of Argyll, Montrose led his reduced company up Spey and into Glen Truim, with the mighty mountains ever closing in and the forests dropping behind. And on, over the dreich high Pass of Drumochter, the very throat of the Highlands, and so into Atholl again. Thus far he had no real trouble; but Atholl was home to not a few of his following, and almost inevitably he lost men there. Nor could he find it in his heart to blame them, and did not call it desertion; with the Campbell coming behind, a man had every reason to prefer to be in his own place, with his family, to protect what he could from the avenger. Nevertheless, he did not risk proceeding much farther south, where he might lose more, the Drummonds, the Hays, even his own Grahams. At Dunkeld he swung off eastwards, by Butterstone and Clunie and Blairgowrie, for Strathmore once again, always having to slow their pace, not too greatly to outdistance Argyll. It was weary work, with a dozen miles a day a maximum progress, and a wet autumn turning into an early winter. At Coupar-Angus, where they had camped five weeks before and Kilpont had died, the Earl of Kinnoull and his Hays took their departure, despite pleas. The King's army now numbered barely 300.

They were close to Ogilvy country again, and Montrose feared the worst. But instead of deserting him, the old Earl of Airlie and his two sons found an extra fifty men, and mounted men at that, and continued with him – warming the Graham's heart as nothing else had done for long. It was a pity that there were not more like the Ogilvys.

It was galling to be so near Old Montrose, Magdalen and the children, and not be able to visit them; but to do so would only have endangered them when Argyll came up. He sent word to his wife to go to Kinnaird meantime, where her father's name and standing would presumably protect them from any Campbell reprisals. And he urged Johnnie to return there also, now that he had sampled soldiering and discovered it less than glorious, and his father to have feet of clay. But the boy clung to him, seeing his sire now as deserted by so many. All but in tears, he pleaded to be allowed to stay. Montrose could not find it in his heart to insist.

Instead of swinging eastwards towards the sea, then, they climbed due northwards over the Mounth again, by the same route of narrow valleys and steep hillsides over which once he had led a hard-riding troop to Turriff – in what seemed almost another life. They went still more slowly now, naturally – but not nearly so slowly as would Argyll if he chose to follow through and over these wild hills where the larger and more heavily equipped the force the greater the difficulties. He believed in fact that the Campbell would not attempt it. For himself, he wanted a day or two's grace, at Strathbogie. The young Lord Gordon there still could produce what he himself needed above all – cavalry. The thought was seldom out of his mind, the hordes of Gordon horse which could be raised from the vast Aberdeenshire lowlands, literally in their thousands. The waste of it all. They could transform his, and the King's, cause almost overnight. Denied them through an old man's stubborn pique and a young man's doubts. It was worth any effort, any sacrifice, to win such prize. Even if he had to go down on his bended knees to Huntly . . . !

By Dee and Don, then, they came at last to Strathbogie, on the 21st of October, with the first snows whitening the mountaintops to the west. The Gordons they passed looked at them askance, doubtful. At the castle, George Gordon, solemn and old-seeming for his twenty-four years, at the head of a swarm of brothers and sisters, received Montrose and his party civilly but warily. They were welcome, he said. His father's house was theirs. But only as guests; not as combatants, it must be understood. And where was Argyll?

Old Airlie cursed Argyll, and by implication the Lord Gordon, and advised that young man to let the Devil look after his own. The King's Grace expected better than that of Gordon. But Montrose was more careful. He conceded that they were only come as friendly visitors, and were grateful indeed for any hospitality Gordon might furnish them, after weeks in the heather. Argyll was far behind, and was not likely to try conclusions with Gordon in Gordon country.

Huntly, it seemed, was still discreetly absent in the far North. And the impetuous Lord Lewis, now nineteen, remained with the Covenant forces of the North-East, somewhere in Buchan. Aboyne, of course, was still in England, fighting for the King. The remainder of the brood were here, and although six years older than on Montrose's first visit, were as noisy, untidy and unruly as ever.

Later, after a chaotic meal, protracted, with a piper strutting up and down the hall, blowing lustily the while, children shouting, dogs barking, and the general chaos which seemed endemic to this establishment even when its master was not present, when he could get George Gordon alone and in quiet, James Graham put the matter to him straightforwardly.

'Once, you told me that you were the King's man,' he said. 'And now the King's cause suffers hurt for lack of horsed men. You can supply such horsed men. By the thousand. And do not.'

'Not I, my lord Marquis. My father.'

'Your father is as good as abdicate. He has left his clan in your hands. Yours must be the decision, now.'

'No! Who am I to go against my father's expressed wishes, in this? To put hundreds, thousands, of men's lives at risk? For a doubtful cause.'

'Your liege lord's cause, my friend.'

'Once, my lord, you said to *me* that our liege lord, having chosen bad counsellors, fell to be shown the error of his ways. That God's cause was higher than the King's.'

'Aye. You do well to remind me. I said it, and meant it. And still hold to it. But, under Archibald Campbell and the fanatic preachers, God's cause has been perverted, shamefully betrayed. The King is still the Lord's Annointed. He gave in to all the Covenant's fair and legitimate demands. And to more. His cause is now God's cause.'

'Many in Scotland think otherwise,' the younger man said.

'No doubt. But when has Gordon – or Graham – acted on the thoughts of others? Think for yourself, my friend.'

'Think you I have not thought a-plenty!' the other cried, his unnatural calm cracking. 'It is not as *I* think – but as my father thinks. He it is who commands, not I.'

'He has left you in the rule of the clan. Himself prefers to bide afar off.'

346

'No. My father is still chief of Gordon. Wherever he is. I only act for him. And he has said that no Gordon shall be lent to the Marquis of Montrose, my lord. That is his express command.'

'But – he is the King's man. Ever has been. He boasts of it. He does not love me, no – and perhaps with reason. But he loves Charles Stewart. Will he sacrifice the King for his hate of *me?*'

'He holds that you are not the King's friend, or ever have been.'

'I am the King's Lieutenant-General. Hold his royal commission.'

'He also holds the King's commission. As Lieutenant of the North.'

'Then should he not be fighting for the King? Using his Gordon host in the royal cause? See you – it need not be used *under* myself. I care not who commands the Gordons – so long as they fight for the King. *You* lead them, my friend. I will give you commission as a major-general. An independent command. Be your own master. Do not serve under me. But co-operate with me, for the King's sake.'

Nibbling his lip, George Gordon shook his head unhappily. 'It is not possible, my lord. I would it were. I would fight with you, serve under you. Gladly. But I will not go deliberately counter to my father's wishes. Would you have *your* son do so?'

It was Montrose's turn to hesitate. 'No-o-o,' he admitted, at length. 'I would not. But, nor would I divorce myself from my responsibilities, and leave my son to face them. With his hands tied. That I would not.'

The other said nothing.

'See you,' James Graham went on again, urgently, 'the King's cause requires your cavalry more than anything. I ask you, in God's good name muster your men. If you will not serve with me, or independent of me – at least have them muster. Argyll will not know what you intend. Will go warily. Give him pause – and me time. Though you do not strike a single blow, will you do this, my friend? Not for me – for Charles Stewart?'

'I . . . I do not know. I shall have to think on it. My father would not have it so – that I *do* know . . .'

'Think, then. Remembering what the King's Grace will

347

expect of Gordon, in his hour of need. Seek the advice of your lairds, if you will. Straloch, your father's chamberlain. Consult your conscience, above all. I will wait . . .'

Montrose waited at Strathbogie for three days, not in the castle but in camp with his men. In that time a few Gordon lairds came to him, offering support – but not the Lord Gordon. They were all small men, and welcomed gladly, with Nathaniel Gordon active in persuading them, some kinsmen of his own. But their offerings did not increase his strength by 200 all told, and less than a quarter of that horsed. The large lairds, with the mounted followings, awaited their lord's commands.

Then, on the 24th of October, the Graham could wait no longer. Word was brought that Argyll was nearer than he had anticipated, less than two days' march away. Worse, this unaccustomed speed was accounted for by the fact that he had been reinforced by no less than fourteen troops of regular cavalry under Montrose's own old lieutenant, the Earl Marischal, who remained loyal to the Covenant, and had been sent north by Leslie, with the Committee of Estates adding the Earl of Lothian as second-in-command in case the Marischal should fail in his duty. The royalist irritation, obviously, was to be disposed of, and quickly. And William Keith, the Marischal, had always been a hot-tempered, hasty young man.

Montrose, ordering an immediate move, went for a last appeal to George Gordon. But there was no moving that unhappy but dutiful son. His father's will must prevail in this matter. He would not muster Clan Gordon. The best he could do, he declared in evident distress, and apparently at Straloch's suggestion, was to offer a single troop of say 100 cavalry, not as any sort of contribution but purely to escort the royalists off Gordon territory. If it served to make the Lord Marquis's force look slightly the stronger, from a distance as it were, that was as might be. But it would return at the limits of Gordon land, and would on no account draw sword on their behalf.

Montrose looked at the young man, his handsome features set. 'Very well,' he said, carefully. 'If that is the best that Gordon can do, in this pass, I accept it. As King Charles's Viceroy. I thank you.'

George Gordon turned and strode to a window, to stare

out. 'I am sorry . . .' he said over his shoulder, his voice choking.

So the King's army left Strathbogie, some 800 strong, with less than 250 of it horsed, and 150 of that number under orders not to fight.

26

WITH THE WORD THAT ARGYLL – OR RATHER, THE MARISCHAL, who in this context was the greater menace – was coming up Donside, circling the Correen Hills, by Alford and Lumsden, Montrose headed eastwards for the upper Ythan and Gight rather than into the wild hills, westwards. On two accounts. In increasingly wintry conditions it grew ever more difficult to feed and forage his host in empty mountains; and there were still vast Gordon lands far to the east, in Formartine and Buchan, remote from Strathbogie, where Huntly's writ might run less strongly, according to Nathaniel Gordon.

They camped that first night in the bare uplands west of Rothienorman, above the Ythan, the Gordon cavalry keeping very much to itself and looked on with suspicion by the rest. The maintaining of adequate scouting parties had been a big problem for long now, owing to lack of the necessary horsed men; but with Argyll's slow if steady pursuit this had been of no great moment, a small cavalry rearguard serving the main purpose, with a few pairs of riders well ahead and to the flanks. At Strathbogie, Montrose had relied on Gordon's own in-built system of intelligence – and that now proved to have been an error of judgment. Next morning, they had barely left camp when couriers arrived, from Strathbogie admittedly, but grievously delayed, almost too late. The Covenant cavalry under the Earl Marischal, it seemed, had moved on fast, far ahead of Argyll's main army, and was now only a short distance behind.

Nathaniel Gordon looked grave when he heard that the

couriers thought the large cavalry force had passed the night in the Culsalmond area – and it took a deal to sober that optimist. If this was true, they could be on them in an hour or two, he declared, knowing the country. Montrose, who was a comparative stranger to these uplands, demanded at once where was the nearest defensive site. It was bare open country of green grassy slopes hereabouts, ideal for cavalry. No use in telling the infantry to disperse and make a bolt for it; they could be ridden down and hunted like hares by hounds. They must fight, whatever the odds. Was there any position which they could reach in time, where they could make a stand? Any Gordon castle, for instance? For such were apt to be set in strong natural sites.

None worth calling strong, the other lamented, amidst a volley of curses. The nearest castle was Towie, a Barclay place and a fine house – but not strong. Fyvie was better five miles to the south. But it was a Seton hold, the Earl of Dunfermline's, allied to Gordon. It stood amongst the Ythan marshes. But the Earl did not live there. And his sympathies were doubtful . . .

'Marshes, you say? Fyvie, amongst marshes? How far?'

'Four miles. Five. In the Ythan valley, north-by-east. The castle stands on a spine of higher land in the flooded valley. A sour place . . .'

'Then Fyvie it is! With all speed. Pass the word. Hasten!'

The infantry almost at a run, they turned in their new direction. And as they went, Gordon of Lethangie, in command of the cavalry escort, drew up to Montrose's side.

'We leave you now, my lord,' he cried. 'My orders are that we be concerned in no fighting.'

'But . . . dear God, man! We have not even *seen* the enemy! At least bide with us to Fyvie. Draw no sword, if you must not – but *be* there. Five-score cavalry, in a prominent place, could save a day, without moving a foot!'

'No, sir – my orders were clear. To leave you at first hint of conflict. And – you intend to fight.'

'I intend to fight!' the Graham agreed, grimly. 'Go, then – and God pity Gordon!'

Nathaniel thereof swore himself hoarse.

One hundred and fifty men short, they reached Fyvie without interception, and found it much as described. The Ythan here sprawled in its fairly narrow valley amidst bogland, water-meadows and scrub, with a long narrow loch to the east. There were islands in the waterlogged vale. Two were linked by a low ridge of higher, drier ground. On that to the south clustered the village – a strange place of turf-roofed huts and wooden cabins, whose folk must have webbed-feet, according to Colonel Sibbald. And on the higher end of the ridge, to the north, soared the tall and handsome brown-stone castle, with drum-towered gate-house and three other great towers, turreted, gabled and splendid, although with an air of desertion. It had been the seat of the ancient Thanes of Formartyne, though much of the present building had been erected within the last century by the great first Earl of Dunfermline, Chancellor of Scotland, grandfather of the present rather feeble lord. Montrose eyed it all assessingly.

'We shall give a good account of ourselves there,' he said, to Johnnie at his side. 'Charles Seton was my friend once. We shall assume his hospitality in his absence!'

'Will . . . will it be bad?' the boy asked. 'We cannot win, can we?'

'No, I fear we cannot win, lad. But it may be that we can keep *them* from winning. With God's help. Which may serve.'

'We cannot all get into that castle. What of those left out . . . ?'

'None of us will be in the castle, Johnnie. It would be but a trap. We will hold this wooded ridge, between the river and that marshy loch. Backs to the loch, which cannot be crossed. Castle on our right flank, village on our left .River and bog before us. Afoot, where cavalry cannot reach us.'

John, Lord Graham, swallowed, and tried not to look dismayed.

Black Pate was away with some of the precious cavalry now, scouting, watching the enemy, reporting back. The Marischal, following the line of their former advance, had eben taken by surprise at the turn towards Fyvie, and had overshot towards the east, on the way to Gight. He had now turned back – but it allowed them a little longer. He was in major strength, in three groups of some 500 each – dragoons, trained heavy cavalry. Argyll, with his thousands of foot, was still miles behind, to the south, but coming up as fast as he might.

That message, reporting 1500 horse, was like a blow at James Graham's heart. But he allowed no hint of his distress to show. His fifty or so remaining cavalry he spread along the summit of the spine, where they were very evident, and, interspersed with scattered thorn trees, might seem rather more than they were. In theory they were commanded by the Earl of Airlie, but in fact by Nathaniel Gordon, who would lead in any desperate action. The foot would be divided into three companies of less than 200 each, to man the west slope of the ridge, amongst the trees and stone dykes – but later. Meantime all must be massed to hold the south approach to the ridge, from the village – for this was the only approach for cavalry, the Ythan and its belt of haughland and water-meadow being too soft for horses. Montrose would have held the village itself, if he could; but his numbers were too small. There was a drystone dyke across the spine about 300 yards north of the houses, with a gateway for the road to the castle. That must be their holding line, with open ground before it. All men with muskets to man that wall.

Hardly were these dispositions completed when Pate Graham and his dozen horsemen came back at the gallop, hotly pursued by a troop of Covenant cavalry, so close had been his shadowing. They clattered through the village, now discreetly deserted by its inhabitants, and into the elongated box which was the royalist position – and a volley of precious ball from O'Cahan's veterans brought down a few of their pursuers, and warned off the rest.

Pate actually had a prisoner with him, a sergeant of Lothian's dragoons captured from a picket they had surprised. He informed that the Earl Marischal was in personal command just behind, with his brother George Keith leading one cavalry group of 500, and the Earl of Lothian the other. Argyll was thought to be some four hours' march away still with more cavalry and some 4000 foot, the latter in two sections, one much farther forward than the other which accompanied the baggage and artillery.

They had not long to wait. In gallant if alarming style, the Covenant horsed host appeared over the skyline of the Cairn Hill shoulder to the south, rank upon rank, in good order, banners flying, a daunting sight.

Soon trumpets were blowing, as the Marischal perceived

the situation, and drew up his squadrons in a great extended line, scores deep. In contrast, the three-score royalist horse, however carefully placed, looked little short of pathetic.

'Thirty times our number!' Pate Graham growled. 'Damned traitors!'

'Not that,' Montrose demurred. 'Misguided, shall we say? Fellow subjects misguided. William Keith was ever head-strong. But no traitor.'

However headstrong, the Keith was not precipitate now. The problems, from a cavalry attacker's point of view, were all too apparent – debarred from making any assault on three sides, and the fourth narrow, and partially blocked by the village, which might well be held. He could not know that Montrose's men were desperately short of powder and shot.

After quite prolonged deliberation, the enemy moved on towards the village. Halting his front ranks just out of musket range, the Marischal dismounted a troop of about one hundred, and sent them creeping forward, skulking behind dykes and hedges and barns, to test the village defences.

When it was established that the houses were not held, the cavalry moved on, but warily, clearly fearing a trap, Mont-rose's reputation as a tactician inhibiting all.

Beyond the village, the spine of higher ground was barely 200 yards wide. There was open, cultivated space, with some orchard, before the first barring drystone dyke with the gate-way to the castle in the centre. Every foot of that dyke was manned, with every musket the royalists possessed. But such was the lack of ammunition that there was not enough for two complete salvoes.

When the Covenant leaders were almost within range, Montrose rose from his hiding-place, ordering a single shot to be fired in the air. 'Will Keith,' he called into the sudden hush. 'You ride under the banner of your King's enemies. It is my hope that you come to place yourself under my com-mand, as His Grace's Lieutenant-General, as is your duty. If so, your past offences will be overlooked. Also those of your company, so be that you serve the King loyally here-after. That on my word. If not, you will suffer my wrath, and the King's forthwith.'

There was a pause, and some laughter from the ranks opposite. Then the Earl Marischal spoke. 'James Graham –

my lord Marquis – I do not wish you harm. My orders are to convey you before the Committee of the Estates. At Edinburgh. I have no lack of men to serve that duty. Many times your numbers. And my lord of Argyll approaches, with a great army. Yield you then, I pray you.'

'I repeat, my lord Marischal – make your loyal duty to myself, as royal representative. Or I open fire on rebels. Quickly, my friend.'

'I tell you, it will not serve, Jamie . . .'

Montrose cut him short, nodding to two marksmen with muskets aimed over the dyke, glowing matches at the ready. They fired, and gravel and dirt spurted into the air a yard or two in front of the Earl's horse.

The beast reared in fright – and not alone in that. Being cavalry, this mounted host had no muskets – which could not be fired from the saddle, requiring supports – but only flint-lock pistols, with less than half a musket's range. In considerable confusion the front ranks reined round on the crowded pack behind. Quite a few pistols were fired, but to no effect. A distinctly unseemly retiral was made to the houses.

'They must attack now,' James Graham called along his lines. 'Hold your fire until you are certain of a hit. But before they gain pistol-range. Every ball must tell. The horse cannot jump this dyke.'

The inevitable charge came quickly. Two troops came spurring forward, yelling, with a third trotting more slowly behind. Knowing that their mounts could not leap that wall, they came bunched, five or six abreast, making for the gateway, some 200 very brave men, hoping by sheer weight and momentum to break through. It was like a clutch at the heart for the Graham to give the order to fire – for this would be sheer massacre, and these were his fellow countrymen. But what option had he?

It was the pistols that fired first, and uselessly, morale-aiders only. Then the slaughter, as the royalist muskets brought down their targets in flailing, screaming ruin. The dragoons had no least chance. The first ranks crashed like ninepins – and the others tripped and stumbled into and over them. The rest sought to spread right and left, inevitably, even though there was no possibility of passing the wall in front. These merely died at closer range and more dispersed.

In only a few seconds, a troop and a half of dragoons were down, without inflicting a single casualty on the defence. The survivors swung away and round, desperately, and ploughed back into the supporting third troop. With good sense, these turned also and streamed back to the village.

'Mary Mother – I'm hoping they will not try that again!' Colonel O'Cahan cried. 'We have used up most of our shot in one stroke.'

'I think not. They will attempt the waterside now,' Montrose said. 'They have no other choice. A score of your best marksmen, Colonel. As near the river as they may venture. Take shot from others. The Master of Madderty's bowmen behind them. Spread along the slope. In cover. You will find good targets, I think.' He sent a trumpeter out into the shambles in front, under a white flag, to announce that the Earl Marischal could recover his wounded, unassailed.

There was a quite lengthy interval thereafter. Then the anticipated infiltration along the riverside haughland commenced. A troop of horse began to pick their way through the reeds and willows there – and quickly were in trouble. In a dry summer it might just have been passable for cavalry horses, but after a wet autumn it was a quagmire. Only by most careful testing and probing could the riders make slow and individual progress. And as they came within range, marksmen with bow and musket picked them off one by one, at leisure. It was a quite hopeless endeavour – so long as arrows and shot held out.

The enemy did not fail to recognise the fact. The attempt was soon called off.

'What will they do now?' John Graham asked.

'They could dismount their men and send them in on foot,' the Earl of Airlie said. 'Men could cross that soft ground where horses cannot.'

'They could. But I do not think they will,' Montrose reasoned. 'They cannot know that we are short of powder and ball. They have only pistols, until they get close enough for lance and sword. They could be shot down while out of range as was the cavalry charge. They will not take kindly to fighting on foot, see you, being regular cavalry. And why should they – when they have us bottled up here, and have only to wait for Argyll's infantry to come up? I say they will wait.'

'And if they do? What will we do then? When my lord of Argyll comes?' his son demanded, voice less than steady.

'We will counter the Campbell as best we may – and pray for God's aid. But meanwhile we shall not waste such time as we are granted. There is much to do, trenches to dig . . .'

James Graham's assessment of the situation was accurate. No further attacks developed. Stalemate had been achieved, meantime.

While the trench-digging and barricade-building proceeded, Montrose repaired to the castle of Fyvie. Its keeper was an elderly kinsman of Dunfermline's, who wanted no worse trouble than he found himself in already. When it was announced that the castle was being taken over in the King's name, he offered no opposition. The Graham did not set about further fortifying the place, however, contenting himself with requisitioning all foodstuffs and forage, and setting up a rough manufactory in the old kitchen for moulding musket-balls, stripping the roofs of lead for the purpose. Fortunately, there was no lack of it. A squad of men were soon working hard.

It was late afternoon before Argyll arrived – and for every minute of that delay Montrose gave thanks. Again they watched the endless files of men come over the shoulder of Cairn Hill, this time with only the officers mounted, in the main. Keenly James Graham watched that vast, slow-moving column, so much less gallant than the Marischal's had been, but more menacing in these circumstances, and assessed its numbers at some 2000. Which meant that this was only about half the Covenant infantry force. Presumably Argyll had left his slower-moving units and baggage behind, hastening on with these. Two or four thousand would not greatly affect the issue, however, as far as the 650 royalists were concerned. What was highly important was that there seemed to be no artillery present. Again the Graham praised his Maker.

The thought of his particular, personal enemy so close at hand had an almost physical effect on the man, incompatible with his God-inclined thanks. He knew a churning within him, almost a nausea. It was sheer hate, he knew, deplore it as he might. He had to control himself sternly.

Archibald Campbell was seldom the man to rush matters.

But with only two hours of daylight left, any attack to be made that day had to be launched quickly. Within thirty minutes of the infantry's arrival, an assault was mounted. As Montrose expected, it was ostensibly on two fronts, the main advance along the riverside, with a diversion straight up from the village. This meant that the royalist force had to be spread out grievously, most of it facing west along the wooded spine, with no massed concentration at the dyke, as before. O'Cahan's men were left to defend that front on their own. They were all now reasonably well supplied with ball, and these were the veterans of the force. But it would inevitably be touch-and-go.

About four companies of foot, something under 1000 men, made the main riverside move, creeping along the reedy bank just out of effective range, parallel to the royalist positions, ploutering and floundering in the marsh and mire but managing to make progress where the horsemen had failed. It took them some time, and there was nothing Montrose might do to stop them. Presently, at a trumpet signal, they halted, and turned to face eastwards forming a quarter-mile front. Then, at another blare, a great hullabaloo developed on the short village front, with musketry and shouting and milling of cavalry. Under cover of this feint attack, the riverside assault commenced.

This was the real test, as all the defenders well knew. Once the enemy infantry won out of the soft ground, it would be hard to halt them – and no doubt Argyll would be throwing in more men than these. They would be well equipped with muskets. To face them, sheltered by the scrub woodland and dykes, plus the trenches, Montrose divided his force left, right and centre. He left O'Cahan and his six-score veterans to hold the short village front, facing south. Along the west-facing river front he put Sibbald, with the remnant of the Athollmen on the left, the Master of Madderty and his bowmen on the right, while he himself took the centre. The cavalry still waited, prominent on the ridge.

At first, the advantage lay with the defence, who had cover, a firm base, and for the time being sufficient ball. In the musketry exchange they undoubtedly were a lot more effective than the enemy, who suffered many casualties, out in the open. But numbers told, and the attackers came on undeterred. And as they advanced, in short rushes rather

357

than concerted charge, more men picked their way along the waterside behind them to take their places. When these were in a position to give covering fire, the first waves made better progress. And once these won their way up onto the firm ground, with broom bushes and the like to hide them, their advance was inexorable.

Thirty yards or so before the thicket woodland, Montrose had had his men dig the first and principal trench, a very rough ditch and rampart amongst tree-roots and stones, with the soil piled into a parapet riverwards. This now proved to be an enormous asset, against which the enemy flung wave after wave of men, between musket volleys, without success, losing large numbers. But the royalists were now running short of powder and although Madderty's bowmen on the right supported them wonderfully, with a vicious hail of shafts in flank, when the powder ran out the trench had to be abandoned, since it then became a death-trap for men fighting only with sword and dirk.

With the first of the attackers actually penetrating the skirts of woodland, and the second wave leaving the water-side more or less unmolested, Montrose recognised that drastic action was necessary if all was not to be lost. He ordered O'Cahan and his Irish and Islesmen to leave their position by the south wall, where they had stood more or less inactive, with no real attack developing from the village, to mount one of their terrifying Gaelic charges, with cold steel, from the left flank. They were to be replaced at the dyke by some of Sibbald's Athollmen. And Black Pate was sent racing, to make a minor cavalry gesture on the right flank, with a dozen or so horse, in the hope that it would be assumed that considerably more would in fact be committed. He sent young Johnnie to Airlie and Nathaniel Gordon sternly for-bidding them and their fifty mounted men to move from the ridge meantime.

O'Cahan's charge was magnificent. One hundred and twenty strong, his company leapt in sword-slashing, yelling fury, shouting their Celtic slogans, bounding slantwise across the scrub-dotted slope above the river, sweeping the advancing Covenant infantry aside like chaff. Montrose had given Pate his trumpeter, and now, with much blowing and to-do, horse-men dashed into action on the right, supported by a lesser but noisy charge of about fifty of Madderty's Drummonds. As the advancing enemy faltered, Montrose ordered a general advance, ridiculous in fact as this might be.

It turned the tide – of this attack, at least. The already wavering ranks broke and ran, pursued back into soft ground by the shouting if far less numerous defenders. As ever when a front breaks and bolts back through a supporting force, chaos ensued.

Montrose did not rush forward with his centre. As commander, he knew what he would do were he in Argyll's or the Marischal's position. A flank attack at this moment, from the village, could change all. Only some seventy Athollmen held the dyke – although the enemy could not know that. He hurried to take charge of them.

He was too late. He had been prepared for a fairly massive infantry assault, under heavy covering musket-fire, on the narrow front; but not for another full-scale cavalry attack over the killing-ground already littered with most of two troops of dead dragoons and their mounts. But this is what emerged from the cluster of houses, tight-packed, rank upon rank of horse, pennons fluttering, trumpets blowing, cheering, a daunting sight for seventy men behind a dyke.

Montrose, while still running, began to shout, saying to hold their fire almost until pistol-range. But the Athollmen were not trained veterans like O'Cahan's kerns, however stalwart. Before their commander's words were able to have any real effect, they had begun to shoot, wildly, haphazardly, at long range. They emptied a few saddles and brought down a few horses – but made no major impact.

Urgently Montrose turned and waved to his impatient horsemen sitting up there on the ridge. Nathaniel Gordon's raised hand and ringing cry answered him, as he dug in his spurs.

Gathering a few men round him to guard the vital gateway through the wall, Montrose shouted to the remainder of the Athollmen to retire a little way, back to the shelter of the tree-trunks, so as to keep out of pistol-range. Shoot from there.

Then came confrontation as the cavalry swept up to the very dyke. They tended to bunch towards the gate, naturally – and it was the leaders who reached it first. Montrose, using a hastily grabbed musket now, saw the pale face of William Kerr, Earl of Lothian, one-time colleague and shot his horse from under him. He saw also George Keith, the Earl Maris-chal's brother, go down with a ball smashing his forehead in bloody horror. Other leaders were crushed against the shut gate itself by the weight of horseflesh behind. The gate's timbers splintered and crashed. But there was no pouring through. The fallen men and horses piled up, to form their own limb-lashing barrier. Some behind did manage to clamber over – and were promptly shot. The gateway held.

All along the wall horsemen were rearing up, ranging back and forth unable to leap it, cursing, firing their pistols, being crushed against the stones by the press coming on. But it was only a drystone dyke, and already men dismounted, delibera-tely or otherwise, were pulling, clawing, at the stones. By keeping below the level of the wallhead, raising their arms to it, these could not be shot – even though they might be trampled down by their own colleagues. It was only a ques-tion of time, brief time, before there would be gaps for a breakthrough.

Then, with ringing cries, the royalist horse thundered down on the rear flank of the Covenant cavalry. Fifty upon 500 is poor odds; but a downward slope, impetus, an attack to the rear, plus sheer desperation, make potent allies. They created major havoc. Montrose caught just a glimpse of his son John charging down just behind Nathaniel Gordon and Sir Thomas Ogilvy – and cursed himself for failing to com-mand the boy otherwise.

Now there was complete confusion on both fronts, men fighting everywhere at close quarters, with little that even the best leadership could do to regulate affairs. Another squadron of Covenant dragoons thrown in at this juncture could have changed the entire scene – but strangely enough was not forthcoming. What did happen was that Magnus O'Cahan and his wild men came storming back, warned by the trumpeting with which the enemy horse had heralded their charge. Just as portions of the wall fell his Gaels with their dripping swords hurled themselves upon the first through the gaps, crouching, to slit the horses' bellies with their dirks, blocking the entries again, even clambering over to launch themselves from the walltop, crazed with the blood-lust.

It was just too much for the now leaderless dragoons. They broke right and left, and streamed off, pursued by the yelling Irish and Islesmen. Both Covenant attacks had failed.

Montrose shouted for his trumpeter to sound the recall.

He was stooping over the fallen George Keith when Johnnie rode up, flushed, eyes alight, sword in slender hand – but, his father was thankful to see, unblooded sword. He gabbled excited words, and Montrose forbore criticism. Then the boy looked down at Keith, and his flush faded. He put his hand to his mouth.

'What now?' Airlie demanded. 'Will they attack again? They have the men . . .'

'I think not,' the Graham answered. 'The sun has set. It is near dusk already. Dark within the hour. They could not mount another attack in time. No, they will wait until morning, I believe. And by morning, God willing, we shall not be here!'

'Ha . . . !'

'Colonel Sibbald – the trumpeter, under a white flag. To the Earl Marischal – not to Argyll. I will not have dealings with the Campbell. Tell the Marischal that he may remove his wounded. Tell him also, with my regrets, that his brother is dead. Pate – see you to the wounded – all wounded. And put those screaming horses out of their pain . . .'

'Permission, my lord Marquis, for my men to collect powder from the dead enemy,' Colonel O'Cahan came to enquire, panting. 'We have scarce a snuffboxful left between us.'

'To be sure, my friend. I think you can do so unassailed, now. And – Colonel, you and yours played a hero's part this day. I shall see that the King hears of it. And recommend that His Grace bestows the accolade of knighthood upon a most valiant soldier.'

The dark Irishman smiled, and bowed. 'A man does what comes naturally, in such pass,' he said lightly. 'But – my thanks. Did I hear your lordship say that we are to be out of this? With the dark?'

'You did. Six hundred cannot fight six thousand for over-long. And when Argyll's artillery comes up, we are lost. On this island in the marsh. We shall slip away under cover of night, secretly. The old man in the castle, Seton, says that there is a way through the bog. To the north-east. A cause-way of a sort, between the loch-head and the Tifty Burn. Just passable for horses, in single-file. He will lead us. I trust

361

him – for he desires only to be quit of us. We shall leave camp-fires burning here, where they may be seen. And steal out when the men have rested and eaten, horses led. Now – go gather your powder . . .'

Four hours later, after replenishing the fires, the royalist army snaked away in utter silence from Fyvie, its castle and its ridge – and found none to interfere with this quiet going, although all the slopes to south and west blazed with the lights of the Covenant host.

The clash at Fyvie would not rank in any annals as a great battle, nor yet a victory; but as a military exploit it was one of the most extraordinary of the troubled century.

27

IN THE GREAT HALL OF THE LARGE AND ANCIENT CASTLE OF Balvenie, in Banffshire's Glen Fiddich, a lofty thirty miles west of Fyvie, Montrose was reluctantly holding a council of war. At least, that is what he called it, though in fact it was nothing of the sort – for he himself knew what he intended to do. It was, rather, an adding-up of accounts, an opportunity for heart-baring – though scarcely his own – and a test, a test of loyalties, of staying-power, of determination. And James Graham had put off making it, almost afraid to do so, until that morning's courier from the South had forced his hand. His was a sensitive nature not difficult to make afraid – however little his fears were allowed to show or to dictate his actions.

In the flickering light of two great log-fires beneath the pointed vaulted ceiling, which but emphasised the grey, wet gloom of the mid-November afternoon, he looked round at the faces of his officers and companions – so pitifully few of them round that long table which could have seated five times their number. He was even glad of his young son's presence there, to help swell the company – to such ebb had they sunk. Besides Johnnie, Pate of Inchbrakie was there, and Graham of Gorthie; the Earl of Airlie and his sons Sir Thomas and Sir David Ogilvy; Colonel Magnus O'Cahan and the Master of Madderty. That was all, all above the rank of captain, in the King's army of Scotland. These, and their host, Sir Robert Innes of Innermarkie and Balvenie, with his son – looking doubtful, as well they might.

Montrose cleared his throat. Thin, worn, he still carried his head high, and his courtesy was consistent. 'So, my friends – there you have it,' he declared, into the argument which had developed. 'Argyll is content to fight, for this winter season at least, with other weapons than sword and musket. Weapons more to his own taste, I think! But sharp, see you – sharp.'

'The man is a dastard!' old Airlie growled. 'We all know that. But that sound men should heed his lying, deceitful words, play his foul game – this is the crowning shame. Betrayal – it is nothing less! The man Sibbald I could believe it of – a mercenary, his sword for sale to the highest bidder. But gentlemen, like Hay and Drummond and Nat Gordon! To buy their skins at the price of their honour! Treachery . . .'

'No, no – not that, my lord. I will not have it so black!' Montrose protested, if a little wearily. 'Do not judge our friends so hard. They have served the King, and myself, so very well. Be not so sore on them because they have not quite so great hearts as your own. These were against a winter campaign, from the start . . .'

'As was I. And am still,' the Master of Madderty interjected.

'I know it, John. And you shall have your say. But do not let us call those who have elected to leave us traitors. Because they have had a sufficiency. The Campbell's blandishments are potent. His promises of pardons, lands, gold, to all who will desert my banner – these speak loud to weary men who have already given so much for the King's cause. I do not find it in my heart to blame them, merely because I myself am beyond the range of the Campbell's generosity!'

'But Nat Gordon . . . !'

'The Gordon has not defected, my lord. Only seemed to do so. Of a purpose. I may reveal it now, within these wall, I think. Nat has gone as my envoy, to the Lord Gordon. Seeming to accept Argyll's offer of indemnity, like the rest, but in fact still in my service. To remain at Strathbogie and seek to play upon his young lord on our behalf. Never forget as I do not, that north of Tay only Gordon can provide the King with the cavalry we require. The numbers necessary. Nat, a Gordon himself, believes that he can work on George Gordon, in his father's absence, to alter his stand. And on Straloch, the chamberlain, his own near kinsman, who has great weight with the young lord. Better that he should be so employed in these winter days than traipsing the Highland hills with us, and no cavalry to command – for that is his worth.'

The Earl shrugged. 'As you will, James. But these others – Drummond, Hay, even Sibbald. If these are not traitors they are cravens at least.'

'Even that I will not allow, my lord. All have shown themselves brave men. Steel, mark you, is not all of the same strength and spring. Some swords will snap before others, if bent too far. As we, my friends, all have been bent those past months. I but thank God for you that remain to me. And pray that I keep you by me, even so, until better days. Colonel Sibbald I grieve over. He fought with me at Morpeth, and rode with Rollo and myself from Carlisle, secretly into Scotland. A good soldier. But . . .'

'But tested, and found wanting!' Sir Thomas Ogilvy put in, shortly.

'Perhaps the testing was too stern? Who am I to judge? Even you, Sir Thomas? Or your brother? Or your noble father, here. I shall not judge *you* if even you are tested too hard.'

'What do you mean, my lord Marquis?' the quiet Sir David asked.

'I mean, my friends, that I have ill news for you. The same courier who brought me news of Argyll's seducing of our friends, brought me other news also. I have scarce known how to tell you. Your brother – and your elder son, my lord – who is my friend and comrade-in-arms, the Lord Ogilvy, we all know was captured in England on his way to Oxford soon after I left Carlisle. Now he has been bought – *bought,* mark you – for gold! For £1000 sterling. By the Campbell. To be *his* prisoner. So hot is his fire. Brought to Edinburgh. Confined in the Thieves' Hole of the Tolbooth, like the foulest felon!' The Graham's voice quivered. 'That any man

364

calling himself Christian, and fighting in the name of religion, should so act ... !'

Sir Thomas had half-raised himself from his seat. But at a gesture from his father he sat again, tense-featured.

'Nothing is beyond the Campbell,' the older man said, carefully. 'I have learned that lesson, ere this. And he hates my house. But . . . Ogilvy will fight him from a pit in Edinburgh's Tolbooth as Ogilvy does from these Highland hills! My Jamie will give *MacCailean Mor* no satisfaction, there or anywhere.'

'It will not be all black hatred, my lord. He will seek to use your son to bring *you* to his heel.'

'Then he is a fool as well as a dastard and a rogue!' Airlie growled. 'Jamie will not yield him a word, much less a whimper. And nor will I!'

Montrose spread his hands. 'What can I say, in face of such steadfast constancy? Save to salute the house of Ogilvy. The King's Grace is fortunate in *some* of his friends, at least!'

'My lord Marquis,' Sir David said, 'we but take yourself as model.'

'Aye, and do not tell us that the Campbell reserves all his spleen for Ogilvy,' the Earl added. 'Since he hates you still more than he does me.'

The other nodded, his handsome face composed, his voice almost expressionless. 'You are right, my lord. Archibald Campbell has not forgotten Graham. I learn that he has ordered the imprisonment of most of my kin and friends. Innumerable of the house of Graham, in the South. My good-brother, the Lord Napier, and his son. Aye, and their womenfolk. Stirling of Keir, and his. John Fleming. And many more. My castle of Mugdock is sacked and despoiled, and much of my other lands harried. Southesk, my good-sire, is to ensure that there is no traffic between my wife and children and myself – on pain of excommunication! And has so agreed. Here is how King Campbell makes war – in the name of the Lord Jesus Christ and no quarter!' With an obvious effort, James Graham controlled the voice which had risen and harshened. 'Forgive me, gentlemen. All this is scarce to the point. Save to sharpen our resolve. What *is* to the point is that I have sure information that Argyll is not now following us, but has turned back. Is making his way down Strathmore for the South ...'

'*Dia!* We gave him his bellyful at Fyvie, then?' O'Cahan cried.

'I think rather that he, at least, has no stomach for a winter campaign in the mountains.'

'In that, on my soul, he shows good sense!' John, Master of Madderty averred.

'You think so? I do not, John. It is a backward step. He has a great army – but has won no battle. He will garner no credit with this – and a general must have credit, as I know to my cost! Covenant Scotland and the Committee of the Estates will only accept his retiral, and a winter's inaction, if *I* do no more. If we are equally inactive. And I do not intend to be!'

'Ha! What means that, my lord?' Graham of Gorthie demanded.

'I mean that we should surely use what we have. However small. Now only 500 men, yes – and no cavalry. But 500 toughened, fast-moving, light of foot, unburdened by gear. Five hundred who can climb mountains, cross bogs, swim rivers, live off the land. You, Colonel O'Cahan – tell us what such a force may achieve, even in winter mountains. You, who have led the like.'

'Anything, my lord Marquis – anything, by the Powers! So be it that *you* lead it!'

'Thank you, my friend. Would that I could be worthy of your so great trust. But at least we can achieve much, where others could not. Or *would* not. And so will not think to look for us. I propose to march through the great hills, up Spey, into Badenoch again. It is Huntly's country, but less under his hand than this. We may gain men there. And from Badenoch slip down through the passes to Atholl, once more. The back door to the country where most of us come from. Drawing men from there into our ranks. And then, gentlemen – strike west!'

'West . . . ? To Colkitto?'

'Partly. But mainly, my friends, to Argyll itself. Inveraray. The Campbell's homeland. Teach *MacCailean Mor* what it means to take up arms against his liege lord. On his own secure doorstep. Without cavalry we cannot fight a Lowland campaign. But we can attempt a Highland one. And the Campbell homeland deserves a taste of war, perhaps . . .'

He knew, of course, that he would have them, with that

366

programme. He could not go on, for the noise, the stamping of booted feet, the banging on the table, the cries of acclaim. Even old Sir Robert Innes, their host, who was scarcely concerned though a loyal King's man, applauded with the rest.

Only Madderty doubted. He declared that they would never get volunteers such as they needed, for a winter's campaign, especially horse, which was the prior requirement. Now that the pressure from Argyll had relaxed, he believed more than ever that they should take a much-needed rest, to regain their strength; and spend the winter months secretly visiting their friends and possible supporters, seeking enlistments rather than actually campaigning.

Montrose acknowledged that there was some sense in this. But he held that there were dangers too. Lose impetus and it might be exceedingly difficult to restart hostilities. Better to keep going – especially when the other side was flagging. Moreover, word of the King's cause in England was not good, and Charles badly required encouraging news from Scotland. It was their duty to give him it, if they could.

He had his way, of course. They would move up Spey, for Badenoch, next day.

It was ten days later that a courier reached them in the Dalwhinnie area, some way north of the grim Pass of Drumochter which linked Badenoch and Atholl, in their camp by the rushing Truim amongst the snow-covered mountains. He was an Atholl Stewart, brother of one of the men with Montrose – and his news was startling. Argyll himself, with a large part of his foot, was less than thirty miles away. He had billeted his men at Dunkeld, on the very verge of Atholl, but was himself now at Blair Castle, pressing the young Earl of Atholl to change his allegiance. He seemed to be settling in for the winter in that area, and was attempting to seduce the loyalties of the lairds round about, with a mixture of threats, promises and money. All his cavalry were dismissed to winter quarters in Perth, Fife and the south.

It was dusk when the Stewart arrived, but despite this, and the windy dark, within an hour the camp was struck, and all were ready to move. Before they set off, James Graham spoke to the assembled company, by the flickering light of the last camp-fires.

367

'My good friends and companions,' he said, 'we face an unexpected challenge and opportunity. Your enemy, and mine, the Marquis of Argyll, is all but within striking distance of us here. Unsuspecting. At Dunkeld, his troops settled for the winter, his cavalry gone south. I had not believed that he would remain so far north, on the verge of these Highlands. He is seeking to lay Atholl under his evil sway. The homes of many of you. Are you with me in surprising the Campbells?'

The throaty roar greeting that left no doubts as to the reaction.

'I need not tell you what it would mean to the King's cause, to all Scotland, if we could capture Argyll ... ! Wait, you! Wait, you! I have boasted of you, my friends, that you can cover more miles of this land in fewer hours than any other men living. Now, prove it! You know the shortest way to Blair, where the Campbell has come to threaten the young Earl. Thirty miles by the roads men follow. But less through the mountains, I am told. How long until you are chapping at Blair Castle door?'

'By daybreak tomorrow!' somebody yelled, and there was a gleeful shout of approval.

'See to it, then. And I with you ...'

So, leaving Lord Airlie to bring on at a more modest pace the older men, those slightly wounded, and such as might hold them back, some 350 of them set out on as major a physical test as could have been devised for an armed force, even mountaineers. It was not a march, more of an endless loping trot, by drove roads, cattle-tracks, deer-tracks and no tracks at all, contouring dark hillsides, ploutering through bogs and peat-hags, crossing high passes, threading woodland, wading rivers. There was half a moon, fitfully shining through scudding clouds, and for late November the weather was reasonably kind. But conditions for travel were appalling nevertheless, and could only have been endured by such men as these, hardened hillmen and veterans, toughened by hard campaigning and challenged to their utmost, travelling light, untrammelled, bearing only shoulder-slung swords, pistols and dirks.

They avoided the long, long bend of the main drove road threading the Pass of Drumochter by heading almost due eastwards, climbing high to start with, up the deep scar of a corrie, or hanging valley, and so over the snowy ridge of Carn na Caim and down over wicked country to lonely Loch an Duin beyond. Here they could turn south down the Edendon River, mile upon mile of it, the watershed behind them. The snows of the upper reaches at least meant that the bogs were frozen hard. But it was a killing journey.

At last the Edendon brought them down into the main central valley of Atholl, at Dalnacardoch where they joined the drove road again, having saved almost six miles. At least they had had no lack of guides, for many of the Athollmen knew even this empty wilderness. They had covered some thirteen savage miles, and taken almost seven hours to do it. Already Montrose was desperately weary, not yet fully himself after his sickness of six weeks earlier. Stewart of Dalnacardoch, roused at two hours past midnight, provided cold venison, raw oatmeal and whisky. All had a little. His son was with the party.

There was still a dozen miles to go to Blair, and before they were half-way down the wide Strath of Garry, it was sheer spirit that was keeping James Graham going, a determination at all costs not to fail the others – and not to betray legs of clay, as well as feet thereof, to young Johnnie who was still going strongly.

With the moon setting behind the black mountains of Craiganour to the north-west, they reached Blair-in-Atholl thirteen hours and twenty-five miles after leaving Glen Truim, a feat possibly unrivalled in Scots military history for any large body of men on foot. There and then, silently, avoiding the township which was the home of not a few of them, they surrounded the great castle, and began to close in.

They were fairly near before the alarm was raised. Montrose had his trumpeter sound the summons and make his presence and identity known. But known only to the Countess, the Earl's mother – not to Archibald Campbell. To the grievous disappointment of all, they learned that Argyll had moved back to Dunkeld the previous afternoon, taking young Atholl with him. Their Homeric efforts had been in vain.

Dunkeld was another twenty miles to the south. And Argyll's main force was there – although in cantonments, unprepared for fighting. Montrose decided to press on. But not yet, hardly yet. Flesh and blood, his own in especial, was capable only of so much. They must have rest, food, refreshment. A few hours ...

It was mid-forenoon before they set out once more, their fine enthusiasm not quite recaptured, though still they went fast, Montrose refusing the offer of a horse. They were almost at the junction of Tummel and Tay, with Killiecrankie and Moulin behind them, when a small party coming in the other direction halted them. It was the young Earl of Atholl returning home.

He was only a little older than Johnnie, and in a great state of excitement. All was well, he cried, to Montrose. All was well. Argyll was fled.

Astonished, unbelieving, the Graham questioned him. It seemed that, while they had slept at Blair, somebody had slipped away, on a fast horse, to warn the Campbell at Dunkeld. And whenever that man had heard that Montrose was so near with an armed force, he had flown into a dire panic, declaring that he was betrayed, that all was lost, that his encamped troops were in no state for fight. And without more ado he had taken horse for Perth and the South, leaving the Earl of Lothian to do as he thought best. He had not so much as taken leave of Atholl.

'But ... but this is madness!' the Graham objected. 'There are less than 400 of us. He must have thousands at Dunkeld. Has the man taken leave of his wits?'

'The messenger did not say but 400, my lord Marquis. He but said Montrose was coming with a Highland host. That was sufficient for *MacCailean Mor!* He believed you on his heels – and fled.'

'Dear God – and this is the man who holds Scotland in thrall! This he who sets himself up against his King, the hope of the Lord's elect!'

'What to do, now? Argyll was escaped; and however unprepared, the camp at Dunkeld was now warned. There could be no surprise. Atholl estimated between 3000 and 4000 men there – and even if their general was a craven, these would not be all the same. More than ten times their own number.

Reluctantly they turned back. Bold grasping of an opportunity was one thing; foolhardiness quite another.

Back at Blair they waited for Airlie to turn up; and then

stayed longer, welcome, to give the Athollmen a chance to
see their own people, and to seek to rally more to the royal
standard. Argyll's extraordinary behaviour aided them in
this – although it was recognised that when Montrose was
gone, the Campbell and his threat would re-emerge. Over
another 100 volunteers were added to their strength.

They were still at Blair, safe behind the closely guarded
Pass of Killiecrankie, when ten days later there were surprising developments on two fronts. Word came from Dunkeld that the entire military scene was changing. Argyll had
gone straight to Edinburgh, where he had had but a cool
reception from the erstwhile loot-licking Committee of the
Estates, who now criticised his generalship. In high dudgeon
the Campbell had there and then resigned his commission as
commander-in-chief of the home forces and shaken the dust
of Edinburgh from his feet – while still, of course, reserving
the right to make all important political decisions. He had
retired to Inveraray and his own territories. What is more,
he had commanded all his Campbell levies, which made up
the main bulk of his present infantry, to return home to
Argyll forthwith, likewise. If the Covenant leadership did
not appreciate his services as a general, they could see how
they got on without him, and his.

Evidently in some considerable confusion the Committee
had been unable to persuade either of the Major-Generals,
the Earl Marischal or the Earl of Lothian, to take on the
thankless task of commander-in-chief. Neither would the
Earl of Callander, commander of the Borders area, consider
it. In desperation they had turned to old Leslie, in England,
and he had sent them an almost unknown individual, one of
his own major-generals, by name William Baillie of Letham,
a veteran of the Gustavus Adolphus wars.

Montrose, although intrigued by the news, was less
delighted than were some of his lieutenants – for he knew
Baillie, and had few doubts that a professional soldier as
commander-in-chief would prove a more potent opponent
than most high-born amateurs. But the resignation of Argyll
was heartening and significant – even though it was only as
general that he was stepping down. He would remain the
political master of Scotland. The tidings therefore, although
an unexpected present encouragement, could also mean
more effective military measures against them hereafter.

The second development was more consistently heartening, and as unanticipated. The day following the first, all at
Blair were excited to hear the distant sound of bagpipes –
intrigued rather than alarmed. Coming from the north, no
attackers would so advertise their approach. All were agog
to see what this could mean. When a large host appeared in
sight, marching down the strath, there was some misgiving.
But when the proud black-and-white Galley of the Isles
standard could be distinguished flying at the head, and
beside it the Red Hand banner of Ulster, there could be no
doubts. Colkitto was back.

Montrose went out to meet the prodigal, forgiving all,
thankful of heart. But as he and his neared the front ranks
of the host, even the mighty figure of Alastair MacDonald
failed to monopolise the attention. For, flanking the blond
giant, was such a galaxy of eagles-feathered Highland chieftains as the Graham had never before seen at one time, fierce-
looking, barbarous-seeming men, dressed in tartans, both
kilts and trews, calf-hide jerkins, antiquated armour and
helmets, with Celtic jewellery, bristling with symbolic arms,
pride emanating from them in an almost visible aura.

'Major-General Alastair – I rejoice to see you,' Montrose
cried. 'With all my heart, I do. And . . . in such bonny
company!'

'Ha, my lord Marquis – I see that you are on your feet
again, by the Mass! I heard that you might have work for
me, once more! And for mine.'

'Always I had that, my friend.'

'Aye. Well, see you – I have brought some kin of mine.
You will not fail to know their names, I think.' He turned
ceremoniously towards his right. 'It is my honour to present
Sir James of Sleat; Aeneas of Glengarry; John of Moidart,
Captain of Clanranald; Alastair MacRanald of Keppoch;
MacIan of Glencoe; MacIan of Ardnamurchan.' He paused
there, for effect – as well he might.

No comparable play-acting was required of Montrose. A
sensitive man, he was in fact concerned that tears of emotion should not well up into his eyes. For this resounding
catalogue represented the greatest clan in Scotland, greater
even than Gordon or Campbell – the Clan Donald Federa-
tion. Here were the chiefs, or their near representatives, of
the age-old dynasty which had been undisputed rulers of

the North-West and the Hebrides for half a millennium. He held out his hand, stirred as he was not forgetting to do so in due order of precedence, the same in which they had been presented.

'Gentlemen – you gladden my eyes and my heart,' he cried. 'I salute the Sons of Somerled!'

That pleased these proud Islesmen, it was clear – although none actually smiled as Montrose grasped each hand.

Colkitto was not finished. 'And here, to present to *An Greumach Mor,* is Clan Gillean. Sir Lachan Maclean of Duart; Hector Maclaine of Lochbuie; Ewan Maclean of Ardgour; Lachlan Maclean of Coll.'

'I greet the great Clan Gillean.'

'Here is Alan of Locheil, Captain of Clan Cameron; Mac-Master Cameron of Letterfinlay; MacSorley Cameron of Glen Nevis.'

'I rejoice to meet the MacGillonie, the Camerons of Lochaber.'

'Moreover, Seumas my friend, here is Duncan Stewart of Appin; Alan Stewart of Ardsheil; Ian Stewart of Invernahyle; and Dugald Stewart of Achnacone.'

'The Royal Race! My salutations . . .'

And so it went on. With meticulous care, Colkitto presented group after group of chiefs and chieftains and captains, all in their due order, rank and precedence. And as heedfully, Montrose acknowledged them, thankful not only for their presence there but that he could remember sufficient of the Gaelic polity and tradition to greet each properly and aptly. For these men were prouder of their ancestry and lineage than any grandees of Spain, the proudest probably in all Christendom, and easier to offend by any failure in address or order. Yet they were some of the finest irregular fighters ever born – and for that the Graham's heart was full. Even though apparently they had brought with them no more than some 500 clansmen, mere token 'tails'. But engage and involve these chiefs, and they could provide their thousands.

That Colkitto was highly pleased with himself over producing this impressive support for the King's wilting cause, went without saying. That they were all probably more deeply imbued with hatred of the Campbell than with loyalty to King Charles was beside the point. Colkitto had been operating for the past month or two on the northern fringes of Argyll, raiding into Campbell country – a proceeding which commended itself to all other western chieftains. However much they might disagree with each other, their antipathy to *MacCailean Mor* was sufficient to produce a kind of unity when opportunity arose to smite the Campbell with some degree of success. Colkitto had promised them such smiting, and consequent rich pickings, in this laudable pursuit.

If the adherence of these Highland chiefs provided its own problems, at least it cleared Montrose's mind as to what must be his next move – something which had been concerning him not a little. Now there could be no question. He had to continue to concentrate on Archibald Campbell. And since the Campbell had retired to his own fastnesses, there they must follow him. Mid-Argyll was a vast natural fortress, of course; and no major assault on its central citadel area had been attempted for centuries – not since the Bruce's campaign against John of Lord in 1308, when the hero-king had won his brilliant victory at the Pass of Brander. Modest hit-and-run raids such as Colkitto had been engaged on, mere pinpricks, were always possible, on the perimeter; but full-scale invasion was something other. There was probably not a commander in Scotland who would even consider it. But, on the other hand, neither Archibald Campbell nor anyone else was likely to expect it, therefore. It had taken the immortal Bruce to do it before. He, James Graham, might humbly try his hand – with God's help. Only so could he make best and enthusiastic use of his imposing new supporters. And the King's cause meantime could as well be served in Argyll as elsewhere.

So it was decided. They would leave Atholl and turn their faces to the west, marching by Breadalbane and Mamlorn. And, God willing, they would teach Archibald Campbell who was king, even in Argyll.

Quickly thereafter Montrose learned how difficult a team he now had to handle. For Breadalbane was itself now largely Campbell territory, stolen from the MacGregors, MacNabs and lesser clans, by the Glenorchy branch of the Campbells. And Colkitto and his friends were for letting the Campbells of Lawers, Balloch, Lochtay-side, Finlarig, Glen Dochart and Strathfillan learn something of what it meant to have the

same name as *MacCailean Mor,* as it were en route. James
Graham's insistence that this should not be was not well
received. Indeed it looked almost as though the authority of
the King's Lieutenant was going to be flouted before even it
was acknowledged – for these men he now spoke to were
little kings in their own way. He declared earnestly that
surprise was the very basis of anything they might achieve
against Argyll. Forfeit that, and they might as well remain in
Atholl. They must avoid all such populous Campbell areas
like the plague, meantime, lest word be sent to Inveraray.
Their turn might come, afterwards . . .

That the Graham had his way, in the end, was thanks
wholly to patient persuasion and nothing to command.

28

GOD, IT SEEMED, ON THIS OCCASION, WAS WITH MONTROSE –
or so decided the Highland chiefs. As well He might be, of
course, since it was the heretical, Covenanting and thrice-
damned Campbell who was equally His enemy as well as
theirs. For that month, from mid-December 1644 to mid-
January 1645, the wind blew lightly but steadily from the
east, cold but dry, frost and clear skies, sun by day, bitter,
splintering starlight by night, such consistent cold as had
not been experienced for long – but dry cold. For moving an
army across the very Highland roof of Scotland, nothing
could have been better. No snow fell – and what was already
there was solid as iron. Rushing rivers were frozen over, and
crossable. Bogs became level, if slippery, highways. The
passes were not drifted up. All the natural hazards of winter
travel in the mountains were modified – for men who could
cope with the cold. This, admittedly, was terrible – but there
was fuel in plenty, for Breadalbane and Mamlorn were well
wooded with the old Caledonian pine-forest. And cattle were

available in large numbers, huddling conveniently on the low ground, not scattered over the ironbound hills – and being Campbell cattle, and therefore free, tasted the sweeter. Whatever the chiefs thought of present Montrose tactics and strategy, they recognised his luck. And acknowledged his energy, and the sustained speed of their going.

They made excellent time indeed, in this epic move – for nobody had thought to transport an army, now numbering some 3000, across the highest and broadest barrier of Highland Scotland, in deepest winter, in memory of man. Even the Bruce had done his Argyll campaigning more seasonably. Leaving Atholl on the 11th of December, they marched south first, to Tay, and then west up Strathtay by Aberfeldy – taking the opportunity to pay a call at Castle Menzies, at Weem, and take into custody Sir Alexander Menzies, who had betrayed Montrose before Tippermuir. His strong links with the Campbells might well make him a useful hostage. Then on down both sides of Loch Tay – carefully avoiding any assault on the Campbell castles there however, much as the chiefs grumbled. In long Glen Dochart they were joined by quite a large contingent of MacGregors and MacNabs, welcome recruits, whose hatred of their dispossessors, the Clan Campbell, was deep and personal indeed. And these saved a bloody encounter at the narrows between Loch Dochart and great Ben More, where a hastily assembled party of Glenorchy men might have held them up indefinitely; and Montrose was shown how to avoid the pass by a secret route on a high terrace to the north. Then up Strathfillan to Tyndrum, where they had a most unexpected adherent – none other than Patrick Campbell of Edinample, brother to Robert of Glenorchy himself, who had quarrelled with his brother and Argyll both, a shifty character but who also might be useful. The long pass of Glen Lochy, under Ben Lui, then opened before them, stark white, bleak savage – but unguarded by man. Through its grim miles they passed unopposed, until the wide lowlands of Loch Awe spread spectacularly before them, a stirring, heart-lifting sight after the close constriction of the mountains. It was the Campbell homeland and very fair.

They had thus reached the borders of the central Argyll citadel in five gruelling days, eighty miles across the high hunched back of the land. And without a single conflict worth so calling. It seemed highly unlikely that any warning could have gone ahead of them, to Inveraray.

Kilchurn Castle, the large and strong main seat of the Glenorchy Campbells, stood in an almost unassailable marshy site at an inlet of the great loch ahead of them. To take that would be difficult and time-consuming, without artillery. But it had to be neutralised somehow – and especially prevented from sending a warning boat up the twenty-three-mile length of the great loch, from which word could be got over the hill to Inveraray on Loch Fyne. Fortunately, Campbell of Edinample, who had been reared here, knew how the lochward approaches to the castle could be blocked by means of a boom across the narrows of the inlet – part of the place's defences against attack by water. The boom was permanently there and only a constricted channel had to be blocked, and no boat could get past. A small party was given this task, and the guarding of the boom thereafter. Montrose was loth to thus use the services of a traitor – but dealing with Archibald Campbell made such scruples too costly.

Farther west still, the mighty jaws of the famous Pass of Brander yawned, barring off all central and coastal Lorne. This was where Bruce had won his great victory, improbable as it seemed. Bruce had not been aiming at Inveraray, however, but at Dunstaffnage, John MacDougall of Lorn's fortress. It was on the MacDougall's consequent fall that the Campbells arose. So Montrose did not require to seek passage of that fearsome gorge between the steep sides of towering Cruachan and the deep black waters of Awe. But it had to be sealed off, nevertheless, lest any enemy assault developed through it, to outflank them. So he sent a detachment of 200 MacGregors and MacNabs, the former once owners of this territory, to stop it – and 200 could hold up 10,000 there, one way as the other.

These dispositions taken, the Graham faced south along the loch-shore.

Loch Awe-side was rich, fertile, long-settled and sheltered territory, highly populous. The loch lay in a north-easterly and south-westerly direction, averaging just under a mile in width. On the eastern side, the access to Loch Fyne area was by a small pass some six miles onward and so down Glen Aray to Inveraray itself, nine miles. But that was the way any attack would be expected to come, and almost certainly it would be kept well guarded. A much less convenient approach was to the north, across high boggy trackless moors to the headwaters of the Shira River, and so down its long waterlogged glen to Fyne. In normal conditions this would be almost impassable for any large body of men, however agile. But with the country frozen solid, it almost certainly could be done. Colkitto, with 500 of the toughest men, would attempt it. But there was still another way over into Loch Fyne-side, almost equally awkward. This entailed proceeding two-thirds of the way up Loch Aweside, to a place called Durran, from which a steep and difficult bridle-path struck off up over the intervening range, eventually to descend into Fyne-side some seven miles below Inveraray, also traversing undrained and evil uplands. This would be Montrose's own route, with the main body.

But there was still another factor to be taken into account. The *west* side of Loch Awe was also fertile, if somewhat less populous, and would have to be taken care of likewise if warning was not to be sent to Inveraray by boat up the loch and then over the hill. Moreover away beyond the head of Awe, the coastal lands of Kilmichael and Kilmartin were densely populated, and could raise thousands of men, who could come up Lord Fyne from its foot, if warned or summoned. The fact was that this whole area, aroused, could produce 10,000 men in a couple of days, and fierce fighters, defending their homes. This must be avoided at all costs. So the veteran John of Moidart, Captain of Clanranald, the most experienced in war of the Highland chiefs, would take another 500, and attend to the west side of Awe, making sure that there was no burning, to send smoke columns of warning high into the still air; and thereafter proceed over into the coastal plain to the south, to block any reinforcement of the central Inveraray citadel from thence.

So the three divisions parted company, with Montrose himself still commanding the best part of 2000 men. Before him, along the eastern lochside, he sent a swift advance party of 300, under Magnus O'Cahan, with instructions to do no fighting but only to seal off any routes and tracks over the hills south-westwards, so that no warnings should go ahead of them; and especially to hold the point, at this Durran, where the main body would branch off, seventeen miles

ahead. No Campbells were to climb up on to those intervening hilltops, to light warning beacons or smoke-signals.

It was midday as they moved off, with a bare five hours
of daylight left to them, and vast mileages to cover. Despite
the temptations of fat Campbell houses, farms and townships,
for Highlandmen with old scores to settle and booty to be
won, Montrose was adamant that there should be no harrying and time-wasting. And certainly no burnings. All that
could wait. They had richer targets ahead. Fortunately, and
advisedly, he had got rid of most of the high-born Highland
firebrands, with Colkitto, who might have felt it incumbent
upon them to demonstrate that they took orders from no
Lowland lord, even though he called himself *An Greumach
Mor*.

They made good time up Loch Awe-side then, despite the
grumbling, with the Campbell population prudently keeping
out of the way, cowering behind their doors and walls, fleeing discreetly into woods and ravines, as well they might, and
putting up no useless resistance at this stage. It was a green
and pleasant land, and ripe for spoiling, all agreed. But they
would be back. There was no snow down here, almost at
sea-level; but the frost remained hard as ever.

Montrose's eyes tended to look across the loch almost as
much as forward. Two things he feared from there – smoke
from undisciplined burnings, and boats setting off up-loch
to bear grim tidings. But neither materialised. John of
Moidart knew his task, and was authoritative enough to have
his men well in hand.

The early dusk found them half-way up the long loch; but
there was to be no halting this night. On they pressed, and
presently a thin sliver of moon rose above the south-westerly
hills slightly to light their way, and to glisten chilly on the
sparkling frost. Montrose sent word that the older and less
able could go slow if they would. Stop if they must. But the
main force must keep going through the night. None would
hear of hanging back, however, with old Airlie and young
Johnnie as examples – both insistent that they were good for
another ten miles at least. Montrose worried a little about
these two. His son was looking thin, these days – as indeed
were they all – but with dark rings to his blue eyes, and a
cough which, though not deep, seldom left him. He certainly
never complained, and seemed to have ample energy, never

flagging. But a father's anxiety was not to be quenched entirely. As for the old Earl, for whom the Graham had acquired a great regard, even affection, he was clearly being taxed to the utmost. He frequently fell asleep at the briefest halt, and collapsed of an evening into a kind of stupor.

At about 8 p.m., three hours after dark, they came up with O'Cahan, and a picket, at Durran, near the loch-shore. He had been awaiting them for hours, of course – but not altogether idly. He had sent most of his men over the bridle-path, to hold the high ground. Some were ahead, farther up the lochside. And others were just back, in a purloined boat, from a visit across the loch to see how John of Moidart was getting on. Their report was encouraging. Clanranald was almost level with this point, and going strong. He would be rounding the head of the loch by midnight. No boats nor messengers had eluded him, at least during daylight.

To take a host of almost 2000, in darkness over a 1200-foot ascent, by a narrow drove road in a rockbound land was a nightmare-proceeding almost beyond contemplation. The ascent, their guide told them – one Black Angus of the Glencoe MacIans – was over two miles long. Then there was three miles of lochan-pocked peat plateau to cover, and the descent of another two miles to Loch Fyne. Only the hard-frozen state of the land made it at all possible. But if one man could do it, Montrose declared, so could 2000. Given time.

It took them, in fact, over six grievous desperate hours, the stumbling across the terribly broken if iron-hard peat-hags of the high plateau quite the direst part of it. But by two-thirty in the morning, most of the now mile-long strag-gling column was down at salt-water, on the shores of the longest sea-loch in Scotland, at Inverleacann, seven miles south of Inveraray. At last, Montrose called a halt. Three hours for rest, he said. He had told Colkitto that he would look for him at the other side of Inveraray, at sunrise.

By 6 a.m. they were on the move again, half-asleep on their feet, cold beef, raw oatmeal and as raw whisky in their stomachs. Fyne-side was less densely populated hereabouts than was Aweside, but even so the passing of such a host could not go unnoticed, even in the darkness, with dogs to give tongue at every farmstead. Occasionally there were cries of men. Whether any raced ahead to warn Inveraray there was no means of knowing. Boats might well be launched on the dark loch to carry the news. That could not be helped.

Dawn of another cold, clear day found them at Dalchenna Point three miles south of their objective. They were on time – and so far they had not had even to draw sword.

Then, presently, ahead of them, distant, faint but clear, they heard the sound of bagpipes on the north-easterly air, many bagpipes, shrilling, ebbing and flowing.

Even as his heart lifted to the sound, Montrose frowned. That could only be Colkitto and the Clan Donald chieftains. None other would blow martial music before sunrise on a winter morning on Loch Fyne-side. The MacDonalds were *ahead* of time, then, not hiding their presence, and presumably not waiting.

It scarcely required the Graham to urge his weary host to greater speed. All perceived the situation. Practically at the run now they surged on northwards.

Rounding an intervening headland of the loch they saw their goal at last, capital of the Campbell's kingdom, a town of whitewashed houses and church spires, with the massive tall castle rising behind and above all. The blue smoke of morning fires was rising from hundreds of chimneys there. Down at the double jetties, fleets of boats lay moored. *MacCailean Mor's* great banner flapped lazily from the castle's topmost tower in the light breeze.

But even as they stared, two developments became evident. Black smoke, thick and billowing, began to rise amongst the blue, and across the still waters of the loch shouts and screams and the clash of steel came clearly though the shrilling of the pipes. And out from the cluster of shipping suddenly shot a large many-oared craft, with a covered canopy at the stern, to set a course down-loch at impressive speed, alone.

'Himself!' Black Angus, the guide, at Montrose's side, cried, pointing. 'The Campbell, whatever! The forsworn, devil-damned craven himself!'

'You mean . . . ? You mean . . . ?'

'Aye – by Christ God, I swear it! That is *MacCailean Mor's* own galley. None other like it, see you. He flees, the dastard – he flees, leaving all.'

Montrose shook his head, wordless. There was neither glee nor scorn in his mind, any more than satisfaction. Rather a sort of pang and anxiety. Would he ever succeed against this man, he wondered? For to fight a man adequately, one had to understand him. And he did not. He just did not know how Archibald Campbell's mind worked. And that, he was well aware, was highly dangerous.

They raced on to the town.

There was little to be done there – save to restrain the MacDonalds' savage ire. Half of the houses seemed already to be ablaze. Colkitto had pressed on, to the castle – whether or not he had guessed the significance of that fleeing galley.

There was only a token defence at the castle. By the time that Montrose reached its walls *MacCailean Mor's* banner was being hauled down, and the chagrined MacDonald chieftains were stamping about, cursing, at the discovery that their quarry was gone. The Graham had the greatest of difficulty in preventing them from putting all within to the sword there and then, and burning the building over them, in sheer frustration – after certain of the treasures had been extracted, of course. It was a fine house, and full of valuables. Argyll's wife and two sons were not there, being evidently domiciled meantime at Roseneath Castle in Cowal, far to the south, on the Clyde estuary – where, retainers informed, the Marquis was now proceeding.

So Inveraray, the vaunted Campbell citadel, fell almost without a blow struck. It was a wonder, an anti-climax of the first order, almost an affront, somehow. Men could hardly credit it, especially the proud chiefs, who went about as though somehow cheated, tricked, offended. Archibald Campbell's credit would never recover from this – at least in the Highlands. But that was scant consolation. Malice was not to be sated.

Montrose sought, with indifferent success, that at least it should not be sated, by proxy, on Inveraray town and district. Some harrying and spoiling there had to be, of course – it was the terms on which Highland armies fought; but whole-sale slaughter, sack and destruction the King's representative forbade in the King's name. Not that his commands received strictest obedience. But at least no more of the town was set alight, and the proposal to hang every able-bodied man on a large extension of *MacCailean Mor's* already commodious gallows – where so many MacDonald clansmen had dangled – was negatived.

A large proportion of the population, in the event, escaped in the fleet of boats, leaving the town to the victors.

That night, in Archibald Campbell's hall, Montrose sat in Archibald Campbell's chair at the head of Archibald Campbell's table, while his colleagues and lieutenants ate and drank the Campbell's provision and made merry. Mac-Donald pipers paced up and down the great stone-vaulted chamber, blowing their hardest; captains and chieftains, many of them already much drink-taken, shouted and sang, banged their flagons and stamped their feet; Campbell serving-wenches skirled and squealed as they ran the gauntlet of lecherous hands; deer-hounds snarled and squabbled over bones and scraps. James Graham was no spoil-sport and enjoyed the relaxation of convivial company with any man. But he was tired, and not being addicted to the bottle, was stone-cold sober – which is a handicap in such circumstances. None better, he recognised that his hard-pushed supporters and allies deserved their recreation and amusement. Young Johnnie had fallen asleep over the table, at his side, and near by, Airlie snored. But if Montrose knew anything of Highland festivity, the noise and excitement would increase rather than lessen, soon the dancing would commence, the trials of strength, the outdoing of one's neighbour in song and story and muscle, and steel might well flash. These clan chiefs were only temporarily in alliance, with each other equally with himself; most of them were at timeless feud and rivalry. By the time such stage was reached, the King's Lieutenant intended to be safely if less than peaceably elsewhere.

It behoved him to say what he had to say soon, therefore, while men might still take it in – since it was important, and the morrow might present no opportunity. He banged on the table with his goblet, he rose to his feet and clapped his hands, Black Pate bellowed for silence – all to no least effect other than to wake up Johnnie Graham, but not the Earl of Airlie.

At length, taking up a great silver tankard half-full of wine, and engraved with the Campbell arms, Montrose suddenly hurled it crashing down the centre of the long table, with fullest force, after the manner of a curling-stone, whereon it smashed aside dishes, goblets and broken meats, spilling its contents and that of others, splashing diners, shouters and sleepers alike, in a spectacular if limited ruin.

This, at least, attracted attention. Men jerked back, startled, and stared. Voices died away – even though the pipes and the hounds still gave tongue.

Montrose smiled at them all, gently, genially, and raised his hand to the pipers – who raggedly choked and wailed to a temporary close.

'My lords, chiefs, friends,' he said, 'a few moments of your time, I pray. I shall not detain you for long. But some matters require your attention, and I crave your patient hearing. Firstly, I would thank you, thank you all, from my heart. These last days, you have done what has seldom, if ever, been done before. What few might have believed possible to be done. You have nursed and coaxed an army across Highland Scotland in mid-winter in five days, most of it in hostile territory. You have made traverse of trackless mountains in darkness. I will not thank you for beating the Campbell in fight, since he did not stay for that . . .'

The roar of derision, abuse and contumely drowned his voice. He waited.

'So much for thanks,' he went on, when he could. 'Now for a word of warning. We celebrate here in Campbell's house – but celebrate what? One man's craven spirit? We have won no victory, gained no battle – save over rock and heather. One Campbell, and he *MacCailean Mor,* has fled before us. But there are others, my friends. You have not, for generations, hated – aye, and dreaded – the Campbells because of one man or one house. There are, I am told, over 150 Campbell lairds who can field over 100 men, some of them up to five times that number. And we are in the midst of their land . . .'

Again interruption, this time growlings and cursings.

'In two days, or three, my friends, 10,000 men could be surrounding this town. We have but a quarter of that, with John of Moidart still at the coast. Nor do the Campbells lack for leaders. Think of these – Campbells of Glenorchy, Auchenbreck, Dunstaffnage, Cawdor, Lochnell, Barbreck, Ardkinglas, Saddell – aye, and a host of others. Men of stature and power.' He paused, and looked down the table at Patrick Campbell of Edinample, who sat beside Sir Alexander Menzies, both not a little uneasy. 'How say you, Edinample? Are there not stark enough Campbell chieftains by the score to lead Clan Diarmid? Even though *MacCailean Mor* plays craven?'

'Plenty, my lord Marquis,' the Campbell agreed. 'And do not forget my lord Earl of Irvine, my lord of Argyll's half-brother. He is banished to Ulster by his brother. But could be back within the week, to Kintyre. Would that he were *MacCailean Mor,* instead of Archibald. Then, I swear, you would not be sitting in this hall tonight!'

That statement was received with mixed feelings by the company, and there were more than unkind glances directed at the speaker – with whom many of the chiefs had been loth to sit down in the first place, and only pursuaded by Montrose's firm notions of courtesy. All, James Graham included, were apt to forget Argyll's half-brother, James Campbell, Earl of Irvine, cordially detested by Archibald and living almost in exile on Campbell lands in Ireland. He was a man of some vigour and ability, it was said. If he came back to lead Clan Campbell in the field, there might be a different story to tell.

'You make your point, Edinample,' Montrose acknowledged. 'It behoves us, therefore, to watch how we go. To recognise that we are not victors in a conquered land – not yet. Let us not behave as such. We cannot *occupy* all this great Campbell land – such would take ten times our number, and more. And be unprofitable, besides. So we must seek to subdue it piecemeal, by careful campaigning. Our task has only begun ...'

There were less than respectful comments, protests, assertions as to what real men could and would do to this Campbell kingdom, claims that no Sassenach would teach true Highlandmen how to deal with Clan Diarmid. Even Colkitto demonstrated a defiant attitude. How much it all was strong liquor talking was not to be known.

The Graham allowed them their say. Then resumed, conversationally, easily, but assuredly. 'You fight under the King's banner. And under my generalship. So long as you do, my good friends, you will heed my commands. Your good advice and offices I will seek on all occasions, as to tactics. But as to policy, my decisions prevail. All understand that, I am sure?'

There was an ominous silence.

'Good,' he went on, smiling slightly. 'We have done great

25

things together, gentlemen. And shall do greater. But in order, and of a set policy. And that policy necessarily forbids widespread pillage and rapine of this country. For nothing is more sure to arouse and unite against us this whole clan and people. Bring them in fury about our ears. This you will understand, I am sure.' He raised a hand as the snarling began. 'Hear me. I say that you shall have your booty and spoil, in full measure. Campbell beasts and gear and goods you shall not lack. But it shall be done decently and in order. On the authority of the King's Lieutenant. I will have no burning and slaying and raping, no lawless harrying of this land. I will not have the King's name soiled, nor the King's cause jeopardised by such, and the wrath which it would stir up. Is it understood?'

Only a few men nodded or said aye to that – and none of them Highlanders, Islesmen or Irish, save only for Magnus O'Cahan.

Montrose looked around at a preponderantly hostile company. He smiled still. 'I do not know how best *you* impose your will and command, gentlemen, on your men. For myself, I intend to hang any in my own command guilty of disobedience to this. It is my belief that your own authority will be no less effectively upheld. I have not heard that any of you are backward in maintaining your supremacy.' He paused, to let that sink in. Then he nodded, and shrugged. 'I end, my friends, as I began – with my thanks and my esteem. And my apology that I should so interrupt your well-earned diversion. The night, and this house, is yours. I bid you enjoy it. Myself, I say a goodnight to you all.'

He bowed and touching young Johnnie on the shoulder, turned and made for the door. The clamour rose behind them.

Up in a small tower bedroom with his son – he could not stomach Argyll's own great bedchamber; Colkitto could have that – James Graham lay listening to the noise from below and riot from the town, long after Johnnie slept. It appeared to be his lot to seem responsible for the sack of towns, hate it as he did. But, dependent on the unpaid armies of fierce lords and chiefs, what could he do? Aberdeen had stained his name. He prayed that Inveraray would not further tarnish it. But he feared that the Campbell capital would not forget its Yuletide of 1644 for many a year.

29

THE SLEET-LADEN WIND SCREAMED AND SOBBED THROUGH the pine-wood where 1500 men lay or crouched, wrapped in their plaids, asleep. When the wind abated for a moment, the noise of the waves on the near-by loch-shore filled the night, in its place. It was the 29th of January, 1645, a month after that celebratory feasting at Inveraray – and dramatic was the change in the circumstances of the royalist army.

Montrose himself was not asleep, nor most of his remaining leaders – for this was only half the company that had taken Inveraray, the rest having gone home with their booty after the age-old fashion of Highland armies. He paced the wet pine-needle floor now, head bent, brows knitted, a man in the throes. Around him his officers watched and waited, huddled shoulders hunched against the storm. None ventured to interrupt the Lieutenant-General now, none were over-ready with advice. It was past midnight, and all save the sentries had been asleep for hours.

Montrose halted his pacing in front of an elderly man who sat, eating cold meat ravenously, on a fallen pine trunk.

'You say that Argyll has 3000 *Campbells*,' he put to him 'Before we left Inveraray we had word, from the South, that the Estates had sent sixteen companies of infantry, Lowland militia, under General Baillie, to *MacCailean Mor*. Are these with him now also? At this Inverlochy? Are they included in the 3000.'

'I know not, lord,' the older man said, his mouth full. He was soaked, dead-weary, but tough, lean, despite his grey hairs, a notable man if an odd choice as courier to send over the winter mountains, Ian Lom MacDonald, the Bard of Keppoch. 'Myself I have not seen them. Keppoch sent me, just, with the word. He said 3000 Campbells.'

'But . . . a mercy, man – it makes a mighty difference! If

it is 3000 Campbells *and* sixteen companies of trained militia, see you, it makes a force twice as strong. How may I decide what I should do lacking this knowledge?'

'Your pardon, lord. I am but a messenger from my chief.' That was said with quiet dignity and reproof.

Quickly Montrose relented. 'Aye – forgive me, friend. I must seem both graceless and ungrateful. *Your* pardon, it should be. You have come far and fast, in evil weather, to bring me this news, and I thank you from my heart. *And* MacDonald of Keppoch. But – my problem is heavy, my choice hard. To press forward, as before? Or to turn back?'

'It is not for such as my own self to advise you, lord. But . . . you might save much of Lochaber, and Keppoch too, from the Campbell's wrath.'

'Aye – there is that also. You do well to remind me.' He did not rebuke the man that his chief, Keppoch, was no longer with the army, but had dropped off at his own country, with his men. 'See you – I am between two fires. Seaforth lies ahead, with 5000, at Inverness. Not more than thirty miles away. And now Argyll, you say, is on my tail, at similar distance, at Inverlochy. If I have to fight, I'd liefer fight the strongest first, while I am fresh. If Argyll has but 3000 of his own Campbells, he is less strong than Seaforth. And in hostile country, where Seaforth is not. But if he is joined by those sixteen companies . . . !'

Pate Graham spoke. 'Strike Seaforth, and you still have Argyll to deal with. Defeat Argyll, and Seaforth and his Mackenzies will melt back into their Kintail.'

'True. Or likely so. It depends on what Huntly said to him. But, if Baillie is now with Argyll we are up against an experienced general. I know him.' He turned back to Ian Lom, the poet. 'You heard no word of this General Baillie, from Keppoch? Or other leaders of Argyll's force?'

'None. Save only that Sir Donald Campbell of Auchinbreck leads, under *MacCailean Mor*. Who fell off a horse to hurt his knee, they do say.'

'More like running away!' O'Cahan commented briefly.

'Auchinbreck? He that was soldiering in Ireland? A hard man, they say. But a trained soldier. If he has Baillie also . . . !'

'Then there will be no doubt which army will be the stronger. To deal with first,' Airlie put in. 'I say, Seaforth

can wait. Even if he has Huntly in his pocket. And is reinforced by that fool Balfour of Burleigh, from Moray and
Speyside.'

This was what had brought Montrose hurrying north-
eastwards from Inveraray five days before, in vile weather
– the information that George Mackenzie, second Earl of
Seaforth, had raised his great northern clan for the Covenant
at last, and marched on Inverness with the declared object
of linking with Balfour's force skulking north of Aberdeenshire. Worse, it was rumoured that he had come to terms
with the disgruntled Huntly, who was still in the far North
somewhere, and that it was his intention to enroll much of
the Clan Gordon against Montrose. The Graham could not
sit at Inveraray, whatever the weather, with such a threat
building up behind him. He had decided to dash north and
deal with Seaforth, before the slow-moving Argyll could
organise the retaking of his kingdom, from Roseneath. But
it seemed that Argyll, for once, spurred on by humiliation,
had moved fast; and instead of merely setting things to right
in his own territories, had pushed swiftly on to bring fire
and sword into Lochaber of the Camerons and MacDonalds
of Keppoch, at Montrose's back.

'Very well,' he said, sighing. 'We turn back. Seaforth can
wait. Let us pray that he does not convince the young Lord
Gordon, whatever success he has had with his father. For
the Gordon cavalry could cost us all Scotland. We turn back,
and at once, gentlemen. This hour we march, storm or none.
See you to it . . .'

And so, thereafter, with even Ian Lom MacDonald saying
that it was impossible, Montrose led his force southwards,
by the selfsame route that the MacDonald had just come.
The normal route, down the Great Glen from this Kilchumin where they were encamped, by the side of the River
Oich, Loch Oich, and the long Loch Lochy, to where Spean
joined the Lochy, was difficult enough, in winter. Did they
not know it, who had just come that way? But thereon the
Campbells would have their scouts out, their advance parties
probing. To avoid them Ian Lom had come from Keppoch,
in Glen Spean, by difficult and hidden ways to the east of
the accepted route, by Glen Roy and Glen Turret, crossing
the watershed of Teanga and so down into Glen Buck and
the Calder Burn. Then avoiding Aberchalder and the gap

into the Great Glen again, he had climbed steeply over another small watershed, high above the Oich's valley, and so down the Cullachy glen to Glen Tarff, the Tarff leading him down to Kilchumin here at the head of Loch Ness. He all but wept at Montrose's declaration that so he would lead them back to Spean and the Lochy. The passes were blocked with man-high drifts, he said; the rocks were glazed with wet ice; the burns were in raging spate; the wind was a yelling demon, on the high ground . . .

The Graham patted his shoulder, and smiled. 'You are an older man than most here, my friend. You, guiding us, will cross it again – and take us with you. We will find no Campbells thereon, I vow! To give word of us. We have done the like before, see you. We will not be put to shame by your grey hairs!'

Nevertheless, as they soon discovered, they had *not* done the like before. There was little comparison, in fact, between the traverse of the hard-frozen heights, on the way to Inveraray, and this storm-lashed hell of soft snow, roaring rivers and steep rock-bound mountains. They could not hasten, with every mile a challenge to muscle, wind and will, a trial, a torment and an achievement. By the direct route they had some thirty miles to cover to Inverlochy, where Lochy joined Loch Linnhe, and where Argyll seemed to have made his base meantime. By Ian Lom's route it was nearer forty. And averaged a thousand feet higher.

No words are adequate to describe that march. None who made it would ever forget a mile of it. Almost at the start they lost three men, swept away in fording the icy thundering waters of the Tarff. Then the fierce rock-climbing ascent of the steep hanging valley of Cullachy, with its half-frozen waterfalls and deep drifts, only two miles up to the watershed but two miles of sheer agony, rising almost a thousand feet, with the south-west, snow-laden gale battering in their faces. Across the bare peat-pitted high ground of Meall a' Chulumain and Druim Laragan they staggered no more than four miles from their starting-point and over four hours later, stumbling over hidden hags and rocks, deafened by the wind, breathless with the cold, weary already.

From the heights they slipped and slithered down a desperately steep burnside into Glen Buck, the valley of the Calder. It was wooded down there, and more sheltered; but the snow lay deeper and the river was in high spate. Daylight found them there. Montrose had been determined that they should get over that intervening high ground before dawn, however stormy a dawn; for though a thousand feet above the Great Glen, they had been little more than a mile from it, parallel, and would have been visible, crossing the open heights, to keen eyes below on the other side of the Oich valley. That danger was now past; and according to Ian Lom there would be no more similar hazards of discovery until they came to Keppoch and had to cross Glen Spean.

The climb out of the head of Glen Buck and over the high tableland of Teanga southwards to Glen Turret was the highest of all the route, reaching 2250 feet, an unrelenting inferno of screaming blizzard, of sleet now rather than snow, for over four miles. It took them almost six hours, men jerking forward with stiff, small steps, numb, almost blind, falling, tripping. Most of this army was bare-legged, in short kilts, with only worn rawhide brogans on their feet. Muscular Highlanders took it in turn to carry the old Earl of Airlie on their backs – to his own almost sobbing protests but the Lieutenant-General's commands. Montrose himself went much of the way his arm linked in his son's. It was mid-afternoon before they were staggering down short Glen Turret.

The wide, major but coiling Glen Roy now lay ahead of them, ten miles of it, in comparative shelter, its extraordinary terraces forming natural roads contouring both sides of it, good as even the Romans could have made – beaches of some forgotten loch, the learned said. Along these they could make better time, even though the soft snow thereon was a hold-up. Half-way down that long glen they rested for some hours, huddled in wet plaids, eating cold meat and raw oatmeal, lighting no fires. Although this was Keppoch country, Montrose was taking no chances. Keppoch itself was only five miles ahead, where Roy reached Spean, and a warm welcome would greet them from MacDonald, Ian Lom assured. But the Graham would have none of it. One tale-bearing traitor, one Covenant-inspired zealot, in the Spean valley, was all that would be necessary to bring to nothing all that they were suffering, he pointed out. One man hurrying down Spean to Lochy, to the Campbells, and all was lost. They would cross Spean by night, avoiding Keppoch, however wrathful its laird might be afterwards. He was willing to pay almost any price for the benefit of surprise.

That they did, then, that evening, leaving the wide mouth of Glen Roy well to the west of Keppoch, in driving rain and darkness, and fording the raging Spean at its wide shallows a mile and more downstream, at Coire Choille, using a human-chain device to help numbed legs and feet support their owners in the ice-cold waters. They turned up the Cour Burn thereafter, in fairly thick woodland – and almost at once ran into trouble, stumbling upon a foraging party of Campbells already camped for the night in the shelter of the trees. Black Pate and his advance-guard made short work of these, leaving none to flee with the news. It was an inglorious brief interlude, the Campbells being cut down as they rose from their plaids, given away by the glow of their dying fires; but it had a most enheartening effect upon the half-starved, half-frozen royalists – first blood in this contest.

On up the Cour and Loin Burns they trudged, and into the ancient pine forest of Lianachain, under the frowning outliers of the mighty Ben Nevis itself – even though they saw none of it.

Dawn found them still in the forest, with the rain ceased and the wind dropping. They were actually crossing another watershed, but a low one this time, no more than 500 feet high, and tree-covered, though the pines were stunted and wide-scattered. It was much less killing going for exhausted men – but still desperately slow. By midday they were dropping down into Glen Lundy – and the Lundy River ran for only four or five miles before emptying itself into the wide Great Glen again, into the River Lochy, only a mile or so above salt-water at the head of the great sea-loch of Linnhe. Inverlochy lay at the junction.

Two hours later they halted, a mile from the mouth of Glen Lundy, still in open woodland. They had accomplished the impossible. Not even the mighty deeds of the old Celtic sagas and legends could outdo the achievements of the last forty hours. Montrose, dizzy with fatigue himself, sought to praise, say his thanks – and could not.

Nevertheless, an hour later, as a murky sunset, the first such for days, was staining the waters of Linnhe and Loch Eil, its westward arm, the Graham and a small advance party under Black Pate, as always, reached the last of the trees in the very mouth of Glen Lundy and gazed out over the suddenly far-flung scene. Remaining carefully within the shelter of the pines, they stared. Directly ahead, wide and level, lay An Moine, the Moss, the flood-plain of the Lochy at the head of the sea-loch. And in strong position amongst its reedy flats, the massive walls of Inverlochy Castle rose on a grassy mound, a great quadrangular stronghold of lofty curtain-walls and rounded flanking-towers, antique in appearance. Semi-ruinous now, it had been the seat of the great House of Comyn, Lords of Lochaber, home of he whom Bruce had slain before the altar at Dumfries. The Gordons had gained it, eventually – indeed it still belonged to Huntly; but they did not use it, and the place was now mouldering away. But strong still.

It was not the castle, however, which held the Graham's interest and concern – even though, if Ian Lom was right, his arch-enemy might well be even now within those crumbling walls. It was the great camp which lay to north and east of it, amongst the scrub alder and hazel, where scores of evening cooking-fires gleamed and sent up blue columns into the sunset sky. He heaved a mighty sigh of relief. The Campbell host had not moved on. Their own desperate journey had not been in vain.

Montrose transferred his gaze to the land itself, its lay-out, features and scope. It was a terrain, from a military point of view, not so very unlike that of Fyvie, though on a much greater scale. There was the castle on its spine of firm ground, and a lot of wet and low-lying land around, with the impassable barriers of the sea-lochs to south and west. A strong defensive position – but this time it was not he who would be defending it. Nor had he any desire to attack such a position. His task was to bring the enemy to battle – but in a position where he himself would have the maximum advantage.

He did not dare peer for very long, in case there were keen eyes watching from that camp, or patrols circled it. Besides, the light was failing. One matter was clear. Whatever strategic surprise he might attain, *tactical* surprise was impossible – at least in actual attack. For, in front of him there was no cover or screening whatsoever. Glen Lundy opened widely on to the flat cattle-pastures. The moment any large force appeared farther forward than these last trees, they would be seen. And they had a mile of these levels to advance over before contact – unless the enemy indeed advanced towards *them*.

Thoughtfully Montrose turned back, leaving Pate Graham, with a picket, to watch there. A night attack might get over the problem of the approach – but bring other and larger problems. He was handling wild and undisciplined troops, however bold – too bold. Without being able to *see* how the battle went, he would be quite unable to control them or the fighting. Night fighting might serve well enough for taking a difficult position; but for actually defeating an enemy army so that it would not reassemble and fight again later, it was of little use. Men could escape in large numbers in the darkness. The attackers would follow, and disperse themselves hopelessly. They might gain the central position, and seeming victory – but with most of the foe undamaged. For his present purposes Argyll had to be defeated in the field, and be seen to be defeated – otherwise their fine and hard-won surprise would be wasted. And it could not be repeated.

He had made up his mind by the time that he got back to his men, wet, cold and hungry, round the first bend of the valley. He conveyed his regrets to all, but they must put out those fires, and no more must be lit. They were less than two miles from the Campbell host, their presence unsuspected so far. It must remain that way. It would be an uncomfortable night – but surely nothing to the discomforts of the past two nights. At least they need not flog their bodies into movement. Tomorrow night, God aiding them, it would be different . . .

Presently Black Pate sent a runner to announce that two mounted patrols had left the Campbell encampment, obviously to make a circuit of the neighbourhood to see that all was well. One was heading in this direction. He requested instructions.

Montrose, half-asleep already, had to think fast. If such a patrol came up this glen any distance, it could not fail to discover them. And, mounted, some would certainly escape back to tell the tale. At all costs that must be prevented. He called for Cameron of Locheil, who was still with him – and who might be expected by the Campbells to be in the vicinity anyway, with his home not five miles away – telling him to take a score of his men and hurry forward to the glen-mouth. Let the enemy discover them. Have a small clash with them, even. Then hurry away southwards, into the Nevis foothills. Draw them away. That should arouse no suspicions of a large force being near at hand. Marauding Camerons, keeping an eye on the Campbell host, were only to be expected.

Locheil gone, all waited tensely. An hour later another runner from Pate Graham came to tell them that there had indeed been a tulzie at the Lundy ford, some small swordery, and then the Camerons had fled off, into the hills, the Campbell horse after them in full cry. None had so far come back.

The encampment relaxed again.

It was near midnight when Locheil got back, grumbling at a frustrating and shameful task. He could have ambushed the wretched Campbells more than once, and ensured that none got back to Inverlochy to tell their story. But that had been forbidden, and he had had to play the feckless poltroon, leading them on into the nightbound hills. He had left them well up the slopes of Sgurr Finnisgaig. They might conceive the Camerons fools and cowards – but they would not conceive an army to be hiding near by.

Satisfied, Montrose thanked him, and resumed his attitude of crouched and shivering slumber. Not that he thought to sleep; too much was on his mind.

Some snatches of uneasy oblivion he did achieve that grim night; but long before dawn he was fully and finally awake, and had said his daily prayer. It was his wont to read a portion in his battered little pocket Bible, which he had always carried everywhere with him, at the start of each new day; but with no fires to give him light he could not do so this dark morning. He repeated a favourite psalm to himself, committed himself and the cause of the Lord's Anointed into God's hands – with especial care sought for his son John – and went to rouse the camp.

Well before daylight all were massed at the wide mouth of Glen Lundy, in a chill drizzle of rain. They watched the fires brighten in the great camp a mile away, as it came alive to another day. Not a man of his host would not have preferred to put all to the test there and then, with no more waiting, to advance under cover of darkness and fall on the unsuspecting foe. But it was not to be. That camp area was no suitable battle-ground; and there were ditches and drainage-channels in the mossy pastures between. Montrose had other plans.

When it was light enough to see what they were doing, and the exact lie of the land, Montrose quietly moved his people forward and some way to the south, extending them into a long line along the skirts of the foothills – which were in reality the first swellings of the mightiest mountain in the land. But he did not move them too far, either forward or southwards – and he kept almost one-third of his numbers back, to hide them behind a long grassy, whin-covered bank, too low to be called a ridge but sufficient to screen them from the west and north. The line he formed with the rest was nearly half a mile long and slightly crescent-shaped, with Colkitto and his Ulstermen on the right, O'Cahan, the Macleans and Islesmen on the left, and, recessed somewhat, in the centre such Highland chiefs as remained, with John of Moidart, Captain of Clanranald in command, with Glengarry. The hidden reserve behind was under another Ulster veteran, Colonel MacDonald, known for some reason as O'Neill, with Locheil and Stewart of Appin. Who was nominally in command of these clansmen was vitally important, since most of them would fight under none save their own chiefs. It made dispositions difficult for a general. The crescent-shaped front faced the Argyll camp and the old castle, at almost a mile's distance. But midway between, rising out of the flood-plain, was a sort of whaleback of firmer ground, not very high admittedly, but solid and fairly wide, with even some rock outcropping, and scattered whins. The previous evening, Pate Graham had pointed it out to his chief as the place for them. Montrose had merely shaken his head. He had perceived another use for it. That was, he prayed, for the Campbells.

At what stage the silent waiting host became apparent to the Campbells in the camp was not evident to the watchers a mile off. Certainly no sudden outcry arose, no obvious alarm. The waiting period had been partly filled, for the Catholic portion of the royalist army – which was the major part of it – by their priests stepping forward and making the sign of the cross with their arms while the men knelt bare-kneed in the wet grass and prayed aloud. There was no snow lying at this sea-level, and the drizzle had ceased; but the chill was daunting, especially for men with empty stomachs, stiff with wet lying. It was Candlemas Day, the 2nd of February. Let them pray.

But chilled waiting, and even prayer, was scarcely the best aid for morale in fiery Celtic troops; and presently, with indications that a wintry, watery sun was rising behind the vast rearing bulk of Ben Nevis, Montrose decided to seek to expedite matters somewhat. He had two trumpeters, his own and Colkitto's, for use in blowing certain basic calls during battle, advance, charge, pause, retire and so on. Now he unfolded the great and handsome Royal Standard – which he had carried these many grim miles wrapped within a plaid around either his own shoulders or his son's – and ordering the trumpeters to sound the Royal Salute, he had the silken banner hoisted high on a lance in the morning breeze, while the mountainsides echoed and re-echoed with the stirring, challenging bugle-notes. A great yell went up from the ranks of the Celtic host – and they would have surged forward there and then had not the leaders sternly held them back.

At last, visible reaction came from the Inverlochy camp. It was not to be credited that they had not been observed hitherto; therefore the enemy must have been making some hurried decisions and dispositions, even though nothing was visible from this distance. But now horns sounded from the Campbell positions and the movement of men became evident and purposeful. Then a flash drew all eyes and a single resounding explosion shook the surrounding hills. A column of water and mud spurted up from the flats half-way between the two hosts. An involuntary indrawn sigh spoke eloquently from the royalist ranks. Argyll could also make a gesture. He had artillery at Inverlochy, even though it was as yet well out of range.

Montrose frowned, but not too blackly. He had hoped that they would not have to face cannon-fire; but he had not excluded the possibility. They would only be field-pieces, here, pray God – in which case they could not have an effective range of over half a mile. He hoped what he had planned might nullify any such, in some measure at least.

Then, to the astonishment of all, Argyll staged another gesture. Three horsemen suddenly emerged from the castle gateway, and went cantering down the quarter-mile track to the loch-shore, plain to be seen. There a number of small fishing-cobles were drawn up on the beach. Two of the horsemen dismounted, clambered into one of these, and were rowed out to a larger craft which lay moored offshore in deeper water. The third turned and trotted back to the castle with the horses.

None who had witnessed what had happened at Inveraray that other early morning five weeks before was in any doubts as to what this meant. That was a similar vessel, probably the selfsame galley in which *MacCailean Mor* had fled that day. Here he was at the same ploy, removing himself to safety before any possible danger could arise for himself.

A howl of execration, contempt and sheer fury arose from the royalist ranks – and was promptly answered by another shattering discharge, and a second cannon-ball – which did not reach even so far as the first. Somebody in the camp, no doubt Sir Donald Campbell of Auchenbreck, was more aggressively inclined than was the chief of all the Campbells. Although aggression could be demonstrated on more than the physical plane.

The galley was up-anchoring and its double banks of oars beginning to impel it out into mid-loch.

'The man is at least consistent!' Montrose declared to Airlie. 'I fear that he will survive us all!'

'For so ill-favoured a creature he rates his own hide high!' Airlie's son, Sir Thomas Ogilvy, snorted. 'Has he no sense of shame? In front of all his people!'

'His sense of his own consequence outdoes all,' Sir David the brother, said. 'After a fashion, there is a sort of pride in it, He cares not what others think of him, knowing himself to be all-important, irreplaceable. Few men, I vow, are made of such stuff!'

Montrose nodded. 'You are right, David. I have come to believe it is not all craven cowardice. The man is unassailable in his self-righteousness – and therefore dangerous. Harder to deal with than a dozen paladins!'

'Aye. And what paladins has he left behind to fight for him there?' Airlie wondered. 'I think we shall soon know. See – he hauls to in the loch. Out of harm's way. To watch. Auchenbreck, his own cousin, has the name of a hard and savage man.'

'But proud,' the Graham added. 'I have heard that he is

notably proud. I pray that he is, indeed. For so I hope to draw him. He has twice our numbers – and will see but part of us. I cannot believe that he will relish his master's careful departure. He will be smarting under it – as any true soldier would. His cannon cannot reach us, here. I believe, I hope, I pray, that he will come out to teach us our lesson, advance to show us that the Campbells are not all poltroons. Get within cannon-shot of us. And to do that, he must do so, directly to yonder tongue of firmer land between us. Or else make a great circuit round to the north. Which would take time, and allow us opportunity to retire and take up new and stronger positions on the hillside. I think that he will come directly at us. Where we want him !'

Very quickly thereafter it became evident that Montrose's thinking had been accurate. To tuck of drum, disciplined companies of foot began to issue from the camp almost straight for them, long columns of musketeers and pikemen, marching four abreast, with banners. The Graham sighed a little at the sight – for this answered his questions to Ian Lom. The sixteen companies of Lowland militia regulars *had* reached Argyll – for only such would advance thus. The odds, therefore, were lengthened considerably.

It was trying to stand idly by and watch the enemy power build up, so much greater than their own, march forth and take up advantageous positions before them, without lifting a hand to interfere. It went against every instinct in the Highland fighting man. But Montrose's orders were emphatic. This battle was to be fought his way, or not at all. Outnumbered three to one at least, no amount of wild heroism was going to serve for victory – although plenty of that would be required also. Only carefully thought-out strategy could win the day for them – with God's help – which was why James Graham had hardly closed his eyes that cold night.

The seemingly unending companies of militia filed steadily forward across the soft and marshy pastures, no doubt congratulating themselves on not being attacked while they were doing so, leaping the ditches and runnels, until they reached the long whaleback of good ground, where they split into two, one half marching on to the extreme right, the other left, eastwards. Clearly they were to form the wings of Auchenbreck's array. The rise was about one-third of a mile long, and averaging some 300 yards in width. Montrose reckoned that 1000 and more of the militia were taking up their stance thereon.

Now the mass of the Campbell irregulars were surging out from the encampment area, not in any orderly ranks. There was no counting these, and however undisciplined, they were known to be fearless fighters. For long they streamed out and across the levels, making it clear that there must be much more of the camp beyond the castle, in the dead ground behind. It seemed as though the whaleback rise could never possibly hold them all.

When at last this great host was all out, came a group of mounted men, not cavalry but Campbell lairds, in the Lowland garb which most of them affected. There were some thirty to forty of these, sitting proudly, some with banners. At sight of them, a long snarling arose from the MacDonald ranks. These were the hated ones, rather than the ordinary Campbell clansmen, these were the oppressors of the Highland West, the rich and able men with the Lowland law in their pockets, the ear of government, the proclivity for being always on the winning side – and the heavily laden gallows-trees. Behind them staggered long columns of men straining and tugging on ropes, drawing two brass cannon, which made heavy going on the soft wet ground. With them came files of shaggy garrons, laden with panniers no doubt containing powder and shot. Finally emerged the reserve and rearguard, more militia and a mixed crowd of clansmen, with some mounted officers.

'It is a great host,' James Graham said. 'Far more than we are. Can we hope to hold them? Those cannon – they bring them near to us. Will they not shoot us down, and we can do nothing? They will be in range, will they not? On that bank?'

'Range, yes,' his father admitted. 'Just. But . . . wait you. More than range is needed. They require a clear field of fire. Do you see them getting it?'

The boy bit his lip. He considered himself to be a veteran soldier now – even though a less robust one than he tried to appear, with an unmanly cough like a bairn and a tendency to shakes and shivers, fight against them as he would. He had, however, no experience of artillery.

Soon his father's meaning, and planning, became evident, to him as to others. The cannon, even when dragged to the highest point of the whaleback, were still too low set to fire over the heads of the massed men thereon, so slight was the rise. And so tight-packed were the enemy that clearing any sort of avenue down which to shoot would be a difficult matter. The great numbers of the foe were here working to their own disadvantage.

Not that Montrose intended to allow them any time for a reappraisal of the situation. As the field-pieces reached the firm ground, and the long teams of haulers pushed in amongst the crowded ranks of clansmen, causing maximum upset, the Graham raised his arm towards Magnus O'Cahan waiting and watching eagerly on the left flank. And with a deafening yell, long continued, his force of Islesmen and Macleans flung themselves forward, at last, in headlong charge, broadswords out.

This tip of the royalist crescent was the nearest of all to the enemy, only about 400 yards separating them from the Lowland militia. These musketeers and pikemen had been in England fighting the Cavaliers, and had never seen or faced a Highlanders' charge – quite the most terrifying and unnerving ordeal in the military experience. Casting aside their plaids, stripped to the waist, dirks in left hand, broadswords in right, yelling their fierce slogans and bounding like deer over the soft ground, 300 of them bearing down on any static body of men, however disciplined, was a fearsome sight to contemplate. Not too much to be blamed, undoubtedly, the officer in command of the enemy right wing was over-early in giving his order to fire – and his men all too eager to respond. At far too extreme a range the matchlocks blazed, and the ball went whistling across the levels amidst impressive clouds of smoke and with a mighty banging. But only one or two men fell as a consequence. And it was highly doubtful whether there would be time to reload the unwieldy muzzle-loaders, as the officers bawled orders to do.

Trumpets rang out again, and horns blew, and the entire royalist front moved forward, not in any charge at this stage, but steadily, sufficiently to further upset worried militiamen.

Montrose halted his centre still outside musket range. But the right wing, under Colkitto, surged into a charge, pipers playing his Ulstermen on, wild Irish screeches rising to a crescendo.

It was more Lowland militiamen who faced them, for the Campbell clansmen mass formed the centre. Colkitto had farther to go than O'Cahan – but his charge was just as fearsome.

Montrose was now dividing his attention principally between O'Cahan and those cannon. There was a great stir and confusion in the middle of the Campbell position and towards the rear, where no doubt the pieces were being manhandled into position and turned to face the enemy, and the ponies with the ball and powder were being pushed through the press. Little could actually be seen because of the dense ranks of clansmen in front. But, by the same token, the cannoneers could not see their targets, and there was just not enough elevation to fire over the heads of their folk. So crowded, indeed, was the whaleback that there was just no room for the cannon and garrons.

On the left, O'Cahan's men reached the rising ground, and went leaping up in full cry, naked steel flashing in the new-rising sun. And without waiting for the impact, the militiamen turned and fled, without getting in a second volley. The ground immediately behind them there was much waterlogged, so they streamed off half-right, back towards the castle area, 500 of them, throwing into some confusion the rear ranks of the Campbells and utterly demoralising their colleagues of the reserve who were still advancing across the levels. O'Cahan's Islesmen, seeming to race after them with unabated enthusiasm, suddenly followed their leader in swinging round behind the main enemy front, between it and the faltering rearguard. Ignoring the massed Campbells altogether, they dashed on towards the rear of the left-wing militiamen facing Colkitto, caring nothing that for much of the way they were splashing through pools and runnels of icy water.

These Lowlanders stood their ground rather better than did their colleagues, but not for long. They had seen what had happened on their right, and they quickly became aware of the extraordinary threat in their rear. The gigantic Colkitto, leading the screaming Irish, was large-enough anxiety, especially as many of the latter had pistols as well as swords and pikes. There was a ragged exchange of fire, with little effect on either side, and the militia front began to waver and cave in.

Montrose drew his own sword, pointed to John of Moidart, and his trumpeter blew the general advance. With a mighty earth-shaking roar the royalist main body of Mac-Donalds broke into a run, like hounds unleashed. And from behind the little ridge at their backs, the reserve emerged, shouting likewise, to take their place.

It was probably the sight of that unexpected reinforcement, even though there were no more than 250 of them, that broke the militiamen of the left. Throwing down their fired muskets, they bolted. O'Cahan was on their left and Colkitto at their backs, so they ran half-right also, north-westwards into the bog.

The Campbell mass stood solid, isolated, on its whaleback, deprived abruptly of flanking cover, and with rear threatened.

Montrose did not actually lead his centre's advance. It would not do to seem to supersede the Captain of Clanranald. He contented himself with remaining in the racing front line – and with keeping an eye on young Johnnie. In the main, his own major part was played. He had brought the two sides to grips, as advantageously as he could. It was now up to others.

Or, almost. Just before the front clashed, he ordered the trumpeter, who stayed almost as close to one shoulder as Black Pate did to the other, to sound a special and repeated call. This was for O'Cahan and Colkitto's men to break off from whatever they were doing, and to concentrate on making a ring of steel round the Campbell position.

And so the real battle commenced. The Campbells still outnumbered their attackers two to one. But they were cramped and crowded in a vast huddle of 3000 men, with no room not only for manoeuvre but for free work with sword and pike. Moreover, only those on the perimeter were in touch with their foes, and the rest, half their strength, could effect nothing. This whaleback was in fact a death-trap, its illusion of firm ground little more than a constricting menace.

The Campbells fought bravely, or rather died bravely; but it could not be said that they fought well – since they could not. Surrounded, restricted, hampered, frustrated, they fell where they stood and were replaced by their fellows, from behind, almost with relief. Soon the MacDonalds, in their element at last, were standing on top of banks of slain, thus gaining desired additional height and reach. And the great circle, or rather ellipse, shrank.

Montrose had fallen heir to some of the garrons which had carried the ammunition, and mounting himself on one's broad back was able to survey the battle from something of a vantage-point. There was little that he could do to affect the issue of the ding-dong struggle. But he was able to summon forward the reserve when the doubtful enemy rearguard looked like reassembling and joining in the fight. And he sent Sir David Ogilvy and a company of Athollmen to silence marksmen in the castle, musketeers who had taken refuge there and were sniping long-distance at any who came within range. For the rest, he circled the fearful conflict, with Johnnie and Airlie, not knowing whether to cheer or to weep. Massed slaughter and bloodshed at close quarters was not to his taste, general or none.

The eventual outcome was not long in doubt, barring unforeseen developments. The Campbells might break out, but they would never gain the mastery now. From the start they had been out-manoeuvred, their advantage in numbers nullified. Their leadership might be brave enough, and conventionally effective, but it had lost the initiative and allowed itself to be trapped in the centre of an ever-narrowing circle. At this rate, it was achieving nothing – even though it might be the last to die.

Colkitto, however, had ideas about that last. Collecting a team of mighty sworders about him, he spearheaded a wedge of smiters in a drive into the Campbell centre, himself out-doing all in the fury of his onslaught, his enormous reach, untiring energy and bellowing bull-like roaring enough to clear a way through the dense pack so long as his back was protected. He was, of course, a superlative captain of gallowglasses, however odd a major-general. Steadily he hacked and hewed a passage through, towards the enemy leadership, still sitting their mounts in the midst.

Montrose, Johnnie at his side, watched fascinated. He saw the giant reach the central group, apparently unharmed. He saw Sir Donald Campbell of Auchenbreck, from horseback raise a pistol and fire at Colkitto. He heard that man's great shout of laughter even amidst all the unholy din so that presumably the shot had missed its mark or done scant damage. And then he saw a huge bare arm and sword-hand come up to sweep the small, neat and grizzled Campbell right out of his saddle, the dirk in the other hand struck fiercely but expertly, once only, and Auchenbreck disappeared in the press while Colkitto strode on.

Whether it was the fall of their principal leader, or the fact that the whole enemy position was now practically cut in two, the Campbells' dogged defence thereafter began to falter and disintegrate. They still fought vigorously, but they were of a sudden concerned with cutting their way through and out, rather than with maintaining a front. It was every man for himself.

Soon the whole battle had broken up into innumerable struggling groups and running men. In every direction the enemy fled – if they could. And after them raced the yelling MacDonalds, Macleans, Camerons and Stewarts, doing at last what they had sought to do all their lives – hunting down defeated Campbells.

At this stage, with all obviously over save individual killing, Montrose would have called off the fighting. He ordered his trumpeters to sound the retiral – and to go on sounding it. He might as well have shouted commands to a pack of wolves. None save the Athollmen, Drummonds and Grahams heeded. The rest were about their own business. The Battle of Inverlochy might be over, well before noonday, for better or worse; the killing was not.

Montrose did his best. He divided his officers amongst parties of the troops who would obey them, and ordered them to protect the Lowland militia who had laid down their arms back in the camp area. He sent out tough men such as Black Pate and O'Cahan to try to halt, or at least limit, the running slaughter. He himself led a company to capture the castle – but the snipers here fled without further opposition. From the ramparts thereafter he gazed out over the scene of his triumph, set-faced – and saw Argyll's antiquated galley starting to speed seawards with all the power of its double-banked oars, even as scores of his clansmen desperately hurled themselves into Loch Linnhe to swim out towards it and safety from their hunters.

James Graham, a patriot, groaned for Scotland.

* * *

That evening, feasting on Campbell provision once more, in the Great Hall of Inverlochy Castle, part-derelict but a palace compared with their quarters of recent nights, Montrose called together such of his officers as were available – many of the Highlanders had just never returned from their Campbell-slaying – and such as were sufficiently sober, and sought to gain a full picture of the situation, its implications, and how fullest advantage might be taken.

The details of the battle, now marshalled before him, were extraordinary, scarcely credible. Although they had sustained many wounded – and one of these, unhappily, had died just an hour before, Sir Thomas Ogilvy, youngest son of Airlie – only three others were dead on the royalist side. Whereas the Campbell slain already counted amounted to over 1500. A large proportion of these, undoubtedly, had been hunted down and despatched as fugitives, and the bodies of many others would no doubt never be found. On the ridge of the whaleback itself, over forty Campbell barons and lairds had died, in addition to Auchenbreck. More than half of the total Campbell army had been wiped out, therefore, a proportion unknown in any battle since Flodden. The Lowland militia had suffered comparatively lightly, the majority of them now prisoners, strictly guarded for their own protection. Not that the Highlanders seemed to have any interest in them – except as a source of booty and matchlocks, despising them as beneath their notice.

Arms, munitions and supplies captured were more than enough to re-equip the entire royalist army – if such a thing there was, any more. This was the question that was worrying Montrose, even as his companions congratulated him, and themselves, on the scale of their victory.

The Master of Madderty summed up the attitude of most of the Lowland officers. 'You have not won only a battle, James – you have here won a campaign, possibly even a war, a nation indeed! For you have broken the power of the Campbells now – that is certain. Argyll will never again put a Campbell army in the field. And Argyll *is* the Covenant, his name and his power its strength. This day we have demolished that name and strength.'

'The Covenant has more than Argyll, John. He is uncrowned king, yes. But do not forget that it has the best-trained professional army in the two kingdoms. Even the man Cromwell has said as much. Sandy Leslie's army. It is in England – but it could be brought home, and quickly, if need be . . .'

'Mercenaries, in the main. At least, its officers, from Leslie downwards. Hired men. Think you they would not quickly perceive who will pay them best to fight for? When *you* sit master in Edinburgh!'

'He is right,' Graham of Gorthie agreed. 'Leslie and his like will not support the losing side, ever. Show yourself master in Scotland, and the army will not come back to challenge that master.'

'Perhaps, friend. But before I am master, or make the King master, in Scotland, I have three other armies to defeat. Four, it may be. Seaforth's at Inverness. Burleigh's in Moray. It may be that they are now one. Callander's in the Borders. And Baillie at Perth – though we know not the size of the force he has there. Or may gather. And he is a notable general.'

'But another mercenary, a paid soldier. As for Seaforth, he is a waverer. It has taken him years to make up his mind to this. Argyll has been at him since '39. He will melt away, with the Campbell prop and spur removed. And Burleigh is a fool. Callander is otherwise, but his is only the reserve army. And I do not believe that he would fight *you*, if he may avoid it. He used to be your own man, signed your Cumbernauld paper.'

'Aye – and he refused the chief command, after Argyll,' Madderty added. 'He will act cannily, will Callander. I say, strike from here swiftly at Baillie, at Perth. Another fast march. He can have no large numbers there yet. Then make straight for Edinburgh, dismiss the Committee of Estates, and call a parliament in the King's name. I swear you would have Scotland in your two hands in a week!'

'Aye! Aye!'

'To be sure. That is the way of it!'

'Strike while the iron glows red . . . !'

It was heady talk, and men rose to it.

James Graham raised his hand. 'My friends – I think you forget one matter, of some import. You would not do so if you were Highlandmen. Donald here, who is one, will tell you, I think.'

Donald Farquharson of Braemar, a quiet modest man,

beloved of all, who had joined Montrose soon after Tipper-muir, sighed. 'You must needs wait, I fear,' he said. 'Until, let us say, the spring. The clans will now return to their own lands.'

The others stared at him.

'It is true,' Ian Lom MacDonald assured. He was already turning over in his mind the mighty fast stanzas of an epic to describe this day's doings for all time to come. 'It is the way, the custom. You will not hold them now.'

'You see?' Montrose asked. 'You have forgot that it was a Highland army which won this fight for us. As only a High-land army could have done. And Highland armies, when they have won a battle, thereafter retire homewards with their booty. Such are the terms of their fighting. Always. Even now we are already missing one-third of our numbers, who have not come back from chasing the Campbells. We shall not see them again, I think. All Argyll, Lorne and Cowal lie open to their raiding. Think you any will march with me to Perth and Edinburgh?'

There was a shocked silence, and then some growling. Again the Graham raised his hand.

'*I* do not blame them,' he declared. 'Most of them joined us only to fight the Campbells. All along I have known that. They have fought, and won. And never was there such booty, so much Campbell treasure. I fear that when we leave Inverlochy, it will be with Colkitto's Irish and Islesmen, the Athollmen and those from Strathearn and Strathmore. Little more than a thousand, all told. Shall I march on the Low-lands with a thousand men?'

None answered him, nor had to.

'It is hard,' he went on. 'In a day or two, when Scotland learns of this day's work, the land will lie all but open for us. Almost for the taking, I believe. Only, I shall not have the wherewithal to take it. I would march on Edinburgh tomorrow, blithely. But I may not.'

'God's curse on them all! What then will you do?' Madderty demanded.

'I think, march north again. Noth south. Send Seaforth back to his northern glens, if we can. Then go talk again with Gordon. Aye, my friends – well may you grimace! But young Gordon, and only Gordon, has the answer to our problem. Perhaps Inverlochy will convince him that his

King's cause is not lost, is worth his support, whatever his father says. Who knows – even Huntly might think again . . .'

At the heavy silence and downcast looks of his friends, James Graham changed his tone of voice, his whole demeanour. Throwing up his head, he smiled. 'Come gentlemen – not so sober! We should be rejoicing, not glooming. I crave your pardon for drawing so long a face. We have won a great victory – and thanks to those same Hielantmen! We have struck a blow for King Charles today such as has not been struck yet in all this long war. I go write the good news to him now. It will, I swear, cheer His Grace mightily. Here at Inverlochy, they do say, stood an ancient capital of our Pictish kings, from whom our liege lord descends. It is an excellent omen. The King's cause triumphs, at least in Scotland, and the King's chiefest enemy flees, discredited before all. This is a day for cheer, not gloom. All who made it possible, I thank from the bottom of my heart . . .'

But when he turned away, that brilliant smile was gone.

30

The great Gordon castle of Bog of Gight was set amongst the spreading and desolate sea-marshes and tidelands of Speymouth, its tall gaunt tower a scowling plaything for the winds that howled and swept across these level wastes, with the boom of the great seas on the long sand-bar three miles distant like the muted roll of artillery in some endless battle, and the sad scream of seabirds and marshfowl serving for the cries of the dying. James Graham, only too well aware of that background of ominous sound, as he was the more immediately obsessed with the grievous sound of his son's difficult breathing, knew a great fear, almost despair. Not a man to be oppressed by conditions or atmosphere or omens, however strong his emotions and vivid his imagination, he nevertheless knew a hatred for Bog of Gight and wished that he might never have come here. Wished more than that, God knew . . .

There was wicked pride speaking in that, wearily he told himself there by the bedside, in the high tower room round which the sea-winds sobbed. He hated Bog of Gight partly because he had once before come to it on a begging mission, seeking aid of Gordon, and had been rebuffed. And now, victor as he was acclaimed, had come again, on the same sorry mission, a beggar, a suppliant – and dreading further rebuff. He had heard that the Lord Gordon, that young man whom once he had felt he could love, was here, at the second greatest of the Gordon castles, the seat from which Huntly took his odd but time-honoured title of Gudeman of the Bog. It was a humiliating posture for any man of spirit, he told himself, the more so for the King's Lieutenant and winner of so many battles – to be soliciting, beseeching a young man barely out of his teens. But the basic situation had not changed, victories or none. To conquer the Lowlands for King Charles, he required cavalry, much cavalry. And Gordon was the only major source of cavalry north of Tay. Now, with Inverlochy behind him, and Scotland ringing with his deeds and wondering what the great Montrose would do next, he was back cap-in-hand at Bog of Gight – to find the Lord Gordon departed for Strathbogie only two days before.

They had marched northwards from Inverlochy and Lochaber in consistently bad weather, driving rain and biting winds. And Seaforth, hearing that they were coming, and what they had done to Argyll, had turned and marched away from Inverness, north-westwards into the remote hills and fastnesses of his own Kintail and Gairloch. Balfour of Burleigh's force was said to be hiding in Banff and Moray, and they had turned south by east seeking him. They had taken the towns which he had so lately occupied, Nairn and Forres and Elgin – but found none to fight. And there, to the surprise of all, they had been joined by the Laird of Grant, with 300 men, fifty of them horsed, the first cavalry Montrose had had for long. This was an encouraging first-fruit of Inverlochy's victory, and a good augury, for James Grant of Freuchie was a notoriously careful character, and had joined the Covenanters as early as 1638 and never wavered in his canny support – indeed was one of the Committee appointed to try all 'malignants' in the North. Moreover, he was married to Huntly's favourite niece. A proud head of a proud line, his grandfather had refused James the Sixth's suggestion that he should make him Lord Strathspey, by demanding who then would be Laird o' Grant? Meantime he had been left in command at Elgin, capital of Moray.

It had been with no lightened heart, however, that Montrose halted at Bog of Gight, and sent only messengers on after the Lord Gordon, to Strathbogie. He stopped because Johnnie could go no farther. The boy had been ailing all the way from Lochaber – that terrible hill-march from Kilchumin to Inverlochy having been just too much for him, after earlier privations. And ever since, he had been shrinking and fading before his father's eyes. Desperately anxious, James Graham had watched him, sought to shield him and protect him in all those winter rains; would indeed have left him behind in some warm house had he dared trust his son to a stranger, in a potentially hostile land. He had even thought of sending him, in Black Pate's care, back to his mother at Old Montrose; but the fever-stricken, dark-eyed boy had pleaded, with tears, not to be parted from his beloved father and hero. Now he lay in this tower-room, in warm bedding and with a great log-fire blazing cheerfully; but still he shivered and was racked with coughing, cold sweat on his young white brow. James Graham was almost beside himself. In the next chamber the Earl of Airlie lay in bed, in not much better shape. Campaigning with Montrose was not for such as these. The old man, hit by the death of his youngest son, and sorely concerned at lack of all news of his eldest, the Lord Ogilvy, imprisoned by Argyll at Edinburgh when last heard of, had travelled latterly in a litter slung between two Highland garrons.

It was the second day of March, in the afternoon. Montrose was roused from sad introspection at his son's bedside, and the boy in uneasy dozing, by the sound of horns blowing at a little distance, ululant above the sobbing wind. Rising, he moved to the window, to gaze out. It was to see a large body of horsemen approaching from the south, down the riverside from Fochabers village. And since no alarm had been given by his pickets, they must be at least ostensibly friendly. Peering, for the window glass was thick and dirty, he saw a banner blow sideways in the wind. It was blue, with three golden charges, two and one. In that country, such could be no other than the three golden boars' heads of Gordon. And the banner bore no difference, tressure, or other mark of cadency.

'Gordon, Johnnie – Gordon!' the man cried. 'And horsed! Scores, hundreds. Do you hear? Gordon cavalry!'

The boy's eyes opened, over-large, glittering, filled with weak tears. No words came, but he licked his lips and nodded, with a caricature of a smile, as his father hurried to the door and went racing down the winding turnpike stairway.

Two hundred Gordon cavalry indeed came riding to Bog of Gight, Colonel Nathaniel Gordon at their head, all gallant cavalier in great feathered hat, gleaming half-armour and thigh-boots. Two others rode beside him – the slight dark figure of the Lord Gordon himself, and his young brother, the Lord Lewis. Montrose, those emotions of his at their tricks, found his throat all but choked as he watched them ride up in jingling proud array. He held out his two hands, wordless.

'My lord Marquis!' Nat Gordon sang out cheerfully. 'I greet you. I acclaim you! And . . . I bring you friends.' And he swept off his hat in a flourish that was both salute and waved introduction of the company.

George Gordon was more quiet, just as he was more quietly dressed, a serious, almost diffident young man, but with a still, grave strength of his own.

'My lord – your servant,' he said. 'Come belatedly, to your side.'

'For that I thank the good God. Welcome, my friend. Welcome to our liege lord's cause.'

' 'Tis to *your* cause, rather, that I am come. Of His Grace's I am less sure.'

'My cause *is* His Grace's, my lord. Only that, be assured.'

'Yet Charles Stewart has not brought me here, sir – only James Graham. You persuaded me to the Covenant. Then the Covenant locked me and my father in cells in Edinburgh. When they freed us, it was on condition that we provided men to fight for the Covenant. *I* would not have agreed. But . . . it was done. I am scarce nimble at changing my coat, my lord Marquis. And my father is hot against you still . . .'

'Yet you are here, friend.'

'Yes. It has taken me much time and thought. But I have come, at length. Against my father's express commands. Because I believe in James Graham. That only.'

'Mm.' Montrose eyed him thoughtfully, and sighed. 'You put a heavy load of responsibility on my shoulders, sir. I shall dread that you find me unworthy. But – so be it. The King's cause and mine are one. I welcome you from my heart – and not only for the men you bring. We shall talk of this hereafter.' He turned to the younger brother with the impatient frown. 'And you, Lord Lewis. Your spirit all Scotland knows. Now, it will serve a worthy cause. I will have work for it, never fear.'

That headstrong, hot-eyed youth, still in his teens but a thorn in the Graham's flesh ere this, shrugged. 'So long as we have an end to talk – talk, and creeping caution and care!' he jerked, his scorn of his sober brother, and of Montrose himself probably, undisguised. If he was the antithesis of George Gordon, he was strangely like his father – strangely, in that Huntly's fox was replaced by Lewis Gordon's wolf, young but unmistakable. James Graham knew well that he would have to watch this new recruit.

'Care I cannot swear to spare you, young man. Nor a modicum of talk. But creeping caution, I think, you may avoid in my service! Nathaniel, my good friend – I rejoice to see you. We have missed you, indeed . . .'

'My grief, to have missed Inverlochy!' that bold man cried. 'But – I have been busy.' He glanced behind to where the Gordon ranks sat their mounts. 'Training these. And others. My lord of Gordon has more to come.'

'A token, only,' George Gordon nodded. 'Give me a week or so . . .'

The Gordons had scarcely been ushered into and installed in their own house of Gight when a second arrival kept James Graham from his son's bedside. These were no additions to his strength, however, even though they were two of his own servants from Old Montrose. They brought a letter from Magdalen his wife, and had been roaming the North-East for days seeking him, having just come from Elgin. He took the letter up to Johnnie's room – which was also his own.

'My lord,' it commenced – and he sighed at that cool beginning, not Jamie, or James or even my dear lord.

I send you greeting, in the hope that you are in health, and that our son John is well. I have heard tell of a great battle in the West, and that Thomas Ogilvy is slain. He was my good friend. Once, as a foolish child, I thought that we might wed. God rest his soul. I hope and pray that you do keep Johnnie from all danger.

My lord James, I must tell you that I cannot go on further as I have done so long. I am less than well, in body as in heart. You have chosen to be neither husband nor father to me or mine. No doubt but that the fault is mine, for I am not of your quality, nor have the heart to partner such as you.

These are evil times and all the land in a stir of trouble. Of which you, my lord, are not guiltless. There is much bitterness here, and threats are made against us. My lord of Argyll has imprisoned your good-brother the Lord Napier, but his son the Master is escaped they say. Also Sir George Stirling of Keir and others of your friends. There is talk of execution. My father fears for the safety of myself and my children, as indeed do I, or I am no heroine and desire but to live in peace. I have therefore left your house and gone to live at Kinnaird with my father and brother. You will not relish this, my lord. I know of your ill-will to my father Southesk. But you do provoke hatred and enmity in others, yet omit to protect your own wife and children. My father is come to some agreement with the Committee of Estates, I thank God. And my lord of Argyll. With him I should be safe. But there is talk of them taking Jamie, as hostage. For your better behaviour and submission. And even little Robert they may take from me. It is my hope and prayer to God that this may not be. But no thanks to you, my lord.

It is my belief that all these threats and reprisals against me and mine who am all innocent of injury to any cause, would be lessened were my Johnnie to be returned to my keeping. So says my father. It is wicked and a sin that one so young and tender should be turned into a man of blood. He is not yet fifteen years. I cannot sleep of a night thinking of him, in war and danger and bloodshed, amongst

*savage men. So, my lord, if you have any heart for me,
and for him, any regard for a mother's feelings and a
father's duty, do you send him again to me at Kinnaird,
where he shall be safe. I am assured that this will commend itself to the Committee and to my lord of Argyll.
You have no right, to be sure, to engage a child in this
your rebellion. James, if you too would come back, with
Johnnie, and forswear further rebellion and war, it would
greatly commend you to your*

sorrowing but dutiful and faithful wife
MAGDALEN CARNEGIE

*The lords Crawford, Maxwell and Reay, of the King's
faction are all captured, and Master George Wishart,
once your secretary. They say they are to be executed.
Also the Lord Ogilvy. Because of your rebellion. Your
excommunication is renewed by the General Assembly.
And the Committee of Estates, have proclaimed you infamous traitor, and forfeited of life, lands and goods.
What have you done, James – what have you done . . .*

The writing tailed away in a tear-blotted scrawl.

For long, unseeing, James Graham stared at the letter,
knowing a terrible hurt, pain and sorrow, almost despair.
When he raised his eyes, it was to his son, lying in a snoring,
restless semi-coma, thin, wasted, broken. Was Magdalen
right, then? Was this the end and price of his victories?
This, and the fate of those friends of his lying awaiting the
axe? Was it all the most shameful, appalling mistake? *His*
mistake, his arrogant faith in his mission and the King's
cause? Was he shockingly at fault, in prideful wrong?

Yet, that pitiful letter, from a wronged and distracted
woman whom he had vowed before God to love and cherish,
the mother of his children – was not right, surely. Nothing
of it was right, true, just? Nothing of true judgment? Those
were the words, in fact, of David Carnegie, of old Southesk,
a man concerned only for his lands, his properties, his position. And behind these were the words of Archibald Campbell's dictation – of that there could be no doubt. Magdalen
would scarcely know it, bue he could read it in every line.

Yet . . . if he had any regard for a mother's feelings and
a father's duty . . . ?

How long he sat there, lower in spirit than he had ever been in all his days, there was no knowing. The noises of an over-full house and a great armed camp came thinly into that high tower-room, and did not touch him. Only the difficult shallow breathing of his son, and the grief of that letter. Head in his hands, he groaned.

The clatter of many more hooves below, and the shouted greetings of men did presently penetrate his tormented consciousness – but this time did not take him to the window. Later a while, Black Pate came to the door, to knock and enter quietly, concern and compassion on every line of his dark, strong features. He looked from man to bed, and drew a deep breath.

'Jamie . . . my lord,' he said. 'Will you go down? Seaforth is come. My lord Earl of Seaforth.'

The other raised his haggard head to look at him, but dully, and did not speak.

'Seaforth, Jamie – the Earl. The Mackenzie himself. He is here. Asking for you. Seeking the King's peace.'

Montrose rose. 'Johnnie is . . . worse,' he said.

'I will bide with him. Go you down,' his friend said, gently.

Obediently, almost like a child, the King's Captain-General went to the door, and out.